John Weeks has been listening to stories all his life. As a child, he loved to hear his grandfather's tales. In adulthood, a career in social work had him listening to people sharing the stories of their lives. He studied Classics and English at Oxford University and has a master's degree in Shakespeare Studies from Stratford's Shakespeare Institute. He and his wife live in a small village in the Shropshire countryside.

For Martina, Eliza, Rory and Serena

John Weeks

FOLK TALES OF OLD EUROPE

AUSTIN MACAULEY PUBLISHERS™
LONDON * CAMBRIDGE * NEW YORK * SHARJAH

Copyright © John Weeks 2024

The right of John Weeks to be identified as author of this work has been asserted by the author in accordance with sections 77 and 78 of the Copyright, Designs and Patents Act 1988.

All rights reserved. No part of this publication may be reproduced, stored in a retrieval system or transmitted in any form or by any means, electronic, mechanical, photocopying, recording or otherwise, without the prior permission of the publishers.

Any person who commits any unauthorised act in relation to this publication may be liable to criminal prosecution and civil claims for damages.

This is a work of fiction. Names, characters, businesses, places, events, locales, and incidents are either the products of the author's imagination or used in a fictitious manner. Any resemblance to actual persons, living or dead or actual events is purely coincidental.

A CIP catalogue record for this title is available from the British Library.

ISBN 9781035818457 (Paperback)
ISBN 9781035818464 (Hardback)
ISBN 9781035818471 (ePub e-book)

www.austinmacauley.com

First Published 2024
Austin Macauley Publishers Ltd®
1 Canada Square
Canary Wharf
London
E14 5AA

I owe much to Anita, for her patience and her typing.

Table of Contents

Plum Brandy – Poland   15

   Chapter One: Kazia and Leon   17

   Chapter Two: The Miser   21

   Chapter Three: The Move   25

   Chapter Four: The Discovery   28

   Chapter Five: The Priest   31

   Chapter Six: The Interview   33

   Chapter Seven: Stories   35

   Chapter Eight: In the Market   38

   Chapter Nine: A Plan Is Made   40

   Chapter Ten: Waiting in the Dark   44

   Chapter Eleven: Intruder   46

   Chapter Twelve: The Chest Is Opened   50

   Chapter Thirteen: Conference   53

   Chapter Fourteen: Plum Brandy for the Priest   56

   Chapter Fifteen: Time Moves On   59

The Castle of Soria Moria – Norway   63

   Chapter One: The Ash Boy   65

   Chapter Two: The Brown Castle   67

   Chapter Three: The White Castle   70

Chapter Four: The Castle of Soria Moria	*72*
Chapter Five: The Golden Ring	*74*
Chapter Six: Homecoming	*76*
Chapter Seven: The Horn Ring	*78*
Chapter Eight: Halvor's Quest	*81*
Chapter Nine: The Wise Woman	*83*
Chapter Ten: The End of the Quest	*87*
Chapter Eleven: The Wedding Banquet	*90*
The White Mountain – Slovenia	**93**
Chapter One: Sophia Begins to Learn	*95*
Chapter Two: The Scholar	*97*
Chapter Three: Sophia Applies Her Learning	*101*
Chapter Four: The Way into the White Mountain	*104*
Chapter Five: Jozef and His Violin	*107*
Chapter Six: Sophia Goes Alone	*111*
Chapter Seven: Trapped	*115*
Chapter Eight: The Violin Plays	*117*
Chapter Nine: Rescue Rewarded	*119*
The Giant with Golden Hair – Scotland	**121**
Chapter One: A Prophecy	*123*
Chapter Two: The Chief Sets Out	*125*
Chapter Three: A Baby Found and Lost	*127*
Chapter Four: The Baby Gets a Home	*130*
Chapter Five: Rediscovery	*132*
Chapter Six: An Encounter with Outlaws	*135*
Chapter Seven: A Wedding	*138*
Chapter Eight: A Quest Begun	*141*

Chapter Nine: Village Puzzles   *144*

Chapter Ten: The Ferryman   *147*

Chapter Eleven: The Giant's Sister   *149*

Chapter Twelve: Knowledge Gained   *152*

Chapter Thirteen: Knowledge Shared   *156*

Chapter Fourteen: Return   *159*

Chapter Fifteen: The Ballad of Duncan   *162*

Maria and the Goat – Italy   **165**

Chapter One: Across the Marshes   *167*

Chapter Two: Grandmother's Cottage   *169*

Chapter Three: Market Day   *172*

Chapter Four: The Storm   *176*

Chapter Five: An Ogre on the Way   *181*

Chapter Six: Flight and Pursuit   *185*

Chapter Seven: Fortunato Transformed   *188*

Chapter Eight: Union and Reunion   *191*

Leaping Ferghal – Ireland   **193**

Chapter One: The Feud   *195*

Chapter Two: A Giant Is Born   *197*

Chapter Three: Revolution   *199*

Chapter Four: Celebration   *201*

Chapter Five: Bull Ford   *203*

Chapter Six: Attack   *205*

Chapter Seven: Escape   *207*

Chapter Eight: O'Flaherty Triumphant   *209*

Chapter Nine: Flight   *211*

Chapter Ten: The Widow   *213*

Chapter Eleven: A Son	*215*
Chapter Twelve: Hollow Victory	*217*
Chapter Thirteen: Ferghal Grows Up	*220*
Chapter Fourteen: Maeve Grows Up	*223*
Chapter Fifteen: Disclosure	*226*
Chapter Sixteen: Decision	*229*
Chapter Seventeen: Arrival	*231*
Chapter Eighteen: A Plan	*233*
Chapter Nineteen: A Meeting on the Island	*235*
Chapter Twenty: The Last of the O'Rourkes	*237*
Chapter Twenty-One: The Last of O'Flaherty	*239*
Chapter Twenty-Two: A Shaking Off of Burdens	*242*
Chapter Twenty-Three: Revelation	*245*
Chapter Twenty-Four: Reconciliation	*248*
Chapter Twenty-Five: A New Clan	*250*
All of You – England	**253**
Chapter One: A Winter's Tale	*255*
Chapter Two: Toads and Frogs	*257*
Chapter Three: Cloud Fairies	*259*
Chapter Four: The Toad's Speech	*261*
Chapter Five: A Parliament of Birds	*263*
Chapter Six: New Names	*266*
Chapter Seven: The Feast	*268*
Chapter Eight: Departure	*270*
Chapter Nine: The Jump	*272*
Chapter Ten: The Landing	*274*
Chapter Eleven: To Bed	*276*

Death in a Shell – Germany   **277**

   Chapter One: A Decision   279

   Chapter Two: The Bounty of the Baltic   281

   Chapter Three: The Timber Trade   283

   Chapter Four: Precious Amber   286

   Chapter Five: Lübeck   288

   Chapter Six: Prosperity and Decline   291

   Chapter Seven: Parting Words   294

   Chapter Eight: Death Comes   296

   Chapter Nine: Recovery   299

   Chapter Ten: Uproar   302

   Chapter Eleven: Confession   304

   Chapter Twelve: Death Goes   307

   Chapter Thirteen: A Story   309

The Tale of Philippe Legrand – France   **311**

   Chapter One: Philippe Lends a Hand   313

   Chapter Two: Labryte   315

   Chapter Three: Journey Plans   317

   Chapter Four: Setting Out   319

   Chapter Five: The Pans   322

   Chapter Six: Water and Salt   324

   Chapter Seven: Encounter on the Way   326

   Chapter Eight: Returns   329

   Chapter Nine: A Mysterious Challenge   331

   Chapter Ten: Finding a Champion   333

   Chapter Eleven: Martin   336

   Chapter Twelve: Negotiations   339

Chapter Thirteen: Preparing for Combat	*342*
Chapter Fourteen: Challenger and Champion	*345*
Chapter Fifteen: A Victor Rewarded	*348*
Chapter Sixteen: A Triumphant Homecoming	*351*
Chapter Seventeen: A New Team at the Forge	*353*
Notes	**355**

Plum Brandy – Poland

Chapter One
Kazia and Leon

Long ago, in a small town in the south of Poland, a girl persuaded her parents to move house.

"I've got an idea," she said. "Why don't we move?"

"What?" her parents asked.

The girl's name was Kazimeira but everyone knew her as Kazia. She was ten years old.

Why were her parents taken aback by her idea? The answer to that question calls for a bit of background about Kazia and her family, about her friend and about the town where they lived.

The land around their town and much of the town itself, were part of the estate of a nobleman who lived in a big house over a day's ride away. From that nobleman many of the townspeople rented their homes and the strips of land they farmed.

The community was not rich but it was lucky in at least one thing. The nobleman employed a bailiff who collected the rents and settled disputes. In many towns and villages bailiffs were hated. They were notorious for cheating their employers and extorting money from their tenants. In Kazia's town, however, the bailiff was an honest man, fair in his dealings.

Kazia's parents were not farming people. Her father was a carpenter and a fine one. Kazia's mother used to joke with him.

"You're too skilled for your own good. When you make furniture, it lasts. So, you don't ever hear from that customer again."

He smiled. "Maybe. But there can be no respect for a man who doesn't do his best. Besides, there are always tools to be mended and wagons to be fixed. Jobs of that sort don't bring in much, but they're enough to keep us going."

Kazia's mother took in washing and did sewing for people. The money she earned did help. They managed to save a bit but day by day, week by week, there was little to spare. Unlike those who farmed, they had to buy their milk, their eggs and their corn in the market.

The town had grown up by a river. Kazia's family and several others occupied a patch of wasteland on one of its banks. The land belonged to the nobleman, but he charged no rent for it. The rains of winter and the springtime melting of the mountain snow swelled the river and it often flooded there.

Kazia's father had built their house himself. It was not much more than a shed. He made it out of lengths of timber he salvaged from here and there. It was small but it was well put together and weatherproof. A prudent man, he built it on stilts, against the flooding.

The riverbank was an unhealthy spot. In winter, it was damp and, in the summer, it was smelly. Cows, oxen and horses were brought to the river to drink. Where they went, flies followed in great numbers.

Besides those who worked the land and those who made things, another group of people lived in the town. They were traders. Many bought and sold cattle. Most of them had bought land from the nobleman and built houses for themselves on it. They tended to keep company with one another and apart from the rest of the town. They had their own place of worship. Amongst themselves, they even spoke a language of their own.

Most of the townspeople appreciated the traders. They brought money and business to the place. The nobleman valued them, for on occasions he had need to borrow money from them. But the rest of the town mixed little with them.

Kazia was an exception. Her best friend was Leon, a child of one of the trading families. He was the same age as her.

There was no school in the town. Even if there had been, Kazia's parents could not have afforded to send her. She helped her mother and father with their work. A lot of the day she spent about the town, looking for jobs that might earn her a coin here and a coin there—running errands, sweeping a yard, watering horses.

Leon had less free time. His people had a school of their own, that was just for boys. But whenever he could get away, he would search out Kazia and they roamed the town together.

The tips they earned from doing odd jobs often caused them to argue.

"You keep the money, Kazia. My folks are not short of cash."

"Oh, no. We're partners. We shared the work, so we share the money."

Leon protested. "Really, I don't need it."

"Look here," said Kazia, raising her voice. "Either we share the money, or our partnership ends now."

"All right then." Leon was always the one to back down.

They worked together and they played together. All sorts of things were washed down the river from towns and villages upstream. One day, Kazia and Leon were playing on the bank and found a couple of barrels.

"I've got an idea," said Kazia. "Why don't we build a raft?"

"Are you sure that's a good idea?"

"Yes, we can do it. And it'll be fun. Come on, help me get these barrels up onto the grass."

Having lugged the barrels out of the mud, they ran back to the place where Kazia's father stored his wood. They pulled out an old plank and a tangle of rope.

After a lot of trial and error, they managed to tie a barrel under each end of the plank. They launched it into the water. The plank was wide enough for them to sit astride it with their legs dangling in the river. They moved off, scooping the water with their hands as paddles.

"Let's pretend this is the river Nile," said Leon.

"Where's that?"

"In Egypt. A hot place, a long way from here."

On the far bank, a man and his son went past in a cart.

Leon pointed to them. "Look," he said. "There's the Pharaoh in his chariot. He's got his second in command with him."

"What's a Pharaoh?" asked Kazia.

As they paddled, Leon told her about Joseph in the land of Egypt. He drew into the story some of the things they could see around them. A distant barn he made out to be Pharaoh's palace. Several cows, over their hooves in mud, were drinking at the water's edge.

"Those are the cows in Pharaoh's dream," said Leon, "the fat cows, grazing on the reeds."

"Wherever do you get all these stories?" asked Kazia.

"We learn them at school."

"I wish I could go to school."

The barrels had floated well enough at first, but they were not water-tight. All this time, they were sinking lower into the water. Leon and Kazia turned about and made back for the bank. Kazia jumped off onto the mud but doing so, she rocked the raft and Leon toppled backwards into the water. He scrambled to his feet and squelched up the bank, wet through and smelling of the river.

Kazia helped him to squeeze as much water out of his clothes as he could.

"I'm going to have to go home now," said Leon. "My mother will be wild."

"Don't worry, I'll come with you and explain. It was my fault, not yours."

"Yes, but you don't know my mother."

Leon's mother was outside their house and saw the two of them approach. She let out a wail. Waving her arms in the air, she shouted at Leon in their own language. She ignored Kazia, who had no chance to utter a sound. Kazia had picked up a few words of this tongue. She made out 'stupid' but for the rest, it was plainly a torrent of wrath and reproach.

Hearing the commotion, Leon's father came out. A big man with a bushy, ginger beard, he let his wife continue her scolding. He smiled at Kazia and spoke to her in Polish.

"Whatever has happened?"

"Leon fell in the river. It was my fault. I tipped him from our raft when I jumped off."

He grinned. "Where were you sailing?"

"We were going down the River Nile."

"Well, well," he laughed, "I've travelled a lot myself, but I've never been as far as the River Nile."

Kazia began to explain but Leon's father interrupted her.

"Don't worry, Kazia. I suggest you run home. It's time I calmed his mother. He's had enough chiding now. What he needs more is a wash and some dry clothes."

Leon's ducking in the river was soon forgotten by everybody; everybody, that is, except his mother. Whether they were working or playing, the time Kazia and Leon spent together was cut short every Friday afternoon, when Leon had to stop and head home. Nearing his house, they would see Leon's uncles, aunts and cousins beginning to gather there.

"What are they all coming for?" she asked.

"We have a meal together at this time every week."

Kazia was envious. She imagined those meals to be feasts and feasts did not feature in her life. She begrudged too that her time with Leon was always lopped in this way.

Chapter Two
The Miser

In this town there was one neglected plot of land. On it stood a wooden house so rackety it looked as if it might be flattened by the faintest puff of breeze. An old man lived there on his own.

The people of the town called him the Miser. He had never shared his name with anyone.

There was a story about him but where it came from no one knew, nor whether it was true. According to this story, the man had been a moneylender in one of the cities in the west of Poland. It was said he charged high rates of interest for his loans. Whenever a borrower fell behind in repayments, he was without mercy in setting the law upon them. He was much hated by the poor of that city.

One night, the story went, a group of desperate men from some of the poorest families got together and set fire to the moneylender's house. He managed to escape with only what he was able to carry. The men had not intended to kill him. They did achieve what they had planned—to burn his house to the ground, and with it the ledgers and papers in which the moneylender recorded their debts.

The moneylender fled the city and travelled east. He stopped when he reached the town where Kazia and her family lived. It seemed to him an out of the way place, where no one was likely to find him. He believed the men who set fire to his house had wanted to murder him and he was terrified they would keep hunting for him with that purpose.

The moneylender bought the plot of land and its house from the nobleman. He paid outright in cash. The life he lived was what caused the townspeople to call him the Miser. He bought meagre amounts of food. Reluctant to talk with anybody, he always appeared desperate to get away from people as quickly as he could. In those parts winters are long and cold. His neighbours noticed that even on the bitterest of days there was only ever a thin wisp of smoke from his chimney. He obviously lavished no more on his stove than he did on his larder.

A day came when one of the market people mentioned he hadn't seen the Miser for several weeks. Somebody else remarked she'd seen no smoke lately from the Miser's chimney. The bailiff heard them talking. He was a regular visitor to the market. He made it his business to know what was going on in the town.

The bailiff paid a call on the town's priest.

"Nobody has seen the Miser for a while, Father. Do you know if he's gone away?"

"I've no idea. He's never set foot in church. He's no concern of mine."

The bailiff decided to go and take a look for himself. He knocked and knocked at the Miser's door. There was no response. He put his shoulder to the door and nearly fell in. The frame was rotten.

Once inside, he caught an unpleasant smell. It was a mixture of dust and dirt, dampness and decay. But there was something more unpleasant still. He found the Miser dead, sitting in a chair. He had plainly been dead some time. The bailiff looked around the place. There was not a scrap of food in the house. Perhaps the man's money ran out, he thought, and hunger and cold had been the death of him.

The bailiff wedged the door shut and returned to the priest.

"I found the poor man dead in his house. He died a lonely death in that hovel."

"We are all alone at the very end."

"I would like you to give him a funeral, Father."

"That's not for me to do. I don't know his name. And more importantly, I don't know his faith, even supposing he had one."

The bailiff brought his fist down with a thump on the priest's desk.

"You will give the poor soul a decent burial, with all the respect you'd hope for yourself." With a shrug, the priest gave way. He knew better than to cross the bailiff.

The next day, the Miser's body was removed from the house. The bailiff called to see Kazia's father.

"To me that house looks in a terrible state. You know about these things. I'd be glad of your opinion."

Kazia's father reached for his boots.

"Let's go right now," he said.

The bailiff made a search of the house. The Miser had been wearing a key on a leather thong round his neck but no lock that it fitted was to be found. He looked for money, hoping to find enough to pay for the burial. There was nothing but a few small coins in a dirty bag. The only document he could find was an old record of military service. The man must have been in the army when he was young. The paper did at least give him a name.

While the bailiff poked about, Kazia's father inspected the property. He was shocked at the state of it. There were few pieces of furniture and gaps in the floor. Splinters of wood and a rusty axe by the stove suggested the Miser had been breaking up furniture and even floorboards to burn.

Everywhere wood was soft and spongy. Rain had been coming in through holes in the roof. There were wet patches and areas of white mould.

"So, what do you think?" asked the bailiff.

"This place is beyond repair. I wouldn't take a single stick out of here, even as salvage. Once we're finished, I'm going to shake my jerkin outside and give my boots a wash at the pump. I don't want to carry any mould or rot back to my own timber."

"What's to be done then?"

"My advice is to burn the place down."

The nobleman was friendly with the governor of the province. Having been given the Miser's name by his bailiff, he passed it on to the governor, who agreed to make enquiries. The nobleman was at that time negotiating the sale of a stretch of his woodland to a timber merchant in Krakow.

While the bailiff was in the city finalising the deal, he took the opportunity to put up notices, asking any relative of the Miser to contact him. The efforts both of the Governor and of the bailiff yielded nothing. Nobody came forward and no more was ever discovered about the Miser.

Kazia's father told his family about the Miser's house. That was what sparked Kazia's suggestion.

"I've got an idea," she said. "Why don't we move?"

"What?" her parents gasped. "We don't have the money to buy a new house."

"But what about the Miser's place?" replied Kazia. "You just said it's in a terrible state and nobody would want it."

"The house is rotten through and through. I told the bailiff he should burn it down."

Kazia would not give up.

"If it's so bad, the bailiff will want to get rid of it. He's not going to ask much for it, and he'll not get much for it."

"Kazia's right there," put in her mother. "We have set by a little money. I daresay, if we spoke nicely to the bailiff, he'd let us have the plot at a price we could afford. But where would we live?"

Kazia was triumphant.

"That's my idea! I'm not saying we should buy a new house. Why don't we move this house there?"

Chapter Three
The Move

"It's a deal," said the bailiff. "You must like a challenge. It's going to take time to put that place into any sort of order."

Kazia's mother smiled.

"We're not afraid of hard work. And once we start growing things, we'll save on what we're spending in the market."

It had taken little for the bailiff to persuade the nobleman to sell the Miser's plot of land. As no relatives to inherit could be found, it had gone back into his ownership. Having already sold it once, he never expected a second payment for it. So, he was content to let it go for a knock-down price.

Kazia's mother visited their neighbours by the river to tell them her news. Once over their surprise, they all offered to help with the move. She began to lay in loaves of rye bread, dishes of curd cheese, jars of pickled cucumber and a barrel of beer.

Nobody would be paid for their labour but those who turned up to help would get a meal at the end of a day's work. One of their friends played the fiddle. He agreed to bring it with him. They would celebrate by singing and dancing when all was done.

The day of the move arrived. Kazia's mother packed their belongings on a handcart which somebody lent them, while Kazia and her father set off to burn down the Miser's house. Kazia insisted on a detour to collect Leon. She didn't want him to miss the spectacle.

Kazia's father had prepared bundles of dry twigs as kindling to get the fire started. While the three of them piled the bundles against the walls of the house, Leon told them the story of Samson. He recounted how a blind man, held in shackles of bronze, had been given the strength to push apart the pillars of a great temple and bring the whole building crashing down.

Kazia's father laughed.

"A mouse with no chains and good eyesight could probably push this building down. But we don't just want it down. We want the site cleared."

When the kindling was in place, he took out his tinder box and lit one end of a faggot.

"Here, you take this, Kazia. This was your idea. So, you set it alight."

"I'll share the job with Leon. That way we can start the fire from both ends of the house." She pulled the burning faggot into two and gave half to Leon.

"Now!" she cried and in unison they threw their torches onto the kindling.

The fire soon took hold. Smoke began to rise. Children, adults and dogs from nearby came to see the blaze. There was a creak and the roof fell in, sending sparks and dust into the air. The watching crowd cheered, and dogs barked. Soon the walls fell in onto the roof. In no time what was a house became a pile of burning timbers.

Kazia's father had brought with him a couple of pitchforks and brooms.

"You two keep raking the fire up. I want every stick to go. And when the ashes are cool enough, sweep them in a pile over there. Mother will be along soon with the cart. I'm off back to the river to see to the house."

When Kazia's father built their house, setting it on stilts was not his only precaution against flooding. He reasoned that if the water rose really high, it might be better to float the house than let it fill. So instead of using nails, he fixed it to the stilts with pegs. It was an easy task to hammer them out and then the house was free.

Some time back, he had fitted a new axle to a friend's hay wagon. That friend came to help, driving his wagon, pulled by a pair of oxen, down to the riverbank. Kazia's father and his neighbours passed stout poles under the house. Lifting them on their shoulders, they raised the house from its stilts, carried it up the bank and set it down on planks laid across the back of the wagon.

On its slow progress along the lanes, the wagon gathered spectators. By the time it came into sight, it looked to Kazia and Leon more like a holiday procession than the delivery of a big load. When the house was finally set down on the ground, people cheered and clapped and whistled. The bailiff came by to wish Kazia and her family well. He shook all three by the hand.

Kazia's mother supervised the unpacking of the handcart. Once she had emptied it, she spread its boards with all the food and the beer. Friends and neighbours were urged to tuck in. People sat on the wagon. The fiddler began to play. They sang and danced, ever more lustily as the beer went down. Nothing could persuade Leon to get to his feet, but Kazia danced until exhaustion and the fading light brought their celebrations to a close.

Leon was home later than usual.

"So, what kept you?" demanded his mother. "You smell like you've been in a smoke house."

"I've been helping my friend to move a house."

"Listen to the boy. We send him to school and what happens? Still, he talks like a peasant. You mean your friend moved house."

"No," insisted Leon. "We moved the house, from the river to where the Miser used to live." Leon told them all about his day.

"And what did you get for all that work?" his mother wanted to know.

Leon's father smiled.

"It sounds to me that you got a valuable lesson—about what can be done when people pull together."

Chapter Four
The Discovery

The bailiff was right. Kazia's family had taken on a big challenge.

The piece of land where the Miser's house had stood was an oblong strip, which stretched back from a lane. About halfway along, near one edge stood an oak tree. Beyond the tree, the land sloped down a little.

If it had ever been surrounded by a fence, that had long ago fallen down and rotted away.

Nevertheless, Kazia's parents were easily able to distinguish it from the neighbouring plots. The strips of land on either side were planted with crops or showed beaten earth, where chickens ran. Their plot was a tangled wilderness. Clumps of brambles flourished everywhere, their long stems arching up into the air, fresh ones of green and dark red climbing over dead, brown stalks. Where brambles did not cover the ground nettles and thistles grew, some to waist height.

Kazia's father levelled the place where the Miser's house had been. He sank flat stones into the ground. One more time his friends from the river came and together they lifted Kazia's house into its final position, raised on blocks of wood resting on the stones.

At the end of the plot, where the land fell away, he built a little wooden hut to house their privy. He carved a heart-shaped opening high in its door.

The family worked at clearing the ground and sometimes Leon came to help. They dug up the thistles. They cut the bramble stems leaving stumps in the ground. When the stems were dry, they piled them around the stumps and set fire to them, to burn out the roots and to fertilise the soil with ash.

Kazia's father built a fence round the plot. It was never a regular fence, for he put it up a bit at a time, as he managed to lay his hands on odd pieces of timber. But it was stout for all that, enough to stop pigs or horses getting in.

Kazia and her mother set to on digging over the soil. Her mother bought cabbage and beetroot seeds from the market. They began to prepare the ground for planting.

It was tough going. The soil had not been turned over for many years, so breaking it up was a hard slog. Once they started digging, they unearthed all sorts of things. Rocks were hauled out and dragged over to a pile in one corner. Rusty horseshoes came up, old nails, bits of broken pot, an old leather bucket, a broken knife blade. One day Kazia's mother dug up a short length of lead pipe.

Nothing was wasted. They heaped all the finds in another pile. Old horseshoes and nails could be sold to the blacksmith. Broken crocks would improve the drainage of the soil. Even a small piece of lead might be reused on roofing.

From time-to-time Kazia poked around amongst the bits and pieces to see if there was anything she could play with.

"What do you think this was for?" asked Kazia one evening, putting the lead pipe on the table.

"Not there, Kazia," shouted her mother. "We're going to eat at this table. You don't know where that's been."

Kazia's father picked up the length of pipe.

"That's strange," he said. "Look at the ends."

"Now you're putting soil on the table," scolded his wife. "Take it outside."

"Just a moment. Look, somebody has gone to the trouble of sealing both ends with wax. Why would they do that?"

"Why would the pair of you let your soup go cold? Put that filthy thing down and get on with your supper. You can look at it as much as you like once we've finished."

Kazia bolted down her soup. She was intrigued by what her father had said.

Once they had eaten and cleared everything away, the three of them went outside. Kazia's father fetched one of his saws. He cut the pipe along its length and prized it open. Inside was a rolled-up piece of paper.

"Oh!" groaned Kazia. She had hoped to see something more exciting than a piece of paper.

Her mother unrolled it. The paper was damp. Words were written on it and amongst them, a few numbers.

"I wonder what this is," she said.

Neither Kazia nor her parents were able to read or write.

"I've got an idea," said Kazia. "Why don't we take it to the priest? He'll tell us what it says."

"Good thinking," said her mother. "We'll go in the morning. He's never seen about the town much before midday, so he's bound to be at home."

Chapter Five
The Priest

Kazia thought of the priest when she saw the piece of paper had writing on it. Many times, she had heard people talk of the priest's plan to start a school in the town.

The priest had arrived amongst them five years before. On learning the town had no school, he decried the ignorance of its people and their apathy in failing to get one going.

In fact, efforts had been made before his time to make good the lack. The bailiff had tried to persuade the nobleman to dip into his pockets.

"It would cost you little, my Lord. Giving up one of the houses for a school building would mean but a small loss of rent. Your only outlay would be modest, just the salary of a live-in teacher, who would keep the property in good order."

"Oh, no! Once they start learning, they'll become discontented. Before we know it, people will begin to drift away to the city."

The bailiff held back from reminding his employer that when it came to his own children, he paid for tutors to instruct them in French and Latin. Instead, he pressed the argument of self-interest.

"If our people could read and write, your Lordship, they'd be able to learn better ways of looking after the land. And if they improve their plots and get more yield from them, that can only be good for your Lordship's estate."

The nobleman laughed.

"Nonsense! What improves the land is hard work, not book learning. You don't need to read to plough a straight furrow. I'll hear no more of this. You stick to collecting my rents. Let others busy themselves with charity."

The priest boasted he himself would set up a school. People were impressed. Kazia's parents were determined to scrape together enough money to be able to send their daughter to school.

They wanted her to get a better start in life than either of them had.

As time went on, townsfolk would ask the priest what progress he was making.

"Be patient," he always replied. "These things take time to sort out."

Disillusion set in. Years passed and no sign of anything being done. Some in the town tackled him.

"So, where is this school you promised?"

"The Church is poor," he replied. "If you gave more, I should get on a lot faster."

In the end, people gave up hope of ever seeing the promised school. The subject became a joke. Whenever it came up, somebody would smile and say: "The priest is going to set up a school for our children. It'll be ready in time for them to send their grandchildren to it."

"Is Father expecting you?" asked the housekeeper when she opened the door to Kazia and her parents.

"No, but we need him to help us."

Had it been anybody else she would have turned them away, but she knew Kazia. Many times, she'd sent Kazia to the market to fetch things, paying her with a coin or with eggs.

"He doesn't like to be disturbed in the morning."

"We won't take up much of his time. We have something which could be important. We only want him to explain it to us."

"Very well. Come this way."

The housekeeper led them along a corridor to the door of the priest's study. She coughed loudly and knocked hard on the door.

Chapter Six
The Interview

For all the noise the housekeeper made, Kazia's mother thought she caught the sound of snoring from within the room.

They waited. The housekeeper knocked again, even harder. After another wait, a fuddled voice called:

"Come in."

The housekeeper opened the door and ushered in the family. The study was warm and stuffy. It gave out a sweet, sickly smell. The priest was sat in a chair by the fire. At his side was a table. On it stood a wine glass and a half empty decanter of liquid, gold in colour.

Ignoring the family, the priest glared at his housekeeper.

"Did I not tell you that I do not care to be interrupted when I am at my work?"

"Forgive me, Father. These are good folk and they have come to ask for your help."

Kazia's mother spoke up.

"We're sorry to interrupt your labours, Father." On the word 'labours', her eyes went to the decanter at the priest's elbow. "If you will do us this small service, we shall leave you in peace."

The priest waved his hand, and his housekeeper withdrew, closing the door behind her.

"Well, what is it? And please be brief."

Kazia's mother explained what they had found.

"We're curious to know what the paper says, Father. But none of us can read. Just tell us and we shall go straight away."

For the first time, the priest looked interested.

"Wait a moment," he said. Having struggled up from his chair, he tottered over to a desk on the far side of the room, opened a drawer and took out some spectacles.

He sat back down in his chair.

"Here, pass it to me."

He read the piece of paper silently to himself. He paused. And he read it again. There was another pause, even longer this time. He peered at them over the top of his spectacles.

"You say none of you can read?"

"No, Father. We neither read nor write."

"Have you shown this to anybody else?"

"We've shown it to no one but you, Father." The priest studied the piece of paper again.

"I'm sorry to disappoint you. This is just a recipe for plum brandy. It lists the ingredients and how much to put in."

"We already know a recipe," said Kazia's mother. "I learned it from my mother. She learned it from hers. It goes back in my family I don't know how far."

The priest smiled.

"Well, as you can't write either, you'll have no need of the paper. I'll keep it," he said, folding it and slipping it into the pocket of his waistcoat.

"And now, if you'll excuse me, I have work still to do."

They thanked the priest and trooped out of his study. After saying their farewells to the housekeeper, they trudged home in silence.

They were disappointed. None of them could say what they had expected to learn from the writing on the paper. But they had hoped for something more interesting than a recipe for plum brandy.

They were not people to brood. They had always too much work to waste time fretting. They got on with the chores of the day.

Chapter Seven
Stories

Kazia met up with Leon. She told him about their find and their visit to the priest.

"Keep it to yourself, though," she said, more out of embarrassment than for any other reason.

"I know a story about mysterious writing," said Leon.

"What happened?" Kazia asked.

"There was a king. He gave a feast in his palace. He invited a thousand people to join him. Huge amounts of wine were laid in for them all to drink. He liked to show off. His father had stolen lots of precious things from the people he conquered. This king fetched out all the gold and silver cups for his guests to drink their wine from them.

"While they were busy drinking, a mysterious hand appeared. The fingers of this hand wrote some words on the plaster of the wall in the palace room where they were feasting.

"The king was amazed and frightened. He couldn't read the writing. In his palace he had wise men. It was their job to give him advice. He got them to look at the writing, but they couldn't tell him what it meant.

"Everybody in the palace was baffled. The king felt terrified. Desperate to get to the bottom of the mystery, he promised a reward for anybody who could read the words. He would give purple robes and a gold chain to the person who told him what they meant.

"The king's wife had an idea. She suggested he should consult somebody called Daniel, who was a holy man."

"I suppose you might say our priest is a holy man," put in Kazia.

"Perhaps," Leon replied. "Anyway, they fetched Daniel to the palace. He wasn't at all interested in the reward."

"I would have been," said Kazia.

"Me too. But this Daniel had his mind more on God than on treasure. He had no trouble reading the words. And it turned out they weren't good news for the king. They were a message to tell him that his reign would soon be over."

"Was the message right?"

"Oh yes. Daniel got his reward but that very night armies of the king's enemies invaded his territory. They took over his kingdom and put the king to death."

"I think we'll settle for a boring recipe," said Kazia, "rather than a message like that. Is that another story you got from school?"

"Yes, it is."

"I wish I went to your school."

"If you did, you'd have a job to read these stories. The words we're speaking now, when they're written down, go from left to right across a page. But in the language of these stories, the words go the other way."

"Doesn't that spoil the story, when you're told how it ends right at the start?"

"No," said Leon. "It doesn't work like that. The words run a different way across the paper, but they still tell the story from the beginning."

"Whichever way the words go," said Kazia, "they're good stories. I like to hear them."

That evening, Kazia and her parents sat down together for their supper. As always, they talked about their day and about what they had seen and done.

"I've been thinking over our visit to the priest," said Kazia's mother.

"So have I," said her husband.

"What I can't understand is why anybody would bury a recipe for plum brandy."

"And remember," said Kazia's father, "whoever did it went to a lot of trouble-writing it down from memory, finding a bit of lead pipe, cutting it to the right length and sealing the ends with wax."

"It's not as if it's a rare or secret thing. There can't be a family in this town that doesn't know how to make plum brandy. When the fruit is on the trees, we're all at it. We've got three bottles on the shelf ourselves. It just doesn't make sense."

Kazia's father nodded.

"And I'll tell you what's been bothering me. Why was he so keen to check that none of us can read and, what is more, that we hadn't shown the paper to anybody else? Perhaps the plum brandy was a tale he made up, so he could keep to himself whatever the paper said."

"Would a priest play a trick like that?"

"Maybe this one would. But one thing is for sure. We'll never find out now. He was careful to hang on to the paper so we can't ask anybody else."

Kazia was quiet but she took in all her parents said. In bed that evening, before she went to sleep, she turned things over in her mind. She thought back to Leon's story of the mysterious hand and the message which at first nobody could understand. Perhaps the paper in the lead pipe was their mystery.

Chapter Eight
In the Market

The next day was market day. Kazia was up and out early. She hoped to earn tips from the stallholders. They valued help unloading produce from baskets, carts and wagons.

It turned out to be a gainful day. Kazia was paid for filling horses' nosebags with oats. She swept up their droppings too. She was given a pocketful of flour for helping a miller's children to drag some sacks to his stall.

By mid-morning, the market was at its height. Geese cackled in their pens. Stray dogs barked when shooed out of the way. Handcarts creaked along between rows of stalls.

People had flooded into the town from villages all around. They shouted greetings to one another. Buyers haggled about prices and shook hands to pledge deals. Sellers bellowed above the noise, urging people to come and see what marvellous things they had for sale. Chickens clucked and bystanders laughed when one escaped and was chased by a boy. Donkeys brayed from under the trees where they were tethered.

As the morning went on, the smells of freshly dug carrots, parsnips and turnips mixed with those of wood smoke and cooking. Cauldrons of beetroot soup and cabbage soup were warming. Dumplings stuffed with meat and cheese were roasting on stoves.

Kazia was surprised to see the priest. She remembered her mother saying he was rarely seen out before midday. Appearing to be in a hurry, he made his way between the stalls as quickly as his plump figure would allow and he kept his head down.

Curious, Kazia decided to follow him at a distance to see where he was going. She had been given a broom to clear the alleys of rubbish, so she had no problem going after the priest, sweeping as she went.

He made straight for the stall of the town's blacksmith. Without haggling over prices, he bought a pick-axe, a shovel and a lantern. Eager though he was to get away, the priest could not avoid talking to the blacksmith.

"We don't often see you here, Father. Is your housekeeper unwell?"

"No. I do try to help her when I can."

The blacksmith smiled. He knew the housekeeper. She would be amused, he was sure, by the priest's suggestion that he helped her.

"So what are these for, then? Are you going to start digging the foundations of our new school?"

The priest scowled.

"I'm waiting for a miracle before I begin—the miracle of seeing you set foot inside my church."

Unabashed, the blacksmith asked again.

"So if they're not for building, what do you want them for?"

"There's a fox in my garden. It's taken over a rabbit hole, so I'm going to dig it out. Not that it's any business of yours. You mind your forge and I'll see to my parish."

With those words, the priest turned and stumped away with his purchases.

Kazia saw the blacksmith pull a face at the priest's back. She caught his eye and they exchanged grins.

Chapter Nine
A Plan Is Made

By mid-afternoon the market had begun to wind down. People were setting off home.

Kazia went back and handed over her earnings to her parents. They congratulated her on the fruits of her hard work. She told them about the priest and what she had seen him buy in the market.

"That's interesting," said her mother. "He finds out we've dug something up and he rushes out to buy things for digging."

"Don't forget the lantern," Kazia said. "If he's going digging, it looks as if he plans to do it in the dark."

"Whatever is he up to?" Kazia's mother narrowed her eyes. "You don't suppose he fancies digging around on our land?"

"Perhaps he liked that plum brandy recipe. He maybe thinks there's a crop of recipes growing in our soil."

They all laughed.

"Seriously, though. There's something going on. He may be our priest, but I don't trust him."

"I've got an idea," said Kazia. "Why don't we stay up and keep watch tonight?"

"And how are we going to do that?"

Kazia pondered for a moment and then spoke.

"You two could wait indoors. Snuff out the lamp at the usual time and make it look as if we're all asleep in bed. I'll wrap up warm and hide behind the little room with the heart. There's a good view from there and there'll be moonlight. If the priest does come, I'll sound the alarm. You can run out of the house and catch him, red-handed."

Kazia's father was not keen on her idea.

"If he wants to get cold and muddy wasting his time, I'm happy to let him."

"Well, I'm not. I'm not having him mess up the work we've done to start growing vegetables."

Kazia's mother was firm, and her husband soon came round. There was still some time before supper. After Kazia had worked much of the day in the marketplace, her parents were happy for her to go off and play for what was left of the afternoon.

Kazia said nothing to them. She shot straight off to find Leon. She couldn't wait to tell him what was going on. Nor did she intend to leave him out of this adventure.

"I wish I could be there," said Leon, when Kazia outlined the plan to him.

"That's why I'm telling you about it. We'll keep watch together. Two lots of eyes and ears are better than one."

"How do I get away, though?"

"I couldn't do it myself," said Kazia. "There's only a bit of curtain between my bed and my parents' bed. But you've a bedroom of your own. You must be able to sneak out somehow."

"I suppose I could climb out of the window and onto the roof of the shed."

"Exactly. And you'd easily jump down from there."

"Yes. And I could climb back up on the water butt. I'll be there. I promise."

"Good. Make sure you put on something warm. Once it's really dark and you think it's safe, come along to my house. Remember, if you get caught, not a word to your parents."

"You can rely on me."

Kazia said little during supper. She was thinking of the best way to tell her parents she had invited Leon to keep watch with her.

As the light faded, they heard the sounds of the town settling itself down for the evening. A couple of dogs barked at one another. Geese cackled as they were herded into their pen. In the distance two men sang, walking to one of the inns. A woman called to a child to come indoors. Soon no more was heard.

The silence was broken by a tap on the door. Kazia was expecting it, but both her parents jumped. They opened the door.

"Leon, whatever are you doing here at this time of night?"

"Let him in. I can explain," butted in Kazia, before Leon was able to utter a word.

Kazia told them she had invited Leon to come and keep watch with her. It would be safer, she argued, if there were two of them out there in the dark.

"I'm not sure what danger you're expecting," objected her mother. Turning to Leon, she asked, "Do your parents know you've come here tonight?"

"No, they think I'm asleep in bed."

"What are they going to say when they find out you've left the house and come here?"

"My father will be angry, and he'll punish me. Then, he'll sit me down and we'll talk about it. I think he'll understand. He's told me about lots of adventures he had when he was a boy."

"This is not an adventure," said Kazia's father. "I'm not happy about this. I think I should take you home right now."

"Oh no," pleaded Kazia. "Do let Leon stay. If there are two of us, we'll keep watch all the better. And we can make sure one stays awake."

The discussion went on for a while and Kazia pressed her case. In the end her parents came round. Her mother knew Kazia and Leon were close and she was keen to encourage their friendship. Her father would have been happy to march Leon back and deal with his father, but he was less enthusiastic about tangling with Leon's mother. He had heard something of her from Kazia.

"Very well, then," said Kazia's mother. "But how are you two going to sound the alarm?"

Kazia grabbed an iron pot and a ladle from a shelf by the stove. She hit the pot hard, and the clang filled the house.

"Now, you give them a burst of your singing, Leon," she said. Leon threw his head back and let go at the top of his voice.

"Stop, stop," cried Kazia's parents. "What on earth is that?"

"It's one of the Songs of David—'Lord, who may dwell in your sanctuary?' There's a man who sings them in our synagogue. He has an amazing voice. I want to do that when I'm old enough. I've been learning the songs. And I practice, trying to sing like him."

"Well, if we do have an intruder tonight and you bellow that out, you'll scare him out of his wits."

"That's just what we want," said Kazia.

Her mother fetched blankets for them both. Her father lit a lantern and led them down to the little house with the heart. They settled themselves behind it. A couple of minutes later, they saw Kazia's mother indoors snuff out their lamp and the house became no more than a shape in the darkness.

Chapter Ten
Waiting in the Dark

Kazia and Leon had a long wait. As their eyes adjusted to the darkness, the stars seemed to become brighter. To pass the time they tried to find patterns in them. The game did not last long. They could not agree and soon got fed up with arguing.

A snuffling, scrabbling noise nearby made them both jump. By the moonlight they could just make out a hedgehog poking about in the soil, probing for worms.

A ghostly, cream coloured shape flapped over their heads without a sound. An owl was on the hunt for small creatures moving on the ground.

Beginning to feel cold, they huddled together. They heard a dog bark far away but around the house nothing stirred.

"How about one of your stories?" whispered Kazia.

Leon thought for a while. "I know one about a man who tried to steal things," he said at last.

"Go on, then. I'd love to hear it."

"It's about the Israelites. At the time of the story, they were led by a man called Joshua. Your Jesus is named after him."

"I didn't know he was named after anybody."

"Well, he was. Anyway, Joshua's job was to lead the Israelites across the River Jordan, so they could occupy all the land between the river and the sea. That's what God had promised them."

"Why did he promise it?"

"The Israelites were his favourite people. He said if they did what he told them, they could have all that land."

"I didn't think God had favourites."

"Look, if you're going to argue with me, I won't tell you the story."

"Alright, alright. Go on. I won't say any more."

"There were other people already living in this land. They all had to be overcome if the Israelites were to take it from them. That was a tough job. There were lots of well defended cities and they were all going to have to be conquered in turn.

"For the Israelites this was a holy war because it was part of their deal with God. One of the rules of a holy war was that every victory won belonged to God. That meant that nobody was allowed to carry off for himself any of the things they captured.

"The first city in their way was Jericho. That was a challenge. It had strong walls. The king of Jericho knew the Israelites were coming and he was ready for them. But with help from God, the Israelites managed to capture the city. Once they were in Jericho, they collected lots of gold and silver and precious things. Because of the holy war rule, the treasure wasn't shared out amongst themselves. Instead, they stacked it up in a storeroom in God's Temple.

"Their next target was a city to the west of Jericho. It was smaller and looked like an easier target. But they were wrong. The army from that city defeated the Israelites and sent them running for their lives. Now the tables were turned. The Israelites were terrified that word of their defeat would spread to all the cities on that side of the river, rousing them to get together to drive them back across the Jordan.

"Joshua was puzzled. He couldn't work out how his army had been beaten by such a small force. He asked God what was going on. God explained that he had given the other side victory to punish the Israelites. 'What have we done wrong?' Joshua wanted to know. God told him that somebody amongst the Israelites had stolen some of the treasure which was taken during the sacking of Jericho.

"Joshua was determined to get to the bottom of the matter. He gathered all the Israelites together and questioned them. Eventually, a man called Achan confessed. He admitted stealing some of the treasure. He said he'd hidden it in his tent.

"Joshua sent some of his people to search Achan's tent. They discovered he'd dug a hole in the ground covered by the tent. In the hole he'd buried the treasure—a heavy bar of gold, lots of silver coins and a beautiful robe."

"What happened to Achan?" asked Kazia.

Leon put his fingers to his lips.

"Shssh! Look! There!" he whispered.

Chapter Eleven
Intruder

Kazia peered in the direction of Leon's pointing arm. She saw a dim light moving from the lane towards the fence, halfway down their plot of land. It swayed as it came. She guessed somebody was carrying a lantern. Whoever he was, he must have shaded it to cast most of its glow downwards, lighting his footsteps.

The figure reached the fence. He seemed to be carrying tools, for Kazia caught a glint of bright metal as he reached over the fence and dropped them onto the ground on the other side.

The figure clambered over the fence. He did so with difficulty, for he was wearing a long black cloak, with the hood pulled down over his head. When finally over, he stood for a moment or two looking around. Then, he gathered up whatever it was he had brought and made straight across the plot for the oak tree on the far side.

As the figure walked, Kazia had enough moonlight to be able to make out his silhouette. She could see he was plump. Few in their town enjoyed a lifestyle that made them put on weight.

"That's got to be our priest."

"Quiet," Leon hissed.

When the figure reached the tree, he put down what he was carrying. He positioned himself with his back pressed against the trunk and lifted his lantern. Its light enabled Kazia and Leon to see him peer down at a piece of paper.

"That's the paper we showed him. And he's not going to make plum brandy by moonlight."

"Will you be quiet, Kazia? He'll hear you and make off before we can find out what he's up to."

The figure picked up his things and began to walk back across the plot. This time he paced in a deliberate way, as if measuring the distance. He stopped. One of his tools was a spade. With it, he made a mark in the soil. For a couple of minutes, he stood on the spot, looking up at the stars, as if getting his bearings. He turned and began pacing in a different direction, this time towards the little house with the heart.

"He's coming this way," gasped Kazia.

"Not another word. He'll be in earshot soon."

To their relief, the figure stopped and made another mark in the ground. There he began to dig. He started vigorously. In little time he had raised a pile of soil by a hole.

Kazia and Leon were close enough to hear him grunting with the effort. As he dug deeper, the work became harder. He threw off his cloak. His other tool was a pickaxe. He began to swing it, prising up stones from the bottom of the hole. He was making enough noise for Kazia and Leon to be able to whisper in safety.

"Shall we sound the alarm now?"

"No," said Kazia. "Let's wait and see if he finds anything."

He continued wielding the pickaxe. They then heard a different sound—a hollow thud. The figure stopped at once. Going down on his knees, he peered into the hole. Having risen, he dug with a new frenzy, trying to free whatever it was at the bottom. Puffing hard now, he lay down at full length, his arms into the hole, tugging and pulling.

"Jesus and Mary!" he blurted out.

"Is he saying a prayer?" Leon asked Kazia.

"I don't think you'd call it praying."

With much heaving and groaning, the figure at last managed to drag a wooden box out of the hole. He collapsed back on the heap of soil, panting.

Kazia squeezed Leon's arm.

"Now!"

Leon launched into his song at full volume. Kazia knew what was coming but, in the darkness, he made even her jump. She recovered and joined in, banging the ladle on the iron pot with all her might.

The figure grabbed his lantern and tools. He tugged at the box trying to lift it or at least drag it with him. But it was too heavy. He left it and ran for the fence.

Kazia and Leon kept up their noise, expecting any moment that Kazia's parents would dash from the house and lay hands on the intruder. But at the house nothing stirred. The intruder clambered over the fence. As he jumped down on the other side, he dropped the pickaxe on his foot. With a howl of pain, he hobbled away into the darkness.

Inside, Kazia and Leon found her parents fully dressed lying on their bed. They were fast asleep.

Kazia was cross.

"Wake up, wake up. You've let him get away." She gave her mother a shake.

"Oh dear. We're sorry. We sat here on the bed waiting. We heard nothing for ages and ages. We must have dropped off to sleep. But what did you see?"

"It was him alright. It was the priest. What's more, he had our piece of paper. But come and see what he dug up."

They lit their own lantern. Kazia and Leon led her parents to the hole the priest had dug. The wooden box was heavy, but Kazia's father was strong and he was able to carry it back into the house. He set it down on the floor and they gathered round to examine it.

The chest had been in the ground for some time. The wood was damp and in places it was beginning to rot. It was fastened at the front with an iron padlock. Both the padlock and the iron hinges at the back were encrusted with rust.

"That's going to take some time to open," said Kazia's father.

"Yes, and it'll not be done tonight," her mother said. "If you can get here tomorrow morning, Leon, we promise we'll not try to open it until you're with us."

"Don't worry. I'll be here."

"Good, and in return will you promise to say nothing about this to anyone?"

"I promise."

Kazia's mother was pleased to get Leon's promise. It was not so much that she wanted to keep the finding of the box a secret. Embarrassed by the behaviour of the priest, she did not want to give Leon's people grounds for thinking badly of the Church.

Having already slumbered deeply when they should have been on watch, Kazia's parents were unable to get to sleep that night. Leon clambered onto the roof of the shed below his bedroom window and managed to enter without rousing anybody in the house. But by the time he got into bed, he was too excited to sleep.

He took some sharp words from his mother next morning for the number of times he yawned over his breakfast. Kazia lay awake most of the night, wondering what could be in the chest.

Chapter Twelve
The Chest Is Opened

A drill, hammer, chisel, knife and crowbar—the next morning Kazia's father assembled the tools he needed to open the chest.

Kazia hopped around the house, chattering all the time. In the end, her mother set her to cleaning the stove to keep her busy. Even as she worked, she buzzed with questions.

"Do you think Leon's parents found out about last night? What if he's been kept at home as a punishment? Is this one of the days he has to go to school? What do we do if he can't make it this morning? How long do we have to keep our promise if he doesn't show up?"

At last, though, Leon arrived. The chest was on the floor where it had been put the night before. Kazia's father tipped it back, so it sat on its hinges. Kazia and Leon held it steady, one on each side. He took his drill. Turning and turning, he bored a number of holes in the wood, close to one another and in a circle around the lock on the front of the chest.

Once the circle was complete, with hammer and chisel he set to, knocking through the wood between the holes. Soon a jagged disc of wood, with the padlock still on it, came away from the body of the chest. He rested the chest back on its base. There was just enough of a gap between the body and the lid to push in his crowbar.

The rust had stuck the iron hinges, but it had bitten deeply enough to make them thin and brittle. As he levered the lid, the hinges suddenly broke with a crack and the whole of it came off.

Inside was a leather bag, tied with cord. Kazia's father lifted it. With a slash, he cut the cord and tipped the bag out on the floor.

They jumped at the sound of a shower of silver coins hitting the wooden planks. There was more money than any of them had ever seen before. They all stared. Kazia broke the silence.

"Is there enough here to pay for me to go to school?"

Her mother laughed.

"There's enough here, Kazia, to set up a whole school."

"Just a moment," said her father. "There's a bigger question before we get to that—who does this belong to?"

"Your father's right. I like your idea about school. But before we start spending it, we have to sort out whether this money is ours."

Kazia and Leon scrambled about the floor on their hands and knees retrieving coins, while her parents heaped the pile in handfuls back into the leather bag.

"I think we should talk to the bailiff before we do anything else. He played fair with us when we bought this land. We should play fair with him."

Kazia's mother agreed.

"Off you go, Kazia. If you can find the bailiff, ask him if he would be kind enough to call. Don't tell him about this. Just say we would like to talk to him about something important."

Kazia shot out of the door without waiting for Leon.

"It's best to let her go, Leon. Racing about the town, she might burn off some of her excitement. You can help us tidy up."

While Leon swept up the wood shavings, Kazia's father gathered his tools.

"Whoever this belongs to," he said, "how are we going to keep it safe? This place isn't secure."

"You're right. Perhaps one of us will have to stay in the house all the time to guard it, until we get everything sorted. Unless, of course, we rebury it."

"My father might be able to help," said Leon.

"In what way?"

"He and his friends keep their money in a strong box. It's made of iron. It was built in when our house was put up, so it can't be moved, even when it's empty. There are five locks on it and each one has a different key. My father has one and so do four of our elders. They all have to be together for it to be opened."

"But would they let us store this silver there?"

"I'm sure my father would be happy to help you. I can't say about the others, but I bet he'd be able to win them round."

Kazia's parents looked at one another.

"Alright, then. Let's ask him," said Kazia's mother. "You go and fetch your father, Leon. You can tell him we've found some silver. But please don't say anything about the priest."

Leon shot off home.

Chapter Thirteen
Conference

Leon was not gone long when they heard a wagon pull up in the lane. Kazia jumped down from the seat and led the bailiff into the house.

"Good day to you," said the bailiff. "You're lucky to have caught me. I'm off to Krakow early tomorrow. I have estate business to do there. I won't be back for six or seven days."

Kazia's father poured the adults each a glass of plum brandy. They sat at the table. Her mother set before the bailiff a chunk of rye bread and a dish of curd cheese.

They told him the story of the lead pipe, the piece of paper, their visit to the priest and his night-time foray into their plot. The bailiff took a handful of coins and looked at them. To gauge their weight, he lifted the leather bag.

"Do you remember the story that went around when the Miser first turned up here?" They all nodded.

"Well, it makes sense now. This must have been his money. If his old place had been burned down and he was frightened of it happening again, he'd want to make sure he kept nothing inside his house. We did find an old key round his neck. I'll bet that was the key to this chest."

"But why bury the instructions for finding the chest?"

"I guess we'll never know the answer to that. He wouldn't have wanted to keep them in the house. Perhaps he wanted double security by burying two things. Maybe he had a way of remembering where he'd buried the lead pipe. One thing is sure. When he became old and frail, he was never going to be strong enough to dig the chest up, even supposing he wanted to spend some of his cash."

"All this is very interesting," said Kazia's mother. "What we really want to know is does this belong to us now?"

The bailiff laughed.

"Of course it does. And good luck to you," he said, taking another swig of plum brandy.

"Really?"

"Look," replied the bailiff. "You bought this land legally. You didn't trick anyone to get it. My master was paid once when the Miser bought it from him. It only went back to him because we couldn't find anybody to inherit it from the Miser. When you bought the land, my master was paid a second time. In my book, he can have no claim on the silver. Nor am I going to prompt him to think he has."

Kazia and her parents looked at one another. The truth was beginning to sink in. All this money was theirs to spend.

The bailiff broke the silence.

"If you'll allow me, I do have a suggestion."

"Go ahead."

"Well, on the way here, I was talking to Kazia. She's keen to learn. You must know that. Your good fortune could make it possible for the town to get that school we've been waiting so long for. It wouldn't take much. There'd be plenty left for yourselves."

"We've been thinking the same thing," said Kazia's father. "But we wouldn't know how to go about it. We're going to need help."

"Don't worry," the bailiff answered. "You can count on me."

"There are two things, though," said Kazia's mother. "We don't want anything said about the priest and his part in this."

She explained that Leon had been with them and that his people might help in keeping the cash safe.

"I understand. I shall share that with nobody else. But I will keep in mind what you've told me. It may serve our purpose if I let him know what we've learned about his behaviour. What was the other thing?"

"If we can use some of this money to get a school going, I'd want people to be told it was an anonymous gift."

"That'll be no problem."

Kazia's father poured another round of plum brandy. They talked more about the school idea. The bailiff thought it would be possible to find a teacher in Krakow, somebody willing to move to their town. If it was a live-in job, there would be only a small outlay on a salary. And that would be offset by whatever families were charged for their children to go.

While they were talking, there was a knock at the door. Leon had returned with his father.

There were greetings and more plum brandy.

"Peace be with you all," he said, "and may that peace not be upset by your treasure."

Leon and his father joined them at the table. He set down a canvas bag he'd been carrying over one shoulder.

"Leon has told me of your find. I'm happy to keep the money safe—at no charge, as this is between friends," he said, smiling at Leon and Kazia. "But why am I wasting time? Let's get down to business."

Leon opened his father's bag. He took out a roll of paper and laid it flat on the table, keeping down the two ends with empty glasses. He fetched out a small enamel pot, stoppered with a cork.

Next came a quill and a knife.

While Leon sharpened the quill and uncorked the ink, his father fetched out an iron balance and a set of weights. He stretched up, slung a cord from one of the ceiling beams and hung the balance on it. Taking coins at random he put one at a time on one of its pans, holding the marker in the middle still, while he placed weights in the other pan. When the marker, on release, stood still and vertical, he took another coin and did the same again. He tested six in that way.

He grinned. "All sound!"

Having written down the weight of the coins, he counted them, stacking them in piles. The bailiff then counted them. They agreed the number. Leon's father wrote a receipt, setting out all the details of the money. The bailiff read it aloud to Kazia's parents. He signed it as a witness, and they added their marks.

Leon's father picked up the leather bag.

"I shall go now and put this in our strong box."

"I'll come with you," said Kazia's father.

"I'm sorry. That cannot be. My colleagues and I are happy to keep your treasure safe for you. But as for being present when we open it—that is something we cannot allow. You will have to trust us. Whenever you want any of the silver, let me know and you will have it at once."

Kazia's parents spoke together.

"Very well. We trust you."

Chapter Fourteen
Plum Brandy for the Priest

"I think we should pay the priest another visit," said Kazia's mother the next day. "And we should go before the bailiff gets back from Krakow."

Her husband frowned.

"Whatever for?"

"Well, I know he tried to rob us. But if it wasn't for him, we would never have all this money. We should be charitable. And besides, I want to see if he'll confess once we show him we know what he was up to."

"As you wish," said Kazia's father. "But don't expect me to talk to the man."

"Why don't we take him some plum brandy?" suggested Kazia.

"That's a good idea. We've got plenty." Her mother reached up and took from a shelf one of several earthenware flasks. She stood it on the table.

"It's early yet and we've got things to do. But we'll go before midday."

Kazia had another idea. This was one she chose not to share with her parents. Once she was sure they were both out of sight, she took the flask and eased off the stopper. Going outside, she went behind the house and poured about a quarter of the brandy away into the soil.

Back indoors she took down a wooden ladle. On the floor, in a corner, where it was cool, was a large earthenware crock. Every couple of months Kazia's mother made a batch of sour cabbage and Kazia helped her. They would sit together and slice cabbage leaves until they had a pile of shreds. Her mother packed a layer into the crock.

Kazia's job was to sprinkle an even helping of salt between each layer. When the cabbage and salt layers were two thirds of the way up the crock, they spread a cloth over them. On top of the cloth went a wooden disc, which they weighed down with two heavy stones. The salt drew liquid out of the cabbage and the pressure of the disc squeezed out more. They left the crock to stand. Every few days they had to draw off the liquid.

Kazia dipped in the ladle. She topped up the brandy flask with the juices from the cabbage until it was nearly full again. Replacing the stopper, she gave it a good shake. She put the flask back on the table where her mother had left it.

They told his housekeeper they had come to thank the priest and to give him some plum brandy. She showed them to his study and ushered them in. This time, he did not wave her away.

The priest remained in his seat. He avoided looking straight at any of them.

Kazia's mother spoke up.

"We wanted to thank you properly for explaining what that paper said. So, we've brought you some of our own plum brandy."

The priest shifted in his seat.

"Thank you," he stammered. "That's good of you."

Still he did not stir. There was silence in the room. Kazia's mother held up the flask. She was adamant she would not go over and hand it to him.

The housekeeper broke the silence.

"Come on, Father, take your gift."

The priest heaved himself out of his chair. As he crossed the room, he walked with a limp.

"I'm sorry to see you limping," said Kazia's mother. "Did you drop something on your foot?"

The priest coughed. "No. It's gout. I suffer terribly from gout."

Having taken the flask, he slumped back into his chair. There was silence again.

"Are you not going to try some?" Kazia's mother asked.

"No, no. I never drink during the day."

His housekeeper's eyebrows shot up. She looked at the glass at his elbow. It was still sticky with the dregs of his last draught.

"If that is all, I really must get on now with my work." They turned to go. In the doorway, Kazia's mother paused.

"By the way, Father, did you sort out that fox?"

"Fox? What are you talking about?"

"I heard you had a fox in your garden, and you were going to dig it out."

"Oh yes—the fox. Yes, that's all sorted."

"I'm glad to hear it," replied Kazia's mother. "Foxes are sly creatures. If they come onto your land, there's no knowing what they'll try to steal."

The housekeeper closed the study door behind them. Instead of leading the way back along the corridor, she put her finger to her lips and motioned them to wait a moment outside the door. She cupped one hand at her ear, urging them to listen. A few seconds passed.

Then they heard a pop come from the room, the sound of the stopper being pulled from the flask. The housekeeper grinned and winked. That was the sound she had anticipated. Kazia's parents smiled. Kazia smiled too, but for a different reason.

The housekeeper turned to show them out. Then came a sound she had not anticipated.

Through the door they heard a burst of coughing, spluttering and spitting, followed by a torrent of curses which prompted them all to hasten to the front door.

"It must have gone down the wrong way," whispered the housekeeper.

Kazia said nothing but she thought to herself, *No, it's gone down the right way, just the way I wanted.*

Chapter Fifteen
Time Moves On

When the bailiff returned, he went to see the priest.

A couple of days after his visit people were astonished by two items of news which buzzed through the town by word of mouth. They had given up hope of it, so they were amazed to learn that a school was at last to be founded. What staggered them even more was the plan to set it up in rooms of the priest's house.

The bailiff was true to his promise to help Kazia's parents manage the business. He spoke to the nobleman.

"Your Lordship should know that I shall be spending some time helping to get the new school going in the town. I shall do it in my own time. Your Lordship can be assured his estate will suffer in no way because of it."

"I am not happy. Your job is estate management, not education."

"I know your Lordship's views about schooling. But this is something that will be popular with the people of the town. It has become possible through an anonymous donation and that is what I have put about. People have already started to guess that the benefactor must be your Lordship. I have no intention of correcting them. And my own involvement in the work will seem to confirm that idea. Your Lordship stands to gain much credit in the town at no cost."

To the nobleman that proved a winning line. But another thought weighed with him as much. He could see his bailiff was dead set on this. The man was deemed to be the best bailiff in the whole province. If aggrieved, he could have his pick of jobs on other estates.

"Very well then. But see that it's in your time, not mine."

Kazia's father helped with the work to make the rooms ready. One was to be the teacher's accommodation, the other the schoolroom. As the bailiff predicted, it was not hard to find a teacher. A young man moved to the town to take the job.

The school was ready to start within three months of the finding of the Miser's chest.

The bailiff organised an opening ceremony. Everyone in the town was invited. The children were to sit on benches at the front of the crowd. Kazia's mother and her friends planned a feast of food to be shared afterwards. The nobleman wrote a speech and had his manservant dust his old military uniform.

The priest was invited to attend to bestow a blessing on the new venture. When no reply to the invitation came, Kazia's mother called at the priest's house. She found his housekeeper flustered.

"He's gone," she said. "I don't know what to make of it. Your invitation came and the next morning he was off like a shot. All he would say was he would send a cart later to collect his things."

Kazia's mother said nothing.

There was plenty of money besides for Kazia and her family. None of them wanted a new house. They were content for Kazia's father to build an extension, so Kazia could have a room of her own.

Kazia's father built a workshop and a store for his timber. He got a horse and cart too. He was able to spend more time making furniture. Word of the quality of his work spread. He had orders for pieces from as far away as Krakow. With the cart he was able to deliver his furniture and to show off pieces in other towns to attract more business.

Kazia's mother invested in seeds. She showed herself talented at growing things. They were able to feed themselves and produce enough to sell surplus vegetables and herbs in the town market. One patch of their land she set aside as an orchard. She planted plum trees. In future they would make their plum brandy from their own fruit.

They did not forget their friends and neighbours down by the river. They made it known that if any family from that part of the town could not afford to pay for schooling, the children would have their education at no charge.

To their surprise, Kazia's parents managed to keep secret their discovery of the Miser's hoard of silver. Townsfolk knew they were friendly with Leon's people. They assumed they had borrowed money from them and that using the money well, they had prospered.

Kazia was the first pupil to be enrolled in the new school. She was quick to learn and soon picked up reading and writing. In the evenings, after their work was done, she sat with her parents and taught them to read and write.

As they moved into adulthood, Kazia and Leon saw less of one another. By his middle years, Leon had become a celebrated teacher amongst his people. They travelled from towns and cities all over Poland to seek his advice and hear him talk. He was revered for his emphasis upon the duty of charity to others.

Kazia became a teacher herself. She was finally appointed head of the school, which her parents' money had founded. She never forgot the time she spent with Leon. In all her work with children and young people there were two things she stressed—the importance of respecting people different from oneself and the enrichment to be gained from stories.

The Castle of Soria Moria – Norway

Chapter One
The Ash Boy

"For goodness' sake, Halvor," said his mother, "stir yourself, lad."

Halvor lived with his mother and father in a house near the mouth of a fjord. He liked to spend all his time sitting by the fire.

Halvor's parents loved their son, but they worried about him. Were it not for their scolding he would have been content all day long to loll in the wooden armchair by their hearth.

"That fire needs fresh logs," his father said.

"Mmh," Halvor murmured, but he did not stir.

He would sit there staring into the grate. He imagined faces and creatures in the flickering flames. When the fire sank, he used to take the poker and stir the ashes, shaping them into seas and valleys and mountains.

Because of that his mother and father called him 'the Ash Boy'. Their friends from the nearby village happened to hear them using the name. Soon everyone in the village called Halvor, 'the Ash Boy'.

They were a poor family. Halvor's parents owned a couple of fields. On their land, they kept a few cows and sheep. Most years they barely managed to make sufficient to feed themselves.

When Halvor became old enough they were keen he should take a job, but he could settle at nothing. They found a place for him with the baker who supplied most of the people in the village with their bread. They got him work with the carpenter who made the wooden racks on which villagers hung fish to dry. They even persuaded the local blacksmith who fashioned axes and chains for the woodcutters working in the forests. The outcome was always the same. After a day or two, Halvor would give up and drift home.

"That's not for me," Halvor would say.

"So what is for you?" his father demanded. "Are you going to sit your whole life by that fire?"

Halvor shrugged. He slumped back into the armchair and sat stirring the ashes in the grate.

"You're beginning to look like a beggar, Halvor," his mother said. "Until you can earn some money, you'll have no new clothes. There's only so much patching I can do before your things fall to pieces."

"Don't fuss, mother," Halvor replied. "That doesn't bother me."

If Halvor was to marry, it was likely to be one of the young women of the village. But when he went out, the young women would call after him.

"Here's the Ash Boy."

"What do you dream of Ash Boy?" one of them asked.

"Logs and pokers," the others shouted in a giggling chorus. "Logs and pokers."

Although he had become a shabby figure, they could see he was a handsome young man.

They were sure, though, that he would never make anything of himself.

One day a sea captain knocked at the door of their house. He had dropped anchor in the mouth of the fjord. He asked for directions to the village, where he wanted to buy provisions.

"How would you like a life at sea, young man?" he asked, looking at Halvor sprawled in the armchair by the fire.

"Fishing is a hard life," Halvor replied. "I've seen the boats from the village sailing past to the fishing grounds out at sea. And I've seen them coming back after being out the night long in all weathers."

"Do I smell like a fisherman?" laughed the captain. "I sail the oceans of the world. I go where I please. I pick up a cargo here and I offload a cargo there. I might dock in a dozen different ports in a year. If you join my crew, you'll get to see places you can only dream about here."

"Now, that does sound like the thing for me," answered Halvor. "I'll go with you."

His mother and father were sad he was leaving them. They were pleased though that at least he had found something which interested him. They said their farewells and Halvor went off with the captain.

Chapter Two
The Brown Castle

The ship sailed from the fjord. At first the weather was favourable. For seven days they had good winds, and they covered a great distance. A storm then burst upon them. The storm raged for three days and three nights. Early on, the ship's rudder was smashed. The battered vessel was driven wherever the wind and the waves took her.

When the storm had passed the captain had no idea where they were. The ship was becalmed off the coast of a land no one on board recognised. The captain dropped anchor. There was much work to be done to repair the storm damage. Ropes had to be re-joined, torn sails had to be stitched and there were broken timbers to be replaced.

"I've none of the skills you need," said Halvor to the captain. "Can I go ashore and look around while the repairs are done?"

"No," said the captain. "What better chance will you have than now to learn those skills?"

"But you promised me I would see exotic lands and strange sights."

The captain was reluctant, but Halvor persisted. At last, he agreed to let him go.

"Mind you keep an eye on the weather," the captain ordered. "I want to be ready to raise anchor whenever we get an offshore wind. As soon as you feel a wind blow, head back to the beach."

One of the crew rowed Halvor ashore. He walked up the beach onto the sand dunes above it. From there he looked inland.

Halvor had seen enough of his parents' work to be able to tell whether or not land was well managed. The fields he could see looked neglected. He saw nobody at work. The whole countryside had the appearance of being deserted.

Halvor set off to explore. Soon, he came upon a road and decided to follow it. Meeting no one on the way, he pressed on. After a while, he felt the beginnings of a breeze. He thought to himself, *it would do no harm to keep walking a little longer.*

It was late in the afternoon when Halvor spotted a castle in the distance. He could see round towers and high walls. The castle was built of brown stone and topped with jagged battlements. He guessed there must be people there. That thought reminded him he was hungry. He made for the castle to see if he could get something to eat.

Halvor reached the castle. As he approached, he looked from window to window but saw no sign of anyone. He tried to walk softly but in the silence his steps sounded loud on the wooden drawbridge. There was no one on duty in the guardroom. He continued into the courtyard. By the side of a well a broken pitcher lay on the ground where it had fallen. In many places weeds were growing between the cobbles. Crossing the courtyard, he came to an opening. He went in and found it led to the castle kitchen.

At the far end of the kitchen was a door, which Halvor opened. Beyond was a corridor lined with more doors. The first one was ajar, and he could hear sounds of movement behind it. Looking in, he saw a beautiful princess with long, brown hair. She sat working at a spinning wheel.

"Who are you?" cried the princess. "What brings you here?"

Before Halvor could answer, she went on, "You'd better get away quickly. This is my castle, but a troll has taken it over. He keeps me prisoner here. He's a fearful creature. He has three heads. If he finds you, he'll gobble you up."

"I'm grateful for the warning," replied Halvor, "but I've been walking all day. I'm tired and hungry. I could do with gobbling something myself, if I may, before I go."

The princess led Halvor back to the kitchen and showed him where to find food. When he had eaten, the princess pointed to a sword hanging on the wall.

"As you are staying, can you take that sword down?" she asked. "See if you can swing it about you."

Halvor went over to the sword. He found it so heavy, he was unable even to lift it from its hook.

"Well," said the princess, "in that case you must take down the flask beside it. Drink from it. That's what the troll does every time he goes off to lay waste to the land and to steal from people."

Halvor lifted down the flask, removed its stopper and took a drink. As soon as he had swallowed, he felt a tingling in his arms and shoulders. He reached up, took the sword and brandished it in the air. Now, he waved it about his head as if it was made not of steel but of straw.

"I can take on any troll now," cried Halvor.

A moment later Halvor heard the sound of footsteps from the corridor. He jumped behind the door. He was just in time. The troll pushed it open and poked its three heads into the kitchen.

"I smell a stranger here," roared the troll. "Who has dared to enter this castle?"

"You'll find out soon enough," shouted Halvor, leaping from behind the door. With one sword stroke he cut off all three of its heads. The troll fell dead on the kitchen floor.

The princess was delighted. She clapped her hands and danced around the kitchen. But then she stopped, and her face became downcast.

"Oh, if only my sisters were free too," she said.

"Where are they?" asked Halvor.

"They too are both held by trolls," she told him. "One of them is imprisoned in her castle ten leagues from here. My other sister, the youngest of us, is kept captive by the most terrible troll of all. He has locked her in her castle and that lies another ten leagues further still."

"Very well," said Halvor, "I'll see if I can help them. For now, though, I'd better get rid of this body."

The magic potion still seemed to be effective. Halvor was able to lift the body of the troll and its three heads. He took them and threw them into the castle moat.

Chapter Three
The White Castle

The next morning, as soon as it was light, Halvor set off for the second castle. Knowing he had far to go, he took a stick with him.

He walked all day without stopping to rest or eat. As evening began to draw in, he saw a castle some way off. The castle was faced all in white and high above its walls clustered slender turrets.

Halvor kept going for he was eager to reach his goal. He shuddered as he passed under the spikes of the castle portcullis. His footsteps echoed in the emptiness of the courtyard. In places the white walls were stained by water which had run down from broken rain spouts. Dead leaves had blown into piles in some of the corners. Meeting no one, he made his way to the kitchen. There, in a back room, he found a beautiful princess with long, blond hair. She was working with bobbins on a cushion, making lace.

"Who are you?" she asked. "Why have you come to this place? You must leave at once. There is a troll here. He has six heads. He'll eat you, if he gets hold of you."

"I don't doubt you," replied Halvor, "but I'm weary and famished. I've been on the road since first light. If his six mouths haven't consumed everything, may I have something to eat?"

The princess showed Halvor the pantry. He helped himself to some food and slumped down on a stool by the fireplace.

"Since you will not go at once," said the princess, "I would like you to take down that sword hanging there. Can you swing it about you?"

Halvor tried but he could not move it.

"Take the flask next to it and have a drink," the princess suggested. Halvor did so and immediately felt strength surging through his body.

"I'm ready for that troll now," he declared.

No sooner had he spoken those words when he heard a grunting sound from the other side of the door at the back of the kitchen. He ran over and hid behind it. The troll pushed the door open and lumbered into the kitchen.

"I smell a stranger here," it bellowed. "Who has dared to enter this castle?"

"I'll show you," answered Halvor. With those words, he jumped out and sliced all six heads from the troll's body with a single blow of the sword.

The princess was overcome with relief at her release from captivity. She sang with pleasure.

But then she broke off her song.

"Oh, if only my sisters were free too," she said.

Halvor told her of his adventure in the first castle and how he had already freed one of her sisters. He assured the princess that after a night's sleep he would set off in the morning to find the castle where their youngest sister was held prisoner.

Halvor took the troll's body and its heads and threw them over the castle walls, where they rolled down onto the bank below.

Chapter Four
The Castle of Soria Moria

In the morning, Halvor gathered some food together and put it into a backpack. As soon as it was light, he set off to find the third castle.

He walked all day without stopping. Towards evening his road began to take him in the direction of a deep valley. The day was fading. The valley had already begun to fill with mist. Beyond the mist rose a range of mountains, blue in the distance.

Halvor gasped at a new sight. Just visible above the crest of the mountains was a golden castle. By now he had already seen two castles, but this one dazzled him. Its walls and bastions were all of gold. Behind the walls were lofty chambers, adorned with golden pinnacles and golden chimneys. The tiles on the roofs were golden and they glinted in the light of the sinking sun. The golden castle seemed to illuminate both the mountains around it and the sky above it.

Halvor stepped off the road onto the grass at its edge, which was strewn with rocks. For a long while he stood there motionless, staring in amazement at the golden castle. It shone as if the sun was inside it, sending its golden light streaming out of every door and window.

The golden castle drove from his mind all thought of the food in his bag. He set off again and quickened his pace. It was a long climb over the mountains, but Halvor did not falter.

He reached the golden castle as it began to grow dark. He strode in and made for the kitchen. In one of the rooms off the kitchen, he found the third princess. She was sitting at a table writing, with open books spread before her. For the second time that day Halvor stopped and gasped. She had long, golden hair. He had never seen a lovelier young woman.

"Welcome, sir, to the Castle of Soria Moria," she said. "My name is Aurea, and this is my home. I'm afraid I cannot entertain you as I should. My castle has been seized by a troll. He is holding me captive here. You must leave without delay. The troll is a cruel monster. He has nine heads. If he catches you, he's sure to tear you to pieces."

"I'm sorry to learn of your plight, princess," said Halvor, bowing to her. "But I can't walk away and leave you in the clutches of a troll. Besides, I neither ate nor rested on my way here. I've covered ten leagues today, so before I do anything I should like to refresh myself, if I may."

She led him to the kitchen. While Halvor took the food from his bag, the princess fetched him a golden plate. As he ate, she warmed some milk in a pan over the fire, mixing in a little honey and sprinkling it with nutmeg. She served it to Halvor in a golden goblet.

"If you're going to stay and face the troll," the princess said, "you'd better take down that sword hanging on the wall. See if you can handle it."

Halvor tried, without success.

"Then take that flask," said the princess. "Whenever the troll sets out from the castle to attack and rob people, he has a drink from it. Drink some yourself."

Halvor did as the princess told him. Straight away he felt the muscles of his arms and shoulders swell with new strength. He had hardly put the flask down, when he heard a shuffling sound in the corridor beyond the kitchen. Halvor grabbed the sword and leapt behind the door. The troll burst into the kitchen.

"I smell a stranger here," screamed the troll from all its nine mouths. "Who has dared to set foot in this castle?"

"Halvor dares and Halvor will free this princess." Shouting those words, Halvor jumped from behind the door. He swung the sword through the air and cut through all nine of the troll's necks. Its heads rolled in all directions over the kitchen floor.

Princess Aurea gave a shriek. But her horror soon gave way to joy that she was no longer a prisoner of the troll. She threw her arms round Halvor and hugged him.

He was still strong from the magic potion. He picked up the troll's body, while Aurea gathered the heads. Together, they piled them into a handcart. Halvor pulled it down to the river which flowed beside the castle and threw everything in. The remains of the troll were carried by the river out to sea, where they were eaten by gulls and fish.

Chapter Five
The Golden Ring

News of the rescue of Princess Aurea spread quickly. The servants and officers of the castle who had been driven away by the troll returned. People came out of hiding and went back to their villages and farms.

The other two princesses soon joined their younger sister. There was great merrymaking at the Castle of Soria Moria. The three sisters were so grateful to Halvor and so admiring of him that they all said they would be happy to be his wife, if he chose. Halvor offered his hand to Princess Aurea, for he felt her to be the kindest of the three. She accepted with joy.

The celebrations at the Castle of Soria Moria went on for days. Halvor joined in the feasting and the fun. But after some time he became quiet and wore a thoughtful look. Aurea noticed the change in him.

"What's the matter, Halvor?" she asked. "Are you no longer happy here with us?"

"It's wonderful to be with you all," replied Halvor. "But when I see your glee at getting back together, I can't help thinking of my father and mother. I would so like to see them again."

"That'll be no trouble," Aurea laughed. "You have only to do as I tell you."

She fetched gorgeous clothes for Halvor. She gave him a damask shirt, a doublet adorned with embroidered figures and a woollen cloak of crimson. Into his hand, she put a purse full of gold pieces.

"Now take this ring," she said. "I recovered it from the hoard amassed by the troll. Put it on your finger."

Halvor did as she told him. He felt the ring warm and heavy. It was made of pure gold.

"It's a magic ring. When you're wearing the ring, you can wish yourself, or anybody, to go wherever you want. Your wish will be granted immediately. But you must be careful not to take it off. Once the ring leaves your finger, you will never again be able to make its magic work for you."

"Oh, how I wish my father and mother could see me now in all this finery," said Halvor.

The moment those words left his lips, Halvor was transported from the Castle of Soria Moria and set down by the front door of his parents' house.

Chapter Six
Homecoming

Halvor knocked on the door. His mother and father were amazed to see before them a handsome young man dressed in rich clothes. They did not recognise Halvor, and he did not immediately reveal himself to them.

"Good evening to you," said Halvor. "May I stop for the night in your house? It's getting dark. I shall not be able to continue my journey until the morning."

"Ours is a small house, sir, and we're poor people," they said. "We've no food of the sort you must be used to eating. Nor do we have the kind of bed we imagine you must sleep in."

"Don't worry," Halvor replied. "If you'll let me stop with you tonight, I shall be happy to sit over there. I can sleep in that armchair by your hearth."

The couple felt uneasy having such a grand person in their house. But they were hospitable folk. They would never turn away anyone who asked for shelter under their roof. They welcomed Halvor in and shared their supper with him. After they had eaten, Halvor settled himself into the old wooden armchair by the fireside.

"Do you have any children?" Halvor asked.

"Yes, sir, we have a son. His name is Halvor. He went off to sea. We've heard nothing from him since."

"How old is he?"

"He'd be about your age," said the wife. "But he would look nothing like you. We loved Halvor, but he was a dreamer. He would never settle into a job, and, without wages he could buy no new clothes. I had to patch and darn all that he wore."

The couple began to get ready for bed. The husband went to fetch a pillow for their guest, while his wife cleared away the supper things. Halvor sat and stared into the fire. The flames had died down by this time. He took the poker and began to poke the ashes. The wife came back to see if he wanted another log. The embers in the grate lit up Halvor's face as he bent over the ashes, stirring them with the poker.

"Halvor, it's you," she cried. Halvor's father and mother wept tears of joy.

They hugged and kissed Halvor. There was little sleep for any of them that night. They sat up together a long time. The couple had many questions. Halvor told them how he had slain three trolls. He told them of the three princesses and that he was betrothed to the youngest of them. He told them of the Castle of Soria Moria. They were reluctant to take it, but Halvor gave his parents the purse full of gold pieces.

Chapter Seven
The Horn Ring

The following morning, after a late breakfast, Halvor and his parents walked along the fjord to the harbour. The couple were eager to share their good news with friends. As for Halvor, he was keen to show the people of the village what had become of the Ash Boy.

When Halvor and his parents reached the harbour the fishing boats had not long returned, having been out all night. The young women of the village were gathered at the quayside to welcome home fathers, brothers and husbands. Many were there to work. They stood at trestle tables in their aprons, gutting the newly landed fish and dropping them into barrels.

At the sight of Halvor the young women stopped and stared. Theirs was an out of the way village. Few of them had seen a nobleman before.

When Halvor revealed who he was, they were astonished. No longer did they laugh at the Ash Boy. They crowded round him. He recounted how he had overcome the trolls. He spoke of the Castle of Soria Moria. He described the beauty of the princesses and told them he was to be married to the youngest and the loveliest of the three.

"Ah, so you're still a dreamer then, Halvor," one of the young women said with a grin. "You're only saying that to make us jealous."

"I wish the princesses were all here," he replied, "and then you would see for yourselves how beautiful they are."

Halvor had forgotten the golden ring. In that instant, the three princesses were standing at his side. The young women of the village had been astonished to see Halvor. Now, at the sight of the princesses, they were struck dumb. They curtsied as one. The princesses too were surprised to find themselves suddenly in a strange place, but they did not show it. They smiled at the staring villagers.

Halvor was delighted. He hurried the princesses off to meet his father and mother, who were at the village inn, celebrating his return with a group of their friends. The princesses were glad to meet Halvor's family and eager to see his home. Halvor and his parents led them back to the house.

In the days that followed, Halvor walked the princesses round the village and introduced them to all the people he knew. That did not take long, for it was a small village. Halvor showed them the places where he used to go when he was a boy—the paths along the fjord, the lake on the mountain side and the tracks through the forests.

The princesses enjoyed seeing these new places and they admired the beauty of the fjord.

But after a while they began to feel low. Just as Halvor had missed his parents when he was away, so they were beginning to miss their own homes. The three of them talked it over. They agreed in the end to take the golden ring from Halvor and to use it to return to the Castle of Soria Moria.

They drew lots to decide which of them was to carry out their plan. By chance it fell to Princess Aurea. That was hard upon her. She had come to love Halvor and did not want to be parted from him. But she loved her sisters too. She could see they were pining to get back to their own land.

One afternoon Halvor took the princesses for a walk by the lake. They sat to rest on the grass at the water's edge. Halvor lay down. Aurea stroked his hair and soon he was asleep. She eased the ring from his finger. In its place she slipped on a ring made from horn. The princesses wished themselves back to the Castle of Soria Moria.

When Halvor woke he was alone. Thinking the princess must have strolled on out of sight, he walked around the lake, but he could not see them. He searched for them in the village. He raced back to his parents' house. Nowhere could he find the three princesses.

Halvor happened to look down at his hand. He saw that in place of the golden ring he was wearing a ring of horn. He guessed what they had done. Halvor was in despair. He knew he would lose his love forever, if he could not find his way back to the Castle of Soria Moria.

Princess Aurea was in despair too. As soon as she and her sisters had been transported back, her first thought was to use the ring again.

"Now, ring," she ordered, "bring Halvor back here to me." Nothing happened.

"What's wrong?" she cried. She called her sisters. Each in turn put on the ring and wished for Halvor's return.

Still nothing happened.

"I don't understand," wailed Aurea.

"Perhaps the magic is spent," said one of her sisters. "Maybe carrying all three of us to Halvor's village and back again drained whatever charm was put into the ring."

Aurea fell into her sisters' arms and wept bitter tears. They did their best to comfort her.

"In time, Aurea, your pain will lessen," they said. "Who knows—it may be better for Halvor to make his future among his own people?"

Aurea was not to be consoled. She knew that if Halvor could not find his way back to the Castle of Soria Moria, she would lose her love for ever.

Chapter Eight
Halvor's Quest

Halvor told his mother and father that Princess Aurea was gone.

"I must leave you again," he said. "I must find the way back to the Castle of Soria Moria. If I have to, I will walk the world for the rest of my life."

Halvor's parents were sad, but they could tell he had made up his mind. They urged him to take back the purse of gold pieces. He insisted they should keep it. He doubted whether he would ever return, so he wanted them to be comfortable in their old age. They continued to press him. At last, wishing not to upset them, he agreed to take three of the gold pieces. They shed many tears before Halvor left.

Halvor walked for days, for weeks, for months. He asked everyone he met if they knew the way to the Castle of Soria Moria. He would stand at crossroads and question people going this way and that. He approached the pedlars who tramped from village to village with their packs. He fell in with travelling players who journeyed by cart to perform plays in the courtyards of inns. He visited markets to talk to the traders who moved from place to place selling their wares. He spoke with drovers as they herded their flocks of sheep and goats up to mountain pastures and down to sheltered valleys as the seasons changed.

No one knew the way. No one had even heard of the Castle of Soria Moria.

On one road Halvor got talking with a man leading a horse. Although he lay down to sleep every night heavy with disappointment, Halvor was unwavering in keeping on with his search. He thought that with a horse he might be able to reach more distant places and question people who had seen more of the world.

"Will you sell me your horse?" Halvor asked.

"Well," said the man, "I've not thought of selling him. He's a good horse. He and I have gone a long way together. We do turn and turnabout. I ride him for a while. Then to rest him, I'll walk for a while beside him. I reckon he's worth at least three gold pieces."

"I'll give you two for him," Halvor said. "That's all the money I have."

Halvor was set upon holding back one gold piece in case he should need it. He told the man of his love for the Princess Aurea and of his quest to return to the Castle of Soria Moria. The man agreed at last to sell the horse for two gold pieces.

Halvor pressed on, riding and walking by turns. He travelled the pilgrim roads, falling in with bands of travellers going to and from Bari, Cologne, Galicia and many another shrine. They had tales to tell of miraculous things but none of them knew the way to the Castle of Soria Moria. He visited riverside quays and seaports to meet bargemen and sailors. He frequented warehouses to talk with merchants from the east who dealt in silks and spices, merchants from the north trading in furs and merchants who brought ivory and gold from far away in the south.

Halvor could find no one who had heard of the Castle of Soria Moria.

Chapter Nine
The Wise Woman

The weeks and months of Halvor's quest stretched into years. Because he was not prepared to spend his last gold piece, he was obliged to cadge food and even to beg. Sometimes he would earn a few coins for helping travellers whom he met on the road, by carrying a pack for them or letting them ride a little way on his horse. He used to visit inns. He would sit down by strangers and tell them his story. Often one would buy him a drink or share with him a bit of their meal.

One evening in a village inn, after he had spoken with every customer, Halvor put his question to the innkeeper.

"I've never heard of it," said the innkeeper, "but there's somebody in these parts who might know."

"Who is it?" demanded Halvor. "Tell me, please."

"The road from the village leads through some woods. There's a wise woman who lives in a cottage deep in the wood."

"Does her wisdom run to castles?" Halvor asked.

"That, I can't tell. She does know about plants and herbs. There's many folks in this village who've been cured by her remedies. She knows about the constellations of the stars and the movements of the planets. People with troubles go to her and they generally come away the better for it."

"Thank you," said Halvor, "I'll go now."

Although both Halvor and his horse were tired, they set off at once down the road into the wood. It was nearly dark before he saw a light in the window of the cottage.

Halvor knocked on the door. It was opened by a woman some years older than his mother.

"Good evening, young man," she said. "What are you looking for?"

"How do you know I'm looking for something?"

"I live well away from the village," she replied. "When people come to see me they seldom want just to chat."

"I'm trying to find the way to the Castle of Soria Moria," said Halvor.

"Ah!" said the woman, smiling. "I've heard of the Castle of Soria Moria. You'd better come inside."

Halvor was smiling too now. In all his travels this was the first person he had met who had heard of the Castle of Soria Moria. He tied the horse to a bush and stepped inside the cottage.

"From the look of you, young man, you have journeyed long and far," said the woman.

Halvor glanced down at himself. He saw his clothes were tattered and his boots cracked and caked with mud.

"Sit down there by the fire," the woman said. "I'll fetch you something to eat and drink."

By the hearth was a wooden chair. Halvor sat down and stared into the fire. He thought he could see the golden Castle of Soria Moria in the flames leaping around the logs burning in the grate.

The woman returned with a jug of water, some soup and a lump of bread. Halvor began to eat, for he was hungry.

"I've heard of the Castle of Soria Moria," she said, "but I don't know how to find it."

At her words Halvor's head sank over his soup bowl.

"Do not despair, young man. I don't know the way myself. But my friend, the Moon, may be able to help you. The Moon must have passed above it at some time."

While Halvor sat eating, the woman went outside. It was a clear night. The Moon shone in the sky.

"Moon, Moon," called the woman. "Can you tell me the way to the Castle of Soria Moria?"

"No, I can't," answered the Moon. "I've passed over it but on a cloudy night. I couldn't see where it lay."

The woman went back inside to Halvor.

"The Moon can't help you," she said. "Clouds hid the way from her. But do not fear, young man. I'm sure the West Wind will soon be here. He blows both above and below the clouds. Nothing escapes him."

While they waited for the West Wind Halvor finished his meal. He sat by the fire with the Wise Woman, and they talked.

"Wherever the Castle of Soria Moria is," she said, "I guess it must be a long way off. You've walked far already. When I was outside, I saw your horse. He's strong, but I doubt whether he's fast. If you are to reach the Castle of Soria Moria soon, you'll need to go more quickly than he can carry you and more quickly than you can walk yourself."

She went to a cupboard and fetched out a pair of fine boots.

"These are magic boots. When you wish it, they will carry you a hundred paces for every one step you take."

"Thank you," said Halvor.

"They're not a gift," replied the woman. "I don't give my help for nothing. What will you pay me for these boots?"

Halvor felt the last gold piece in his pocket. He was still not prepared to spend it, sure that at some time he would be in even greater need.

"I'll give you my horse," he replied. "You said yourself he's strong. He's served me well. He'll do the same for you."

The Wise Woman said nothing for a moment.

"You're probably right," she answered at last. "You've worked him hard. He deserves a rest. There's plenty of grazing in this part of the wood. And he'll be company for me. I accept your offer, young man. Let's drink on our deal."

She fetched a bottle, and they shared a beaker of ale as they sat before the dying fire. Halvor stared into the glowing embers. He picked up a poker and stirred them.

He heard a roaring sound in the chimney. The windows of the cottage rattled. They felt a draught under the door.

"That must be the West Wind," said the woman. She ran outside. "Wind, Wind," she called. "Can you tell me the way to the Castle of Soria Moria?"

"Yes, of course," said the West Wind. "If you follow me, I'll take you there. I'm due to be at the Castle of Soria Moria tomorrow. They'll have washing for me to dry."

The woman rushed back into the cottage.

"Hurry, young man! You must put on the boots and follow the West Wind. Hurry! He waits for no one. You'll need all the speed those boots can give you to keep up with him."

Halvor jumped up. He pulled on the boots and ran outside with the Wise Woman. He embraced her and patted the horse farewell. Then he turned and wished that he might run as fast as the boots could make him go.

Halvor's first step took his breath away, for he flew through the air. The faster he ran, the faster the boots carried him. As the Wise Woman had predicted, it took all his efforts to keep up with the West Wind. He sped along through the night. He had no time to gaze about him, but he was aware of the stars which seemed to be racing across the sky above him. From time to time, he would cross a river lit by the moon, making it look like a silver ribbon lying on the ground.

Morning and daylight came but the West Wind did not slacken his pace. Halvor was grateful he had enjoyed rest and food at the Wise Woman's cottage, for he had to call upon every bit of his energy not to be left behind. On he ran, over cultivated fields, through dense forests and over great tracts of moorland. He ran past farms and villages and towns.

Chapter Ten
The End of the Quest

At last, in the afternoon, the West Wind began to slow. Halvor saw before him the Castle of Soria Moria. He knew joy for the first time in a long while as he looked once again upon its golden walls and pinnacles gleaming in the sunshine.

Very soon now, he thought to himself, *I shall be back with Aurea.*

Halvor stopped at the river beside the castle. Looking about, he could see people had been busy in the water meadows. Everywhere, on the grass and over the hedgerows, sheets and cloths had been spread out to dry.

Halvor was exhausted. He sat down close to a group of laundry maids.

"You look as if you've been busy," he said to one of the young women.

"Yes, sir. We've been washing all morning. We were beginning to despair of getting it all dry, but you seem to have brought the wind with you. If it keeps blowing, we may get it finished in time."

The laundry maid noted Halvor's fine boots, but she noted, too, the shabby and dusty state of his clothes.

"Are you a guest at the castle, sir?" she asked.

"Not exactly a guest. I'm a traveller. But I've travelled long and far to reach the Castle of Soria Moria."

"We've got guests here today from every kingdom and country round about," said the laundry maid. "I've never seen so many people staying in the castle. And all that makes more work for us."

"Is it a festival, then?" asked Halvor.

"Why, no, sir! It's a wedding. Straight after tonight's banquet, the Princess Aurea is to be married."

"Married?" gasped Halvor. He went cold. It seemed to him that a single word had turned all his joy to misery. "Who is she to marry? How has this come about? Tell me."

"She is to marry a prince, sir," answered the laundry maid. "Is that so strange? Princesses will marry princes—that's the way of the world. He's a handsome young man, the son of the king who rules the lands across the mountains. And a lucky young man he is. Suitors came here from all over to seek her hand in marriage.

"There were princes, counts, dukes and noblemen of every kind. She held out against them for a long time. There was a rumour she already had a love in some distant place. I don't know the truth of that. Anyway, both of her sisters were keen to see her married. In the end, she gave way."

Halvor could hardly speak. The West Wind brought their conversation to an end. As he mumbled his thanks to the young woman for her story, the wind, with a sudden gust, lifted one of the sheets and blew it across the meadow. The young woman sprang to her feet and raced after it.

Halvor trudged up to the castle. At dark moments during his travels, he had comforted himself by imagining how he would feel when he walked again through the gatehouse and into the courtyard of the Castle of Soria Moria. Now, he sauntered in with his head down.

As the laundry maid had said, the castle was full of people. Guests were still arriving. Grooms were watering horses and unhitching them from carriages. Serving men tottered by bearing logs for the fires and the ovens. Sides of boar and venison were carried to the kitchen. Men rolled barrels of wine over the cobbles. Everyone was busy. The din of talking and shouting filled the courtyard.

Halvor alone was silent. He wandered about, dodging the porters and maids who rushed this way and that. He sat for a time by the well and stared up at the windows which overlooked the courtyard. He hoped he might have a glimpse of Aurea, but even that hope came to nothing.

It began to grow dark. Guests started to gather for the wedding banquet. Lords and ladies in elegant robes crossed the courtyard and made their way into the great hall. Halvor hung back in the shadow of a doorway until he thought everyone was inside. He hoped to slip in without being noticed. He mounted the steps up to the hall door.

"Where are you going?" said a voice.

At the top of the stairs one of the castle guards barred his way. The man looked Halvor up and down. He noticed his fine boots. but he also saw that Halvor's clothes were torn and dirty.

"I think you've missed your way, young man," he said. "The stables are over there."

"Please let me pass, sir," pleaded Halvor. "I've travelled long and far to be here this evening."

"You'll not travel a step further, unless you can show me your invitation," the guard replied. Halvor thought for a moment. He reached into his pocket.

"Would it help if I showed you this?" He fetched out his last gold piece. The guard grinned. After looking round, he snatched the gold piece.

"Stand at the back of the hall," he said. "Mind you keep by the door. Stay out of trouble. If anyone complains, I'll have to throw you out."

Chapter Eleven
The Wedding Banquet

Halvor slipped inside the great hall. It was lit by candles set at intervals on the tables and by the logs which blazed in the fireplaces along its walls. Between the candles there were pools of darkness. There was much smoke too. Halvor had no difficulty keeping out of sight at the back. He made as if he was an attendant, waiting should his services be needed.

The hall was long. Halvor peered up to the high table at the far end. At last, he spied Aurea. She seemed to him even more beautiful than he remembered. Her two sisters sat on one side of her. He guessed the man on her other side must be the prince who was to marry her that night. Halvor decided he must do something now or lose his love for ever.

The banquet was under way. Great quantities of food and drink were being served. There were so many guests that every servant in the castle had been called upon to help with serving. It happened that waiting at the table closest to Halvor was the laundry maid with whom he had spoken that afternoon. She recognised Halvor and gave him a smile.

When she next came to the table, carrying a dish piled with fruit, Halvor beckoned her.

"Miss, I shall be in your debt forever," he said, "if you will do a service for me."

On the table next to him stood a goblet of wine. Halvor took it. He drew the horn ring from his finger and dropped it into the wine.

"Will you take this to the Princess Aurea and ask her to drink the health of a stranger?"

"I will, sir. You brought us a good drying wind this afternoon," she said with a laugh, "so I owe you a favour."

By that time the noise in the hall was tremendous. All along the benches guests were talking with one another. Some were calling for more wine. In a gallery a band of musicians was playing.

Nobody took any notice of the laundry maid as she walked the length of the hall to the high table. She stopped before the Princess Aurea. Making a curtsey, she delivered her message.

Aurea was surprised, but she understood the young woman was only doing what one of the guests must have asked of her.

"Very well," she said, giving the laundry maid a wink. She accepted the goblet. "Good health to the stranger, whoever he may be."

As Aurea tilted the goblet to take a sip of wine, something hard touched her lips. Placing the goblet on the table, she dipped in her fingers and fished out the horn ring. Aurea recognised it at once. Her heart began to thump, and her cheeks reddened.

Halvor must be here, she thought to herself.

She felt sure he was watching her at that moment. She peered down the hall, but for all the bustle, the shadows and the smoke she could not see him. She decided to give him a sign. She closed her fingers around the horn ring and raised her hand above her head.

The prince gave her a puzzled glance.

That wine must have been sour, he thought to himself, *and she's shaking her fist at the serving wench.*

Aurea sat back in her seat and thought hard. She realised she must do something now or lose her love for ever.

Aurea summoned her chamberlain. He came and bowed to her. She whispered in his ear.

The chamberlain strode to the end of the high table. He banged his staff of office three times on the tabletop.

"Pray be silent," he announced. "The Princess Aurea will now address the company." The hall became hushed. As Aurea rose to her feet her heart was beating even faster.

"Honoured guests," she began, "my first task is to thank you all for travelling to the Castle of Soria Moria to be with me on my wedding day."

Her words were greeted with loud cheering. The warmth of the response from her guests encouraged Aurea. The chamberlain waved his staff to call again for silence and she continued.

"Many of you will be here because you know the prince. Some of you will be here because you know my story. I have a question to put to you. Who do you think most deserves my hand in marriage—the prince who has asked me to be his wife or the man who delivered me and my sisters from our imprisonment by trolls?"

There was silence in the hall. In a shadowy corner at the back another heart now began to beat fast.

"Is it to be the prince?" asked Aurea.

There were loud shouts of support from around the hall. The prince had many followers.

"Is it to be my deliverer?" she asked.

The explosion of noise made Aurea jump. Guests roared their approval. They clapped. They banged fists and tankards on the tables. They stamped their feet on the stone floor. Their choice was beyond doubt.

It took a time for the uproar to die down. At last, the chamberlain managed to restore silence in the hall. Aurea smiled at the assembled company.

She called, "Halvor!"

Out of the shadows at the back stepped a young man dressed shabbily but for a pair of fine boots. In years to come, when Halvor related the story to his children and to his grandchildren, he would tell them he did not walk the length of the hall, he flew.

Halvor and Aurea were married that night. The prince and his followers returned to their own land. It was said he soon found another bride.

As for the laundry maid, she was appointed to be Princess Aurea's principal lady in waiting and became her most intimate friend. When the couple had children, she was their godmother. Their firstborn was a girl, whom they named Favonia.

Those boots never again sped Halvor aloft, but they kept a bit of their magic. They never wore out. Halvor wore them for the rest of his days.

Aurea devoted much time and effort to restoring the fortunes of those whose lands had been devastated and whose valuables had been plundered by the trolls.

Halvor and Aurea lived together in lifelong love. Never again did they know the pain of separation, nor did they ever leave the Castle of Soria Moria.

The White Mountain – Slovenia

Chapter One
Sophia Begins to Learn

Long ago, in the land of Slovenia, there was a girl who was curious about everything. Her name was Sophia.

Sophia's father was a Duke. She lived with him in his palace on the side of the White Mountain. The Duke's lands stretched as far as the eye could see in every direction.

The Duke became aware of Sophia's curiosity when she was a small girl. He used to walk with her in the palace gardens and she would ask him question after question.

"Father, where do bees go when it's cold?" Sophia wanted to know. "Why can birds fly, and rabbits can't? Why do some trees drop their leaves in autumn while others don't?"

"Oh dear," said the Duke. "Those are all good questions, I'm sure. But I'm afraid I don't know the answers."

The Duke was proud of his daughter's curiosity. He consulted his Secretary and instructed him to summon to the palace all the most learned men to be found. When they were gathered, the Secretary sat down with them and together they drew up a programme of teaching which covered all the branches of knowledge.

The more Sophia learned, the greater became her curiosity. The Ducal palace had a library. Its collection of books had been built up over generations. The Duke himself seldom ventured there.

But when Sophia was not working with her tutors she loved to read in the library. She dipped into volume after volume, following the threads of whatever interested her at that moment.

Led by her curiosity Sophia learned quickly. Her tutors were amazed. They too were often embarrassed by the questions she put to them. But Sophia was not one to show off. When she grew to be a young woman she still loved to walk with her father. The terraced gardens of the palace looked upon the town below the White Mountain and over the fields beyond. As they walked arm in arm along an avenue of lime trees, Sophia would tell her father about her studies.

"Dear child," he said, "my own father engaged a whole pack of tutors to teach me, but I've learned more from you than I ever did from them."

Sophia became a skilled musician. She played the violin. For all its grandeur, the palace was chilly in winter. Fingers stiff with cold cannot handle a bow or stop strings. Sophia asked her father's steward to make sure her fires were kept burning all day. The steward ordered logs to be delivered every hour to Sophia's chambers. The job of bringing the logs from the courtyard fell to Jozef, one of many lads who fetched and carried in the Ducal household. Jozef had only seen Sophia in the distance, but he loved to hear her playing the violin. He used to linger in the corridor after setting down his load of logs.

One day, the steward found him there.

"What do you think you're doing, young man?" he demanded. "Why are you idling here?"

"I'm listening, sir, to the beautiful music."

"Get back to your work at once. The Lady Sophia does not play for your pleasure, fellow."

Jozef's family was poor. They lived in the town at the foot of the White Mountain. Like many of the townspeople, they worked for the Duke. Early in the morning they would trudge up the mountain to the palace. At the end of the day, they trudged back down to the two rooms they rented in an old house off the town square.

Jozef's mother worked in the palace kitchens. His father helped to look after the Duke's horses. Often, they were required to sleep at the palace. If there was a big dinner to be prepared in the evening, Jozef's mother would have to work late and sleep over on the floor of the laundry. If the Duke and his guests were riding out to hunt early in the morning, Jozef's father would have to bed down in one of the hayloft to be up before first light.

They had too little money to send Jozef to school. As soon as he was able to be useful, he was given odd jobs about the palace. He was paid no wages but sometimes he would get a tip for sweeping out the stalls in the stables or for drawing water from the well in the courtyard.

Chapter Two
The Scholar

Sophia continued her studies and learned more every day. As she read, she came across mention of a learned scholar who lived in a far-off castle. The scholar did scientific experiments. He was reputed to practice alchemy and to know much about the ancient lore of Slovenia.

"Father," said Sophia to the Duke, "I've read of a scholar who is celebrated for his knowledge. I'd love to meet him and learn from him."

"Ah Sophia, you're always curious to find out more. Don't you have enough tutors?"

"I'm grateful, father, for all you've done for my education. But this man seems out of the ordinary. I do so want to find out what he can teach me."

"Very well, my dear, I shall see what I can do."

The next day, the Duke called for his Secretary to join him in the long gallery. The Duke liked to walk there with the Secretary whenever they had weighty matters to ponder. Portraits of his ancestors hung on the gallery walls. The Duke imagined that their wisdom wafted down over discussions which took place beneath their gaze.

"My daughter tells me of a learned scholar who she would like to teach her," began the Duke.

"I believe I know of the man, my Lord," the Secretary replied.

"Indeed?" said the Duke. "Did I not ask you to bring all the most learned men here to share their knowledge with my daughter?"

"You did, my Lord. But this scholar will not take pupils. He is embarked upon a great work. It is a book in which he intends to draw together all that is known about our lands—their history, their geography, their folklore."

"That is all very well," said the Duke. "But my daughter is desperate to learn from him. How are we to persuade the man? I am willing to pay well."

"I do not believe money will sway him, my Lord."

"Then what are we to do?" asked the Duke.

"I do have an idea. Over the years, your Lordship has been generous in his donations to the monasteries in his domain."

"They do much good work to relieve the poor," the Duke replied. "I know where my duty lies. But what has that to do with the matter in hand?"

"Those monasteries, my Lord, hold many ancient manuscripts. They guard them jealously and will not let them out of their hands. I imagine this scholar would like to consult those documents for the book he is writing. I am sure your Lordship's generosity would prompt a positive response from the abbots if your Lordship was to request to borrow the manuscripts.

"If they were to be made accessible to him only in the palace library, I think the scholar might be persuaded to visit your Lordship and to divide his time between studying them and teaching the Lady Sophia."

The Duke smiled. "As ever, my Secretary is astute in solving problems."

The Secretary bowed. "As ever, your Lordship is gracious in acknowledging the efforts of his servants."

The next morning, the Secretary and a couple of his men set off on horseback for the castle where the scholar lived. Their journey took them over mountain ridges, through olive groves and vineyards and past meadows dotted with hayricks. They stopped to refresh themselves and to water their horses at villages on the way.

In two days they reached the castle. A servant led the Secretary up a spiral staircase which rose into the scholar's study and twisted up through the room to quarters above it. The scholar, an old man with a white beard, was sitting at a table beneath a window. The table was covered by a Turkish rug. On the rug lay piles of books and rolls of charts.

"Greetings to you, sir, from my Lord, the Duke," said the Secretary.

"My thanks to his Lordship. But I fear he'll have sent you for nothing, if you come wanting me to tutor some young nobleman for him."

"I am not here on behalf of any young nobleman," replied the Secretary.

"I'm relieved to hear that. Years ago, I used to give way to requests and take pupils. I wasted much time. In my experience, the sons of Dukes are more interested in hunting and fencing than in the pursuit of knowledge. So, what is it you want?"

"My Lord has learned with interest of the great work you are undertaking."

"Really?" said the scholar.

"Indeed. His Lordship would like to hear more of it, so that he may know how he can help you."

"Come and see, then," said the scholar.

He beckoned the Secretary to a map on the wall behind him.

"These are our lands," said the scholar. "They are small. We have never been the seat of an empire subjugating others. Instead, for many centuries we have been the subjects of greater powers beyond our borders. But through every hardship we have held onto our language and the things which make us different from other people—our way of life, our traditions, our songs and our stories.

"I want to write those things down, so they can be handed on to the people who come after us. Things will change in the future, I know that. But people have nothing, if they have no knowledge of what they have been."

"That is a noble task," said the Secretary, "and one his Lordship is eager to support."

He told the scholar of the manuscripts which the Duke was gathering from monasteries. The scholar was excited.

"But is there nothing the Duke wants from me in return?" he asked.

"Well, my Lord does ask that you divide the time of your stay in his palace between studying the manuscripts and teaching his only child."

"Aha," said the scholar, "so there is a pupil at the back of all this."

"No ordinary pupil, as you will find out if you grant the Duke's request. Your pupil would be the Lady Sophia, the Duke's daughter."

"I'm afraid your Duke has been misinformed about me. I know nothing of dancing or lace-making."

"I'm afraid that you, sir, may have been misinformed about the Lady Sophia. Her Ladyship is a person of exceptional intelligence. She excels in grammar, logic and rhetoric. She is proficient in Latin and Greek. She plays the violin and her compositions have earned admiration from the finest musicians in the land."

The Secretary drew a bundle of papers from his bag. He had taken the precaution of getting Sophia's tutors to write down their opinions of her abilities.

"I am impressed," said the scholar, after reading them. "I agree to the Duke's request. But I insist upon one condition. No one else is to be present while I instruct her."

"My Lord will, I am sure, be happy to accept that," replied the Secretary.

The Secretary rode straight back to the palace. His two men stayed behind. They hired a coach. The scholar stood over them and supervised the loading of his things. There were boxes of the books he thought he would need to consult. There were bundles of notes containing the material he was collecting. There were folios, the first volumes of his great work. And a trunk full of pens, compasses, protractors, measuring rods and geometrical shapes.

"We have stowed everything, sir," said one of the men, "exactly as you ordered. But may we now ask you a question?"

"Certainly," said the scholar.

"There is just room for the two of us on top. And the coach is full of your luggage. So, where are you going to ride?"

The two men had to unpack everything. This time, they tied some of the largest boxes onto the roof of the coach. The scholar was then able to squeeze himself inside.

Chapter Three
Sophia Applies Her Learning

Sophia was overjoyed to meet the scholar. On his part, a single conversation with her was enough to show him that the Secretary had exaggerated neither her intelligence nor her curiosity.

They agreed a programme of work. During the mornings the scholar instructed Sophia in arithmetic, geometry and astronomy. The afternoons he passed on his own in the library studying the manuscripts, while Sophia practised her violin.

This arrangement kept Jozef busy. He continued to bring logs for Sophia's fires. In spite of being reprimanded by the Duke's steward, he lingered whenever he could to listen to Sophia playing. He thought the music magical. In addition, he had to supply the three fireplaces in the library. The abbots had insisted their manuscripts should not be allowed to get damp while they were on loan to the Duke.

The scholar copied out passages and made notes in his notebooks. He got through great quantities of ink. The Duke's servants, Jozef amongst them, were sent out many times to pick galls from the oak trees in the woods on the lower slopes of the White Mountain. Those oak galls, crushed and mixed with rainwater, were one of the ingredients in the scholar's ink recipe.

At length, the scholar had got from the manuscripts all that he wanted. He returned to his castle. Sophia had gained a lot from his teaching. In particular, she discovered the beauty of numbers. She was to use her new skills sooner than she expected.

The Duke had a younger brother. He lived in the palace and was a member of the Duke's court. Sophia noticed her uncle was often deep in conversation with the same group of the Duke's followers. One day she happened to walk through the east wing of the palace. She came upon this little band sitting in one of the corner turrets. They broke off their conversation as soon as they saw her approach.

"Good day, Uncle," said Sophia.

"Good day to you, Sophia," he replied.

"I wonder what you were talking about."

"We talk of nothing, my dear, which needs trouble you."

"I didn't say I was troubled, Uncle. I'm curious to know why you and your friends huddle here to talk, away from everybody else."

"We're making plans," he replied. "The hunting season will soon be upon us. We huntsmen are competitive. My friends and I are considering how we can bag the biggest prizes."

Later that day, when Sophia passed back through the east wing, she spotted a piece of paper on the floor. On it she recognised her uncle's handwriting, but she could make no sense of what he had written. She guessed the note must be in code. She hid it in a fold of her gown and hurried back to her chambers. Having copied it, she took the original back to the east wing and placed it on the floor where she had found it.

Sophia sat up long that night. She searched for patterns in the writing which might suggest words. She looked at how often certain letters occurred and tried to match them with the frequency of letters in ordinary writing. At last, after many failures, she cracked the code. The paper revealed a plot. His brother was going to arrange for the Duke to have an accident while out hunting.

It was not to be fatal. But he was to be put out of action long enough for his brother to seize power.

In the morning Sophia went to the Duke.

"Father, you should read this. It's something my uncle thought would be seen by no one but him and his confederates."

Having read the letter, the Duke ordered the palace guards to bring his brother before him.

The brother confessed at once. He feared the Duke would banish him or even put him to death.

"Forgive me, my Lord," he said, "I've been foolish."

"You have indeed," replied the Duke. "I wonder what you would have done with me if you had succeeded in your plot. But enough of that. As an act of penance, you will undertake a pilgrimage. You will walk on foot to Galicia, to the shrine of St James and you will return on foot. When you are back, you will come and give me an account of what you have learned, both of the world and of yourself."

"Your Lordship is more merciful than I deserve," said the brother. "When I return, I shall do everything I can to regain your Lordship's trust."

The Duke had long respected Sophia's wisdom, but from that time she became his principal advisor. He consulted his daughter on all decisions about the management of his lands and his relations with neighbouring nobles.

Chapter Four
The Way into the White Mountain

Time passed and a messenger arrived at the palace. He brought a package for Sophia. It was a bundle of papers. The scholar had copied out and sent her a chapter of the book on which he was working.

In that chapter the scholar wrote about the rivers, the plains and the mountains of Slovenia.

Sophia was fascinated by what she read.

"Father, I beg you. Do send for the scholar again. He has found out so much about our lands. I am curious to learn from him the answers to many questions."

"What sort of questions, my dear?"

"Why are there mountains in some places and plains in others? Why is our own mountain white? Why do we have lakes which disappear and reappear at different times of the year?"

"Enough, enough," said the Duke. "I will get our Secretary to pay him another visit. But remember, Sophia. The scholar is an old man. He may not be willing to keep travelling backwards and forwards to satisfy your curiosity."

The Secretary again made the journey to the scholar's castle. This time he did not have to work at persuading him. The scholar respected Sophia's intelligence and curiosity. Even so, he was reluctant to interrupt his work.

"I don't know how many years I have left," he said. "I cannot afford to break off from my studies."

"My Lord understands that," replied the Secretary. "His Lordship has a proposal which may help you to quicken the pace of your research. If you will consent to another visit to give instruction to the Lady Sophia, the Duke will send a scribe back with you on your return. The scribe will do all your copying.

"In addition, the Duke will place his courier service at your disposal. His Lordship knows you correspond much with learned colleagues in other lands—

in Bologna, in Paris and in Oxford. His couriers will speed up your exchange of letters with them."

"I agree to the Duke's request," said the scholar. "But I insist upon one condition—that no one else should be present when I instruct the Lady Sophia."

"My Lord will, I am sure, be happy to accept that," replied the Secretary.

The scholar arrived at the palace and was soon busy with Sophia. He had gathered much information about the lands around them from written sources. But what excited Sophia's curiosity most was not what he had read, but what he had heard.

The scholar had spent time visiting villages to listen to those who told stories at inns and at county fairs. He had travelled to hear singers who performed at wedding feasts. None of them could read or write. But in the tales and songs which they had by memory they kept alive a wealth of folklore and legend.

The scholar revealed to Sophia that he had heard of caves inside the White Mountain.

"In one village I visited," he said, "I met a woman who shared with me a magic spell. She said the spell opened the way into those caves."

"Then we must go at once and try it," said Sophia.

"One moment, young lady. The woman warned me. The magic of the spell has its dangers. It will work only at midnight. And one can stay in the caves for no more than an hour. If one does not leave within an hour, the entrance will close. Nothing will open it again."

"I shall make ready," declared Sophia, "and we'll go tonight."

She sent for the steward and told him she would be up late that night with the scholar to work on an experiment. She asked for two lanterns, two oil lamps and an hourglass. The steward hurried off and ordered the things. It was Jozef who carried them to Sophia's chambers.

In a back wall of the palace there was a gate which led onto the side of the White Mountain. Once outside, Sophia and the scholar walked for some time up a track. They came to a rock face. The scholar thought it might be the right spot. He uttered the spell. Sophia listened and repeated it several times under her breath. She was determined to memorise it for herself. After a moment they heard a rumbling sound and a door opened in the rock.

Sophia and the scholar stepped into the cave. The blackness was total. They lit the two oil lamps and left them by the opening. They needed the more powerful light of the lanterns to see their way as they began to explore. Sophia was sorry she had not put on something warmer, for it was cold. They went forward slowly. For stretches, the ceiling of the cave was low, and they had to crouch.

Some of the ways were slanted and they passed along steadying themselves with their hands against wet rock. Pools of water blocked their way in places. They had to skirt them over beaches of pebbles. All the time they heard the sounds of dripping water.

"Look at that," said Sophia. She pointed to thin tubes of rock which hung down from the roof of the cave, like strands of yarn set solid. Great rock icicles, the colour of cream, tapered down from the roof. Their rippled surfaces glistened wet in the light of the lanterns. Columns rose from the floor. Some were pink. Some were brilliant white and sparkled with crystals, as if made of salt.

"Look," called Sophia. "Over there. That looks like a shaft of moonlight. There must be an opening to the sky. Let's go and see."

"No, my Lady," said the scholar. "It is easy to forget the time. We must go back. Remember, anyone who outstays an hour will find the opening shut for ever."

"Very well," said Sophia, "but I do want to learn all about these caves."

They made their way back to the opening, where the oil lamps were still burning. They picked them up and returned to the palace.

The next day the scholar said his farewells to the Duke and Sophia and set off back to his castle. He had been eager to go inside the White Mountain himself, but he was satisfied with what he had seen. He was keen to get back to his work and to start using the scribe and the couriers.

Sophia was so excited she had hardly slept all night. As soon as the scholar was gone, she was in the library. She made notes of what she had seen and sketches of the rock formations. She began to work through all the volumes she could find which had anything about caves. What she read stoked her curiosity to find out more. She must, she decided, make a second journey into the White Mountain.

Chapter Five
Jozef and His Violin

Jozef, too, loved to see and to learn, but he was obliged to turn his curiosity to everyday things. Whenever he was in the town, he liked to stroll about the shops and the market stalls. He loved listening to shop-keepers, stall holders, pedlars and travellers, always curious to learn where they had been and what they had seen.

One day he watched a miller delivering sacks of flour to a local baker. The baker had a set of scales outside the front of his shop. He weighed the sacks and paid the miller. It was a blustery day. For a moment the wind lifted the miller's cloak. Jozef noticed that beneath his cloak he had two large canvas bags, hung on leather straps over his shoulders.

The miller offered to carry the sacks to the yard behind the shop. The baker was serving on his own, so he accepted the offer of help. Jozef followed the miller and watched him from out of sight in a doorway in the alley.

The miller set the sacks down in the yard. He looked round to check he was unobserved.

Jozef saw him sink his hands deep into the flour. Out of each sack he drew a heavy stone. He put the stones into the canvas bags and refastened his cloak. Jozef ran back to the front of the shop. He told the baker what he had seen. The baker, a big man, grabbed the miller as he came out of the alley. He reweighed the sacks and took back the money the miller had tried to cheat from him.

The baker thanked Jozef. That morning he had made a tray of baked dumplings, filled with apple, walnuts, cinnamon and cream. He took the biggest one and handed it to Jozef. Jozef was delighted. His family never afforded more than ordinary bread. But Jozef was astonished when, on top of that, the baker gave him a gold piece. That was more money than he had ever held in his hand.

Jozef thanked the baker for his generosity. Eating his dumpling, he turned in the direction of the shop which was his favourite of them all. It was owned by a woman who sold and repaired violins. Whenever on errands in the town, Jozef went out of his way to pass this shop.

He admired the violins in the window. They showed all the shades of colour from brown to orange. Jozef marvelled at the minute lines of grain in their wood. Some of the violins were decorated with dots and diamonds in mother of pearl. The scrolls on some were carved with the heads of lions and dolphins. They had pegs topped with tiny finials of gold and ivory. Having heard Sophia make music, Jozef longed to own a violin himself and to learn to play.

While he stood gazing, the woman came out.

"Come in, young man. Take a closer look."

"Oh, no thank you," replied Jozef. "I was just passing by. I must be on my way." He turned to go, but the woman stepped forward.

"Nu, come inside and look round. You stare into my window again and again. You want me to believe you're not interested?"

Jozef was embarrassed. He knew he would need not one but a great many gold pieces to buy any of her violins. But the woman pressed him. He felt it would be rude to run off, so he followed her into the shop.

It was both shop and workroom. From one corner came the fresh smell of newly sawn wood. Blocks of spruce and maple were piled on the floor. A stale, vegetable smell wafted from a stove in another corner, where pots of glue and varnish were warming. On a wall behind a workbench there was a row of nails and hanging from them were hammers, knives, chisels, scrapers, gouges and drills.

"What is your name?" the woman asked.

"Jozef."

"Ah, Jozef was the name of my father, of blessed memory. Take your time. Look around. Fetch one down and get the feel of it."

"I couldn't do that," said Jozef. "I've never held a violin. I shall be too clumsy. I couldn't bear to drop one."

"Let me be the one to worry over that," she answered. "Go on. Take one."

Jozef looked about the shop. The woman was so insistent, but he was frightened to pick any of the fine violins. Then he spotted one on a shelf at the back. Once a handsome instrument, it was now in a sorry state.

There had been an inlay of light-coloured wood making a decoration of vine tendrils and leaves down its ribs. In many places the inlaid wood had fallen out. The spaces left had filled with grime. It had no strings and all its pegs but one were missing. The soundboard was dull and scratched.

"May I see that one?" said Jozef, pointing to the shelf.

"You have made a wise choice," said the woman. "Though it is the violin that chooses the player."

Jozef was not sure what she meant, but he took the violin from her. As it had no strings, he tapped its soundboard with one finger. For all its poor condition, it made a lovely sound.

"The violin is magical," said the woman.

"Yes, I know," said Jozef.

"Do you really?" she asked, with a smile.

"Yes, I've many times heard the Duke's daughter playing."

"Well, gold is needed to make this violin play," said the woman. Jozef took this to be her first move in negotiating a price.

"I've only got one gold piece. That's all the money I have," he said.

"For you, I will sell it at a special price—one gold piece. It should go to one who will give for it all he has."

Back out in the street, Jozef was pleased with his purchase. But he dreaded what his father and mother would say. Having earned a whole gold piece, within minutes he had spent it on an old violin he could not play.

Jozef told his mother and father about his adventure, and he showed them the violin.

"You've bought a violin without strings or a bow?" said his father. "You're a fool, Jozef. What do you think the Duke would say to me if he sent for his carriage and I took him just one wheel?"

"Leave him alone," said his mother. "The lad has ambition. Everybody has to start somewhere. You go on all the time about carriages and horses. Don't forget. When we first got together, all you had was an old donkey."

She turned to Jozef.

"Take no notice, son. None of us can play an instrument. You'll be the first in our family to take up music."

Jozef's father could not stop himself from telling everyone how stupid his son had been. In no time, all who worked in the palace had heard about Jozef's violin.

One day when he walked into the washhouse, one of the laundry maids said to him: "Hey, Jozef, can I join your orchestra? I can't play and I don't have an instrument, so I should be just the person you're looking for."

Another time one of the gardeners called Jozef over.

"When you next come with a load of manure," he said, "I've got a new wheelbarrow for you. Both handles are missing, there's no wheel and its bottom has dropped out. But I hear you're smart enough to get by without all the right bits and pieces."

Jozef laughed with those who made fun of him. He was happy with his violin. Whenever he had any free time, he would tuck it under his arm as he set off for a walk. He liked to tap out a rhythm on it, keeping time with his steps.

Chapter Six
Sophia Goes Alone

Meanwhile, Sophia was planning her second journey into the White Mountain. Her researches in the palace library had raised more questions and she was curious to find the answers. Were the colours in the caves different because the rocks were different or did the colours come from things in the water trickling over them? Did the flowing water she had seen come from springs inside the mountain or were there streams which flowed in from outside? If water did run in, were any creatures swept along on the current and were they able to survive in the dark and cold inside the White Mountain?

Sophia gathered together the things she would need. Because of the cold inside the mountain, she decided to take her warmest cloak. The cloak, embroidered with thread of gold, was a gift from her father. She checked that her tinderbox had plenty of spare linen. She wanted to be certain she could kindle a flame if her lantern blew out. She put a loaf of bread into her cloak pocket in case she felt hungry.

Sophia had kept the lanterns, the oil lamps and the hourglass from the first journey. To make sure she would not run out, she sent for the steward and asked him to bring her three leather flasks of oil. The steward had them fetched from the palace storeroom. He called Jozef and instructed him to carry them up to Sophia's chambers.

"What can the Lady Sophia want with all this oil?" Jozef asked.

"Curiosity is not for the likes of you, lad," replied the steward. "Yours is to do what you're told and not to ask questions."

A little before midnight Sophia slipped out of the back gate and made her way up the mountain path. As she approached the rock face, laden with all her things, she stumbled and fell against a bramble bush. She spilled nothing and with a tug she was able to free her cloak from the thorns.

She uttered the spell. Again, she heard the rumbling sound and a door opened in the rock.

As before, she placed an oil lamp inside the opening and set off to explore.

On her own, Sophia made faster progress, but she had to walk with care. Some ways ended in cliffs above gorges whose bottom she could not see. She came upon a stretch of water. At one end there were horizontal layers of rock where a waterfall must once have poured into the lake. The waterfall was gone but it had softened the steps, to look as if they were covered by a white carpet.

Sophia at last spotted the shaft of light she had seen on her first visit. She made for it and found herself in a gigantic, vaulted space, ten times higher than the great hall of the palace. There was an opening way above her. It was a waxing moon that night and its light streamed in. She saw bats flittering in and out through the opening.

Before her was a lake. At its edge grew several trees. Sophia was curious to know whether birds had flown in carrying the seeds or whether they had been washed in by the streams which fed the lake.

Sophia checked the hourglass. It was time to make her way back. She decided to collect some rock samples as she went. Soon she became distracted, searching for better and better specimens. She caught sight of the oil lamp ahead but at that moment she heard the rumbling sound. Sophia dropped the rocks and ran as fast as she could. When she reached the spot where the opening had been, it was gone. She could find no trace in the rock that a door had ever been there.

Sophia remembered the scholar's warning that if she stayed for more than an hour, she would be shut in forever.

The next morning Sophia's maid was alarmed to find that her lady's chambers were empty.

She told the Duke and the Duke sent for his Secretary. The Secretary organised a search of the palace, but Sophia could not be found. The steward reported Sophia's request for extra oil flasks. The maid said that Sophia's best cloak was missing. She must, they guessed, have left the palace by night.

"My Lord," said the Secretary, "you may wish to look at these papers. I found them in the library."

"Why, this is Sophia's handwriting," said the Duke.

"So it is, my Lord. The Lady Sophia has made notes about caves. And she has written that these drawings show the cave system of our own mountain. I believe the Lady Sophia may have found a way to get inside the White Mountain."

"Then we must search the mountain without delay," said the Duke.

The palace guards were sent out at once. They were local men, so they knew the White Mountain well. They searched every path and probed every crack. Although they spent the whole day scouring the mountain, they could find no way into it.

The Duke was desperate. He sent for his Secretary to walk with him in the long gallery.

"Whatever are we to do?" he asked.

"With the papers I found in the library was a chapter of the scholar's book. Your Lordship will remember that he sent it to the Lady Sophia. In that chapter, he writes of many places to be found in our lands. It occurs to me that the scholar may know something of caves inside the White Mountain."

"You may be right," said the Duke. "We must send for him. If Sophia is trapped underground, we have no time to spare."

"I shall go myself, my Lord, as soon as it is light. This time, I fancy, we shall not need to offer the scholar anything. He became fond of the Lady Sophia. He will be alarmed to know she is missing. In the meantime, it will do no harm for your Lordship to offer a reward to anyone who can find your daughter."

"An excellent idea," said the Duke. "Take this down and make it into a proclamation."

The Duke dictated and his Secretary wrote. The Duke promised to give half of all his lands to anyone who restored his daughter to him. At those words, the Secretary raised an eyebrow. He hoped the Duke would not regret such a promise. But he did not object, for he could see how frantic the Duke was.

The proclamation was copied out and by the time the Duke retired to his bed, dark though it was, riders had been despatched in all directions to nail the proclamation on barns, on church doors, in market places and at cross roads.

At first light the next morning, the Secretary and a couple of his men set off on horseback for the castle where the scholar lived. This time, they commandeered relays of the fastest horses at every stage. In that way, they managed to reach the castle in a day.

Meanwhile, word of the proclamation travelled fast. People of all kinds flocked to the palace. Nobles journeyed there to comfort the Duke on his loss. Huntsmen arrived with packs of hunting dogs. Wise Women came, who were famed for their success in finding lost things. Some brought with them spells and charms of their own.

Priests turned up and organised a vigil in the palace chapel to pray for Sophia's safe return. And a good many adventurers made their way to the palace, in hopes that a lucky find might make them rich.

Jozef's mother was kept busy in the kitchens preparing food for the visitors. His father had much work to stable all the horses and to find places to park all the carriages and wagons. Jozef himself, and every pair of hands in the palace, were occupied kennelling dogs, waiting at tables and running messages.

Late in the evening of the next day, the Secretary returned. He was shown straight to the Duke.

"My Lord, I bring bad news."

"What is it?" asked the Duke.

"When I reached the castle, I learned that the scholar had died two days before. If he had any secret knowledge of the White Mountain, it has perished with him."

"That is a blow," said the Duke. "All my hopes rested on him. For two whole days, people have been trying to find an opening or to break their way into the White Mountain. All have failed. There must be something else we can do."

"I confess, my Lord, I am at a loss. The searching must continue, of course. But perhaps first thing tomorrow, before anybody goes onto the mountain, some of us should walk up in the quiet and just listen. If the Lady Sophia is trapped, she may try pummelling the rock walls inside the cave."

"Very well. We shall do that," the Duke replied. "But I'm beginning to feel I may have lost my dear child forever."

Chapter Seven
Trapped

When Sophia saw that the opening had closed, she tried the spell, but nothing happened.

She picked up a stone and pounded the rock, but it made no impression. She had seen how thick the rock face was when she entered. It was plain that, even if there was anybody on the other side, they would hear nothing.

Sophia sank to the ground and wept. Her tears were tears of anger. She was cross with herself for not heeding the scholar's warning.

Sophia did not weep for long. She blew out the lamp to save oil but left it there to mark the spot. With her lantern, she made her way back to the place with the opening above it. She found a ledge well above the level of the lake. Wrapping her cloak around her, she lay down. After some sleep, she thought, she might be better able to weigh up what to do.

When Sophia woke, she could see, from the sky visible in the opening above, that it was day outside. She examined the trees by the lake. They were plum trees and laden with fruit. She knelt and drank some of the water. Around the trees lay fallen branches and twigs. She gathered a bundle. With her tinderbox she lit a fire to warm herself. She broke a small piece from her loaf and ate it.

"I'd better be sparing with the bread," she said to herself. "Once I've finished that, I'll have nothing but plums. I suppose a bat must fall to the ground from time to time. I wonder how roasted bat tastes."

Sophia decided to walk around the lake. On her way, she had to cross a number of streams flowing into it. On the far side, she discovered a broader stream which flowed out of the lake. She started to follow it in the hope it might lead her out of the White Mountain. But after only a short distance it ran away into the darkness down a gap in the rocks through which she would never be able to squeeze.

But that stream gave Sophia an idea. Back by the plum trees she topped up the oil in her lantern from one of the leather flasks. What was left in it she shared out between the other two flasks. Into the now empty flask she stuffed her handkerChief. It was embroidered with the Duke's crest.

Anyone who found it would know at once it was hers. She sealed the flask and made her way back to the stream. She threw it into the water and watched it bobbing away on the current. She hoped the stream would carry it out of the mountain, where it might be seen and fished out by somebody.

Sophia had another idea.

"What if I light a fire," she thought, "and put fresh, green wood on it? That's likely to give off a lot of smoke. If I can make enough smoke, it may drift out of the opening. Somebody might see it."

Sophia got her fire going. She broke growing branches from the plum trees and piled them on. They made a lot of smoke. But the air in the vault was still. The distance up to the opening was vast. None of the smoke rose that far.

Chapter Eight
The Violin Plays

It was now the fourth day since Sophia had gone into the White Mountain. Searchers had tramped all over it. They had hammered at every patch of exposed rock and probed every opening, down to the narrowest crack. They achieved nothing. Many who had come roused by the Duke's proclamation began to drift away.

For the first time in days, Jozef was able to take a break from running around waiting upon visitors. Although it was late, he thought he would go up the White Mountain himself. He knew it well, but he had no idea how he might succeed where everyone else had failed. He set off a little before midnight. As always, he took his violin with him, tucked under one arm. There was a full moon, so he had no need of a light.

Jozef was climbing a path when he noticed something glitter in the moonlight deep inside a bramble bush. He reached in, taking care not to catch his hand on the thorns. He drew out a long, golden thread. He did not know it, but that thread of gold had been pulled out of Sophia's cloak when she snagged it there.

Jozef held up the golden thread and looked at it. The words of the woman in the shop came into his mind.

What was it she'd said? he thought to himself. *Gold is needed to make this violin play. Just suppose*, he wondered, *that she wasn't talking about its price.*

Jozef tied the golden thread to the tail piece of his violin. He pulled it taut and wound the other end round the only peg. He had no bow, so he plucked it.

Jozef was astonished to hear the violin produce a melodious sound, as if it was a human voice. He did it again. Each time he plucked the string, it seemed to sing another word. He heard a rumbling sound. A door opened in the rock by him.

Sophia, too, heard the rumbling sound. She had been trying to sleep but pangs of hunger kept her awake. She jumped to her feet, lit her lantern and with all haste made for where the opening had been.

Jozef, meanwhile, peered through the doorway. It was black inside and he could see nothing. He hesitated for a moment before stepping in. As he entered, he struck his foot against something on the ground. Kneeling down, he picked it up. He stepped back out of the cave to examine it in the moonlight. He recognised it as one of the oil lamps he had carried up to the Lady Sophia's chambers.

Jozef looked back into the cave. This time he could see something, a point of light moving in the distance. Then he heard something too, the sound of running footsteps. He moved back and the next moment Sophia ran out of the cave. She saw Jozef and threw her arms round him.

"Good sir, you have saved me. But for you, I should have been shut inside the White Mountain forever."

"Here, my Lady," he said, "take my arm. Let me help you back down the path."

Chapter Nine
Rescue Rewarded

There was great amazement and great rejoicing that night in the palace when Jozef led Sophia in. The Duke was sent for at once. He had been unable to sleep. He was on his knees at prayer in the chapel.

"Dear Sophia," he said, "my prayers have been answered."

The Duke took Sophia in his arms. Both of them wept tears of joy.

"As for you, young man," said the Duke, "we shall be in your debt forever."

The kitchen staff, including Jozef's mother, had stayed at the palace overnight. They were roused and asked to prepare a meal for Sophia. She ate all that was put before her—all, that is but for the dessert.

"Here, my Lady, is a dish of ripe plums," said a serving maid.

"Excuse me," Sophia replied, "but I shall give the plums a miss. It may be some time before I can face another one."

Sophia and her father sat together into the early hours of the morning while she told him her story.

The next day the Duke called Jozef before him.

"You will know of my proclamation, young man," he said. "I now give you half of all the lands I possess. I give them to you gladly. What you have restored to me is more precious than anything I own."

"I am grateful, my Lord," answered Jozef, "but I cannot accept them. I am not one to be an owner of land. And besides, I should make a poor job of it."

The Duke was troubled by Jozef's response. He turned to his Secretary.

"Please talk to Jozef and persuade him. I am a man of my word. If it becomes known that my daughter was found but I did not hand over the reward I promised, my honour will be stained."

Jozef and the Secretary withdrew. They spent some time together in the Secretary's office.

At length, the Secretary reported back to the Duke.

"Jozef and I have agreed a proposal we should like to put to your Lordship. We suggest your Lordship issues another proclamation. In that proclamation your Lordship might first of all thank those who travelled from afar to the palace to lend support and to search the White Mountain. Then it would be appropriate to give the news that the Lady Sophia is found and that her rescuer was, after all, Jozef, a local man.

"As one of your loyal subjects, he does not wish to see your Lordship's estate broken up to give him a reward. Therefore, your Lordship has awarded Jozef a payment, to be made every year, equal to the income of half your lands."

"An excellent idea," said the Duke. "Come here, Jozef and let me embrace you."

The first thing Jozef did with his new wealth was to buy a house in the town for himself and his parents.

His father left the Duke's service and Jozef bought a small farm for him. There he bred horses, importing new stock from Spain and Italy to improve the local breed.

Jozef's mother loved her work in the palace kitchens. She had no wish to leave. But she worried about the welfare of many of the young women who came from the town to work in the palace. Their poverty made them vulnerable. She put some of Jozef's money aside and drew upon it to relieve their families and to help many of them to better lives.

Sophia was sad to learn of the scholar's death and to discover that his great work lay unfinished. She took it upon herself to complete what he had begun. She had hundreds of maps and engravings produced to illustrate the book. When at last she felt it was done, she paid for it to be published in his name as a memorial to his learning.

Jozef hired a tutor to teach him to read and write. He was quick to learn but he never became as fond of books as Sophia. Jozef's great delight was music. He had the old violin restored and Sophia taught him to play. He soon became Sophia's equal in skill. They composed and played together and gave great pleasure to all who heard them. The joy they found in making music became in time a joy in one another's company. Jozef and Sophia fell in love and were married.

When the Duke died, they became joint rulers of his lands. Admired and respected by all, they lived happily ever after.

The Giant with Golden Hair – Scotland

Chapter One
A Prophecy

In Scotland, long ago, there was a Chief who always thought he knew better than anyone else.

As a young man, he had led some of his followers into battle. He ignored the advice of those more experienced in fighting, believing he knew better than them. By sheer luck and because his crazy attack was such a surprise, he chanced to overcome the enemy. That victory persuaded his people to choose him as their Chief.

As a Chief, he had command of a castle. His people lived there with him. Most of them were related to him in some way or else they had sworn allegiance to his family.

When the Chief's wife gave birth to their first child, a girl, there was great rejoicing. They named her Margaret. He ordered a feast to celebrate. Men rode out in numbers to hunt deer and wild boar to supply the castle kitchens. Carts groaned under the weight of the wine barrels brought to the great hall.

Among the guests was an elderly lady. The sister of the Chief's grandmother, she was respected by all, for many times she had shown she could foretell the future. At the top table, she was honoured with a seat close to the Chief.

As the evening went on and as he drank more and more wine, the Chief boasted of the beauty and the cleverness of his baby daughter.

"When the time is right," he said, "I shall choose a fitting husband for her myself."

"I think not, young man," said the Chief's great aunt. "Others will decide the man to marry your daughter, not you."

"Nonsense!" he shouted. "I know what I shall do better than any foolish old woman. I shall marry my daughter to the son of a Chief or perhaps even to the son of a king from beyond these lands."

The woman had not intended to say more, but the Chief's words provoked her.

"I'll tell you something you don't know," she said. "Your daughter will marry a man born on the same day and at the same hour as her. And he will be a working man, the son of a poor fisherman."

"I do know one thing," the Chief roared. "I don't have to sit here and listen to you talking rubbish."

He threw the dregs in his cup into the woman's face, jumped to his feet and stormed out of the hall.

The Chief's wife ran after him, up to their chambers.

"Shame on you, husband," she said, "to insult one of your own family and a lady who is esteemed by all."

"You know nothing of these things, woman," he said. "I shall decide who marries the girl and that's an end of it."

"Surely it matters little who decides, or what her husband is," she said. "What is important is that he proves a loving husband, and they are happy together."

"I shall not be contradicted at my own table," said the Chief, "nor in my own chamber."

His wife was used to the Chief's ways. By the next day, she had soothed his temper. Once calm, he began to think about what his great aunt had said.

"Suppose she can see something of the future," he mused. "I'm not going to sit back and let that happen. I know how to put a stop to her nonsense."

The Chief summoned his most trustworthy men.

"You are to go out and scour these lands," he ordered. "You're to look for the son of a fisherman. The child must have been born on the same day and at the same hour as my daughter. When you find him, bring him to me. I don't care what you have to do. Bring him without fail."

Chapter Two
The Chief Sets Out

The men left the castle. They separated and each one made off in a different direction. They rode over stretches of moorland dotted with heather and gorse. They squelched across marshes and peat bogs. Their horses scrambled over rock-strewn ridges. Between mountains, they passed along wooded glens. Occasionally, the sky was clear, and the sun shone. More often, it was grey and cold. Some days, they were soaked by drizzling mist. Strong winds chilled them.

They journeyed in search of fishing folk. Making for the coasts, they commandeered boats to carry them across the sea to offshore islands. They sought out lochs, burns, rivers and estuaries.

Everywhere they asked the same question.

"Have you a new-born son?" Everywhere they were disappointed. Baby boys there were, but not one born on the same day and at the same hour as their Chief's daughter.

The men gradually straggled back to the castle, weary and with only failure to report. If any of them was expecting to be thanked for his efforts, he was disappointed. With each return, the Chief became more and more cross.

"Give up this search now," his wife urged. He had shared nothing with her of his plans. She was troubled though, when she thought what he might do, if he did find the baby boy.

"Let the matter rest." She pleaded, "Who knows? Things may turn out for the best if we leave them be."

"Nonsense," he replied. "Three months gone, and my men achieved nothing. It's always the same. If you want something done properly, you have to do it yourself. I know how to go about finding a baby, if they don't."

The next morning, the Chief ordered his horse to be made ready. He filled one of his saddle bags with gold pieces. He bade his wife farewell and rode from the castle at a gallop.

Once he was out of sight of the castle, he slowed down to walking pace. He wondered how to begin his search. In truth, he had no more idea than his horse which direction to take.

The Chief rode this way and that. In every place, he asked the same question his men had asked. In every place, he got the same answer. Nowhere could he find a fisherman's son born on the same day and at the same hour as his daughter.

Chapter Three
A Baby Found and Lost

One afternoon, weary from two months of wandering the land, the Chief came to a beach. Sore from being so long in the saddle, he tied his horse to a bush in the dunes and went down to walk along the sands.

Some way off, he saw a man wading and bending down in the water by a line of sticks.

Curious to know what the man was doing, he went over to him.

"That looks like cold work," the Chief said.

"Aye. It's cold enough," replied the man.

"What are you doing?"

"I'm catching fish or rather I'm trying to."

"I don't see any nets or lines," said the Chief.

"Nor will you," answered the fisherman. "With these sticks, I've planted lines of hurdles in the water. As the tide goes out, the hurdles steer any fish on the land side of them into the baskets I've staked in the sand."

"Are you having any luck?"

"No," the fisherman said. "Some months back, I had a great haul. I won't forget that night. I was lucky in more than just my catch. When I got home, my wife had given birth to our son. A full five months have gone by since then. In all that time, I've hardly caught a thing."

The Chief held his breath. *This must be the baby,* he thought to himself. His daughter was now five months old.

"At what hour was your son born?" he asked.

"I live by the tides," said the fisherman. "So I mark them well. Low tide that night was an hour before midnight. I had so many fish, I took an hour to carry them up to our cottage. When I got in, the wee boy was but an hour old."

The Chief smiled. His daughter had been born an hour before midnight.

"I've travelled long and hard," he said. "It's growing late. May I stop the night at your cottage, before I go on my way?"

"We are poor people," replied the fisherman, "and all the poorer now that my luck with the fish is gone. We can offer you little. But you're welcome to share what we have. I'll turn no one away who comes to my door."

A few hens were scratching in the dirt outside the fisherman's cottage. It was not much more than a single room, warmed by a fire in the middle of the floor. In a corner stood a table and a couple of chairs, in another corner a bed.

The fisherman's wife sat cross-legged on the floor. Cradling her son in her arms, she was singing to him. Seeing a visitor, she rose and put the baby down in a wooden crib by the fire. He lay there, kicking his feet and waving his arms.

"He's a handsome boy," said the Chief. "And that's a fine crib."

"He is that," replied the fisherman's wife. "And he has the sweetest nature."

"We may be poor," said the fisherman, "but we're rich in our neighbours. One of them works at floating timber down the river nearby. He made us the crib from a piece of oak that came into his hands."

"You're rich too in having a child," said the Chief. "My wife and I have no children. We have money enough and plenty more. We would give much to have a child of our own."

The fisherman was not a greedy man, but the Chief's words brought a thoughtful look to his face. He felt ashamed he could not provide better for his family.

The Chief spotted that look. He took his saddle bag and tipped onto the table a pile of gold coins bigger than any the fisherman and his wife had ever seen.

"All this I will give you," he said, "if I may take the boy and bring him up as my own. With this money, you can make a fresh start. You're both young. You may have many more children. My wife and I will give this boy opportunities you could never put his way. You'll be doing him a favour if you accept my offer. And when he's a young man, he'll come back to you."

That night, the fisherman and his wife slept little. They lay by one another, turning the matter over in whispers. The wife was reluctant. She could not bear the thought of parting with her first born. Her husband, though, was desperate for them to break out of their poverty. At length, he persuaded her.

In the morning, the fisherman and his tearful wife shook hands with the Chief on their bargain. They took his gold coins. He tied the crib across his saddle and rode away.

The Chief's first thought was to find a place out of sight and run his sword through the baby. But the rocking movement of the horse had lulled the boy to sleep. He could not bring himself to do violence to a sleeping child. He decided it would be better to drown him. It would be risky, he reasoned, to use the river near the fisherman's cottage. He rode on for several hours until he came to another river. He threw the crib in and watched it float away downstream.

"So much for the predictions of foolish women," he said to himself. "I know how to see off a fisherman's son. And anyway, when that crib gets tipped over, it'll be the current or the rocks that drown him, not me."

The Chief remounted his horse and rode off. It took him several days before he found his way back to the castle.

"How did you get on?" asked his wife when he returned.

"We have no need to fear any fisherman's son now," he replied.

"But how can you be sure of that?"

"I know what I know," he said.

The Chief was determined not to tell his wife what he had done. She noticed he had come back without a single gold coin. Her guess was he must have found the baby boy and had paid his parents to take their son far away.

Chapter Four
The Baby Gets a Home

The crib was well-made. Being watertight, it floated for some distance down the river. At last, it bumped against a dam of stones built a little way out into the stream.

Later that day, a man walked along the riverbank. He and his wife lived in a cottage downstream. He was a fisherman too, but he fished the river, not the sea. He caught the salmon, the trout and the eels which migrated along the river. The dam was of his making.

The man saw the crib. He kept stacks of spare poles in places along the bank. He fetched one and with it pulled the crib free of the dam. Wading in, he lifted it from the water.

At first glance, he'd known it to be a crib, but he was astonished to find a baby inside. No longer soothed by the sound and the motion of the water, the baby greeted him by starting to cry.

The man carried the crib in his arms and hastened back to his cottage. As he approached, his wife heard the howling of the baby. She came out to see what was going on.

"You'll never guess what I've got here," said the man.

"Well, unless somebody is tormenting a piglet, my guess is you've got a crying baby. From the noise it's making, the wee one is either cold or hungry or both."

"Take a look then," said the man. She peeped into the crib.

"That's the bonniest child I've seen in many a year. But whose is it? How did you come by it?"

Her husband began to explain how he'd been out walking, how he'd spotted the crib, how he'd grabbed a pole, how he'd freed the crib from the dam, how astounded he'd been.

"Hush your blether, man," she interrupted. "Let's inside and settle this wee one."

They went into the cottage. The wife placed the crib by the fire. She put some milk in a pan and set it over the fire to warm. When she picked the baby up, it stopped crying.

"What are we to do, wife?"

"I'll tell you what we're going to do. I'm going to feed the wee thing. You're going back along the river to see if you can find anyone who knows anything about it."

The man set off back. He walked for miles upriver. He crossed by a ford and returned down the far bank. No one was about. Nothing could he find to shed any light on the baby in the crib.

All was quiet in the cottage when he got back. The baby lay in the crib by the fire, kicking his legs and waving his arms. Whenever the wife looked into the crib, she was rewarded with a smile.

"This is the sweetest wee boy," said the woman.

"What now then?" asked her husband.

"The way I figure it, someone has abandoned the poor boy," she answered. "We've never been blessed with children of our own. And at our age, it's not likely we shall be. I say we keep him."

And they did keep him. They could not have cared for him better if he had been born their own child. They called him Duncan. When he could talk, he called them 'mother' and 'father'. From the age of five, he went out with the man, helping him with his work.

In that way, he learned much about the river and about the forest through which it flowed. He grew to be a handsome young man and a loving son to the couple.

Chapter Five
Rediscovery

Eighteen years had passed since the day of the Chief's bargain with Duncan's real parents.

His daughter had become a young woman. In addition to her many qualities, she was skilled in poetry and music. She and her mother spent much time together. They enjoyed one another's company.

The people of the villages around the castle who kept sheep and goats were much troubled by wolves. Packs of them came by night after their lambs and kids.

The Chief declared that something must be done about the wolves. He summoned a hunting party, to be led by himself. The huntsmen would seek out their dens and kill the wolves. The villagers gathered to see them off and cheer them on their way.

The hunting party rode for many days. They searched for the wolves in forests, in glens and on mountain sides. They went a great distance from the castle. One day, as they rode through dense cover of oak and birch trees, they came into a clearing and from there, they glimpsed a high plateau some way off. They decided to make for that and set off at a gallop. The Chief lagged behind at the rear of the troop.

"Wait," he called to them. "You're going a long way round." They pretended not to hear him and rode on.

"Fools!" he shouted after them. "I know how to find my way out of a forest, if you don't."

The Chief took his own way through the trees. Soon, he was lost. He stopped for a rest and wondered what he should do to find his men. After a while, he rode on again through the trees.

He came to a river. By the bank was a cottage. As the Chief approached, a man came out.

"Has a troop of huntsmen passed this way?" the Chief asked him.

"No. Not a soul."

The man looked at the Chief. He could tell from his horse and saddle he was someone of substance.

"You look weary, friend. Will you not come inside to rest awhile and sup with us."

The Chief dismounted and went in. The man introduced him to his wife. She began to prepare a meal. The Chief sat down and warmed himself by the fire.

He was sitting there resting when a young man came in.

"We have a visitor, son," said the man.

The young man bowed to the Chief.

"Can I do anything for you, sir?" said the young man.

"I'm tired. My horse is too. Would you see to him for me?"

The young man went outside. He fetched oats and water for the horse. Having taken off its saddle, he began to rub the horse down.

"He's a handsome young man," said the Chief.

"He is that," replied the woman. "And for all that he's strong and brave, he has the sweetest nature. No mother could ask for a better son."

The woman set a spit over the fire to roast some rabbit her son had caught in his traps. The man fetched barley ale and poured the Chief a beaker full.

The Chief sat back. Taking a mouthful of ale, he looked about the room. He saw something which made him choke. He spluttered and ale ran down his chin. He wiped his beard, coughed and pretended that some of the drink had gone down the wrong way.

"That's a fine piece of work," he said, gesturing to the object in the corner.

"Aye, it is," said the woman, interrupting her husband who had been about to reply. "Our son spent many a peaceful hour in that crib. He was a contented baby. He slept well."

"There's an interesting story about that crib," said the man.

His wife looked hard at him. She had been going to say no more. But he took no heed of her.

"We call the young fellow our son," he went on, "but he was not born to us. We found him in that crib. I was out by the river one day. I saw it stuck against one of my dams. And what should be inside but a bonny baby boy."

The Chief went pale. The man's words bore out what he feared the moment he recognised the crib. That baby boy had not drowned. It had grown up to become this young man.

"Most interesting," stammered the Chief.

"Are you not feeling well?" asked the woman.

"No. I'm not. All that riding has been too much for me. May I stop the night here, to regain my strength?"

"Of course," she replied, "you're welcome to share what we have."

The Chief wanted time to think. He said little over the meal. Making a show of being exhausted, he retired to bed early.

For most of that night he lay awake. He turned the problem over and over in his mind. What should he do to see off this threat to his daughter once and for all?

Chapter Six
An Encounter with Outlaws

By daybreak, the Chief had fixed upon a plan. At breakfast, he pretended to be unwell.

"You have been most hospitable," he said. "I fear I'm not well enough to travel on. If you'll let me stay awhile, I'll pay you for my keep. May I ask your son to take a message to my castle? He can ride my horse. It will know how to find its way back. I'll give him a letter for my wife. In the letter, I'll ask her to send a wagon to carry me back."

"I'll gladly do you that service," said Duncan.

The Chief always carried with him paper, a quill and a small pot of ink. He took them from his saddle bag and wrote the letter. The couple and Duncan watched. None of them was able to read or write. When he had finished, the Chief folded the paper. He took out some red wax, which he warmed at the fire. He sealed the letter with the impress of his ring.

"It's likely to be some way," said the Chief, "maybe two days' journey."

"In that case," said the woman, "you'll be needing this."

She gave Duncan a leather bag. In it she put some salt fish, a couple of oat cakes and a flask of water.

Duncan slung the bag over his shoulder. Having bidden farewell to his mother and father, he mounted the Chief's horse and rode off.

The Chief smiled. *I know I'll not see you again, fellow,* he said to himself.

Through the forest Duncan held a loose rein, allowing the horse to go where it chose. The Chief had said the horse would know how to find its way back to the castle. As the day went on, Duncan began to doubt that. He realised the horse was plodding along, not knowing where it was going. As evening began to draw in, he saw he was lost, far from his home and deep in a part of the forest he had never before explored.

Duncan started to look for a place where he might safely lie down for the night. Along a narrow path almost hidden by trees, he noticed a hut. He got off the horse and led it down the path. By the door of the hut was a stack of peat, cut and dried ready for the fire. A wisp of smoke rose from the roof. He tied up the horse and looked around. He called, but no answer came. The hut was empty.

Inside, the fire was barely alight, so he put on some fresh peat. There were sheepskins and goatskins on the floor. It was clear that people slept in the hut.

Before eating, Duncan went out and found a patch of grass. He tethered the Chief's horse there to graze. Back inside the hut, he sat by the fire and made a meal of the food his mother had given him. He was tired from the day's riding. Pulling some of the skins over him, he lay down by the fire and fell asleep.

The hut belonged to a band of five outlaws. They were desperate rather than wicked men. Most of them had been driven off their own land, having been on the losing side in feuds between different Chiefs. By day, they ranged through the forest, only coming back to the hut to sleep.

They lived by taking deer and boar from the hunting grounds which were the preserve of the Chiefs and their followers. Whenever they caught more than they needed for themselves, they shared their spoils with the villagers living roundabout.

When the outlaws returned that night, they saw the horse. Their fire, they knew, ought to have gone out by then. A fresh top layer showed them the peat stack had gone down and there was still smoke rising from the roof.

"We have an intruder," said one of them. "Nobody make a sound. We'll see who it is." They crept inside and found Duncan asleep on the floor.

"My word, that's a handsome lad," said one of the outlaws. "Who can he be and what's he doing here?"

"We'd better be careful. We don't want to wake him," said another. "If this place gets known about and we're recognised, we'll have to move on."

One of them drew back the sheepskin Duncan had pulled over him.

"Look," he said, "there's a letter tucked in his jerkin."

He pulled the letter out.

"I'd know that seal anywhere," he said. "It's the seal of the Chief I used to follow. I was his steward. Until, that is, he banished me from his castle."

"Why was that?" asked one of his comrades.

"He always knew better than everyone else. I put up with it for a long time. But one day, he countermanded my instructions for the planting of a crop of oats.

The result was a lot of our people had a hard and hungry time. I told him he'd blundered. And for that he had me thrown out of the castle."

"Is this young fellow the Chief's son, then?" asked another outlaw.

"No. He has only a daughter. She'd be much the same age as this young man. Anyway, look at his hands. Those are the hands of someone who earns his living by his own toil."

"So what does the letter say? You're the only one of us who can read or write."

The man drew his knife. Having warmed it by the fire, he used it to prise the seal from the paper without breaking it. Unfolding the paper, he read it.

"So does it say where he's going?" one of the men asked.

"Yes—to his death."

"What?"

"Hush. Let me read you what it says. It's a letter from the Chief to his wife. In it, he writes, 'This is the one. I know what we must do. As soon as he arrives, you are to order my men to take him down to the dungeon. They must put him to death immediately'."

"Whatever can he have done to deserve that?" they wondered.

"I don't know," said the reader, "but I do have an idea of my own."

He fetched paper, a quill and some ink which he kept in a box. Copying the Chief's hand, he wrote out a fresh letter. In that one, he put, "This is the one. I know what we must do. When he arrives, you are to have this young man married to our daughter without delay."

As for the Chief's order for a wagon to be sent, that he left out. He folded the paper and stuck it down again with the Chief's seal. He tucked the new letter back into the young man's jerkin. The Chief's letter he burned on the fire.

"We must be away now, comrades," he said. "It's a night out in the forest for us. We mustn't be here when this young man wakes. By the time we come back tomorrow evening, he'll have gone on his way."

Chapter Seven
A Wedding

Duncan rose early. He put more peat on the fire to keep it going and arranged everything in the hut as he had found it.

This time he decided to trust his own wits, not the Chief's horse. When he came to a clearing, he climbed to the top of an oak tree. From there, he spied the castle in the far distance, and he could see which way to go. Late in the afternoon, he reached the castle.

The two men in the gatehouse recognised their Chief's horse. They levelled their pikes at Duncan. They were satisfied, though, when he showed them the letter bearing the Chief's seal. They let him pass. One of them led him into the castle courtyard and offered to show him where the Chief's wife had her chamber. Duncan would not go until he had drawn a bucket of water from the courtyard well to refresh the horse.

He was shown into the presence of the Chief's wife. He bowed low before her and handed her the letter. She read it.

She looked into his face.

"Do you know what this says?" she asked.

"I believe, madam, that it contains some instructions from your husband."

"To what purpose?"

"I saw your husband write the letter, madam, but I do not have the skill of reading, nor did he share with me what he'd put."

She looked at him again. Her eyes moved from his head to his feet. Although he bore the signs of having been in the saddle for two days, he still made a handsome figure. She saw before her a tall young man, fair haired and broad of shoulder.

"Well," she said, "my people will show you to a room where you can refresh yourself. You must eat this evening with me and my daughter."

Alone again, the Chief's wife frowned. After reading the letter a second time, she sent for her daughter.

"Did you see the young man who rode in this evening?" she asked. Margaret turned her head away.

"I may have seen somebody."

She did not want her mother to mark her blush. From her chamber window, Margaret had watched the young man cross the courtyard and draw water from the well. She liked what she saw.

"He brought this letter from your father. Read it, my dear." Margaret read the letter. This time, she could not hide her blushes.

"I'm not surprised," her mother said. "Your father has long had fixed ideas about whom you should marry. What does surprise me, though, is his choice. Your father has never been the best of judges. If he told me an egg was good, I should have to smell it to be sure."

Margaret giggled.

"But this young man does seem a fine fellow," she went on. "He has an open face and a lovely smile. His manners are good too. I've said he is to eat with us this evening."

Margaret said nothing.

"You don't need to worry," said her mother. "I'll not have you marry anyone against your wishes. Meet him. Take your time. Get to know him and see what you think. Then tell me what you would do. I'll stand by you, whatever you decide. And if it is not to your father's liking, I'll settle that with him."

Their evening meal together was a success. The first impressions of both mother and daughter had been favourable and they soon found they were not mistaken. Duncan was good company. He talked well. He told them much of his life by the river and in the forest. His love for his parents and his fondness for the land where he lived came across in all he said.

He also listened well. He asked many questions about life in the castle. He was eager to learn how mother and daughter spent their time. By the end of the evening, Margaret liked Duncan a lot and he liked her.

With her mother's blessing, she spent much time with him over the following couple of days.

They walked together to visit some of the villages scattered around the castle. They rode together along the tracks in the nearby forest. And when the drizzle and mist settled in, they sat together by the fire in the great hall of the castle. Margaret played her harp and sang ballads to Duncan.

By the time three days had passed, liking had turned to love on both sides. Margaret revealed her feelings to her mother, who agreed she should ask Duncan to be her husband.

"Remember your father's letter. He said we should waste no time. So if the young man consents, we'll have your wedding this very day."

Duncan was overjoyed. They were married that afternoon. To celebrate the event, the castle was decked with flags. A feast was held. Singing and dancing lasted long into the night.

Chapter Eight
A Quest Begun

Meanwhile, back at the cottage, the Chief was becoming more and more cross. No wagon had come to carry him back to the castle. Although they were too polite to show it, Duncan's parents were becoming more and more fed up with the Chief's crabby temper.

At length, the Chief decided to make his own way back. His hosts knew a woodcutter who lived in the forest. The woodcutter had an old donkey which carried his bundles of firewood. The Chief hired the donkey and paid the woodcutter to lead him out of the forest.

The Chief reached the castle. He was a tall man. At the sight of him plodding in under the gate on an old donkey, the toes of his boots scraping the ground, the two men on guard had to avoid looking at one another, for fear they would burst out laughing.

"Good of you to put out the flags to celebrate my return," said the Chief. "I know how fond you are of me."

The two men kept looking straight ahead. They said nothing.

It was lucky for them that the clopping of the donkey's hooves on the courtyard cobbles masked the sound behind it in the gatehouse, the clanking together of steel helmets as the two men fell into one another's arms, with tears of laughter running down their cheeks.

The Chief made his way up to his wife's chamber. She welcomed him home.

"Did you get my letter?" he demanded.

"Yes," she said. "I got your letter. We did just what you said. And look! Aren't they a handsome couple?"

She gestured to the window.

"A handsome couple? What are you talking about?"

He strode to the window and looked out. Duncan was walking by with his arm round Margaret's waist.

"They were married yesterday," said the Chief's wife. The Chief scowled.

"Give me my letter," he snapped.

She handed the letter to him. Having read it, he stormed out of the room. She heard a crash as he slammed the door of his own chamber.

The Chief stood and gripped the stone mantle above the fireplace. He thought hard. He was not going to let his wife or anybody, know he had been hoodwinked. He thought back to what his great aunt had said at the feast eighteen years ago.

"So, the old fool got that much right," he said to himself. "My daughter has married the son of a poor fisherman."

He threw himself into a chair. He sat turning the matter over in his mind.

"She didn't say how long the marriage would last. What's done can be undone. I only have to find a way to get rid of him."

As he thought about his great aunt, he recalled a story he'd heard her tell many times. She used to talk of an island, far, far away. On that island lived a giant, a ferocious creature. The giant had a head of golden hair—the golden hair of knowledge, she called it. Anyone who was able to get even a single hair from his head would gain great knowledge.

What appealed to him now was the end of the story. She always finished by saying that over the years many men had gone to search for the giant but not one of them had ever returned alive.

The Chief sent for Duncan. He snarled at him when he entered the chamber.

"I suppose you're feeling pleased with yourself."

"I am feeling lucky, sir," replied Duncan, "that someone as fine as your daughter asked me to be her husband."

"Pah!" snorted the Chief.

"You seem unhappy, sir," said Duncan. "I want to make my wife happy but that cannot be if you are troubled. If there is anything I can do to banish your sadness, I will do it."

"I'm pleased to hear you say that," said the Chief. "I'm unhappy because I don't know all that a Chief should know."

"I doubt I can help you there, sir. I'm no scholar."

"There is something you can do for me. On an island far from here lives a giant. He's a kind and generous fellow. He has a head of golden hair, the golden hair of knowledge, I've heard it called. To anyone who finds his island, he'll give some hair from his head. A person who possesses even one of those hairs will, through its power, gain great knowledge. I'd like you to find that island and bring me three of the giant's hairs."

"I'll try," said Duncan, "if you think it will make you happy."

"I know it will," said the Chief.

"When do you want me to start?"

The Chief smiled. "Right away," he said. "The sooner you go, the sooner you'll be back."

The Chief called his wife and daughter. He told them Duncan was about to set off on a quest. Margaret protested.

"Father, we were married only yesterday. Surely this can wait?"

"I know what is best, girl," he replied. "Spend one more night with your husband. He is to be off in the morning. He'll be back with you in no time."

The Chief's wife frowned at him. She turned to Margaret to comfort her.

"Take heart, Margaret, my dear. Duncan is a bright young man with a winning way. He's bound to find people who will help him with his quest. We must put our confidence in him and wish him a safe return."

The Chief said nothing.

In the morning, Duncan was given a horse and saddle bags packed with food and money.

Duncan, Margaret and her mother all shed tears at their parting.

Chapter Nine
Village Puzzles

Duncan travelled long and far. He rode across sandy beaches. He followed tracks on the top of sea cliffs and heard the crash of ocean waves breaking on jagged rocks below. Many times he left his horse with crofters and took ferry boats to distant islands. He sailed with fishermen on their trips after the shoals of herring. Everywhere he asked about an island which was home to a giant with golden hair. Nowhere did he meet anyone who had heard of such an island.

He soon got through his food. After a while, he had spent the money too, having bought food and paid for lodgings. He was cold, wet and hungry when one day he approached a village, where he hoped to find someone who might give him a meal and shelter for the night.

He saw a group of the villagers gathered in one of the field strips behind the cottages. They were talking loudly, and some shook their heads.

"Welcome, stranger," said one man, as Duncan rode up to them.

"You seem to be troubled, sir," said Duncan. "Do you have a problem?"

"Aye, we do that," replied the man. "Come and see for yourself."

Duncan dismounted and the man led him over to a team of oxen, who were yoked to a plough. The blade of the plough was broken in two.

"Something has happened to our land. We cannot understand it," the man explained. "The ground has become as hard as iron. We cannot get a plough into it. We've tried by hand, but every spade and hoe in the village has been shattered. We can't make as much as a crack in the soil.

"Already, we're having to travel to markets far off to buy oats and barley. If this goes on, we shall have to leave our homes and find new land."

The man sighed. "Enough of our troubles, young man. Where have you come from and where are you bound?"

"I've travelled long and far. I'm on a quest to acquire three hairs from the giant with the golden hair of knowledge."

"We could certainly do with some of that knowledge," replied the man, "if you succeed in your search."

"Well," replied Duncan, "if you will give me a bed for the night and a little of your food, I'll come this way when I return, and I'll share whatever knowledge I've gained."

The villagers agreed and made Duncan welcome. One of the village women had a spare bed in her cottage and she took Duncan in. Over a meal of oat cakes and goat's cheese, he told her his story.

The woman pursed her lips. "I've heard tell of this giant. I fear your Chief means you no good, young man. All the tales I've heard agree that the giant is a ferocious creature. They say no man who has set out to find him has ever returned. That's why no one from this village has ever made the attempt. But there's one thing I remember. In your hunt for the island, you'd do better to leave the coast and push inland."

"Thank you," said Duncan. "I'll try my luck that way."

After a sleep in a comfortable bed and a breakfast of porridge, Duncan said his farewells to the woman and to her neighbours. He repeated his promise to return with any knowledge he gained.

Taking the woman's advice, Duncan turned inland. He rode on for many days. He crossed marshy moorland, pitted with small lochs and littered with boulders. He tramped drovers' tracks and climbed mountain ranges.

One day, looking for a place to lie down and rest, Duncan saw a village. As he rode in, he came upon a number of villagers clustered round a well. Some were peering down the well. Others seemed to be arguing. Duncan pulled up beside them.

One man turned to him.

"Welcome, stranger," he said.

"What is wrong?" asked Duncan. "You seem to be agitated."

"We are indeed," the man answered. "We can't understand what has happened to our well.

"This well supplies the whole village with the sweetest of water. There is water in it still and at its usual level. Drop a stone and you'll hear it splash. But we can't draw a single bucketful. Whatever we lower down comes up empty every time. We have to fetch water now from far off. We'll soon have to abandon the village and find somewhere else to live."

The man shrugged. "That's our problem, young man. But what of you? Where are you headed?"

"I'm travelling in search of an island, the home of the giant with the golden hair of knowledge."

"Knowledge is what we need," replied the man, "if we're to sort out our well."

"In that case," said Duncan, "in return for shelter and a meal, I'll share with you any knowledge I've got when I come back this way."

The villagers were pleased and welcomed Duncan amongst them. They found space for him in one of the cottages. Sitting by a peat fire in the evening, he explained to the wife of the family how he had been asked to undertake his quest.

The woman shook her head.

"I think your father-in-law has misled you. This giant is far from being kind or generous, if the stories I've heard are true. No one from these parts has ever dared to look for his island. They say that those who do never return. But if you're determined to keep searching, I do recall one thing I've heard tell. Seek an island set not in salt water, but in fresh water."

"I am determined to keep looking," said Duncan, "so I'm grateful for your advice."

Chapter Ten
The Ferryman

The next morning refreshed and having eaten well, Duncan assured the villagers he would come back and tell them whatever he had learned. He set off once again. He began to search for freshwater lochs big enough to have an island with a castle.

One day, he was riding on a hillside thick with pine and birch trees. He came to a clearing and saw below him a loch. Way out in the middle of the water was an island and on it stood a castle.

There was a square tower at one end, where an eagle had made its nest. He watched the bird rise, swoop down and skim over the water as it went in search of prey.

Duncan wove his way through the trees down to the shore. He saw an old man sitting in a rowing boat. The boat was motionless in the shallow water at the edge, but the old man gripped the oars in his hands.

Duncan got off his horse and walked over to the boat.

The old man looked up.

"Who are you?" he asked. "And whatever are you doing in this place?"

"I've come a long way," Duncan answered. "I'm searching for the giant with the golden hair of knowledge."

"You've come to the right place then. I'm the ferryman. I row to the castle and back twice a day, every day of the year. In that castle lives the giant with the golden hair of knowledge, and his sister too. What do you want with him?"

"I want three hairs from his head."

The ferryman laughed.

"Listen to me, young man," he said. "Over many years, I've rowed a lot of brave fellows over to that island. Not one of them have I ever seen again. So, I've promised myself I'll take no more men to die there."

"If you'll carry no one over, why do you keep rowing to and fro twice a day?"

The man groaned.

"I wish I knew," he said. "I'm sure there's magic in it. I've tried everything, but I can't get out of this boat. I can't remember now how many years I've been stuck here." Tears came into his eyes and rolled down his cheeks into his beard. "How much longer must I endure this before I die with these oars in my hands?"

"But that's where I might be able to help you," said Duncan. "If I succeed in taking hair from the giant, I might get to know how you can break free of whatever magic is holding you in its grip."

The man looked at Duncan and said nothing for a while. Then he spoke.

"I like the look of you, young man. It'll be an awful shame if the giant kills you. But I guess you're my only hope of ever getting out of this boat. You're certainly the first one who's thought how the knowledge might be good, not just for himself, but for me too. Alright, I'll take you over."

Duncan thanked the old man. He took off its saddle and bridle and tethered the horse where it could reach plenty of grass. He sat down in the stern of the boat and the man rowed him across the loch to the island.

There was a crunch and a grating sound as the prow and the keel rode up over the pebbles of a small beach. Duncan stepped out.

"Good luck to you, young man. I hope I shall see you again."

"You will," said Duncan, "if you're here at this beach tomorrow morning. If you pick me up, I promise I'll share with you whatever I find out."

"I'll be here," the man said. "There's but one piece of advice I can give you. Do what you can to make friends with the giant's sister – if, that is, you stay alive long enough."

Duncan nodded, waved farewell and set off for the castle.

Chapter Eleven
The Giant's Sister

As Duncan clambered over the rocks on his way from the beach, he noticed tiny white flowers peeping through the crevices between them. He picked some as he went.

When he reached the castle, he faced a huge wooden door. His fist made little sound upon it, so he picked up a rock and banged with all his strength. The door was opened and before him stood a woman of great height. Duncan was tall himself, but the top of his head was below her shoulders.

Duncan bowed.

"Good day, my lady. Will you accept a gift of flowers from a visitor to your castle?"

The woman looked at him in amazement.

"Who are you and whatever are you doing here?"

"I've come in search of the golden hair of knowledge. Will you help me in my quest?"

She looked down into Duncan's face.

"You do realise, don't you, that we're giants?"

"Aye," said Duncan. "I can see that I'm smaller than you. But I can tell from your apron and from the flour on your hands that you are the mistress of this castle."

The woman stared at Duncan, astonished. Then she spoke.

"Come away inside. If my brother catches sight of you, that'll be the end of our conversation and of your life."

Stepping through the door, Duncan bowed again and handed the woman the flowers. They were a bunch, but in her hand, they looked like a single bloom.

She smiled. "Thank you, young man. It's a good while since any man, big or small, has given me flowers."

She led Duncan to the castle kitchen. Along one wall was a fireplace so big, he could have walked into it without stooping. In the grate, logs were burning which would have needed a heavy horse to shift. She motioned him to sit on a bench beside the table where she had been working. On the table was a huge oval dish, a loaf of bread and a couple of wine bottles. There were heaps of cut herbs.

"How do you come to be living here in this lonely place?" asked Duncan.

"The castle was built long ago. In those days, the people of these parts were harassed by raiding parties from the northern isles. They built this castle on the island as a place of refuge. When the raiders came, all the people from the villages and farms around the loch would flee here over the water. They built it big to house many people and to store plenty of provisions should they need to stand a long siege."

She carried on working at the table as she talked. The herbs she chopped and ground. From the loaf, she grated a pile of breadcrumbs.

"When the raids stopped, the castle fell out of use. Its size made it ideal for me and my brother. And being isolated, it would keep us out of the way of ordinary people. To be different is not easy. My brother is a troubled soul. He's savage to everyone he meets. I promised our mother I'd look after him and try to keep him out of trouble. And that's what I do."

"From the look of what you're preparing," said Duncan, "you take care of your brother well."

"Yes, and he'll be here soon. He's fishing on the far side of the island. He'll be back any time now with his catch, to go with this sauce. You'd better hurry and tell me your story. And then you must be off, out of here."

Duncan told her how the Chief had come to his parents' cottage. He described the warm welcome he received when he got to the Chief's castle. His talk was mostly of Margaret, of her smile, of her liveliness, of her skills in music and poetry. He loved her, he declared, more than anything.

"And yet," said Duncan, "I've spent only two days with Margaret since we were married. I set off straight away on this quest."

"But whatever made you seek us out?" asked the woman.

"It's not me, but the Chief who wants the golden hair of knowledge. He's asked me to bring him just three hairs from your brother's head. With them, he says, he'll be happy. He wants to possess all the knowledge a great Chief should have."

The woman sighed. "Thanks to that hair of his, my brother knows all manner of things," she said. "But I can't say it has made him happy."

"On my journey here," Duncan added, "I met other people who are desperate for knowledge. I would so like to be able to help them, if I can."

Duncan told her of the villagers who wanted to know why their ground had become as hard as iron, of those who wanted to know why they could no longer draw water from their well and of the ferryman who wanted to know why he was unable to step out of his boat.

He was explaining how the ferryman had agreed to pick him up next day, when they heard the crash of the castle door being slammed shut. That sound was followed by the thump of heavy footsteps on the stone floor of the corridor to the kitchen.

"Quick. He's coming," said the woman. "Climb into that chest. And keep still. Your life depends on it."

Duncan clambered in. She lowered the lid. It was an old piece. The lid had warped with age so that it no longer sat flat on the body of the chest. Through the gap Duncan could see the kitchen and hear the crackle of the logs burning in the fireplace.

He held his breath. He had no idea what the giant's sister was going to do.

Chapter Twelve
Knowledge Gained

The giant shoved open the door and stomped into the kitchen. He was carrying a pike. It was the biggest pike Duncan had ever seen. He slapped it down on the kitchen table. The thud made the dish jump into the air and the bottles clinked against one another.

"Goodness, you've done well today, brother."

"Aye," said the giant. "I knew this big one was lurking in the reeds. I just needed patience and the right lure to entice him out."

"Well, you deserve a drink. You draw off some ale, while I make our supper."

The giant ambled over to a barrel on a wooden stand at the back of the kitchen. From it, he filled an earthenware flagon. He sat on the bench and put the flagon to his mouth. In one go, he downed a quantity which Duncan guessed would keep two ordinary men in drink for a whole evening.

The woman dressed the fish and doused it in the sauce she'd prepared. She set the dish by the fire.

"That'll take some time," she said. "We'll need to cook him slowly, so the flesh comes easily off his bones. You fill up again and come and sit by the fire."

The giant refilled the flagon and drank it empty again at a single gulp. His sister fetched a rug made of sheepskins stitched together. She spread it before the fire.

"Come and lie down," she said, "while I draw some more ale."

The giant sat on the rug. His sister handed him the flagon, which he drained again.

"Lie you down," she said, "and rest your head on my lap. You've earned a nap before we eat."

He stretched himself out on the rug. His sister knelt beside him, and he laid his head on her lap. The warmth of the fire, the effect of the ale and the soothing touch of his sister's fingers as she stroked his golden hair soon sent him to sleep. In no time he was snoring loudly.

His sister wrapped one of his hairs around her finger and gave a sharp tug.

"Hey," said the giant, waking from his sleep. "What are you doing, sister? You're pulling my hair."

"Oh, I'm sorry," she answered. "I dropped off myself and I was having a terrible dream."

"What was the dream about?"

"I dreamt there was a village a long way from here. And in that village, the people were troubled because their land had become as hard as iron. They were no longer able to plough it. They would give anything to know what to do to be able to work their land again."

"Ah, if only they knew," said the giant. "A witch has cast a spell on their land. In a corner of one of the fields, there's a beech tree. If they pour ale into the ground at the foot of that tree, they'll be able to dig there. When they dig down, they'll find an iron key, which has locked up the soil. They must get their blacksmith to heat that key in his furnace and hammer it into a new horseshoe. Once it's no longer a key, the spell will be undone. Now let me get back to sleep."

With that, he laid his head back on his sister's lap. He was snoring again in a few moments.

His sister wrapped another hair round her fingers and pulled it out.

"Ow! You've woken me again. Whatever are you up to?" said the giant.

"While I was dozing, I had another dream," said his sister. "I dreamt of another village, even further off from here. In that village was a well which used to supply the people with the sweetest of water. But now, whatever they try they can't draw a drop from it. They would give anything to know what to do to get their water back."

"Ah, if only they knew," said the giant. "A travelling pedlar visited that village. When he asked for a drink, he was turned away. To pay them back, he cast the evil eye upon their well. They must put out word to every pedlar round about them. They must invite them all to a feast in their village. And at that feast, they must announce a promise that every pedlar who comes their way will always get a free jug of ale from them. If they do that, they'll draw water again. Now stop bothering me with your dreams and let me rest."

Soon, Duncan heard again the loud and regular sound of the giant's snores. His sister wrapped a third hair round her finger and tugged it out.

"I'm getting angry now, sister," the giant shouted. "Don't tell me you've dreamt about another village."

"No, not another village, brother. But I have had another dream. I was dreaming about the ferryman who rows back and forth to our island every day. I dreamt he was doomed for all time to keep rowing to and fro and that he would give anything to know how he was ever to get out of his boat."

"Ah, if only he knew," said the giant. "There's a water spirit living in this loch. She heard the ferryman boast about his rowing, so she put a curse on his boat. He'll row to and fro for all time unless another man sits down in it and freely offers to take the oars from him. Now, you drink some ale. That'll wash those dreams out of your head. Hush yourself and wake me no more."

The giant lay down fully on the rug and his sister rose, as if she was going to refill the flagon from the barrel. She had not crossed the kitchen before he was slumbering once more.

She lifted the lid of the chest and helped Duncan out. She whispered.

"Did you hear all that?"

"Yes, I did," he answered. "Thank you for what you've done. You are both kind and clever."

She unwound the three hairs from her finger and handed them to Duncan. He put them into the purse hanging from his belt.

"Now, you must be away from here before my brother wakes."

As they crossed the kitchen on tiptoe, she paused at the table. She tore a hunk of bread from her loaf and gave it to Duncan. She led him back to the castle door and bade him farewell. Before he stepped out, Duncan took her hand and lifted it to his lips. He kissed her hand.

"Once again, thank you," he said. "I shall be in your debt forever."

"Away with you, now. And mind you keep out of sight. Give my regards to your new wife. She's a lucky young woman."

Duncan made his way in the darkness back across the island towards the beach where he had landed that afternoon. Brought up in the forest, Duncan knew how to make a shelter for himself. He found a hollow spot that was dry. There he stacked branches to shield him from the wind.

Hunkering down against the cold, he nibbled his piece of bread. He thought of the warmth of the fire in the castle kitchen, he thought of the smell of the pike cooking in its sauce, but most of all he thought of the kindness and cleverness of the giant's sister.

Chapter Thirteen
Knowledge Shared

In the morning, the ferryman steered his boat onto the beach, just as he had promised. He looked at Duncan in amazement.

"I little thought I would set eyes on you again, young man," he said.

"Your advice was good and I'm grateful to you," Duncan replied. "I'd have failed but for the help of the giant's sister."

Duncan jumped into the boat. He did not sit down. He lay flat on the bottom of the boat.

"When you rowed me across yesterday," he said, "I was lucky the giant was fishing on the far side of the island. I don't want to risk him spotting me this morning. If he did, he would make trouble for his sister. I wouldn't want that."

Duncan pulled his cloak over his head. He lay still and covered in the bottom of the boat while the ferryman rowed it back across the loch to the shore.

Duncan stepped out onto the shingle.

"I've kept my promise," said the ferryman, "so what about your promise to me?"

Duncan shared with the ferryman what the giant had revealed of the curse of the water spirit.

"You must wait for someone to sit in your boat and freely offer to take the oars from you. Only then will you be able to get out. That person will bear the curse from you. He'll be condemned to row to and fro in your place for all time."

"Thank you," said the ferryman. "I can do nothing now but wait for that day to come."

Duncan said farewell to the ferryman. He found his horse and re-saddled it. He set off, retracing his route so that he would pass through the two villages he had visited on his way to the castle.

When he came to the village where no water could be drawn from the well, he made straight for the cottage where he had slept for the night. The family were surprised and delighted to see him.

"So you did achieve your quest?" asked the wife.

"I did," said Duncan.

"And did you get any knowledge about our well?"

As he had promised, Duncan shared with them what the giant had revealed of the evil eye cast upon the well by an aggrieved pedlar.

Without delay, the villagers came together. Men were sent off on horseback in every direction. They spread word at inns, at county fairs and in marketplaces that every pedlar who could make it to their village would be made welcome at a feast.

Duncan was desperate to return to Margaret, but the villagers would not hear of him leaving before he had joined in the feast. Pedlars flocked to the village in great numbers. Every family contributed food. Those households that brewed ale made provision to brew more, so that the village would be sure of always delivering on its promise.

The feast was a riotous affair. Before it was over, the village elders proclaimed to their guests that to every pedlar who came their way from that day they would give a free jug of ale.

By the next morning, just as the giant had predicted, the people of the village were once again drawing sweet water from their well. Duncan tried in vain to decline their gifts. Such was their gratitude that they gave him a donkey and loaded it with two bags of gold.

Duncan said farewell and resumed his journey. After many days he came to the village where the ground was hard as iron. He sought out the woman who had sheltered and fed him at her cottage. She was amazed to see him and made him welcome.

"So were you successful?" she asked.

"I was," said Duncan.

"And what knowledge did you obtain about our land?"

As he had promised, Duncan shared what the giant revealed of the witch's spell.

The villagers lost no time. They found the beech tree and having soaked the ground beneath it with ale, they retrieved the key. A crowd of villagers gathered to watch their blacksmith make it red hot and beat it on his anvil into a new horseshoe.

Duncan was longing to be on his way and reunited with Margaret, but the villagers feasted him that night. They insisted he should be the one to take the reins next day behind their first team of oxen. When morning came, the whole village turned out and paraded behind the oxen as they plodded up the main street and onto the land.

Just as the giant had predicted, the plough cut through the soil as if it was butter. The people had seen Duncan's two bags of gold. Nothing he said would turn them from their determination to match that. They loaded his donkey with another two bags of gold.

At last, Duncan said his farewells and set off on the final stage of his journey back to Margaret.

Chapter Fourteen
Return

They had been together for only a short time, but Margaret was bereft when Duncan rode away from the castle to begin his quest. For the first couple of days, she walked about the villages they had visited and rode the forest tracks they had followed. She tried to remember all they had said to one another and to fix in her mind the image of Duncan at her side.

"He'll be back with you in no time," said the Chief and smiled.

"He's a fine young man," said her mother, taking Margaret's hands in hers. "His quest is a hard one. But the people he meets will warm to him. They are sure to help him on his way."

Margaret turned to music and poetry to soothe her sorrow. She found comfort in putting her feelings into words and fashioning those words into rhymes and verses. She wrote of her love for Duncan, of her pain at their parting and of her longing for his return.

Twice every day, Margaret would walk the whole circuit of the castle battlements. She looked in every direction, hoping to see Duncan approaching.

One morning she spied not a solitary rider, but a man on horseback leading a donkey. She rushed down from the battlements, along the corridors and out into the courtyard. The minutes she waited there seemed to her like hours, but in a short time, Duncan rode in under the gate.

The donkey behind him clopped slowly over the cobbles, weighed down by its saddlebags. Duncan jumped from the horse. He and Margaret hugged one another. Those working in the courtyard and the men on guard smiled and cheered and clapped.

The noise reached the ears of the Chief and his wife. They came down from their chambers.

Margaret's mother threw her arms round Duncan.

"Welcome home, son," she said.

The Chief scowled.

Duncan bowed to him. He opened the purse that hung from his belt.

"I have done what you asked, sir. I now give you three hairs from the head of the giant with the golden hair of knowledge."

The Chief said nothing. His wife broke the silence.

"Off you go, you two, to your chamber," she said. "I'm away to the kitchens. We'll have a feast to remember tonight to celebrate Duncan's return."

In no time, the castle was bustling with activity. Fresh logs were piled on the kitchen fires. Joints of venison were set to roast. Men fetched up barrels of wine and ale from the cellars. Maids collected baskets of eggs and filled dishes with apples and blackberries.

Margaret's mother busied herself organising the preparation of the feast. The Chief sat alone in his chamber and examined the golden hairs. Even those few began to have their effect upon him. He knew now there was nothing he could do that would rid him of this young man. But he was excited by the gold Duncan had brought back.

"I know many folks," he said to himself, "who would heap gold on me in return for just one of the giant's hairs. If that young fellow can fetch away three, I'm sure I could get a lot more than that."

The feast was a wonderful occasion. The candles in the great hall of the castle lit up smiling faces on every side, but none smiled more than Duncan and Margaret.

Duncan rose to his feet to address the company. The spoke of his joy at being reunited with Margaret. He thanked those who had worked hard to put together such a feast at short notice.

"Many of you will have heard," he went on, "that I've come back with gold. I'm not going to keep it for myself. I have Margaret and, in her, I have all the riches I want. The gold I shall share out. Every person, whatever their place, will get an equal portion."

A riot of rejoicing greeted Duncan's words. People's pleasure owed more to relief than to greed. Decisions taken by the Chief down the years had done little to increase and much to diminish the wealth of their community.

The feasting resumed. As they sat together at the high table, Duncan began to tell of those whom he had met on his way to the giant's island.

"Never mind that tale," the Chief interrupted. "All I need to know is the route. I'm going to go myself and get more of the giant's hairs."

"Sir, I would advise against that," said Duncan.

The Chief snorted. "If you were able to come away with three hairs, I'm certain I can do better."

Before his wife or Duncan could say another word to dissuade him, the Chief rose to his feet. He announced to the whole company that he himself would be setting off the next day to visit the giant with the golden hair of knowledge.

There was loud applause in the great hall. The news that their Chief would be away for some time went down well.

Chapter Fifteen
The Ballad of Duncan

The next morning, the Chief left the castle. He took Duncan's donkey with him loaded with food for his journey.

After travelling many days, he reached the loch with the giant's island. Down on the shore, he saw the old man sitting in his boat.

"I want to cross the loch to that island," the Chief said.

"You're talking to the right person then. I'm the ferryman. I row to the castle and back twice a day every day of the year."

The Chief got into the boat and sat down.

"You're very old to be going to and fro every day. I know a thing or two about rowing. Let me take the oars or we shall be ages crossing the water."

The ferryman let go of the oars. The Chief was surprised to see that, although he was old, the man at once leapt nimbly out of the boat.

The ferryman smiled. "You're welcome to take my boat. Even if your rowing is not good, you'll have time enough to perfect it."

The Chief spat on his hands, took the oars and rowed out into the loch.

At his castle, they never again heard word of their Chief. A year and a half after he had set out, his wife declared she was positive he would never return. She went into mourning for a week. From the end of that week, she ever afterwards spoke of herself as a widow.

She met with the elders of the community. They needed little debate. Every one of them wanted Duncan to be their new Chief. Duncan agreed. He turned out to be a wise choice, leading his people well and always pursuing the best for them. Under his direction, they prospered and lived in peace with their neighbours.

Duncan went to see the couple who had brought him up as their own. He invited them to come and live in the castle. They declined, for they loved their cottage on the riverbank and did not want to change their lives. But frequent visits were made between the cottage and the castle. The wife and Duncan's mother-in-law became great friends. Their friendship deepened when they shared the role of grandmother to Duncan and Margaret's children.

Duncan searched for and found the hut where he had slept when he was travelling with the Chief's letter. He spoke with the five outlaws and persuaded them they no longer needed to live as fugitives. They joined Duncan's followers and used their forest craft and their hunting skills for the good of the whole community. The man who had changed the old Chief's letter became Duncan's steward.

Margaret taught Duncan to read and write. He read his wife's poems and through them came to value her abilities even more. But he still loved hearing her recite them more than reading them himself.

Margaret's poems were handed down to her children and, by them, to her grandchildren. Copied many times and shared with others, they became well known throughout Scotland. Lovers, particularly those separated, turned to them and found in them their own feelings beautifully expressed. For making those poems, she came to be known to following generations as Margaret the Makar.

Duncan told Margaret the full story of his adventure, from the moment he first met her father. She made his story into a ballad. Every year, they celebrated their shared birthday with a feast in the great hall of the castle. Every year at the climax of the feast, Margaret sang the ballad of Duncan's adventure.

Duncan was a loving husband. He and Margaret lived together happily for the rest of their lives. And the Chief? About rowing, at least, he did come to know better than anyone else. And, back and forth, twice a day, he is probably rowing still.

Maria and the Goat – Italy

Chapter One
Across the Marshes

In Italy, long ago, there was a girl who fell in love with a goat.

The girl's name was Maria. Her parents were poor. They lived in a small town deep in a valley. Making pots was their livelihood.

One day, they had an order for wine jars. The order came from a farmer whose lands were to the south of their town. Three years before, he had planted new slopes with vines. Now he wanted to be ready for the extra grape harvest he was expecting. He wanted a lot of wine jars, and he was eager to have them quickly.

Maria was only a few months old at this time. A neighbour agreed to look after her while her father and mother toiled day and night to make the wine jars. When they had finished the order, they hired a wagon and set off to deliver them to the farmer.

A stretch of marshes lay in their way. Most travellers avoided them. They were unhealthy and they were haunted by brigands. People preferred to travel south by boat, along a canal by-passing the marshes.

"What shall we do?" Maria's father asked his wife. "We've paid a lot for the wagon. The boat fare is going to take even more of our profit."

"That's not all," replied his wife. "All the loading and unloading is going to take time and the boat won't set off till it's full. I want us to get done and back to Maria as quick as we can."

They decided to push on across the marshes. They delivered the wine jars. The farmer was pleased with them and handed over their payment. They returned home without mishap.

But not long after they got back, both Maria's parents fell ill. Their neighbours looked after Maria again, as they became more and more unwell. Within a short time, both of them died.

The neighbour went to the parish priest.

"I am torn, Father," she said. "This child has lost both her parents. She is the dearest creature. If I could, I would love her and keep her as my own. But we are poor ourselves. We have three children. The Lord knows what a struggle we have to feed and clothe them. What are we to do?"

"Calm yourself, my child," said the priest. "I baptised Maria and I remember she has a grandmother. The woman lives somewhere up in the hills. I'll ask around and find her."

There was a local man who traded with those farming the slopes above the town. Over the years, he had got to know all the households up there. He was able to tell the priest where Maria's grandmother lived. The priest saddled his donkey and set off up the hills.

Maria's grandmother was a widow. Her husband had worked at a quarry. By saving from his wages, they were able to buy a field and to build a cottage in one corner of it. They put up outhouses behind the cottage where they kept chickens and a couple of pigs. A pond was the home of their ducks and geese. In the field, they had some olive trees. One day, the grandfather was helping to cut a large block of stone when he tripped on a rope and fell from it to his death.

The priest found Maria's grandmother in her field, hoeing the soil around rows of artichokes.

She was distressed to learn of the deaths of her daughter and son-in-law. The priest took her into the cottage. He poured wine for them both and they sat and talked.

"The poor child," she said. "Of course, I'll take her in, Father. Both of us have only one another now. I've been on my own for more than ten years. But the passing of time doesn't make it any easier. She'll be company for me. It's a long while since I looked after a little one, but I'm sure we'll get on well."

Chapter Two
Grandmother's Cottage

Maria and her grandmother took to one another straight away. Neighbours who kept flocks helped her, so that for the first couple of weeks, she fed Maria with the warm, fresh milk from their goats and sheep.

Once Maria learned to walk, she followed her grandmother everywhere. She loved the animals. She used to chase the hens and the ducks. The geese, though, she kept clear of, for they could be fierce. Her grandmother often sat outside the cottage spinning wool or preparing beans in a bowl on her lap.

Maria liked to sit on the ground at her side. She collected stones and twigs. She pretended the stones were pigs and with the twigs, she made pig sties for them.

Maria was a bright child. Soon, she was asking all sorts of questions.

"Grandmother, why can our ducks and geese swim but the hens can't? Will the pigs lay eggs if we keep feeding them? We don't plant them, so where do the mushrooms come from?"

"Heavens, child! What a lot of questions you ask. But I've a question for you. How come those old olive trees grow so slowly, while you grow so fast, I can hardly keep up with you?"

Maria was a great help to her grandmother. She collected the eggs and fed the pigs. And when the time was right, she helped to harvest what her grandmother had grown—tomatoes, rocket, beans and artichokes. As she grew up, her grandmother was happy for her to venture further from the cottage. Maria wandered over the hillside to collect wood for their stove. In the autumn, she went gathering chestnuts.

Her grandmother baked them and ground them into flour to make cakes. When she was out, Maria always kept alert to spot tufts of wool caught on thorns. She collected the wool and took it home. When there was enough, her grandmother would spin it and dye the yarn using plants Maria had picked from the hillside. Grandmother made most of the clothing she and Maria wore.

Every day, Maria walked down the hill to get water from a spring. One day, when she returned to the cottage with a full pitcher, her grandmother said: "I'm glad to see you're careful with that pitcher, Maria."

"I try to be careful with everything," replied Maria. "I know if we break things, we can't afford to buy new ones."

"You're a good girl, Maria. But that's not the only reason. Come and sit down with me for a moment. It's time I told you about that pitcher. You see, it's special. It was made by your father and mother."

Maria sat down. Her grandmother told her about her parents and about their house in the town. She described the cart they used when they went to collect clay and the kiln her father built in the yard behind the house where they fired their pots. She said they were overjoyed when Maria was born, and they loved their baby with all their hearts.

She told her how they had travelled across the marshes and how they had both died of fever caught from the mosquitoes there. She explained how the village priest had brought her to her.

Maria listened. She said nothing. At the end of the story, she gave her grandmother a hug.

They lived a lonely life on the hillside. Sometimes, Maria stopped and talked with women at the spring. When the shepherds and goatherds led their flocks from the valley to graze the upland pastures, they passed the cottage. They always shouted a word or two of greeting to Maria and her grandmother.

Maria looked forward to the markets held in the town. When the seasons were kind to them and things flourished, they had produce to sell or exchange. Sometimes they harvested more beans and salads than they needed for themselves. Maria had soon learned where to find mushrooms and they sold well in the market. At the end of the year, Maria and her grandmother would spread sheets on the ground below the olive trees.

They hit the branches with poles to bring down the olives. The man who had helped the priest find Grandmother had an olive press. On a market day, she took her olives to him. On the next market day, she collected her oil. Often Grandmother walked down into the town with a basket over her arm, full of eggs to be sold. Maria led the way, waving a stick as she drove a couple of geese before her down the path.

Maria and her grandmother enjoyed their visits to the town. The market was always full of noise and colour. Often, they met the neighbour who had looked after Maria when her parents were ill. Every time the neighbour was surprised that Maria had grown since their last meeting.

In a corner of the town square, there was a tiny chapel. Inside its walls were painted with images of saints. Sometimes Maria and her grandmother went in to light a candle in memory of her parents. From time to time the market fell on the same day as a festival. Then there were flowers everywhere, a procession and much merrymaking. On those days, her grandmother kept Maria close at her side. She was afraid the child would wander off and get lot in all the bustle.

Chapter Three
Market Day

The years went by, and Maria was a child no longer. The shepherds and the goatherds noticed there was now a pretty young woman living at the cottage. They stopped shouting silly jokes as they went by with their flocks. Now in passing, they tried to make themselves look as tall as they could.

Grandmother realised it was time to give Maria more freedom.

"You don't want to be stuck with me all the while, Maria. Next market day, why don't you go off on your own and have a look round?"

"I'd love to do that, Grandmother."

The day of the market came. The year had been a hard one. A fox had got into their patch and had killed all but one of the chickens. The weather had been harsh too. Frosts had nipped their vegetables just at the time when they needed warmth and sunlight. Grandmother had only duck eggs to sell and half a sack of artichokes.

Maria and her grandmother made their way down into the town. As usual, the market square was full of people and animals. Pens had been set up in the middle. In the pens stood oxen, cows, sheep, goats and geese, all of them waiting to be sold. Around the square were stalls selling produce of every kind.

The noise was tremendous. Mooing, bleating and cackling filled the air around the pens. Stall holders called out to attract customers. Pedlars walked amid the crowds, shouting the beauty of their ribbons, their brooches and their pins. Gypsies hammered away at copper pots and pans.

Grandmother could not afford a stall of her own. She found a stretch of wall, where she was able to set out the eggs and the artichokes. Maria noticed an old barrel. She rolled it over for her grandmother to sit on.

"Are you sure you're going to be all right on your own, Grandmother?" asked Maria.

"Don't you worry about me, child. I'll be fine here. You go and look round. Here's a bit of money. Get yourself something to eat when you feel hungry."

"Shall I come back to you here?"

"No, it won't take me long to sell the little we've brought today. I'll have a wander round myself too. When the market starts to pack up, we can meet by the fountain."

Grandmother did sell all her eggs and artichokes. But she got less than she hoped. She walked around, greeting and stopping to talk to people she knew. An old friend of hers stood at the doorway of his cantina, a tunnel he had cut back into the rock to make a place to store his wine. He drew off a beaker full and handed it to her.

Knowing how poor she was, he refused any payment. From one of the stalls, she bought a piece of sausage to go with the wine. As she ate the sausage, she thought of the two pigs she'd had to sell one by one to buy things they needed.

The afternoon drew on. Stall holders began to pack up their goods. The pens in the square emptied. Some led away the new livestock they had bought. Some made ready to trudge home with the animals they had been unable to sell. Grandmother made her way to the fountain. She sat down on the rim of the pool and waited for Maria.

She waited and waited. Maria did not come. She began to feel anxious. After waiting some more, she decided to go and look for her. She walked all over the town, up steep cobbled alleys, under stone arches, into tiny courtyards, along dark passages and past countless stone steps before doorways. There was no sign of Maria anywhere.

Grandmother returned to the square to take another look there. At last, she came upon Maria. She was in one of the pens. She had not seen her before because she was sitting on the straw, with one arm around the neck of a small goat.

"Isn't he beautiful, Grandmother?" she said.

"I've been waiting for you for ages, Maria. Have you been here all the time?"

"I couldn't leave him," replied Maria. "All the other animals have now been sold or taken back but nobody has collected this little one. Just look at him. He's so handsome."

Grandmother looked at the kid. It had a black and white face and long ears which drooped down. It was a fine creature; she could see that. But goats had never interested her.

"Come along, Maria, it's time we were setting off back."

"Oh, Grandmother, there's no one to take care of him."

"It must belong to somebody," said her grandmother, "otherwise it wouldn't be here for sale."

"Please, Grandmother, can we buy him?"

"Whatever would we want a goat for?"

"He'd be no trouble, Grandmother. I'd look after him. You know goats will eat anything and they forage for themselves. We wouldn't have to buy any feed. I could make a little home for him where we used to keep the pigs. Do say yes, Grandmother. He'd be company for me."

Of all Maria's arguments, it was the last one which made the difference. Grandmother did worry that Maria might come to resent their lonely life on the hillside.

"I'm making no promises," she said. "You stay here with the kid. I'll go and talk to somebody about it."

It was the man who pressed her olives who had charge of the market. He was talking to some men, giving them instructions for taking down the pens.

"Who does that kid belong to?" Grandmother asked him.

The man frowned. "Now, there's a puzzle," he said, "I didn't see who brought it in this morning. Nor did any of my men. And nobody has come to see if it was wanted."

"How much would a kid like that fetch?" asked Grandmother.

"Not much. Most people are after nanny goats. They want milk, to make cheese. There's not much call for Billy goats. Most of them end up in the pot as goat stew."

"Can I buy this one?" Grandmother asked. "Maria has fallen for it."

"Are you sure? Don't forget, little kids grow to be big Billy goats. They can be a handful. They'll get through any fence you put up. They'll eat anything they find. And they soon smell awful."

Grandmother sighed. "I know, I know. But Maria has set her heart on the creature. And it'll be company for her."

"Very well," said the man. "But I can't sell it to you. It doesn't belong to me. I guess whoever does own it wants it off his hands. He's dumped it here today. As far as I am concerned, you can have it for nothing. If anybody does turn up to claim it, I'll let you know."

Grandmother thanked the man. He gave her a length of rope.

"Tie this round its neck," he said. "You'll need to lead it back to your place."

Grandmother returned to Maria. She found her stroking the kid and tickling its ears.

"The goat is yours," she said.

Maria clapped her hands. "Oh, thank you, Grandmother."

"Remember though," said her grandmother. "It's going to be your job to look after it."

To their surprise, they had no need of the rope. The kid walked at Maria's side all the way to the cottage.

Maria set to work as soon as they were home. She would not sit down to eat or drink until she had cleared out the shed where they used to keep their pigs. She made it comfortable for the kid, putting down some fresh hay and filling a trough with water.

That evening, as they sat together Maria asked her grandmother.

"What do you think we should call him?"

Grandmother smiled. "I don't know, I'm sure. We've kept poultry and animals all our lives. But they weren't pets. We never gave them names."

Maria was silent for a while.

"I know," she said. "I'll call him Fortunato because it was my good luck I saw him in the market today."

Chapter Four
The Storm

Fortunato seemed set on proving wrong everything the man in the market had said about Billy goats. When Maria and her grandmother were working in their field he made no attempt to wander off. When they harvested their vegetables and salads they were able to leave them heaped on the ground. Fortunato stole nothing.

He seemed content to feed on leaves and the bark of trees and to nibble the thorny scrub that grew on the hillside. He browsed for himself when he was out with Maria. That was just as well. Times were hard. Maria and her grandmother had nothing to spare.

Fortunato went with Maria everywhere. In the morning, the first thing she did was to go and see Fortunato in his shed. He joined her when she went down to the spring for water. He was at her side when she set off to find berries and mushrooms. When she went to collect firewood, he trotted at her heels.

Maria began to take Fortunato when she and her grandmother went to market. The people of the town were amazed to see a Billy goat jogging along with her. Those who didn't know her name started to call her 'the goat girl'.

Grandmother's prediction turned out to be right. Fortunato did provide Maria with company. She loved him and she was always brighter when he was with her. He also took her mind off their deepening poverty. Maria and her grandmother had to work harder and harder to make enough to feed and clothe themselves.

Grandmother's eyesight was getting weaker, but she had taught Maria to sew. Maria started to take in bits of sewing work to earn extra money. She would collect things on market day and, having done what was wanted, return them at the next market.

Maria had got to know the shepherds and goatherds who moved their flocks over the hillsides. All of them watched their own animals but they looked out for one another too. They took care to keep a close eye on the weather.

One day, a goatherd saw a dark cloud approaching. Driven by strong winds, it was moving at speed towards the hillside. The goatherd shuddered at the sight, realising a storm was heading their way. Maria and Fortunato were by a small clump of trees at some distance. The goatherd shouted across to them and waved, beckoning them to follow him.

Other herdsmen had seen the cloud too and were moving in the same direction. There was no time to get back down into the valley. There was a cave on the hillside, and they were looking to shelter in it. They drove their sheep and goats into the cave. Maria and Fortunato joined them. The animals were packed closely together. There was nothing to do but wait out the storm.

The herdsmen knew about animals. They could see the kid had grown into a fine beast.

Some of them were jealous of Fortunato, for the goat got all Maria's attention. She had no time for any of them and, to their surprise, Fortunato showed no interest in any of their nanny goats.

"Why is he so stand-offish, Maria?" they asked. "Are our goats not good enough for him?" They were even more amazed that he didn't smell like a Billy goat.

"Do you perfume your goat, Maria?"

She laughed.

"I don't have to," she replied. "Without my help, he already smells sweeter than you."

Their banter helped pass the time while the storm raged outside. The gusts of wind were ferocious. Rain poured down in torrents. Maria began to worry about her grandmother alone at the cottage.

The storm passed. The herders led their flocks out of the cave. Maria hurried home with Fortunato. As she approached the cottage, she was appalled by what she saw. Maria rushed inside.

"Oh, Maria, thank goodness you're safe," cried her grandmother. "I was terrified at the thought of you out on the hillside in that storm." They hugged one another.

"I'm alright, Grandmother. But what about you?"

"When it started, I closed all the shutters. Your grandfather knew all there was to know about stone. He built this cottage. I reckon it's as solid as the hillside itself. But have you seen the damage?"

Maria groaned. "It looks awful out there."

"I thought I'd be able to hear nothing above the roaring of the wind," Grandmother went on. "But suddenly there was a terrific crash. Our two best olive trees have gone over. And just look at the field. There was so much rain in such a short time. I guess the stream above us couldn't take it. It must have burst its banks. It's washed away everything we've planted. And it's left behind mud and stones from the bed of the stream."

They held one another tight as they stood in the doorway of the cottage and looked out at the filthy, smelly mess that was once their field.

The remaining daylight hours of that day, Maria and her grandmother spent shovelling mud and heaving stones from around the cottage. At dusk, they sat down together.

"I don't know where I would be without your help, Maria. You work so hard for us every day. And lately you've sat up every evening sewing too. We were just about getting by. But this storm changes everything."

"Don't be downhearted, Grandmother. It'll be hard work, I know. But we can clear things up and get started again."

"I'm getting no younger, child. And I've no right to expect more from you. We have to ask for help. Tomorrow is market day. I'm going to ask people in the town to come up and help us clear the field. And our friend with the olive press will know whether there's any chance of righting those two trees."

"I'm sure people will help us," said Maria.

"But we also have to help ourselves, child. We must sell that goat." Maria gasped.

"Oh, Grandmother. No, no!"

"Listen to me, Maria. We don't have any choice. This is a time for survival, not for pets."

"But I love Fortunato. I couldn't let him go. He doesn't cost us anything. And you told me the man in the market said male goats don't fetch much."

"That's true, Maria. But we'll get something for it, at least enough to buy some new seed to plant. We can't live on eggs and berries."

"But I couldn't bear the thought of somebody else taking him away. And who knows what they would do to him?"

"I don't want to fall out with you, Maria. In all our time together, we've never quarrelled. But on this, I'm going to stand firm. At tomorrow's market, we'll sell the goat. And that's the end of it."

Maria's eyed filled with tears. She ran to her room, threw herself down upon her bed and sobbed. She was still lying on the bed when she heard her grandmother blow out the lamp and close the door of her own room.

Maria could not sleep. Before long, she heard the sound of her grandmother snoring. Maria rose. She tiptoed out of her room and slipped out of the cottage. Inside the shed, she threw her arms round Fortunato's neck and hugged him. The goat rubbed its head against the side of her face.

"Oh Fortunato, we must go and go now. Grandmother wants to sell you. She doesn't wish you any harm but she's desperate. With me gone, there'll be one less mouth to feed. And she's got friends in the town who'll help her. I'm the only one who can help you. I love you and I won't be parted from you."

She led Fortunato from the shed. By chance, the moon was nearly full, so she was able to see her way around the mud to the path down the hill. She walked quickly and Fortunato trotted at her side.

Before they reached the town Maria turned off the path.

"This way, Fortunato," she said. "We're well known in the town. I don't want to risk anyone there seeing us. Come on. I want us to get as far away from here as we can before the sun comes up."

They skirted the town. Maria could see below her the tiled roofs of the houses shining in the moonlight. From some of their chimneys the smell of wood smoke reached her, a reminder that others were snug indoors at this time. Once around the town, they went down again into the valley to follow the course of the river which flowed below it. The way down was steep.

The river had cut a narrow gorge in the volcanic rock. Above them were cliffs, thick with oak trees. They made their way along the riverbank, weaving between trees and bushes. Maria heard the hiss of a porcupine shaking its quills at something in the undergrowth. Far away, an owl hooted. Fortunato was sure footed, but Maria stumbled sometimes, scratching her legs on thorns.

When the sun rose they climbed the valley side and came out onto a plain. Beyond it, Maria saw a line of hills clothed with trees. Although they had already walked for hours, she was keen to reach cover. They pressed on. At last, they entered the forest. Fortunato was still trotting at her side but by now Maria was exhausted. Not only that, she was also afraid.

"Oh Fortunato, what have I done?" she said. Maria sat on the ground, leaning her back against a tree.

"I don't know where we are. I've got nothing to eat. And I've no idea where we're going to go."

Chapter Five
An Ogre on the Way

"Maria," said a voice.

Maria jumped. She looked around her.

"Who's there?" she shouted. "Show yourself."

"Maria, I spoke to you," said Fortunato.

Maria gasped. "You can speak?"

"Yes, Maria, I can speak. But I can only speak when somebody close to me is in great danger."

"But how—?"

Fortunato interrupted. "Now is not the time, Maria. Trust me and do as I say. Look inside my ear."

Maria smiled. She could not believe what she was doing but she lifted one of Fortunato's drooping ears. She looked and saw there a tiny piece of cloth.

"Take it out," said Fortunato. Maria drew out the piece of cloth. "Now unfold it and spread it on the ground."

Maria did as she was told. As she unfolded the cloth, it grew in size. When she laid it on the ground, food began to appear on it.

Maria laughed. "This is magic. Look! Here's bread, cheese, salami. Is it real?"

"Yes," said Fortunato. "Now eat."

Maria sat down and ate. She was hungry after walking so far.

"But tell me, Fortunato. How do you come to be able to speak? And how can you work magic?"

"No questions for now. Just trust me and do as I say. I promise you will come to no harm. Make haste and finish eating. We have to press on. There is somebody I must find. We must make for the tower."

When Maria had eaten her fill, she folded the cloth, which shrank to its former size. She put it back into Fortunato's ear.

They set off again. This time, instead of trotting at Maria's side, Fortunato led the way. He was taking a path out of the forest.

But before they were clear of the trees, a loud roar startled them both. A huge figure jumped out from behind an oak. An ogre stood with his legs astride the path, barring their way.

Maria clutched Fortunato. She trembled. The ogre was a fearful creature. The skin of his face was blotched. He smiled at them. Maria thought his teeth looked as if they had been filed to points. He dribbled from parted lips.

"Where are you going, young lady? I see you've found a friend of mine."

"I don't know what you're talking about," said Maria. "I'm going to market with my goat. Now, please, let us pass."

The ogre frowned. With one hand, he held a sack over his shoulder. With the other, he pulled his cloak open to reveal a sword hanging at his belt.

"Don't be afraid, my dear. I'm not going to hurt you. But there's something you must do for me. Then you can go on your way."

"What is it?" Maria asked. She still held Fortunato close to her.

"I've been hunting in this forest all morning," said the ogre. "All I've got to show for my efforts are two rabbits. I'm tired out. And besides, I'm not much of a cook myself. You will come with me to my tower and bake me a rabbit pie while I have a rest. Once you've done that, you'll be free to leave."

Maria was ready to argue with the ogre. But with his last word, he grabbed Fortunato by one of his ears and began to drag him along the path. Maria was not going to let anyone take Fortunato from her, not even an ogre. She followed him in silence.

The ogre led them out of the forest. Some way off, Maria could see sunlight sparkling on the waters of a lake. Across the lake, she made out a tower.

The ogre never let go of Fortunato's ear. He grunted from time to time but said no more.

When he stumbled on loose rocks, he gave Fortunato a kick, as if it had been the goat's fault.

They trudged around the southern shore of the lake and reached the tower.

"Here we are at last, my dear," said the ogre. "You go inside. The fire in the kitchen should still be alight. Put some logs on for me while I tie up the goat."

Maria went in. One whole side of the kitchen was a stone fireplace. The fire in the grate was still burning low. Maria found a bin of logs. She piled some over the embers.

She looked around her. From the rafters hung bundles of herbs. Some of them she did not recognise. Around the walls were shelves full of pots, jars and flasks. In glass bottles, there were liquids of every colour. Some of them seemed to hold small creatures floating in oil. Maria did not care to look closely. In front of the grate stood all manner of pans and cauldrons. There was a wooden table before the fireplace and on its knives, cleavers and pestles of every size.

Outside the tower, the ogre took a rope and tied Fortunato to a post by the door.

"So, we meet again, my friend," said the ogre. "I thought I'd seen the last of you when I dumped you in that market. Never mind. I'll look forward to some goat stew tomorrow."

The ogre bent down and whispered in Fortunato's ear: "But today I'm going to sample a dish I've never tasted before—girl pie!"

The ogre laughed and went inside.

"Well done, young lady," said the ogre, looking at the fire. "We'll soon have a good blaze. Now, I want you to make some pastry for my pie. You'll find flour butter and salt in that cupboard over there. And in the corner, there's a flagon of water. I'm going to have a sleep in my room. But be warned. I'll be in earshot, only next door. And I'm a light sleeper. Don't even think about trying to make off."

"But when I've done the pastry, can I go?" asked Maria.

The ogre grinned. "Of course, my dear. Once the pie is ready to be baked, there'll be nothing more you can do."

The ogre ambled off to his room. Maria fetched the ingredients for the pastry from the cupboard. She made a point of clattering the bowls, the tubs and the spoons, so the ogre would think she was hard at work.

All the time, she listened. Soon, she heard snoring coming from the ogre's room. She took a sharp knife and without making a sound, she went outside to Fortunato. She cut the rope and set him free.

"Thank you," said Fortunato. "You are in great danger, Maria. It's you he plans to bake in that pie, not the rabbits. Listen to me and do what I say. With your knife, cut three tufts from my beard."

"But what will they—?"

"Never mind, just do it. And hurry, for the ogre will wake soon." Maria took Fortunato's beard in one hand and cut off three tufts.

"Go back into the kitchen and lay them in a line on the kitchen table. Come straight back. But make sure you bring some salt with you."

Maria shot into the kitchen. She placed the three tufts of hair on the table. She had no money in her purse, so having dipped her hand into the salt, she stuffed a fistful into it. In no time, she was back outside with Fortunato.

"Come on," he said, "we must get away from here." They ran from the tower down the hill towards the lake.

As they set off, the ogre woke from his sleep. He sat up on his bed and called out.

"How are you getting on in there, girl?"

In the kitchen, the first tuft of hair spoke in Maria's voice.

"Fine. I've sifted the flour and I've rubbed in the butter."

Satisfied, the ogre lay down and went back to sleep.

A couple of minutes later, the ogre stirred again.

"You must be nearly finished by now, girl," he shouted.

"Not long now," said the second tuft of hair. "I've mixed in the water and I'm just letting it rest for a moment or two."

The ogre stretched himself out for another nap. After a short while, he surfaced for the third time.

"You'd better be done by now," bellowed the ogre. "I'm starving."

"Yes, I'm done," said the third tuft. "I've rolled it out and I've lined the pot. It's ready for the meat to go in."

The ogre chuckled. He got up from his bed. He went to the corner of the room and picked up an axe which was leaning against the wall.

He strode into the kitchen and looked round. There was no one there. He threw the axe to the floor.

"So, he thinks he can outwit me, does he?" snarled the ogre. He ran up the stairs of the tower. From a window, he saw Fortunato and Maria hurrying down the hill towards the lake. The ogre bounded back down the stairs. Pausing only to fasten on his sword belt, he dashed from the tower and ran after them.

Chapter Six
Flight and Pursuit

When Maria and Fortunato reached the shore, they stopped. The lake was vast and almost circular.

"Where do we go now?" asked Maria.

"We need to get back to the river valley. It will take too long to go round the lake. We must cross it."

"But I can't swim."

"That's no problem," replied Fortunato. "I can swim well enough for both of us. You just hold tight round my neck."

"What about the salt?"

"Take off your belt, Maria and use it to tie the purse onto my horns. I'll keep my head above water all the time."

Maria did what Fortunato said. They waded into the water. The coldness took away Mara's breath. She put her arm round the goat's neck and gripped tightly. Fortunato was a good swimmer. They made rapid progress across the bottom corner of the lake. Maria helped by kicking her legs behind her.

They were about halfway across when they heard a roar behind them. It was followed by a splash. The ogre had jumped into the lake and was swimming after them. He was not an elegant swimmer. He swallowed a lot of water as he went along. But he was strong. The sound of him thrashing through the water became louder and louder behind them.

They were not far from the shore when Maria looked back.

"Oh, Fortunato," she cried. "He's going to catch us."

"Don't be afraid. Take the salt and throw it into the water behind us."

Maria grabbed her purse and tipped it out. As the salt hit the water, every grain seemed to multiply into a hundred grains. The water fizzed and turned grey as the salt dissolved in a mass of frothing bubbles. The ogre stopped swimming. What they heard behind them now was his coughing and spluttering.

Maria and Fortunato made it to the far side. Fortunato shook the water from his fur like a dog. They found the path into the forest and ran for it.

The ogre meanwhile stumbled towards the shore. His eyes were smarting from the salt and he could hardly see. Again and again he fell over on the rocks. By the time he was out, his hands and knees were grazed and bleeding. The salty water made the cuts sting. The salt had gone up his nose.

He snorted and spat, trying to clear it. Having swallowed a lot of salty water, he was sick several times. Sitting down on the beach, he howled, he cursed and he swore. He vowed the most horrible vengeance on Fortunato.

Maria and Fortunato made good progress. They walked with haste along the path and Maria's clothes soon dried.

They were halfway through the forest when Fortunato stopped.

"What is it?" asked Maria.

"Hush for a moment," said the goat. He put his head down and listened. Maria could hear nothing, but Fortunato picked up the rhythmic thump of heavy feet beating on the forest path behind them.

"It's the ogre. He's on our trail again."

"I've got an idea," said Maria. She picked up a fallen branch and used it to beat down the undergrowth at the side of the path, making a track leading from it. A short way along the track, she put her purse on the ground.

She placed it so that its brass buckle caught the sunlight. She tore off a strip of cloth from the bottom of her skirt. A little further along the track, she snagged the piece of cloth on a bramble.

They carried on through the forest. Just as Maria intended, the ogre, when he reached that spot, thought the two of them must have turned aside from the main path. He found the purse and the piece of cloth. He spent a long time crashing around in the brambles and the thorns, searching for more signs that his quarry had gone that way.

Maria and Fortunato used the time to good effect. They cleared the forest and crossed the plain. Maria was relieved when at last they dropped down into the river valley. Fortunato slackened his pace. They reached the narrowest point of the valley, where it became a gorge between cliffs.

A little beyond there, Fortunato stopped. Both he and Maria took a drink in the river. He seemed to be in no hurry to move on and he spoke no more. While he nibbled at some scrub, she listened to the sounds of the river and the birds.

Then a less pleasing sound struck her ears. From out of sight beyond the bend in the river behind them, she heard the bellowing of the ogre.

"I'll catch the pair of you," he roared. "And when I do, I won't bother with cooking."

Maria jumped to her feet.

"Look inside my other ear," said Fortunato. She lifted the ear and looked. She saw a pea. "Take it out. Now, go back along the path."

"But the ogre—"

"Trust me, Maria. Go back until you are just short of the spot where the gorge is narrowest. Wait there. When you see the ogre reach that place, you are to throw the pea. Don't throw it at the ogre. Throw it at one of the cliff faces. And as soon as the pea has left your hand, turn and run back here as fast as you can."

Maria clutched the pea. She put her arm round Fortunato's neck and kissed the goat on his nose. Then she turned and set off back along the path in the direction of the ogre's shouts. Her heart was beating fast. Her legs felt wobbly, and she wondered if she would be able to make them run when the time came. But she had learned to trust Fortunato.

She chose her spot and stopped. By now, she could hear the thud of the ogre's feet. He came around the bend. Maria waited for a few moments. She was surprised at her own calmness, standing there without moving as he ran towards her. She threw the pea at the rock face, turned and fled back down the path.

Chapter Seven
Fortunato Transformed

When the pea hit the cliff, there was a mighty explosion. Maria was running with all the speed she could make. She felt the force of the blast as if she had been kicked in the back by a horse. It lifted her off her feet and threw her face down on the ground. She tumbled over but was not hurt. Having scrambled to her feet, she ran on until she got back to Fortunato.

As she ran, there was a roar and a crash. Part of the cliff, shattered by the explosion, plunged down into the valley. She threw her arms round Fortunato's neck and held him tight.

Soil and fragments of rock fell around them. For a time, they could see nothing through the cloud of dust. When it cleared, Fortunato said to Maria.

"Come on, let's go back and look."

"I don't want to," replied Maria. "It'll be too terrible."

"We must find the ogre, Maria. That is my only hope."

They picked their way back along the path, now strewn with the debris of the explosion and the rock fall. Maria spotted the ogre's sword and picked it up. They could see no sign of the ogre.

Then, as they stood scanning the jumble of boulders, they heard a moan. What they had taken for a rock was the ogre's head. His hair was matted with dust. He had been buried up to his neck in the avalanche.

The ogre groaned. "Set me free. Please, set me free."

"Set me free first," answered Fortunato.

"I can't," said the ogre. "Just help me out of this and then I'll set you free."

"We both know you can. Why should I trust you now, after all you've done? Besides, it's going to need two pairs of hands to shift all these rocks off you. One young woman and a goat are never going to manage it."

The ogre grunted, "Very well, then."

He muttered a string of words. They were in a tongue Maria had never heard before. There was a flash and, where the goat had been, crouched a young man, on his hands and knees. The young man got to his feet, stretched himself and smiled at Maria. She stood staring, her mouth open in bewilderment.

"Get on with it then," said the ogre. "It's your turn to set me free now."

"Yes," said the young man. "I'll set you free, for all time."

At those words, he snatched the sword from Maria's hands and with a single stroke cut off the ogre's head. It rolled across the ground. Blood spurted from the trunk. Maria put her hands over her eyes and turned away.

The young man picked up the ogre's head by its hair and hurled it into the river. A kite sitting in a tree on the opposite bank heard the splash and took off. The bird spotted the head being carried downstream and flew after it.

"I'm sorry, Maria, that you had to see that," said the young man. "It was the only way to put an end to all the evil he has done."

"But who are you?" she asked. "And what are you?"

"Here, takes my hand. I'll explain everything. We're not far from your grandmother's cottage. She'll be desperate to know what has happened to you. Let's walk back there. As we go, I will tell you my story."

Maria nodded. They clambered over the fallen rock and back onto the path by the riverbank. From there the way was easy, but the young man did not let go of Maria's hand, nor did she withdraw it.

"I live in Rome," he said. "My father is a merchant. He has a warehouse on the bank of the river and a ship in which he goes on trading voyages. When I came of age, I expected to join him on his trips. My mother was keen that I should. But my father had different ideas.

"He wanted me to study before I got into the business of buying and selling. He knew of a man in the city who for many years had studied at the University of Bologna. My father paid him a sum of money and I became his apprentice."

"Are you married?" asked Maria.

The young man squeezed her hand.

"No, I am not. At first, all went well. The man had indeed studied much. I learned a lot from him, particularly about the hidden properties of things. But, as time went on, I began to realise that his real interest lay in magic and the dark arts. He had gathered a collection of old volumes full of spells, incantations and tales of wizardry. He pored over them day and night.

"More and more, he made it my job to gather the ingredients for his potions and charms. I became frightened when I found he had discovered the secret of shape shifting. He was able to change himself into all sorts of forms. He liked to turn himself into an ogre, for in that guise he was able to frighten people and rob them of the rare and precious things he needed for his magic.

"He soon found it difficult in the city to hide what he was doing. So he searched the countryside and came upon the tower by the lake. In the shape of an ogre, he terrified the family living there and drove them out. Having turned the tower into his study and laboratory, he forced me to work there for him.

"I noticed that each time he changed back from having been an ogre, some feature of the ogre lingered in him. He was taking the form of an ogre so often he ended becoming one.

"I decided to run away. But he discovered my plan. He said I knew too much about what he was up to, so he would have to do away with me. But he thought it dull just to kill me outright. He had a more amusing plan. I had managed to steal a little of his magic.

"You saw me use it. And I was able to snatch a charm to make sure I could still speak a little. But my powers were no match for his. He turned me into a goat. He had me dumped in that marketplace, certain I would be taken off to be slaughtered."

"What is your name?" asked Maria.

The young man smiled. "I did have a name before, of course," he said. "But it was my good luck to be found by you, Maria. So, from this day I shall answer only to the name you gave me—Fortunato."

They walked on together in silence. It was evening when they climbed the valley slope onto the hillside path and caught sight of Grandmother's cottage.

Before they reached it, Fortunato stopped. He looked at Maria and took both her hands in his.

"When we left here, Maria, you told me you loved me, and you would never be parted from me. You said that to a goat. I wish with all my heart you would say those same words to me as a man."

"Let this stand for those words," said Maria. She leant forward and kissed Fortunato.

Chapter Eight
Union and Reunion

Maria's grandmother was overjoyed to see her safe. She welcomed Fortunato and was astonished to hear his story. She was happy to give her blessing to their marriage, for she had always known that one day Maria would leave.

The next morning, Maria and Fortunato went down into the town. The ogre's sword was ornate, and Fortunato was able to sell it for a good price. He and Maria insisted that Grandmother should have half the money. They wanted to help her to put her land in order again.

Fortunato was keen to be reunited with his own parents and to introduce Maria to them. They made for the city, by way of the ogre's tower. Maria lit the fire again in the kitchen but this time not for a pie. Fortunato gathered the ogre's books of magic and burned them to ashes.

In a nearby village, they found the family who had been driven out by the ogre. Fortunato handed back the tower keys. He gave them the rest of the money from the sale of the sword, so they could restore the place to be their home again.

Fortunato's mother and father were overjoyed and astonished too. They gave their blessing to the couple, and they welcomed Maria into their family. At first, they were unhappy about the idea of their son changing his name. But as they got to know Maria better they accepted it. They came to see how fortunate he was to find such a fine wife.

Maria and Fortunato were never parted again. When Fortunato set off on trading voyages in his father's ship, Maria always went with him. In time, Grandmother was no longer able to tend her field. She moved to the city where Maria and Fortunato cared for her. She lived long enough to be proud of becoming a great-grandmother. Maria and Fortunato lived together in loving harmony for the rest of their lives.

Leaping Ferghal – Ireland

Chapter One
The Feud

I'll tell you a story I had off a Connemara man. It was already an old tale, he said, when his grandfather told it him.

Long ago, there were two clans living on the west coast of Ireland, the O'Rourkes and the O'Flahertys. Their lands were close to one another. A stream flowed there, running westwards to the sea. The O'Rourke village lay on the south side of a ford across the stream. The O'Flahertys lived on its other side, to the north.

They were farming people. Some land they cleared for growing crops but mostly they lived by their cattle and sheep. A lot of rain fell then, as it does now. It made for rich grass and their livestock thrived on it.

Theirs was a harsh world. Peat bogs stretched in every direction. The peaks of distant mountains were shrouded much of the time in cloud. Mist lingered long in the valleys. Even the mountain slopes were boggy but in summertime their upland pastures gave grazing to the livestock. Few trees could withstand the cold winds and winter storms that blew in from the Atlantic. People burned peat to keep warm.

Although they were neighbours and shared a common way of life, the O'Flahertys and the O'Rourkes had been feuding longer than anyone remembered.

How it began, nobody could tell. Perhaps they fell out first over the right to graze a pasture or over the line of a cut of peat. Whatever their dispute was, they inflated it as the years went by into a full-blown feud.

The people of each clan held a low opinion of the other. Their mutual scorn they passed down through the generations.

"Those O'Rourkes," an O'Flaherty would say, "they have so little brain, they couldn't find a hole in a ladder."

On the other side of the stream, the O'Rourkes said: "Those O'Flahertys are a feeble lot. If you twined all their courage together, you could pass the thread through the eye of a needle."

The two clan Chiefs both entertained travelling bards. Whenever one arrived in their village, they would make him welcome. They feasted and paid him for the songs he sang and the stories he told.

At the end of a day, when they had done their work, each Chief's chosen people gathered in his hut. The rain might be drumming on the thatch and the wind shaking the skins hung over the doorway, but they sat warm in a fog of blue smoke from the peat fire.

A visiting bard would pluck the strings of his lyre and entertain them with old legends and new tales. To flatter his hosts, he sang of the skirmishes between the O'Flahertys and the O'Rourkes. He embroidered their squabbles so they sounded like battles fought by heroes of the past.

For much of the time, the two clans put up with one another. Their feud was kept alive with a deal of boasting and taunting but mostly they traded gibes, not blows.

Now and then, though, there was a clash. An O'Flaherty might find a stock fence broken. An O'Rourke might spot one of his stacks toppled over. However slight the offence, it was always taken amiss. Harsher words then were uttered and sometimes, clouts were exchanged. A bout of tit for tat followed. With time, these spats tended to peter out and people resumed the routine dictated by the seasons and their livestock. Life was tough. Just getting by claimed most of their energy.

Chapter Two
A Giant Is Born

So, what is it, you'll be asking, that makes this a story worth the telling? It's hardly news that neighbours seldom get on with one another. There were feuds like this the length of Ireland, from the Skelligs to the Giant's Causeway.

To answer that question, I shall have to go back, back to a point before Ferghal, the hero of this story was born. At that time, the feud took a wicked turn. It came about through a change in the O'Flaherty clan.

Their clan Chief had a son. When his wife gave birth, the women of the village came to marvel at the size of the baby.

"You poor thing," they cried, throwing up their hands in horror, "however did you deliver such a monster?"

To be sure, he was a huge baby, with an appetite to match. He grew at amazing speed. In no time, he was able to walk, and no sooner could he walk than he began to run. He stood above other children of his age. Those who saw him guessed him twice as old as he was.

When the men of the village were out on the land, tending cattle or cutting peat, some of the women would take baskets and trek to the coast. Children with enough stamina for the walk went with them. On the beaches, the women gathered shellfish. The children were not there to play. Small hands and fingers were good for feeling into crevices and under rocks. They were set to work, searching for crabs and sea snails.

On these forays to the coast, villagers first came to grasp the strength burgeoning in young O'Flaherty. He seemed to have hands of iron. Clenching a fist, he could punch a limpet free of a boulder with his bare knuckles. He used to pick up mussels, crush their shells in one hand and gulp them down raw.

"We're going to have bother with this one when he's a man," said the Chief to his wife.

"Away with such talk," she answered. "Isn't he going to be a fine, handsome fellow?"

Handsome he was. But many a time through his boyhood years, his father had to visit families in the village, to return a stolen chicken, to replace a smashed spade or to placate parents whose children his son had bullied.

When he reached manhood, young O'Flaherty was a giant. His strength matched the size of his body. Having huge hands and a terrible grip, he liked to intimidate others by showing off his might. One of his knacks was to take a horseshoe in one hand and, closing his fingers, bend the two ends to meet. Out on the bog, he picked up rocks that would have taxed three men and hurled them further than anyone imagined possible.

Young O'Flaherty learned early of the feud and took it up with relish. On the slightest grounds, he was for storming across the stream to fight the O'Rourkes. When checked by the Chief, he was angry. He grew more and more resentful of his father's curbs.

Chapter Three
Revolution

The showdown between father and son came one night in the Chief's hut. Many of the clan's men had gathered to hear a visiting bard. It happened that the bard recounted a battle between two clans. He told of fearless feats in the fray, but his narrative was drenched in blood. Long was the catalogue of those on both sides slain in his story of slaughter.

When the bard finished, the Chief rose to his feet to give the traditional toast of thanks. But that night, he went further.

"Do you mark this story well, son of mine. There is glory to be won in battle, to be sure. But only when the cause is just. Even then, a wise man will pause to ponder on the blood that will be shed and on those to be made widowed and fatherless."

The assembled host was hushed. Those who welcomed the Chief's words and those irked by them—all were shocked to hear him rebuke his son before the men of the clan.

Young O'Flaherty jumped to his feet.

"Wasn't that a fine way to thank our guest? He gives us a stirring tale and you mither on about women and children."

Laughter from young O'Flaherty's supporters greeted his words.

The Chief raised a hand to silence them.

"Is it not enough that you have no respect for your neighbours, that you must now disrespect your father and your Chief?"

"Respect must be earned, old man. And it's earned by showing courage, not by talking of it." The comrades of young O'Flaherty roared their approval.

"Enough. I'll chop no more words with you. Be gone from my hut. And take your rabble with you."

"Indeed, I will not. It's time this clan was led by a man ready to do more than just suffer the O'Rourkes. How many here are with me?"

A great number bellowed their support for the Chief's son. Those loyal to the Chief saw they were fewer.

"I'll hear no more of this," declared the Chief.

He stormed from the hut, followed by those still true to him. They left to a chorus of jeers and cackles from young O'Flaherty's people.

Chapter Four
Celebration

With his father gone, O'Flaherty and his supporters clustered round the Chief's barrel of heather beer. They celebrated their triumph, with round after round of toasts to their new Chief.

O'Flaherty's mind was on more than drink. Many times, he had watched his father unlock the wooden chest which stood at the back of the hut. Only the Chief had a key. He kept it on a leather thong round his neck. In that chest, the Chief kept his hoard of weapons.

O'Flaherty took a peat spade and began to hammer at the lid of the chest. It was a sturdy piece, made of oak. But O'Flaherty mustered all his strength. After a dozen or so blows, he managed to smash a hole in the lid. He got his fingers into the opening and, straining the muscles of his arms and hands, he ripped the wood apart.

Howls of delight rose from his supporters. He held them back while he chose for himself a great wooden club. A free-for-all followed as men pushed and pulled, reaching into the chest and grabbing for themselves swords, battle-axes, daggers and clubs. In moments, the chest was empty, and the mob armed with battle gear. A cheer went up as O'Flaherty lifted it and dropped it onto the open fire. They set about draining the barrel of beer.

The bard was a smart fellow, able to smell trouble. He wanted none of it. Up and ready at first light the following day, he mounted his pony and rode away.

O'Flaherty and his supporters, befuddled by the night's drinking, rose late. O'Flaherty himself was first to wake and knew at once what he had to do. With a slap here and a kick there, he roused the others.

He ordered them to collect everything in the hut that belonged to the Chief and his wife. He had them carry it all outside and hurl it in the mud.

Some of the young men thought this a shabby act but they kept their thoughts to themselves. Most of them were still elated by their rebellion. They wondered, though, what would follow.

O'Flaherty had no such doubts. Having sent for another cask of heather beer, he ordered them to fill their cups.

"You're men now, not sheep. You've got battle gear, weapons you've only ever seen in your fathers' hands. And who was it giving them to you?"

"You did! You did!"

"Well then. Lift your cups and pledge your loyalty to your new Chief."

"Our new Chief!" they roared. "Our new Chief!"

Every cup was filled again. When they had emptied the cask, O'Flaherty led them, bawling and stumbling, round the village. At every hut, he shouted to those inside to step out. Waving his club in their faces, he demanded every man to swear allegiance to him as the new Chief of the clan.

This was a dark day for the O'Flahertys. Many in the village, not just the old Chief, felt the shame of it. Whenever the role of Chief passed from one man to another, the old Chief was always held in respect. His counsel would be sought, for he was the one who over decades had led them, the one who understood the stars, who knew the tracks across the bog, who read the weather signs and who settled their disputes with one another. It was the old Chief who carried in his head the history and traditions of the clan.

Chapter Five
Bull Ford

Having made off in haste, the bard did not know the outcome, but he shared what he had seen with those he met on his way. The O'Rourkes learned soon enough of the turmoil amongst the O'Flahertys.

No O'Rourke could boast of the size or the strength of young O'Flaherty. But amongst them, just as amongst their neighbours, there were hot-headed young men ready to egg one another on to do rash things.

"Now's the time to land a blow on those O'Flahertys," said one of them to his friends. "They're on the back foot and that's just the moment to strike."

"We're with you," came the response. "But what'll we do?"

"I have an idea," said another. "Do you mind that great bull they think so much of?"

"The one with white horns?"

"The very one."

"Well, what of it?"

"How would it be if we hid the beast and made them think they'd lost it?"

"That would make them mad, to be sure."

"Shall we do it then, lads?"

"Let's do it," was the cry from every side.

The young men set off as light began to fade. They crossed the stream by the ford and found the bull. A fine bull he was, of massive bulk. The O'Flahertys had polished his horns, which shone in the evening light.

The bull stared at these strangers and snorted. They managed to get a rope round his neck. He may have thought they were leading him to the stream to drink, for he plodded with them. At the ford, he stood in the water and drank.

The bull knew which way his own grazing lay. He knew too he had never crossed the stream. The O'Rourkes tugged the rope. The bull would not budge.

Tossing his head, he ripped the rope from their hands, and it fell into the water. They retrieved it and some pulled, while others got behind and pushed. The bull bellowed.

The O'Rourkes slapped and shouted. One of them took off his cloak and got it over the bull's head. That worked. Once he could no longer see, the bull became calm and let himself be led up the far bank. From that struggle and from what followed, the place was ever afterwards called Bull Ford.

Not far from the stream, towards the O'Rourke village, there was a gulley. A cluster of oak trees had taken root there. They were thin and stunted but the hollow gave them enough shelter from the wind to survive. The young men got the bull down into the dip and tethered him, on a long run, to the stoutest of the trees.

On their return to the village, laughing and singing, they stopped at each hut to boast of their deed.

Word soon reached O'Rourke himself. The clan Chief stormed out of his hut. The rage on his face brought silence and a halt to the progress of the riotous rabble.

"You fools!" he shouted. "What do you think you've done?"

"'Tis only a bit of fun. We've not robbed the O'Flahertys. We just wanted to trick them."

"You don't know the O'Flahertys. They'll not smile at this. Where's the bull?"

"Down in the gulley. Don't worry. There was nobody out. Nobody saw us take him."

"Get back to your families," ordered the Chief, "every one of you. At first light, you'll be outside my hut. It's too dark now but as soon as morning comes, we shall take that bull back. And in front of me every one of you will apologise to O'Flaherty himself for your folly. Now be gone."

The young men slunk away, heads bowed, into the darkness.

Chapter Six
Attack

Those young men were mistaken. They had been seen.

Cows were left out to graze on the upland pastures. Women went from their villages to milk them where they were. One of the O'Flaherty women was trudging back with two full pails when something of the commotion at the ford carried to her on the wind. She looked that way. At first, she saw nothing but as the young O'Rourkes led the bull up the bank, she spied the glint of its white horns. She guessed what was afoot.

"We'd best tell O'Flaherty," she said to her husband back in their hut. "There'll be fury from him if the bull's gone and he's not told."

There was fury and more.

"That's it," roared O'Flaherty. "We'll put an end to this feud once and for all."

He seized the club that had been his father's and dashed from the hut. He was furious, to be sure, but he rejoiced too. Here was his chance to bolster himself as the new Chief of the clan.

O'Flaherty's shouting shattered the quiet of the night. He summoned his followers to his hut.

The gathering buzzed, agog to know what was doing. O'Flaherty brought them to order with a flourish of his club.

"Those thieving O'Rourkes—they've only gone and stolen our prize bull." Cries of outrage went up on all sides.

"Are we going to let them get away with that?" demanded O'Flaherty.

"No, no, no!" they cried.

"You're too right, we're not. We're going to finish off the O'Rourkes, once and for all. I don't want a single one of them left alive. Are you with me?"

"We're with you, Chief," they clamoured.

"Get your battle-gear then and make ready to march. We'll show them what it means to steal from the O'Flahertys. And light your torches. When we've done, there'll be only smoke and ashes to show where that pack of thieves lived."

Led by O'Flaherty, the rabble ran for the O'Rourkes' village. They held high their torches. The flickering flames glinted on their newfound battle-gear. They felt themselves a worthy band of warriors sallying out to avenge a wrong.

"Look, Chief," one of them shouted. "There's our bull. We've found what we came for."

O'Flaherty did not even turn to see. No longer caring about the bull, he drove on his men.

Some in the O'Rourke village heard the yelling of the O'Flahertys as they charged. Grabbing their weapons, they rushed out to defend their homes and families. Their attackers fell upon them. They had both numbers and surprise on their side. One group cut down the defenders, while another set about torching the huts.

In his own hut, O'Rourke, the clan Chief, heard the din and jumped to his feet. He decided in an instant he would take no weapon with him, to show he wanted to talk, not fight.

The Chief dashed out. At once, he was face to face with young O'Flaherty. He was a tall man himself and long of leg, but O'Flaherty stood head and shoulders above him, so big was he.

The Chief held out his hand.

"Come, man, we must stop this and talk, or more innocent folk are going to be killed."

O'Flaherty swung his club.

"This does all my talking for me," he yelled, smashing it against the side of O'Rourke's head and felling him to the ground. He dropped down, knelt on O'Rourke's chest and closed his fingers round the throat of the fallen man. Those fingers did not release their iron grip until they had throttled the life out of him.

Springing to his feet, O'Flaherty grabbed one of his men who was racing by.

"Here! Hand me that torch. Mine is the right to burn their Chief's hut to the ground." With those words, he thrust the torch into its thatch.

Chapter Seven
Escape

Inside was O'Rourke's young wife. She had been sick that morning so she had not stirred all day.

She cowered in terror at the shouting and screaming. Above the din, she heard O'Flaherty's triumphant yell. Moments later, she saw flames taking hold in the roof of her hut.

It had a single door. She knew what to expect if she ran out that way. Grabbing her husband's axe, she dashed to the back of the hut. In frenzy, she hacked at the wall. She was able to smash a small opening in it. Squeezing through, she crouched on the ground outside.

Behind her, the roof was now ablaze. Before her, she saw a line of torches. One group of O'Flaherty's men had formed a ring around the village to make sure no-one got away in the darkness.

Her hand went to her throat. She clutched a leather pouch which hung about her neck. In that pouch was a small stone.

Death was pressing close on every side. So whatever was she doing, you may wonder, at such a time to fiddle over a stone? That was no ordinary stone. Bide a moment, while I tell you how it came to her.

Away years back, when she was a girl, she was alone minding her parents' hut. They were out tending their cattle. An old woman, a stranger to the village, appeared at her door.

"There'd be no chance, I suppose, for a weary traveller to rest awhile?" the old woman asked.

She was of a mind to turn her away. The old woman was in a bad state. Nor would her parents be happy with her letting a stranger into their hut when they were away. But she could not bring herself to leave the old woman to the weather, so she invited her in.

Setting her by the fire, she warmed some milk. She fetched a ladle and filled a bowl with gruel from a pot keeping warm on the hearth stones.

The old woman's feet were wrapped in bandages, muddy, wet and bloodstained. Having heated some water in a pan, she bathed the woman's feet. Her mother had put aside an old apron for rags. She tore it into strips and helped the old woman re-bandage her feet.

"Do you mind now, if I doze for a moment or two?" asked the old woman.

A troubled look came over the girl's face.

"Fear not," said the old woman. "I need only a short rest. To be sure, I shall be out of here and on my way before ever your mother and father are back."

She kept her word. By the time the girl had cleaned and put away the bowl, the pan and the scraps of cloth, the old woman had woken and was making ready to leave.

"You've been kind to me, my dear. Let me give you something."

From deep in her skirts, she drew out a leather pouch, strung with a cord.

"There's a magic stone inside. You must use the magic only when your life is in danger. Swallow the stone and it will save you."

"What will the stone do?"

"That, I'll not tell you. Know only that you'll be able to get away from mortal danger. But remember this. The magic will serve you just once. It'll last only for as long as it's inside you. Once you pass the stone out, its magic will be gone forever. Now take it. Be sure you keep it round your neck. You never know when you'll need it."

The girl's parents smiled when she told them of the old woman's visit and her gift. They were wise to the tales of travelling people. But they said nothing and were content for her to keep it round her neck.

That, then, was the stone O'Rourke's wife took from the pouch. It was not a time to dither.

She put the stone in her mouth and swallowed.

Chapter Eight
O'Flaherty Triumphant

For all the shouting of men, the screams of women and children and the crackling of flames, O'Flaherty nevertheless heard the sound of wood splintering, as O'Rourke's wife hacked through the back wall of the hut.

He sneered. "You'll not escape O'Flaherty that way."

As he strode round the side of the blazing hut, he caressed the end of his club, readying to fell another victim.

He reached the rear of the hut. There was a hole. But no one was there.

He saw only a hare bound away at speed, running a zigzag course to dodge through the line of men holding torches.

O'Flaherty chuckled. "Go your way, hare," he shouted after the fleeing creature. "You'll be the only living thing to get away from here this night."

O'Flaherty mustered his men. They trooped back through the village, their way lit by burning huts. They did to death anybody they found still alive and seized everything they could carry off.

Whooping and hollering, they tramped back to their own village.

Their women, left behind, smelled the blaze in the distance. The wind carried to them not only the cries of the people but also the howling of dogs and the squealing of pigs terrified by the flames.

"What have you done?" they demanded of the returning men.

"We've done for the O'Rourkes," sniggered O'Flaherty.

"Those poor folk."

"Hush your snivelling. Fetch us beer. We've done thirsty work this night."

"Did you find the bull?"

"Never mind the bull. Tomorrow will be time enough to fetch him back. It's drink we're looking for now. Get it!" barked O'Flaherty.

Some men slunk away to their own huts. If they expected a welcome home, they were disappointed. They were put to shame for their deeds, berated by mothers, by wives and by sisters.

O'Flaherty summoned them all back to join him in celebrating their victory with a barrel of beer. They heeded his call, for they feared his wrath more than the upbraiding of their women.

What was left of that night and the hours into next morning, they spent carousing. The barrel was drained. Brawls broke out as men bettered one another's boasts of who had done most. They scrapped over the swords and spears stripped from slain O'Rourkes.

There was little sleep that night amongst the O'Flahertys. It was the middle of the day before many stirred. They woke with sore heads. Many had sore hearts.

Their new Chief alone had no regrets. He stomped from hut to hut, rousing the men.

"Come on. We're going back. There's the O'Rourkes' livestock to be rounded up."

Drizzle fell as a grey mist over the land. A cold wind blew it, making everything wet. They trudged back across the ford. The sight of the sacked village chilled them even more. Wisps of smoke rose from heaps of ash. Cows bellowed in discomfort, not having been milked. Dogs nosed at bodies on the ground, as if trying to wake their owners.

Men felt ashamed.

"This was not well done," some muttered.

"Get to it," shouted O'Flaherty. "Round up those pigs. You there, collect all the chickens. And you, bring the cows down to the ford. Let no man take for himself. I shall be the one who sorts our spoils."

"What are we to do with the dead?" one man asked.

"We'll leave them for the crows and the wolves, that's what we'll do."

"No!" shouted the man. "We should bury them and show some respect."

O'Flaherty turned on him and swung his club. He smashed it so hard against the man's arm, he shattered the bone.

"You'll do as I say, or you'll join the O'Rourkes lying dead in the mud."

Chapter Nine
Flight

I must leave O'Flaherty now, to tell you what became of O'Rourke's wife.

"Go your way, hare." That, you'll remember, was O'Flaherty's shout.

She heard him. But no longer did she hear understandable words. What she picked up was sound, the sound of the terrifying animal that went upright on two of its legs. The stone had turned her into a hare. The last thing her human mind registered was the throttling pain as her body shrank.

The hare bolted. No hare chooses to run towards men, but it had fire and noise at its back.

The hare zigzagged across the ground, making for a dark space between the torches before it.

The hare ran and ran. It came to a hill. Pausing, it rose on its hind legs. The noises made by the giant animals reached it on the breeze. To the hare, those noises meant only one thing – pursuit.

It set off again, turning this way and that a thousand times. Its fur became wet from the dew on the grass. Briars scratched its legs. But every sound urged it on. Fear possessed its whole being.

The hare switched the direction of its run again and again. It swerved aside to go through a flock of sheep. Catching the scent of rabbits, it made a detour through their burrows. It dashed amid a herd of deer. To the hare, pursuit meant dogs on its trail, so it tried all it could to mix its own scent with the scents of other creatures.

Thud. The hare was yanked to a stop and thumped into the turf. With the impact came a searing pain in a hind leg. A snare had caught it. The hare hurled itself forward. The pain burned deeper as the loop of twine tightened around its leg. But fear was more intense than pain.

At intervals, exhaustion took over. The hare fell down on its side, panting and unable to move. Moments later, it revived and at once leapt forward to bolt, only to be jerked back to the ground. The fur of its hind leg was soon wet, not just with dew but with blood.

Then, in one of those frenzied bursts to break free, the hare passed the stone. O'Rourke's wife became herself again. She lay wet, cold and breathless on the grass, her left ankle racked with pain.

Terror of pursuit still throbbed through every part of her, but slowly human thoughts began to return—where was she, what had she done to her ankle, where was she to go?

She shivered. Her fingers stiff with cold, she nevertheless managed to untie the noose of twine which had cut into the flesh of her ankle. Tearing a strip of cloth from the bottom of her skirt, she wrapped it round to staunch the blood.

Mist covered the ground. But in the distance, a faint curl of smoke rose. A smell came to her, one she recognised. It was the smell of a peat fire. There must be a village, she thought, somewhere nearby.

She set off to find it, limping and stumbling over tussocks.

The hare had kept to the south of the stream. Further inland, the line of the stream turned south, blocking the way of O'Rourke's wife. Probing along its bank, she heard at last the tinkling of water running shallow over gravel. She had found a ford. The water was icy cold, but it numbed the throbbing pain in her ankle.

Ever afterwards that was known as Safe Haven Ford, for across its O'Rourke's wife found refuge in her flight.

Through the mist, she began to make out the blurred shapes of huts. Staggering for the nearest one, she tried to call out, but her breath and strength were gone. A gasp was all that left her lips as she fell in the mud. The last sound she heard as she closed her eyes was the barking of dogs.

Chapter Ten
The Widow

A widow lived in that hut. The barking of the dogs roused her from sleep. She rose and lit a lamp from the fire. Draping a cloak over her shoulders, she stepped outside to see what had alarmed them.

She found the dogs sniffing at a heap in the mud. Her eyesight was poor. With one foot, she gave it a poke. It stirred. It was a person. She bent down and her lamp lit the face of a woman lying there senseless.

The widow shook her, and O'Rourke's wife came round for a moment. She helped her up and led her inside the hut.

"Lie down there, my dear," she said, spreading her cloak on the ground close by the fire. She heaped on more peat. Having warmed some milk, she stirred in a blob of honey. O'Rourke's wife was too weak even to prop herself on an elbow. The widow sat down and supported her in her arms, putting the drink to her lips.

"Whatever brings you to be walking alone through the night? Where have you come from? And how did you do that to your ankle?"

O'Rourke's wife sipped the milk and said nothing. When she had drained the bowl, she sank back in the widow's arms. Her eyes closed.

The widow nodded. "You're right, my dear. Sleep is the best remedy for many an ill. I'll not disturb you till you're ready."

The widow laid her down. She bent to take a closer look at the woman's ankle. The cloth bound round it was bloody, but the wound seemed no longer to be bleeding.

"The poor thing will come to no harm," she said to herself, "if I leave tending that till the morning."

Taking a blanket from her own bed, she covered the sleeping figure. She lay down herself but slept only in snatches, looking now and again over to the stranger asleep by her hearth.

O'Rourke's wife slept on into the morning of the next day, but the widow was early up and about. She fetched out some clean clothes for the woman. Skilled at healing, she ground together herbs, roots and berries to make a salve to rub on the woman's ankle. A pot of porridge she put to keep warm by the fire.

Alarm gripped O'Rourke's wife on waking. She sat up and looked about her. She had no idea where she was, nor how she had got there.

"Be calm, my dear. You are safe here."

"But where am I?"

"There'll be time for talking. First, get some of this porridge inside you." She did not argue. Sleep had refreshed her, but she felt faint with hunger.

"Here, give me your leg while you eat. We need to wash that wound and put something on it."

The widow unwound the filthy cloth. With warm water, she bathed the ankle. Having rubbed on some of the salve, she put on a clean bandage.

"How come you to cut yourself like this?"

"I gashed it on a sharp rock."

The cut looked too deep and too regular for that to be true, but the widow chose not to challenge her guest.

Chapter Eleven
A Son

By now, you're maybe saying to yourself, "Why ever is this story called 'Leaping Ferghal', when it's gone a deal of a way and I've still not heard a word of the man?"

Didn't I warn you when I started that I'd have to go back a bit first? Well, I've done that. And now's the time, at long last you'll be thinking, for the hero of this story to come into view.

O'Rourke's wife soon recovered her strength. She would tell the widow nothing of what happened to her, but she was eager to show her thankfulness.

"I can't be sitting here while you wait on me," she said. "You've been more than kind. There must be something I can do for you."

"As it happens, there is." The widow pointed to the wooden frame leaning against the wall of the hut. "Do you see my loom?"

"Yes, and a good one it looks."

"So it is. But I've got it into a tangle. My eyes are not what they were. The other day, I tripped and stumbled into it. I managed to kick the warp stones this way and that. They've got themselves in a knot. For the life of me, I can't see to unravel it."

With a steadying arm from the widow, O'Rourke's wife hobbled to the loom. Her eyes were sharp and her fingers nimble. A skilful weaver herself, she soon undid the tangle and got all the yarns hanging down straight again.

O'Rourke's wife proved some help to the widow. Before she could walk again, she sat carding by the hearth. The widow was able to spin while she watched a pot on the fire and busied herself about the hut.

For years, the widow had supported herself by making cloth and sewing for others.

Neighbours paid for her work with eggs, milk, peat and sometimes even a duck or a chicken. An extra pair of hands made a difference. What they earned together was enough for them both.

The widow had seen and learned much in a long life. O'Rourke's wife had not been with her many weeks when she guessed the young woman was expecting a child.

"The poor soul must have had trouble, wherever it is she came from," the widow said to herself. "I'll not stir it up by pressing her to share more than she's ready to tell."

When O'Rourke's wife was sure of her condition, she spoke of it to the widow. Far from being upset, the young woman was thrilled. She had lost her husband, her home, her friends and her neighbours. But now she would have a child of her own. Through the child, something of her husband would live on. She said nothing of that to the widow, but she shared her joy and the widow rejoiced with her.

During the hours of her labour, unable to sleep, she had time to think. She resolved to tell her child nothing of its past. That was behind them and behind them, she wanted it to stay.

She gave birth to a son. He was a handsome baby, fair-haired and long of body and limb. She named him Ferghal.

Chapter Twelve
Hollow Victory

Their neighbours' onslaught upon them doomed the O'Rourkes but it turned out to be a dark day too for the O'Flahertys.

Wanting his victory to be trumpeted abroad, O'Flaherty put out word for bards to visit his village, to learn of his exploits and to make a story of it.

Travelling bards have to earn their food and shelter. A little gilding of facts to flatter a Chief help in that cause. They might perhaps inflate a lucky chance into a brilliant strategy. What is vaunted in a story as a march of matchless endurance may in reality have been no more than a tramp across a bog.

Nor is there any harm if folk who come afterwards are spurred to admire and emulate those of bygone ages, overlooking that they were people like themselves, people who sometimes slipped over in the mud or dozed off at the hearth and let their fire go out.

Word had spread quickly of O'Flaherty's massacre of the O'Rourkes. No bard was willing to lend his tongue to celebrate the slaughter of innocent women and children and the wiping out of a whole clan. Out of curiosity, a few accepted O'Flaherty's invitation. They listened to him, they said they would give the matter some thought, and they slipped away as soon as they were unobserved.

O'Flaherty's grip on the clan became as strong as that of his fist. From then, nothing held him back from his chosen course of robbery and violence. His people followed him not out of respect but from fear and he led them into many a fight with clans round about.

In the chaos of combat, an arrow or a spear was sometimes sent his way from the hand of one of his own people. O'Flaherty seemed to lead a charmed life. None of them found its mark.

Gigantic in stature and awesome in strength as he was, O'Flaherty was not stupid. Glad that his people were afraid of him, he knew he could not trust them.

He decided to make a stronghold for himself alone, one he could defend against all comers.

The bog around the village was dotted with ponds and lakes. In places, outcrops of rock rose from the peat. Some of those outcrops made islands in the water.

Near O'Flaherty's circle of huts was a small lake with an island in the middle. Drawing on all his might, O'Flaherty gathered boulders on the lake shore. Heaving them up one by one, he hurled them out into the water. Advancing from pile to pile, he laid down a line of steppingstones to the island. He set them so far apart that only someone with his height and stride would be able to leap from rock to rock. On the island, he built himself a house of stone and roofed it with reeds cut from the margin of the lake.

When he had finished, O'Flaherty moved his belongings from his hut to the house on the island. By then, he had taken a wife. He lifted her in his arms and jumped her across the stones to their new home. From that day, she lived there as a prisoner, while her husband came and went at will.

He continued his campaign of raids on neighbouring clans. His band of henchmen in the village was kept loyal with shares of the plunder he amassed. For the others, menace was enough to hold them in thrall.

In time, O'Flaherty's wife became pregnant. She went into labour alone, while he was on his way back from leading yet another foray. He returned to find she had given birth to a baby girl.

Having had no help with the delivery, his wife had lost much blood. She died the next day.

O'Flaherty took the baby to the village.

"I want a woman to come and look after this," he demanded, "and to keep house for me."

People looked at one another in dismay. They could think of no woman in the village so desperate she would take that job.

To their shock, though, one did step forward.

"I'll do it," she said. "I'll look after the dear thing."

She was a young woman who had been widowed early in her marriage.

"What is her name?"

O'Flaherty scowled.

"I had a name for a son, a boy who would follow me. But now I care not. You give it what name you will."

"Then she shall be Maeve," said the woman. "From her crying, the poor child must be hungry. I'll warm some milk. When she's fed, I'll go with you."

O'Flaherty carried them both over the water to his house. Back in the village, people were at a loss to know whether they felt sorrier for the baby or for the woman.

Chapter Thirteen
Ferghal Grows Up

Ferghal had a happy childhood. He was loved by his mother and by the widow. When he learned to talk, he called the older woman 'grandmother'. She welcomed that. In every way she was a grandmother to him.

The people of the village did not welcome strangers. And this newcomer would say neither who she was, nor where she came from. But the fact that the widow had taken her in weighed in her favour. In time, they saw and valued the young woman's skill at the loom.

As soon as he was able to walk, Ferghal helped with the work of the family. Going out with his mother, he learned to know the berries and the lichens they used to dye their wool. He enjoyed wandering on his own to collect them. He fed their few chickens and gathered the eggs.

When he became older, he began to spend more time with other boys, roving the countryside about their village. On his long legs, he could outrun them all.

One day he came home excited. He told his mother his friends had shown him how to make and set snares to trap hares.

She frowned. "You go back right now," she ordered. "You take those snares up; do you hear me?"

"Why? Everybody catches hares."

"Never mind. You're not to do it."

"But mother—"

"Not another word. I'm telling you—never hurt a hare. They're magical creatures. You never know what harm you may be doing. Now, go and do as I say."

Ferghal trudged off. He did as his mother had told him, but he was careful to do it unseen.

He said nothing to the other boys.

Another time he asked, "What do I say, mother, when they want to know who my father is?"

She put her arm round him.

"Just tell them the truth, son. Your father is dead, and you never knew him. There is nothing more to know."

Ferghal grew to be a handsome young man. He had curly yellow hair and wore his beard cut square. With each year, he seemed to become taller. He stood above all those of his age. They joked about his height and his long legs.

"You'll soon need one hut to lay down your head," laughed one, "and another for your feet."

"That'll never do me," replied Ferghal. "I shall lie down here in Connacht and stretch my legs into Ulster."

He moved on from stacking peat turves to wielding the spade himself. At the end of the day, when work in the fields and on the bog was done, the young men would gather round a fire. They sat and talked.

"My father may not be Chief," boasted one of them, "but it's in honour of his swordsmanship that the bridge over yonder bears his name."

"That's nothing," another retorted. "The yew tree below the hill is named from my grandfather, for the strength of his spear arm. He threw a spear from a hundred paces. It went so far into the tree; it took two men to pull it out. Even then, the head stayed fast in the trunk."

A third joined in. "Spears are one thing but it's a sling that needs real skill. Up on Wolf Hill, my uncle tracked down a she-wolf that had attacked his stock. It was night. He had only the moon to see by, but he launched off a stone and took out that wolf's eye."

Ferghal stared into the fire and kept silent. His friends could brag of the feats done by men in their families. He had nothing to pitch in himself.

As they do, the young men turned their talk to the girls of the village. They discussed their qualities, they shared their own hopes and they calculated their chances. Still, Ferghal kept his peace.

One fellow turned to him.

"What about you, Ferghal? Who do you fancy?"

Ferghal hesitated. Before he could answer, another put in.

"I can't see any girl's father welcoming a bond with two women."

Ferghal rose to his feet. He towered over the speaker, who shrank back.

"I'll not rely on the fame of others," he declared. "I'll win a bride by my own hands." He turned and strode out into the darkness.

Chapter Fourteen
Maeve Grows Up

While Ferghal was free to wander over bog and slope, Maeve spent her childhood and her youth a prisoner on her father's island.

The young woman O'Flaherty brought over was as good as a mother to her. From the start, he had called her 'Nurse' and that is how Maeve addressed her as soon as she could talk.

Nurse loved Maeve and the child drew upon that love. She got little of it, to be sure, from her father. He did not mistreat her, but he had no time for the girl. His only interest was keeping her on the island.

Maeve felt the difference between the two adults in her life.

"Why does he treat me so, Nurse? All I ever hear from him is, 'Girl, fetch that. Girl, clear that up. Girl, make yourself scarce'."

"Mind it not, Maeve, my love. 'Tis the way he is. There'll be no changing him."

Much of the time, O'Flaherty was away leading raids. When their work about the house was done, Nurse would spread skins on the floor in front of the fireplace.

"Come, Maeve, sit down with me. I'll tell you a story."

Nurse had what seemed to Maeve a boundless store of tales. She told of spirits, of fairies and of ghosts. She recounted family sagas and chronicles of clan history. She had narratives of distant voyages, of the feats of heroes and of the trickery of knaves. All this she leavened with songs and rhymes and riddles.

"However did you come to know so much?" Maeve asked.

"Ah, Maeve. That is a story in itself. Away years ago, when I was a girl myself, I used to listen to the bards who travelled from village to village, telling tales and singing songs. When they came to our village, the menfolk would get together of an evening to hear them. It was not thought fit for women.

"On one of those evenings, the men happened to gather in my father's hut. Earlier that day I had twisted my ankle, so I was lying down at the back. My parents were not keen for me to be moved. Being a curious child, I was eager to hear what was going on. I pretended to be asleep. My father promised to keep an eye on me in case I should wake, so my mother left me and went to sit with our neighbours.

"Lying there I heard such things, Maeve. Not every word did I understand, mind you, but the flow, the run of the story and the beauty of the songs—they held me in a spell. From that moment, I was set on hearing more.

"The next time a bard came to our village, I pleaded with the Chief to let me be there to serve the company.

"'It needs somebody small', I told him. 'I'll be able to pass amongst the men. I'll not get in their way. I can fetch turves from the stack to keep the fire going. There'll be beakers to refill and lamps to be topped up.'

"'For one who slept the evening long,' he laughed, 'you picked up a deal of what goes on.'

"The Chief was a kind soul. Maybe he was tickled by the idea of having someone wait on his men. After a word with my parents, he agreed.

"From that day, I served at every performance. I took pains to do what I'd promised. But all the time, I was listening to the bards. The men of the village drank their ale. I drank the stories and the songs.

"I listened hard, Maeve. I hoarded in my memory as much as I could. In the days after a bard's visit, I sang his songs to myself as I drew water from the well. While walking with the cows, I went over the stories I'd heard. It seemed to me wonderful to hold in my head things I'd neither seen nor heard myself. I had things to muse on when I needed a lift out of a dull task or a dreary day."

Maeve grew to be a handsome young woman. She was tall. Long brown hair hung down her back.

Small though the island was, Maeve enjoyed walking its shores. She loved to watch the birds. Collecting scraps of food, she scattered them on rocks. O'Flaherty saw her. He was handy with a sling. It amused him to aim stones at birds. After he killed a couple, Maeve stopped luring them to land. Still, she loved to get outside, and she kept up her walks, relishing the cold, fresh air of early morning.

Being inside was no pleasure when her father was at home. O'Flaherty became more morose as time went on. If he was not going into the village or afar on a raid, he would rise early and settle himself in a chair by the fire. The whole morning, he would spend drinking toasted beer. He warmed a poker in the fire and plunged it into his flagon. Maeve came to hate the hiss it made and the smell that followed. Both Maeve and Nurse kept out of his way.

From his raids O'Flaherty returned with plunder. He cared nothing for amassing riches. For him, the pleasure was more in the taking than in having. Most of it he gave away, using it to buy loyalty from men in his village.

From one raid, he came back with a haul that included an old harp. Scorning it as a thing of no value, he tossed it into a corner.

That was where Maeve found it. She mended the harp. With Nurse's help, she taught herself to play. She had a beautiful voice. Soon, she was able to play while singing the songs she learned from Nurse.

O'Flaherty hated music.

"I'm out of here," he growled, whenever Maeve took up her harp and sang. He would stomp from the house and head for the village to seek his cronies.

Maeve's music carried across the water and was heard by villagers passing that way. They whispered to one another.

"That's the only sweet sound ever to come out of there."

Chapter Fifteen
Disclosure

A shriek pierced the night-time silence in the hut. It came from Ferghal's mother. The scream woke him and his grandmother. They rose and went to her bedside. She was still asleep. In the glow from the hearth, they could see sweat on her brow.

Ferghal put out a hand to wake his mother. Grandmother stopped him.

"Let her be, Ferghal. It'll be a nightmare. Best to let her sleep on."

Ferghal nodded. Grandmother fetched a cloth and mopped the brow of the sleeping woman. That done, she gestured to Ferghal for them both to return to their beds.

The cry and the nightmare behind it seemed out of keeping with the household's peaceful pattern of life. Grandmother carded and spun wool and Ferghal's mother wove it on the loom.

Together they looked after their chickens and cooked their food. The younger woman took over some of the heavier jobs-carrying water and churning butter. Ferghal became skilled with the peat spade. Soon he was able to cut more turf in a day than any other man.

But for all the calm of their routine, the nightmares kept coming. Again and again, Grandmother and Ferghal were roused by his mother's cries in the night. Strange sounds, they thought them, wordless and more like the cries of an animal.

Sometimes, Ferghal's mother woke herself. They would find her sitting up, trembling.

"What is it, mother?"

"It's nothing. Nothing at all. Back to bed with the pair of you and let me be. I shall be asleep again in no time."

But the nightmares came more often. Ferghal's mother lost a lot of sleep. She woke feeling tired. A pained look settled upon her face.

Ferghal was worried. One day when his mother had gone to deliver a length of cloth to a family at the far end of the village, he spoke with Grandmother.

"What are we to do? She can't go on like this. The nightmares are dragging her down."

"You're right, Ferghal. What it is, I don't know. At the back of this must be some trouble she's had."

Out of respect for her wish for secrecy, Grandmother had never told Ferghal how his mother had come to her hut. But she guessed the nightmares must have their cause back then.

"I shall ask her," said Ferghal.

"That'll not be easy. But you're right to try. I doubt your poor mother will have any peace until she can talk of it."

Ferghal chose his moment. A storm rolled in from the sea. The gusting winds and the lashing rain made work outside impossible. The three of them hunkered down by the fire in the hut to sit it out.

"What is it, Mother, in these dreams, that racks you so?"

"Haven't I told you? It's nothing at all. Dreams are just fancies. They'll pass. I'm sure they will."

"There's more to them than that. When you call out, you sound in pain."

"I'm sorry if I wake the two of you. But it's nothing to bother about."

"I'm not bothered about being woken. It's you I'm worried about."

"But I keep telling you. It's nothing."

Ferghal frowned. "Don't treat me like a child. I'm a man. I demand to know what's grieving you."

She looked to Grandmother. If she was appealing for support, she got none. Grandmother avoided her eyes. She too wanted an answer.

A sob rose in the younger woman's throat, which she could not keep down. Ferghal jumped to his mother's side and put his arm round her. She wept and wept. It was a while before she could speak.

"I never wanted to tell you this, but I guess it has to come out. I keep re-living the night Grandmother took me in."

"Go on," urged Ferghal. "I want to hear the whole story."

"You're an O'Rourke, Ferghal. More than that. Your father was Chief of the O'Rourkes."

She told them of O'Flaherty's attack on their village, how he had murdered her husband and slaughtered the whole clan. About the magic stone, she said nothing—save that she was the only one to escape with her life.

Ferghal listened in silence, holding his mother in his arms.

"It comes back to me now in dreams—the noise of the burning and the baying behind me as I ran away."

Ferghal hugged his mother.

"It's good it's out at last," said Grandmother. "The dreams may go on yet a while, but it'll be better for you to talk of it. Do you not agree, Ferghal?"

He was deep in thought. Grandmother's question brought him back to the moment.

"Yes. Much better."

Grandmother poured them all a bowl of milk. They put their bowls to warm on the stones at the fireside.

Turmoil reigned outside. Wind battered the hut and tore at its roof. There was turmoil too in Ferghal's mind. He stared into the fire, heeding nothing of the din of the storm.

"Am I truly the son of a Clan Chief?"

"Indeed you are. And a better man than him never walked this land."

Questions poured from him.

"How did he become Clan Chief? Who were his kin? Did his people respect him? Did he know you were with child? Am I at all like him?"

She answered her son with patience. To her surprise, she did find it a comfort to talk at last of the man she had loved and lost.

Chapter Sixteen
Decision

The days that followed Ferghal spent in a daze. His friends saw his mind was not on his work.

It was plain he was turning over something more important to him than peat.

Finally, Ferghal said one evening to his mother the words she dreaded to hear.

"I've decided, mother. I'm going back there. I have to tackle O'Flaherty."

"Oh no, Ferghal, not that. You mustn't. Don't you understand? I kept it from you because I wanted you to be free of it. The past is the past. Leave it be."

"I know why you said nothing. I don't blame you for that. But try to understand me. All this time, I've been nobody. Now, I know who I am. I have a name at last and I have to live up to it."

"But you don't need to be the slave of your history."

"I'll never be a slave. I'm going to be master of my history."

"Brave talk, my son. But what can you do? One stick doesn't make a fire. You're one young man and there's a whole clan of them. And O'Flaherty himself is a giant and a brute."

"I don't know. But if I do nothing, I'll doom my own clan to be forgotten. The O'Rourke name is mine now. I'm going to make sure people remember it."

For days, she tried to talk Ferghal out of it. Grandmother said nothing. It was not for her, she thought, to come between mother and son. She carried on with her daily tasks, doing what little she could to soothe them both in their upset.

"Very well, Ferghal." His mother sighed. "I see I can't move you," she said at last. "If you'll not waver from going, though I like it not, you'll go with my blessing, not with my curse."

At those words, mother and son fell into one another's arms.

To hold her fears at bay, Ferghal's mother busied herself getting things together for his journey. On the morning agreed for him to set out, she went early to a neighbour's hut to fetch a lump of salted cheese, so he would have something to eat on his way.

Once she was gone, Grandmother beckoned to Ferghal.

"Here, come and help me open this." It was an old box she kept by her mattress.

"Take this, my boy." She drew out a dagger. It had a long blade and a handle of polished yew.

"It belonged to my husband. I don't know what you intend, and I don't want to know. But, sure, when you face O'Flaherty, you'll not want to be empty-handed."

"Thank you, Grandmother."

"Mind you keep hold of it, Ferghal. If once you lose it, you'll have only your wits to rely on."

Chapter Seventeen
Arrival

Following his mother's directions, Ferghal reached O'Flaherty's village with daylight to spare.

He went from hut to hut, giving out he was a wayfarer looking for work. In those days, many a lone man walked the countryside, so his arrival raised no eyebrows.

Men lost their livestock in raids, defeated in feuding they lost their homes and when times were bad, they lost families to disease and famine. There were always those who had no way to live but by tramping the land, offering their toil in return for food and shelter.

At length, one man took him in. He liked the look of Ferghal and was impressed by his size.

Ferghal was keen not to disappoint his host. The next day, he worked long and hard. The man was staggered to see how much peat he cut and how well he did it. That evening, he found an old mattress for Ferghal. He invited him to stay and work for as long as he liked.

The man's wife welcomed him too. She was a weaver of cloth. He said nothing of his mother, but the woman could tell from his interest in her work that he had watched women at the loom and knew something of their skill.

Ferghal got on well with the family's neighbours. To those who asked, he gave only his name, saying he had no clan, nor had he ever known his father. Few did ask. In keeping a check on his tongue, Ferghal did not stand out. Ever since O'Flaherty had ousted his own father to make himself their Chief, the people of the clan had learned to be wary about what they said. They knew he had his spies among them.

Those spies did their work. In no time, they had told O'Flaherty of the arrival of a stranger in the village.

O'Flaherty trusted no one, not even his spies. He went to take a look at the young man for himself. And he questioned the family who had taken him in, to find out what they had gleaned about the newcomer.

Ferghal guessed who the tall figure was, stood watching him one day from the turf cutter's road. By a stack at the roadside, the man leant on a great wooden club. Ferghal kept his head down. He worked on, as if he had not noticed him.

O'Flaherty finally went on his way. From the look of him, he mused, that young man might be handy in a fight.

"But he's a nobody," he said to himself, "a man of no name. Men like that owe loyalty to no one. They can be bought for an egg. He'll not join any raid I lead. Spades, not swords, will keep his hands busy."

Chary though they were of speaking out, the villagers could not hide their discontent. They talked with fondness of the days before the O'Flahertys were hated by the clans around them.

Ferghal heard of O'Flaherty's cattle raids. He learned how some had slipped away into the hills when O'Flaherty was mustering men to take part and how afterwards, he wrought vengeance on their families.

A tall, good-looking young man, friendly in his manner, Ferghal became popular in the village.

"He's a good worker," his host's wife told her husband. "He deserves more than just meals and a mattress." She gave him a green cloak of wool she had dyed and woven herself. Ferghal was grateful, for he had brought little with him.

Several young women in the village grew interested in getting to know him better. Ferghal was courteous in response but still he kept himself to himself. Having led a solitary life, walking the countryside from an early age, he explained, he liked to spend time on his own, roaming and clambering about.

To back up what he said, Ferghal would wander off whenever he was not wanted, making sure villagers spotted him rambling over the bog and the mountain slopes beyond it. In that way, Ferghal hid his real purpose, which was to scout around the lake where O'Flaherty had built his house.

Chapter Eighteen
A Plan

The singing stopped him. Crawling through reeds fringing the lake, Ferghal pulled up and crouched there to listen to the sounds reaching across the water from the house on the island. He could make out only a few words. It was the beauty of the voice that moved him.

He would have liked to stay kneeling there in that spot to hear more but he knew he must press on. He was about to creep forward when he saw O'Flaherty striding to the shore of the island.

O'Flaherty had his wooden club strapped over his back. He paused short of the water's edge to gather himself. Then he took a run and began leaping from rock to rock, in great bounds, towards the far shore.

For all his loathing of O'Flaherty, Ferghal was impressed. Those were huge jumps, led first with one leg, then with the other. Tall and long of leg though he was himself, Ferghal doubted whether he would be up to getting across that way. O'Flaherty made it seem easy but the spans between the stones were daunting.

O'Flaherty was over. He stomped away towards the village. Ferghal knew he had little time, for he wanted to be back in the village himself before he was missed. He pulled up two reeds and knotted them together. At the water's edge, he pushed his reeds out to the first of the steppingstones.

Measuring the distance, he marked it with his teeth on the reed closest to him. He pulled the two reeds back and laid them on the ground. Stepping along them, he counted the length with his feet. All the stones, he thought, appeared to be much the same distance apart.

Ferghal flung his measure into the reed bed and set off at a run back to the village.

His plan was simple—to get over to the island unseen. O'Flaherty had much on his side. He was big, he was strong, and he was ruthless. But he counted on being unreachable on that island. If Ferghal could get across un-spied, he would have surprise on his side. That, he hoped, would shift the odds a bit in his favour. And on the island, O'Flaherty had with him none of his own men.

In the weeks that followed, when he slipped out of the village to roam the countryside, Ferghal took different routes each time but always made his way to the same place, a fold on the lower slopes of one of the mountains. In that fold was a trough of ground where he was out of sight of the village.

Ferghal heaped two piles of rocks, setting them apart a little more than the distance he had measured with the reeds. Time after time he practised leaping from one to the other. He worked particularly hard at it whenever it rained, so he might learn how to keep his footing when the rocks were slippery.

Many a fall he suffered. The men who worked the peat with him voiced surprise to see him grazed and bruised.

"However do you manage, Ferghal, to get so many scrapes and bangs?"

"I like to scramble the rocks," Ferghal replied, "to watch birds. I'm not as sure of foot up there, I guess, as I am here on the bog."

Once he had mastered the distance, Ferghal added more rock piles, stringing together a line of leaps to take at a run. He kept adding to them until he had as many as the number of the steppingstones to the island. After training himself long and hard, he was at last confident he could match O'Flaherty and get across.

Whether those heaps of stones are still there, I cannot tell. What I do know is that, in the years that followed people would go and marvel at them and try leaping for themselves. The place was ever afterwards called 'Ferghal's Rocks'.

Chapter Nineteen
A Meeting on the Island

Ferghal woke early and rose. While the rest of the household slumbered, he dressed. He tucked Grandmother's dagger under the belt round his tunic. Folding his green cloak about him, he stepped from the hut. The dogs outside knew Ferghal by now, so none barked. The village was hushed.

By the time he reached the shore of the lake, the sun was beginning to rise. A wisp of smoke curled into the sky from the house on the island. Somebody there was already awake.

Ferghal drew a deep breath. He stepped out from behind the gorse where he was crouched. There must be no hesitating now, he told himself. He would have to hope that nobody on the island would spot him. He launched into his run up, leapt from the shore and began bounding over the rocks.

He had hoped in vain. O'Flaherty himself was already sat by the fire and into his first beaker of burnt ale but Maeve had gone down to the beach to listen to the birds at dawn.

She was standing on a rock in the water when she saw Ferghal leaping towards her. She screamed. Turning in haste to jump back to the shore, she slipped and fell into the water.

Ferghal had his head down and his eyes fixed all the time on the next pile of rocks, but he heard the scream and the splash. In a glance, he saw Maeve thrashing in the water.

From practicing on the mountain, Ferghal knew there were two things he must do if he was to make all the leaps. He must stick to an even pace, and he must keep driving forward. The young woman had already gone below the water once, but he held to the same speed. If he tried to go faster, he feared, he would fall in himself.

As he landed heavily on one rock, he heard a tink and then a plop. He realised at once what those sounds told him. The impacts had shaken loose the dagger, which had fallen onto the rocks and into the water. But there was no stopping now, if he was to reach the young woman before she drowned.

Ferghal made the island. From the rock where she had fallen, he stretched an arm over the water. She had gone under a second time, but a swirl of her long hair floated on the surface. He grabbed a handful and pulled her up by that. Ferghal hauled her out and laid her down on the shore.

Maeve coughed and spluttered, while Ferghal panted. It was a while before either of them could speak.

"Who are you?" she asked.

"There'll be a time to know that. You're wet and cold. Come, I must get you inside." Without another word, Ferghal took Maeve in his arms and trudged up the beach.

It was a short way to the house. Neither of them spokes.

Maeve chided herself for a fanciful thought. On first sight of the young man, she reckoned he was Lug. Steeped in Nurse's stories and songs, for a moment she imagined Ferghal to be the god, appearing miraculously and come to rescue her from imprisonment. But she could feel the pounding of Ferghal's heart and his breath on her face. This was no god but a man. More disappointing, he was taking her back into the place where she was kept in thrall.

Ferghal was thinking too. This must be O'Flaherty's daughter. People in the village had spoken of her. He had heard her singing. But darker thoughts beset him. He no longer had surprise on his side. Worse still, he had lost the dagger. Now, he had only his own wits to rely on.

With one foot, he pushed open the door of the house and carried Maeve inside.

Chapter Twenty
The Last of the O'Rourkes

"Maeve!" Nurse cried. "What has happened?" She ran to the couple and lifted Maeve from Ferghal's arms.

"Come child. We must dry you and get clean clothes." She led Maeve to their room. O'Flaherty had risen to his feet. He glared at Ferghal.

"By the devil, how did you get here?"

"I came not by the devil, sir, but by my own legs. I leapt across, just as you do."

In O'Flaherty's mind, those words sealed Ferghal's fate. Having found a way of getting onto the island, this intruder could not be allowed to leave it alive. But first, he must find out what had made him come.

"You're the stranger that cuts the peat so well?"

"Indeed, I am."

"Come over here by the fire, boy, where I can see you better."

O'Flaherty took his seat again. At his side was a table. On it was a joint of meat, a carving knife and, beside them, an earthenware flagon and a couple of horn beakers. Ferghal crossed the room and stood in front of the fire. O'Flaherty did not invite him to sit.

"You'll have a drink with me?"

Ferghal nodded and attempted a smile. O'Flaherty poured ale into the two beakers. An iron poker jutted from the roaring fire. O'Flaherty bent down and drew it out. Its tip glowed red. He plunged the end into his ale. It hissed and sent up a puff of steam.

"I like my ale burnt. So, tell me, boy, what brings you to my house?"

Ferghal was at a loss. Planning to take O'Flaherty by surprise, he had not thought to find himself answering the man's questions. Behind O'Flaherty, hanging from a peg in the wall, hung Maeve's harp. Seeing it, Ferghal had an idea.

"When passing this place, I've heard music and song across the water. They sounded beautiful. I came to ask if I might sit and listen to your daughter."

O'Flaherty laughed.

"Songs and harps are for women." He looked Ferghal up and down. "But then, only someone as soft as a woman would dare step into O'Flaherty's house without a weapon in his hand."

By this time, Maeve and Nurse had returned. O'Flaherty ignored them. He reached out and took the carving knife. He set it closer to him on the table, watching Ferghal all the while. He enjoyed scaring people and was glad to see fear in Ferghal's eyes.

"I've heard stories in the village, sir, of your courage and strength."

"Have you now?"

"They talk to this day of your raid on the O'Rourkes."

"And what do they say, boy?"

"They say that many a Chief led his men against others but only O'Flaherty ever wiped out another clan."

O'Flaherty grinned. "Then they speak the truth. That was a night to remember alright. Those feeble O'Rourkes! They'll never steal cattle again. We burned down every hut and killed every last one of them. But fetch me the poker, boy. My ale is growing cold."

Ferghal pulled the poker from the flames.

"And do you know what, boy? O'Rourke himself had the gall to try to parley with me. I knocked him down and with this hand, I squeezed the breath out of his body. He was the last of the O'Rourke's I ever saw alive."

Ferghal was approaching, to dip the poker into O'Flaherty's ale but at those words, he leapt forward and with two lightning jabs, he stabbed the red-hot poker into both of O'Flaherty's eyes.

"No! I'm the last of the O'Rourkes and the last you'll ever see now."

Chapter Twenty-One
The Last of O'Flaherty

Away in the village, people heard O'Flaherty's bellow of pain and rage.

One hand he put to his streaming eyes. Lunging forward he swept the other in an arc before him, trying to grab Ferghal. Too late, for Ferghal had leapt beyond his reach.

O'Flaherty rose and rampaged about the room. He stumbled, this way and that, all the time bawling bitter curses upon Ferghal's head. Ferghal dodged away from him, saying nothing. Maeve and Nurse shrank back, clutching one another. They backed away every time O'Flaherty crashed near them.

It was Nurse who at last managed to quieten him.

"Hush your noise, man," she said. "Shouting will do you no good. Sit you down again. Let me bathe your eyes. I've warm water on the hearth and herbs with healing power. Who knows—we may save some sight yet?"

"Just a glimmer," said O'Flaherty. "Give me just one glimmer of light and I'll hunt that boy down. With these hands, I'll tear the dog into a hundred pieces."

She led him back to his chair. Maeve and Ferghal looked on in silence.

In the side wall of the fireplace was a small wooden door. Nurse opened it without a sound. She had her back to Maeve and Ferghal, so they could see nothing. Both hands she dipped into a box in the cupboard behind the door. Turning, she ignored the pot of water on the hearth and came behind O'Flaherty where he sat writhing on his chair.

"Hold your head up and be still," she said. "This will work upon the pain."

Nurse put her arms around O'Flaherty's head from behind. With all her strength, she pressed into his bleeding eye sockets two handfuls of salt.

The scream from O'Flaherty was louder even than his cry when Ferghal stabbed his eyes. He flailed about, sending the two beakers clattering to the floor.

One hand found the flagon. He tipped ale over his face, trying to wash the salt from his wounds.

O'Flaherty poured a torrent of abuse upon Nurse, abuse I'll not repeat, for fear of scalding the ears of those who hear this story.

"Well spoken, well spoken, O'Flaherty," shouted Nurse back at him. "You show yourself for what you are—as foul of tongue as you are of heart."

"What did you do that for, you venomous hag?"

"I'll tell you, O'Flaherty. You don't recall my husband, do you? You've hurt and killed so many. How could you remember them all? He was one of your men. He was the one whose arm you broke the morning after the O'Rourke raid. All because he wanted to show some humanity to your victims. I don't suppose you know what happened after that.

"The break never mended. Infection set in. He suffered agony for nine days before he died. While I sat at his side, I made him a promise. I said I would watch and wait. I swore to him that somehow, sometime I would find my chance to give you a taste of the pain you gave him."

Nurse sobbed. Maeve put her arms round her.

Ferghal broke his silence, stepping forward and facing O'Flaherty.

"Know now you didn't kill all the O'Rourkes. The Chief's wife escaped. I'm her son."

"Hah! So, you've had your revenges on me now." He spat out his words. "To think of it. O'Flaherty brought low by a boy and by a woman. And I mind well, girl, that you never uttered a sound or lifted a hand to help your father."

Maeve rounded his chair and stood at Ferghal's side, facing the blind man.

"Father!" she cried. "Had you ever been any sort of father to me, you might have earned some help."

O'Flaherty said nothing for a moment or two. Then he sighed.

"Maybe you're right. 'Tis a poor sort of man who doesn't know when he's beaten." After another pause, he spoke again.

"Here, boy. Let's forgive and forget. Come, shake my hand."

Ferghal stepped forward and began to stretch out his hand. Maeve nudged him aside. In one swift movement, she snatched up the bone on the table and thrust that into her father's outstretched hand, keeping hold herself of the other end.

"Ah!" O'Flaherty cackled. "While there's life in his body, O'Flaherty will crush any man who crosses him."

His iron grip closed upon the bone. Maeve tugged, pretending to be Ferghal trying to pull his hand free. There was a crunch as O'Flaherty broke the bone into splinters.

Ferghal grabbed the carving knife and drove it into O'Flaherty's heart. He slumped back in his chair. Maeve let the bone drop. O'Flaherty's fingers stayed locked on the shattered bone even in death.

Chapter Twenty-Two
A Shaking Off of Burdens

"Are you going to do away with us now?" asked Nurse. The two women clutched one another.

"You have nothing to fear from me, I promise you. But there is something I am going to do away with."

Ferghal walked to the door and picked up O'Flaherty's club. He cast it into the fire.

"There! Let that be an end to all killing."

All three stood in silence for a time, watching the flames in the grate.

At length, Nurse spoke.

"Come on, Maeve. We can't undo what's done. Let's you and me clear things up."

The two women began to retrieve beakers, to right stools and to mop spilled ale. Ferghal joined them.

"What you said," asked Maeve, "was that true? Are you really the son of O'Rourke?"

"I am—though I learned it but a short time ago."

While they busied themselves, Ferghal told Maeve and Nurse his story.

"So there are two O'Rourkes," he said, ending his tale, "myself and my mother. She never sought revenge. I can understand that. But it's done. All I wish for now is peace between us and peace between the O'Flahertys and their neighbours."

"I want that too," said Maeve. "But there's something I want first and that is to get away from this place. It's been my prison for as long as I've lived."

Their talk was interrupted by sounds of shouting from outside. People in the village had heard O'Flahertys screams. Many took no notice. They thought it no bad thing if O'Flaherty was in trouble. But those loyal to him took up their spears, swords and axes and made their way to the lake shore.

"O'Flaherty! O'Flaherty!" they called across the water. "What's amiss? Show yourself."

Maeve looked through one of the openings.

"You'd better keep out of sight for now. I'll go and talk to them."

Seeing Maeve, they fell quiet.

"O'Flaherty is dead," she shouted.

The men were silent. None of them wanted to show any reaction. They knew O'Flaherty's ways. Had he forced the girl to say this, they wondered? And was he watching them now to see who amongst his followers would rejoice at such news.

Maeve tried again.

"O'Flaherty is dead. The tyrant is dead. I am free and you are free." A couple of the men smiled.

"It is Ferghal who has rescued me. He saved my life, and he has defeated O'Flaherty." One man raised a cheer. Soon, others joined him.

Maeve called for quiet.

"I need your help now, friends. Go back to the village and share the good news. Put your weapons aside. Come back with your carts, your ropes and your crow bars. And bring your strongest people. I want you to gather all the rocks you can move and fill the spaces between these steppingstones. Make me a causeway. I'll have a good fire and a barrel of ale waiting for you when you get across."

After more cheering, the men turned and trooped back to the village. They did what Maeve had asked. Soon there was a gang heaving rocks and tipping them into the water.

At last, they were over. They crowded inside. Men were aghast to see O'Flaherty's body slumped in the chair, the knife still in his chest.

"Look your fill," said Maeve. "Though he was my father, I'm glad he's dead. He never showed himself a father to me."

A group carried the body out. They heaved it back across the causeway and onto one of the carts. Carrying it over to the edge of the bog, they buried it there in the peat under the shadow of the mountains.

Those who stayed behind clustered round the fire. Nurse, Maeve and Ferghal filled beaker after beaker from the barrel of ale.

One man pointed into the flames.

"Is that O'Flaherty's club?"

"Indeed, it is," answered Maeve. "Ferghal threw it there." She glanced at Nurse. "It'll hurt no one ever again."

The village men looked at Ferghal. More than a few wished in their hearts they had been able to muster the courage he had shown.

"Good health to Ferghal," shouted one of them and a chorus joined in the toast and the cheers.

When the hubbub had died gown, Maeve addressed them.

"There's more to tell but that will save for this evening. Go back now and fetch your families. And bring food with you, whatever you have. We'll feast this night and celebrate our freedom—yours and mine."

After more cheering and much slapping of Ferghal's back, they bustled off to the village, eager to make ready for an evening of merriment.

Chapter Twenty-Three
Revelation

The three of them set to work to make ready the feast. They spread fresh rushes on the floor. Nurse fetched out all the food they had in store. Maeve scoured the island, picking berries and mushrooms. She hauled in the nets O'Flaherty had set and collected what fish were caught. Ferghal heaved in more barrels of ale. Nurse set pans to warm by the fire.

This was a country of few trees. Peat was never enough for O'Flaherty. Whenever timber was to be had, he demanded it was his. He floated logs across the lake and built them into a great stack. Now, Ferghal went back and forth, carrying in logs to keep the fire blazing the night long.

Villagers packed into the house that night. Never before had it seen such jollity. Never had so much food and drink been swallowed there, with so little thought for stomachs or heads on the morrow.

At last, the laughter, the singing and the shouting subsided. Full and tired bodies began to slump.

"Maeve!" one of the men called out, "you said you had more to tell. Give us the tale."

Maeve stood and people hushed to listen.

"First of all, I want to say my thanks. With all my heart, I thank Nurse here. She it was who brought me up. She was my only friend, my only comforter, my only teacher for all the years O'Flaherty kept me shut here."

They drank a toast to Nurse and clapped her long. Maeve raised a hand and quietened them again.

"And I have Ferghal to thank. On those long legs of his, he leapt across the stones and set me free. But more than that, he saved my life. I fell into the lake.

It was Ferghal who pulled me out by my hair. Were it not for him, I should have drowned this day."

Another toast followed and chanting of Ferghal's name.

Ferghal rose to speak.

"What Maeve hasn't told you is how she saved me—if not from death, then from being maimed." He described to them O'Flaherty's guile in feigning a handshake of peace.

"I have thanks of my own to give," Ferghal went on. "I want to thank the family who took me in when first I came here. And I thank all of you who accepted in your village a stranger who would tell you little of himself."

More cheering broke out.

"There is more to tell," Ferghal continued. "To those who asked me, I said I didn't know my father. I spoke the truth. But I didn't tell you I knew who he was. My name is Ferghal O'Rourke. My father was the Chief of the O'Rourkes." Gasps were heard on every side. More than one hand went to the handle of a knife.

"Fear not, friends. I want only peace between us. There are some here tonight who have O'Rourke blood on their hands. But I have O'Flaherty blood on mine. So I can reproach none, nor will I."

Maeve rose and stood by Ferghal's side. She took his hand and raised their joined hands into the air for all to see.

"Look," she said. "We all have reasons to be glad O'Flaherty is no more. Ferghal killed my father. My father killed his. If the two of us can be friends, we can all be friends."

There were a few moments of silence and then the house shook with the cheering, the stamping of feet and the clapping of hands.

It was with difficulty that Maeve called the place to order.

"I have two things to ask. Go back now but come here again tomorrow. I'll spend just one more night in this house. Tomorrow, will you help me tear it down? The stones can go in the lake. We'll make the causeway broader still. But will you carry the timbers back? I'd like you to build two new huts in the village, one for Nurse and one for me."

"We will, we will," went up the cry from all sides.

Weary villagers ambled home. Maeve and Nurse retired to their room. O'Flaherty's house stood quiet for the last time.

Ferghal lay down in front of the dying embers. He did not drop straight off to sleep. Propped on one elbow, he looked into the low flicker of flame in the hearth. He turned over in his mind a thought that warmed him more than the fire—after her gesture to the crowd, Maeve had brought down their hands, but she kept her fingers entwined in his longer than she needed and longer than he had dared to hope.

Chapter Twenty-Four
Reconciliation

Strangers travelling past the lake years after were puzzled to see a causeway to an island on which stood nothing. To those who asked, local villagers told the story behind Stone House Island, the name they had given it.

The new huts for Maeve and Nurse went up in no time. Ferghal returned to the family who had taken him in.

Maeve was not content only to be free. Keen for the O'Flahertys to make peace with their neighbours, she was bent on visiting the clans round about and trying, as far as possible, to return what the O'Flahertys had stolen from them.

Many of the village men thought this was going too far. It would be hard now, they argued, to sort out what came from where. Far better, they suggested, to draw a line under the past and to leave it at that.

Maeve was not to be put off. She talked with the women of the village. They supported her.

They reminded the men they had shown themselves in recent years to be neither the bravest nor the wisest of folk. It was time for them to pay heed to their sisters, their wives and their mothers.

The women brought them round. Objects were turned in and livestock were separated, ready to be handed back.

Ferghal was eager to go and see his mother and grandmother. Maeve asked him first to join her in visiting neighbouring clans. She wanted to show the goodwill between the two of them as proof that the O'Flahertys were true in wishing to live at peace with others. Ferghal agreed at once.

They were successful. People were moved by the story Maeve and Ferghal told. They accepted apologies for past misdeeds. A good many rejoiced on learning O'Flaherty was no more. They sent people to the O'Flaherty village to fetch back what plunder they could. In the telling of their tale, Maeve and Ferghal held hands many more times.

When their journeys were done, Maeve and Ferghal returned to the village.

"Now at last, may I go back to my mother and grandmother?"

"Of course. They must be longing to see you."

"I want you to come with me, Maeve."

"Why? The family reunion is for you."

"I want them to meet the woman who is to join our family as my wife."

"If that is a question," Maeve answered, "this is an answer."

Maeve kissed Ferghal.

Ferghal's mother and grandmother were overjoyed to see him and to find him unharmed.

Thrilled to meet Maeve, they congratulated Ferghal on his choice. Ferghal and Maeve told their story one more time and never did they have keener listeners.

"I'm sorry, Grandmother. I lost the dagger you gave me. It lies now at the bottom of that lake."

"No matter, Ferghal," she said. "Where it is, it'll do harm to no man. 'Tis plain your own wits were enough."

When they had a moment together to themselves, Ferghal spoke with his mother. He asked her if she would come and live with him and Maeve. She gave him the answer he expected.

"There'll come a time for that, Ferghal. I shall not leave Grandmother. She's getting frailer and she needs more help. She looked after me when I was in need. I shall look after her to the end of her days."

Chapter Twenty-Five
A New Clan

To their surprise Ferghal and Maeve found, on their return to the O'Flaherty village, that the women had put together a feast to celebrate their union. There was much revelling that night.

The eating and drinking in time wound to a close. Maeve rose to thank everybody but before she could speak, one of the elders of the clan stepped forward.

"I have something to say," he declared. "While you've been away, we've been talking. We have a settled mind, and it falls to me to tell you what it is."

He turned towards Ferghal.

"When you came here, you proved yourself a good and hard worker. It took cunning, not only long legs, to get over to O'Flaherty's house. In facing him alone, you were brave. You have forgiven those of us who killed your people. That says a lot about the sort of man you are. And in taking Maeve to be your wife, you've shown sound judgement."

Maeve blushed. Ferghal squeezed her hand.

"For all those reasons," he said, "we're asking you, Ferghal, to be our Chief."

Cheering and clapping broke out on all sides.

It was a task for Ferghal to bring them to order so he could make himself heard.

"Thank you for those words. You have done me great honour. But I cannot agree to be your Chief."

Groans were heard all round, and some began to chant: "Chief! Chief! Chief!"

"If I became your Chief, an O'Rourke would be above the O'Flahertys. I want no more of one over the other. We've all seen where that can lead."

They listened in silence.

"I do have a proposal. If it pleases all of you, Maeve and I will share the role of Chief."

Rapturous applause broke out.

"Ferghal and Maeve! Ferghal and Maeve!" they shouted. Ferghal calmed them again.

"Thank you for your trust in us. We want this to be a new clan. The O'Flahertys and the O'Rourkes. Who knows? Before long, there may be children who are both."

Maeve went scarlet. She gave Ferghal a kick.

To Maeve's delight, no one had claimed the old harp. She tuned up and her singing brought a tear from many an eye there.

From that day, the O'Flahertys and the O'Rourkes lived with one another and with their neighbours on good terms, which matched the harmony Maeve coaxed from her harp. A new and welcome peace was enjoyed in that part of the west coast of Ireland.

There now. You have the story as I got it. I hope my tale will shorten the night for those who hear it. And when they do, let them remember me and the Connemara man who told it me and all those long gone who have passed down tales like this one.

All of You – England

Chapter One
A Winter's Tale

"Steady on, Tom."

The boy was heaping armfuls of wood onto the fire.

"We need to keep warm," said his father. "But the stack has got to see us through the winter."

They did need to keep warm. It was a midwinter evening. The morning frost had never melted. Around the cottage, the grass still crunched under foot in the middle of the day. Before dusk, the sky looked full of snow.

Tom was nine years old. It was one of his jobs to fetch wood from the stack piled against the back of their cottage. For poor families, their wood was crucial. If they were to survive the winter, they needed enough, both to keep warm and to cook their food.

Tom's father spent much of the autumn building up the stack. The Lord of the Manor forbade cottagers to cut timber in his woods. They did, though, have the right to gather any that had fallen to the ground. Tom went with his father to forage the woodland. He learned how to tell newly fallen branches from those long in the leaf litter. His father taught him too how to build a stack, placing branches so that, as it rose in height, it stood firm.

Tom and his sister, Judith, who was eleven, lived with their parents and their grandmother.

The cottage that was home was in the Feldon country.

The family rented several strips of land in an open field over Draycote way. Working with their neighbours, they planted crops of wheat, oats and barley. On the patch of land next to their cottage, they grew peas and turnips. When not tending his land, their father worked for the Lord of the Manor, coppicing trees and making pales and posts for fencing. In a corner of the cottage, he kept his axes, which he sharpened every day.

They had long since shut the chickens and geese in their pen, to be safe for the night from foxes. Supper was over. Bowls and jugs were back on their shelf and the trestle wiped clean.

Grandmother had scoured the great pot in which they cooked their pottage. It was back in its place beside the hearth. The pot's outside was black from the flames and smoke of countless fires. Its inside shone, the metal made bright by the rubbing of many hands.

Once everything was cleared away, they drew stools and a settle round the fire. Candles were expensive. For light, they made do with the glow of the burning logs. The wind outside hissed in the roof thatch. Down the chimney came the hoot of a tawny owl in a hollow tree nearby.

"Can we have a tale?" asked Judith.

Chapter Two
Toads and Frogs

Her mother smiled. There was no need for the question, but it had become a family ritual on winter evenings. Judith would ask and her mother would tell them a tale before the children went to their beds.

Grandmother sat with them, sometimes listening, sometimes dozing. In her time, she told the tales. Her daughter had learned them from her.

There were tales of fairies and witches and magic. There were tales of heroes, of journeys, of danger and of quests. Queens and goblins and animals featured in them. To the children, it seemed there must be countless tales stored somewhere in their mother's head.

"Make yourselves comfortable," she said.

Both children were already comfortable and waiting, Judith on a stool, Tom on the settle between his father and grandmother. But at their mother's words, they always shuffled in their seats. The shuffling done, their mother began her tale.

Once upon a time, it was hard to tell a toad from a frog. Toads used to have smooth, shiny skin like frogs. They had strong back legs and liked to jump as much and as far, as frogs do. They croaked like frogs too.

At that Tom did an imitation of a croaking frog, making his grandmother jump. Judith giggled.

"Thank you, Tom," said his mother. "I think we all know how a frog sounds."

There was, though, one difference between toads and frogs. Frogs were simple creatures, in the best of ways. They got on with their lives amongst themselves. They looked after the ponds. They were no bother to other creatures.

Your toad was altogether different—a wily creature, cunning, smooth of tongue and fond, not only of tricking, but also of cheating others.

Now, the time of this tale is the autumn. It was a tough one, following hard on a poor summer. The frosts had come early and often. Berries and fruits were few. Many of the insects had been finished off by the cold and wet. Every creature was finding food scarce.

"I've seen a few years like that," said grandmother.

"Too true, too true," agreed father, puffing on his pipe.

Chapter Three
Cloud Fairies

"I've told you tales of fairies before."

"Yes," said Judith. "Are they in this one too?"

"They are. Have you ever heard of Cloud Fairies?"

Both children shook their heads.

"There are folk," went on her mother, "who seldom look up at the sky. Many believe that clouds are no more than streaks and patches of mist. They are mistaken. We can't see them, but clouds are where the Cloud Fairies live."

"Are they good or bad fairies?" Judith asked.

"Well, some people complain when they send too much rain or when they hide the sun for too long. They are sometimes a nuisance, it's true. But they're good fairies. They know none of our plants would grow without rain and what we do grow would be scorched if we had blazing sun all summer long."

"So, what have they got to do with toads?" Judith asked.

"That's what I'm coming to."

The Cloud Fairies could see all sorts of creatures were struggling to find enough to eat. They felt sorry for them. The Queen of the Cloud Fairies, whose name was Nebula, called all her subjects together to talk over the problem.

"They are suffering down there," Nebula said. "I think we should do something to help them."

The Cloud Fairies agreed, and they mulled over what to do.

One of them said, "They're all finding it hard and, as winter comes on, it's only going to get harder. The ones I feel most sorry for are the birds. Some creatures can hunker down in holes or under leaves for the winter, but the birds who stay here the year long have to brave it out in the open."

"That's true," said another. "And those birds that don't find enough to eat in the day die during the night. If we're going to do anything, I suggest we do it for the birds."

Nebula welcomed that idea. Without more talk, she announced: "We shall put together a feast for the birds. You know what to do. Make everything ready and send out invitations."

Nebula set a date and got the Cloud Fairies busy preparing food for the birds.

The shortage of berries, fruit and insects was nothing to them, for they had fairy magic to wield. The Cloud Fairy Hall, a large room in one of the biggest clouds, was made ready to receive their guests.

The invitations, when they came, stirred a great flutter amongst the birds. A family of long-tailed tits could talk of nothing else as they worked their way along a hedge. They chattered about the feast to come while they searched the branches, some of them hanging upside down to look under the few leaves for something to eat.

Being full of guile, toads liked to lurk out of sight, watching and listening, in hopes of learning something they might profit by.

There was a toad skulking in the ditch at the foot of that hedge. She heard the tits talking of the feast. She listened to them making plans to meet with their comrades to fly together up to the Cloud Fairy Hall.

"So," said the Toad to herself, "if there's free food, I'm going to have some. I shall fly up there with the birds and get my share—and more than my share, if I can manage it."

"But toads can't fly," put in Judith. "They don't have wings."

"Be patient," replied her mother. "Listen to the tale and you'll find out."

Chapter Four
The Toad's Speech

The day of the feast came. The birds began to gather, making ready to set off for the Cloud Fairy Hall.

The Toad got to the meeting place before any of the birds and waited for them to arrive. As each bird flew in, she gave it a hearty greeting. The birds were cool in answer. Unhappy on finding the Toad there, they reckoned she must be up to some misChief.

When most of the birds had flocked together and before they'd had a chance to sort themselves out for leaving, the Toad puffed herself up and launched into a speech.

"My dear friends, I'd like to congratulate you all on your good fortune. This is a wretched time and you are lucky indeed to get help from the Cloud Fairies. But allow me to correct myself. It's not luck, it is merit. The Cloud Fairies are doing no more than acknowledging how richly you deserve their aid."

The birds listened. They said nothing.

"I know well," continued the Toad, "what a struggle you're having to find things to eat. I see you searching the ground, the hedgerows and the trees. I feel for you all."

Still the birds said nothing.

"It upsets me to see what a hard time you're undergoing. And believe me, friends, I do know how hard it is, for I'm not getting enough food myself. We're all suffering this autumn."

A Jay, looking at the Toad's fat body, could hold back no longer.

"Don't give us all that guff, Toad. You'll soon be finding yourself a snug hole somewhere and sleeping out the winter, cosy underground. You should try roosting the night long in a leafless tree in the middle of winter. Then you'd know what it is to suffer."

"You're right, of course, my friend," responded the Toad. "I don't know how that feels. But just imagine, will you, what I go through when frost turns the ground as hard as iron. Lying there, still and underfed, some of us freeze to death. At least, you can fluff up your feathers and flap your wings to warm yourselves in the bitter cold.

"But, forgive me, dear friends. This is not a competition. All of us need to feed up in the autumn. We can all come to grief if a hard winter catches us hungry. Solidarity is what we need in these tough times."

"I think I know what's coming," said a Robin to her neighbour.

"I came here this morning first to apologise to you all. And then to ask you to let me join you on your visit to the Cloud Fairies."

Not a word came from the birds.

"I do owe you an apology. I confess, I've not been the straightest of creatures. So I can understand you being wary of me.

"But I've changed. I'm ashamed of many of the things I've done. I know now that if you do harm to others, sooner or later, harm will come to you. Can we not put the past behind us, friends, and join together in sharing the generosity of the Cloud Fairies?"

Chapter Five
A Parliament of Birds

It was the Raven who broke the silence.

"Withdraw a while, Toad. We need to talk over what you've asked amongst ourselves."

The Toad jumped back. The Raven said nothing but stared at the Toad, tapping its claws on the branch and waiting. At last, the Toad caught on. She leapt further off, this time out of earshot.

"We need a Parliament, so we can decide this," said the Raven. "You know the rules. One at a time. And if you want to speak, flap a wing twice."

They had already agreed a truce, to last for the day of the feast. No bird was to prey upon another. Even so, as they gathered in a circle round the Raven, the Chaffinch perched away from the Sparrow hawk and the Starling kept a distance from the Peregrine.

The Raven called them to order.

"The Toad has asked if she can join the feast. We all know Toad and her ways. This may be another of her tricks. But she claims she has changed. What do you all think?"

"I wouldn't trust her one bit," said a Blackbird.

"I agree," said a Thrush. "She says she has a hard time of it. What does a Toad know of hard times? In the spring, we wear ourselves out brooding our eggs and going to and fro to feed our chicks until they fledge. The Toad lays her eggs and from that time never gives them a second thought."

"I'm not sure that's to the point," said the Raven, "what we have to decide is whether we can trust her."

The Wren flapped a wing twice to signal her wish to speak.

"As you've said, Raven, she tells us she's mended her ways. How will we know whether she has if we don't give her a chance to show us? After all, showing is better proof than telling."

"I'm with the Wren," said a Pigeon. "It would be sad if we didn't allow for any creature to change."

"There are some here who would do well to change their ways," put in a Sparrow. "The Toad has her faults but she doesn't eat other birds' eggs, like some I could name."

With these words, the Sparrow looked hard at the Magpie and the Jay. Both of them avoided her gaze and studied the sky as if they were weighing up the weather.

"Let's have none of that," said the Raven. "We aren't going to settle this by squabbling amongst ourselves."

The Raven turned to the Owl.

"What do you think?" The Owl blinked.

"What did you say?"

"I asked you," repeated the Raven, "what you think about the Toad's request."

"Uh I don't know. I'll go along with whatever the rest of you decide."

The other birds were puzzled that owls were thought to be wise. Settled in their roosts, they often saw owls perched motionless in the branches staring into the gloom of evening. They struggled to believe there was much going on behind those big, unblinking eyes. Some even remarked how fitting it was that part of an owl's call sounded like 'twit'.

None of the family was surprised this time to hear Tom let out a stream of 'Tu-whit, tu-whoos'. When he had finished, his mother took up the tale.

A Nuthatch, clinging head down to a tree trunk, looked up and suggested, "Why don't we think up a test of some sort?"

"That's a good idea," said the Raven, "but we don't have time. The Cloud Fairies are waiting on us and we're ready to go now. We're split on this one. Are you happy for me to make the decision?"

The birds were eager to get to the feast, so they wanted no more talk. They nodded their agreement.

"We've good reason to doubt Toad's word," said the Raven. "But, as some of you have said, we ought to give her a chance to show she's changed her ways. Why don't we take up the Nuthatch's idea and make this feast a test? If she behaves as she promises, we'll have learned to trust her. If she's still up to her old trickery, we'll know never to listen to her again. I can't foresee how it will turn out. But, whatever happens, I have a foreboding it will change things in a big way. Are you with me?"

Most of the birds held up a wing to vote for the Raven's plan. Some who held back at first saw the number in favour and added their votes. A few, the Chough and the Kite among them, kept their wings down, unswayed.

"Carried by a majority, then," said the Raven. "Call Toad back and I'll tell her our decision."

Chapter Six
New Names

Words of thanks gushed from the Toad, when she heard the outcome of the Parliament. She showered praise upon the birds for their wisdom.

"What is more," she added, "I can help you. I'm always picking up news wherever I can. Over time, I've learned a lot about the Cloud Fairies. I'll share what I know. That way you can be sure to do the right things when you're with them."

The Raven asked each bird to lend Toad a feather. Some were grudging but Raven was firm. They formed a line and each bird in turn handed the Toad one of its feathers. She wove them into a pair of wings and fixed them on.

"How can a toad fix on wings?" asked Tom.

His mother sighed. "Tom, this is a tale. If you can believe a toad talked, you can surely believe one fixed on a pair of wings?"

Tom smiled. His mother continued.

With a lot of flapping, she rose into the air. Pleased with herself, she looked back and grinned at the watching birds but in doing so, she slackened the speed of her wing beats. She flopped to the ground, landing in some mud with a thwack.

The birds laughed. The Toad was undaunted. Toads go after worms and slugs in the soil. They like it damp, so a bit of mud doesn't bother them.

The Toad tried again. This time she kept flapping at a steady rate. Soon, she was able to lift herself from the ground and to stay aloft.

They were ready. At a signal from the Raven, all took off and set a course for the Cloud Fairy Hall. The Toad never stopped talking the whole way. At first, many birds ignored her but they could not help becoming interested in what she had to say.

"The Cloud Fairies belong to different crews," she told them. "Each crew has its own job. One of them makes the fluffy, white clouds that sit low in the sky. Another works high up on the wispy streaks. There's a crew that does colouring too. They put in the greys, the dark blues and the blacks ready for storms."

"Like all fairies," continued the Toad, "they can make misChief. They like spreading mist in valleys and around hill tops. It's a good idea not to cross them. Some badgers once cursed them for making their tunnels damp. The Cloud Fairies got to hear of it and straight away, they sent a downpour that flooded out the badgers altogether."

"Their Queen, Nebula, may appear mild but she rules the Cloud Fairies with a firm hand. She expects her subjects and her guests, to listen to what she says and to do her bidding to the word."

It was a long flight. The hedgerow birds had a hard time, for they were used only to flitting short distances. Even the most distrusting of them found the Toad's talk helped to ease the tedium of the journey.

"Oh and there is one thing I do need to tell you about," added the Toad, as if she had just called something to mind.

"They have a custom," she said. "When they invite guests, they like each of them to choose a new name for the day. We don't want to upset them. So each of us should think of a name to use at the feast."

None of the birds had heard of this before. But the Toad was so definite, they reckoned she must know what she was talking about.

"I'll be 'Minstrel'," said the Song Thrush.

"'Guard' is the name for me," the Goose said.

"How about 'Glutton' for you?" said several birds to the Cormorant. The Cormorant made as if she hadn't heard.

The birds spent the rest of their flight thinking of names and testing them with one another. The Toad listened. She said nothing.

They were nearing the Cloud Fairy Hall, when the Jay called out.

"Why so quiet, Toad? Can't you think of a name?"

"Oh," said the Toad, as if she had forgotten about the fairies' custom. "Let me think. Yes, I'll settle for 'All of You' as my name."

Some of the birds grinned to one another. Never had they heard such a silly name.

Chapter Seven
The Feast

"Welcome, birds," said Nebula, as they landed on the steps to the Cloud Fairy Hall. "We know you have been having a tough time. So, go inside and eat your fill, one and all."

The Toad pushed her way to the front.

"Your majesty, may I first say a few words?"

Nebula nodded and moved aside. She was taken aback.

"What sort of bird is this?" she wondered to herself. "It has feathered wings and it flew up here. But where are its beak, its claws and its tail?"

The Toad poured out words of homage to the Cloud Fairies. She trumpeted their kindness. In honey terms, she said all of them would be beholden to the Cloud Fairies the winter long.

Eager though they were to get on with the feast, the birds had to admit she gave a fine speech.

The Toad was done at last. Nebula raised a hand and gestured the birds into the Hall.

"One last thing, if I may, Your Majesty," put in the Toad. "Will you remind us who you have made this feast for?"

"Why, it's for all of you," said Nebula.

The Toad turned to the birds. She smirked.

"You heard what the Queen said. The Feast is for 'All of You'. That's my name. So, it's for me."

In one bound, she cleared the steps and was inside the Hall. The birds trailed after her. They looked on, dismayed, as the Toad launched herself at the spread laid out there.

Nebula was at a loss.

"They must have chosen this odd-looking bird as their leader," she said to herself. "Perhaps it's their custom to give the leader first picking."

Unwilling to embarrass her guests, she signalled to the Cloud fairies and they withdrew.

"Don't worry," spluttered the Toad over her shoulder, her mouth stuffed with earthworms. "When I'm done, they'll be something left for the rest of you."

The birds were outraged. Open-beaked, they watched the Toad move from dish to dish, guzzling without pause.

And many were the dishes, all of them brimming with food. There were hawthorn and elder berries piled up for the Blackbird and seeds in plenty for all the Finches—seeds of dandelion, chickweed, thistle and teasel. A heap of acorns had been collected for the Jay.

This feast was the work of fairy magic, so there was food from different seasons of the year, not just the autumn.

A dish of moth caterpillars had been laid out for the Wren. Ants were there for the Woodpecker, leatherjackets for the Starling and a pile of snails for the Thrush.

Live food had been served too—voles for the Owl, mice for the Kestrel and sticklebacks for the Heron.

The Toad lurched this way and that, grabbing items and cramming them into her mouth. She knocked dishes over in her haste, spilling pondweed and fruit in all directions. In no time, the floor of the Hall was littered with spiders, beetles, aphids and hazelnuts.

Chapter Eight
Departure

The birds shook their heads in disgust at the guile and the greed of the Toad.

At length, she was full. She lay on the floor, so bloated she could hardly move.

The birds stepped forward and began to pick over the mess the Toad had strewn everywhere. Anger had taken away their appetites but out of courtesy to the Cloud Fairies and to leave the Hall clean, they finished what little the Toad had left.

That done, they made ready to leave. Without passing a word between them, they were all of one mind. They formed a line. Each bird, as it came to the front, plucked its own feather from the Toad's wings and turned its back on her in silence.

Drowsy as she was, the Toad kept her brain working. She knew she would soon be stranded on that cloud without wings to fly or even to glide, back to earth. She came up with a plan.

"My dear friends," she said in a fawning voice, "I did say there'd be some left for the rest of you and so there was. I kept my word. What is more, my flattering speech to Nebula may have won her over to give you another feast again next year. I'm not asking for much in return. Just that you take a message to my husband."

The birds kept silent. As each one came before her to snatch back its feather, she renewed her plea.

"No," said the Robin.

"You must be joking," snapped the Linnet.

The Dunnock and the Coot said together, "Forget it."

Many of the birds so loathed the Toad for her trickery, they could not bring themselves to answer her.

Last of all came the Lapwing. She was the Toad's final chance. She begged the Lapwing to have pity.

"Just say a few words to my husband. That's all I want you to do."

The Lapwing looked hard at the Toad. After a pause, she answered.

"What do you want me to say?"

"Ah," beamed the Toad, "a bird with a heart. Find my husband and tell him to gather as much moss as he can. He is to spread a deep layer of moss in a circle on the flat ground near our place. I've long thought you were a deal more clever than the other birds, my friend. I shall not forget this."

Chapter Nine
The Jump

"Now, your Toad," continued the children's mother, "was not the only creature given to tricking others."

Judith grinned. Tom looked at her, puzzled.

"Have you guessed what I'm going to say?" Judith nodded.

"Go on, then. Tell your brother."

"Lapwings make their nests on the ground," said Judith.

"I know that," snapped Tom.

"But listen," his sister told him. "Sometimes, a mother Lapwing will be sitting on a nest and she spots a fox. If she thinks he's coming her way, she'll leave the nest. She moves off and starts flapping about on the ground. She wants the fox to think she's injured. Then, he'll go after her and away from the nest."

Judith's mother took up the tale.

The Lapwing found the Toad's husband.

"I have a message for you from your wife." she told him. "She asks you to collect branches of blackthorn. The longer and sharper the spines are, the better. You're to spread them on that flat space over there, making a circle. Then she wants you to gather heaps of moss. You're to spread the moss over the blackthorn. The spines must all be hidden."

That Toad, no less crafty than his wife, smiled. He didn't know what she was up to. But her plan to hide blackthorn under a covering of moss made him sure this must be another of her tricks. He guessed too that the Lapwing was in the dark, so he said nothing.

The Lapwing flew off. The Toad set about his task. He knew where to find blackthorn with the most fearsome spines.

Up on the cloud, his wife waited. Having gorged herself to bursting, she was happy to sit and let the food go down. Between short dozes, she looked over the edge. At last, she saw it, a green target on the ground far below. She crawled to the edge, steadied herself and jumped.

Chapter Ten
The Landing

Even the Cloud Fairies, way up in the sky, heard the Toad's scream when she hit the ground.

"Did she die?" asked Tom.

"No, she didn't. But she was in a bad way. The fall broke both her back legs. It was a long time before her bones knitted together again. And that was not the worst of it. Blackthorn is nasty stuff."

"It's more than nasty," put in their father. He leant forward and held one hand towards the glow of the fire.

"It's two years since I had a blackthorn spine go into this joint." He waggled his finger. "I was kneeling and I bent to pick up an axe. I lost balance, put my hand out and brought it down, with all my weight, onto a broken sprig of blackthorn on the ground. There's something about blackthorn. The joint swelled. It throbbed red for a week. And look."

He held his other hand by it to show the difference. "After all this time, it's never gone back to the size of the other one. There's nothing in the world more vicious than blackthorn."

"Yes, there is."

They all turned to Grandmother. They had thought her asleep.

"There's one thing more vicious," she said. "Poverty."

The children looked at one another, not knowing what to say. Their parents avoided one another's gaze. Both of them stared at the pot in the hearth. Meals beyond number had been cooked in that pot. It had served them feasts when times were good but they remembered thin fare too, when foul weather, crop failure and rent rises had pinched and gripped the family.

Their mother took up the story.

The Toad was pricked all over, first when she landed and then as she writhed in agony from the pain in her legs.

"Do you remember what I said at the start of the tale?" Judith and Tom nodded.

Once it was hard to tell a frog and a toad apart. This Toad was the mother of all the toads we find today. They take after her. That's why they now differ so from frogs.

Her broken bones did heal at last but her back legs were never the same again. Toads mostly crawl now. If they do ever jump, it's only a feeble hop. They can no longer leap like a frog. Because they're less active, they've grown fatter than frogs too.

Toads are covered all over now with pimples. Those are the scars left by the blackthorn spines. The bright, glistening skin they used to have has become dull and lumpy.

And it's not only their bodies that have changed. Toads are still greedy, it's true. They'll eat all the time, if there's food around. But now they keep to themselves. They'll squat for hours without moving. Their days of hopping about to eavesdrop and to trick others are long gone.

There you have it. The Raven was right. Letting the Toad go to the feast did change things in a big way. The Toad was right, too. The Lapwing was clever and the Toad had good reason never to forget it.

Chapter Eleven
To Bed

"Time to turn in," said their father. "Mother has ale to brew tomorrow and I've got a charcoal pit to fill."

Having set down his pipe, he gave Grandmother his arm and helped her from the settle. Their mother put more wood on the fire to keep it burning the night long.

Judith and Tom pulled out their pallets from the corner where they were stacked. The cottage was a single room. The children slept on the floor in front of the fire. Their father had made a wattle screen down one side of the space. The adults slept behind that.

Lying awake, the children listened to cracks and hisses from the grate as the fresh logs began to burn. They heard scratching noises overhead. The family had settled down for the night but up in the thatch, a couple of mice were stirring.

From time to time, the flickering light of the flames was caught by the blade of one of her father's axes. Judith watched the glint flitting across the cottage wall. She wondered. At the end of the summer, there were always rooks' feathers on the ground. If she collected them, could she make a pair of wings for herself?

Tom gazed at the pot in the hearth. It turned his mind to tomorrow's brewing. Drawing the water would be cold work in this weather. But there was something to look forward to. It was his job to mind the pot on the fire as the water came to the boil. He enjoyed pouring in the malt and the oats. The smell was not pleasing but the warmth, the sound of the bubbling and the swirling patterns he stirred with the ladle—they made up for it.

Their thoughts did not keep the children awake for long. Soon, they were asleep. They did not hear the owl. From its perch in the hollow tree, it hooted again. Owls too like frogs more than toads. For them, it is a matter of taste.

Death in a Shell – Germany

Chapter One
A Decision

Once upon a time, there was a young man who clung too much to his mother. His name was Albrecht and he lived in a cottage on the coast of Germany. Shaded by pine trees, the cottage sat behind sand dunes on a stretch of shore washed by the Baltic Sea.

From boyhood, Albrecht enjoyed walking along the beach, He developed a keen eye at spotting things amongst the rocks and on the sand. Stones veined with lines of quartz, razor shells, crabs' claws—all of them he pocketed and took home to show his parents.

Some of his finds were of use to the family. The pine trees dropped plenty of twigs and branches but wood that burned longer and hotter was often washed up on the beach. Albrecht sometimes returned from his rambles with arms full of driftwood to feed their stove.

Here and there on the beach, Albrecht found little balls of tar. His father was a crewman on a local fishing boat. The boat often sprung leaks. The crew were grateful to get tar to plug them.

The boat, like many along that coast, went to sea following the shoals of herring. The master of the boat sold the herring in the market of the nearby town. If they made a good catch, he paid his crew well. If not, Albrecht's family and all the other families, had a lean time.

The Baltic, as every sea, posed dangers to those who sought their living from it. In the winter, there was fog and sea ice. The gales of autumn were wild.

One autumn night, the boat was caught in a storm. Albrecht's father was swept overboard by a wave. His mates turned the boat around. They shone their lanterns on the water but in the dark and with rain pelting in their faces, they could not find him. The wind increased and the waves heaved higher and higher. For their own safety, they were forced to run for shelter back to the harbour.

His father had been away a lot during Albrecht's boyhood years. Many of the fishing trips lasted for days. Albrecht had grown close to his mother. He was a great support to her in her grief.

Albrecht loved walking and searching along the beach but as the years went by what he came to love even more was that time in the early evening when, with supper eaten and cleared away, he and his mother sat together at their table and chatted.

One evening, when Albrecht was approaching manhood, his mother wore a serious face.

"We have to talk, Albrecht."

He guessed what was coming and got in first.

"I'm not going to sea, mother."

"Albrecht, you know your father counted on you following him onto the crew."

"Maybe, but that's not the life for me."

"Why ever not? You're a young man now. You're big and strong. You're more than up to it."

"I love you, mother. I'm not going to leave you."

"I know you do, son. And that means everything to me. But I can look after myself on my own here. Won't you give it try?"

"It's no good. You'll not persuade me."

His mother threw up her hands.

"So, tell me. How are we going to get by?"

"We have the duck and our geese. I can take eggs to the market and sometimes one of the birds. And I'll sell what I find on the beach."

She frowned. "What do we do when they don't lay? And what kind of a living do you call that, selling bits of firewood?"

"I'm going to stay here with you, mother," said Albrecht, "and I'll keep my feet on dry land. The sea has more to give than herrings and firewood."

Chapter Two
The Bounty of the Baltic

Albrecht was right. The beach did yield a bounty richer than kindling.

In those days, the Baltic was a busy sea. Cargo ships crossed it in all directions. Traders from the north brought furs. Eastern merchants came laden with honey, wax and timber. The west sent bales of wool and cloth. Barrels of salt and beer were carried from the south.

Although they sailed bigger and stronger craft than the fishing boat on which Albrecht's father had served, the crews of those merchant ships still had much to fear when storms fell upon them. To make more profit, captains loaded their vessels as fully as they could but when the winds began to rage they often had to jettison some of their freight to reduce the risk of capsizing. They threw overboard the barrels and the timber they had lashed on deck, for fear of being top-heavy.

Wherever rich merchants ply their trade, there will be pirates who pursue them. In their flight, captains would throw some of their goods overboard to lighten their vessels for greater speed. It was better, they thought, to forego some profit than to be caught and held prisoner for ransom, be sold into slavery or even pitched over the side to drown.

Some of the things jettisoned went straight to the bottom. Most were spoiled by sea water. But barrels and timber were often carried to land by the tides. The wood was of all sizes and kinds, from small pieces, to planks and sometimes even beams. And in all conditions, too, depending on how long it had been in the water.

The other harvest of those shores was amber. The shells and stones attracted Albrecht when he was a boy. But from time to time, he found bits of amber in the sand.

He thought it odd stuff. It felt light and warm to touch. Already an habitual collector, he dropped the pieces into the cloth bag slung over his shoulder.

"What do you think these are, mother?"

One evening, as they sat together, the young Albrecht spread a handful of them onto the table.

"They're amber."

"What's that?"

"Come outside. I'll show you."

She led the boy to the pine trees. Peering at their trunks, she found what she was searching for.

"Look at that." She pointed to a sticky trail which dribbled down the bark of one of the trees.

It ended in a shiny, golden blob.

"That's resin. It's like the blood of the tree. Often, when it's warm, it oozes out of a crack and runs down the trunk. Eventually, it sets. After a long time, it drops off and goes hard. That's what amber is, old bits of tree resin become solid."

"But how does it get into the water? There aren't any trees under the sea."

"It needs somebody cleverer than me, Albrecht, to tell you that."

Albrecht poked the blob of resin.

His mother laughed. "There. Now, you know it's even stickier than the tar you sometimes bring back."

"Come on in, now," she said. "It's time you were in bed—once, that is, you've scrubbed those fingers."

Chapter Three
The Timber Trade

Albrecht's mother was right about her son. The boy grew into a big and strong young man. But Albrecht was eager to prove her wrong in doubting he would be able to support them both from what he picked up along the shore.

Albrecht collected the barrels, the planks and the beams that washed up. Some of it was wood of quality. Even broken barrels often yielded whole staves that could be salvaged.

All his father's tools were still in the cottage. He sawed off the damaged ends of timbers.

With a chisel, he chipped away barnacles and he planned rough surfaces back to smoothness.

He was not one to be content to wait for the tides to bring timber to land. Many a time, his keen eyes spotted pieces wallowing in the sea some way off shore. He was reluctant to see the current carry them off to be beached far away along the coast.

When Albrecht's father drowned, his son made two decisions—first, that he was not going to be a fisherman and, second, that he would teach himself to swim.

It was a challenge. Sometimes, struggling out of his depth, he frightened himself. As he thrashed about in the water, he swallowed many a salty mouthful. But gradually, he caught the knack. With practice, he became a powerful swimmer and gained the confidence to venture far out from the beach. He was strong enough to battle the waves and tough enough to endure the cold of the water.

Sometimes, he swam out to a piece of wood and towed it back to shore. On other occasions, he anchored one end of a long rope under a boulder. Letting out the coil as he swam from the beach, he tied the other end to any timber too heavy or unwieldy for him to drag through the waves. Back on the sand, he hauled it in.

A little way along the coast, at the mouth of the River Trave, there was a harbour. It gave shelter and mooring to fishing boats and merchant ships which served the city of Lübeck, further inland. The harbour quays were always busy with men at work, many of them doing repairs on their vessels.

One morning, Albrecht picked three of the best planks he had collected, put them over his shoulder and walked to the harbour. He toured the quays, stopping to talk with seamen at their work. Several complimented him on his strength in carrying such a weight so far. Albrecht sold all of it. The wood was good stuff. And he was willing to accept lower prices than were charged by the city's timber merchants.

It was a happy young man who walked back to the cottage that day. Albrecht loved to look for the flowers which grew in the sand amongst the grasses and the sedges. At that time of the year, some of the green clumps were dotted with tiny blooms. Most of them were white but by searching he found some tinged with purple. He picked a bunch.

His mother was busy inside when he got home. Albrecht strode in with a smile on his face.

"Here, some flowers for the best mother in the world."

Before she could say a word, he wrapped his arms round her and gave her a hug.

"To what do I owe this?" she asked.

"To this," replied Albrecht and he slapped three silver coins on the table. He told her how he had sold his wood.

"Didn't I say there was money to be got from what the sea washes up? What's more, several men at the harbour said they'd be happy to look at any timber I bring them."

"You've done well, son. I was wrong to doubt you."

"It's not just me. We've done well. And together we're going to do even better. There's no reason now why we should ever be parted."

Albrecht's mother smiled but she said nothing.

Albrecht began to make regular trips to the harbour. Soon, he was well known by the crews of the vessels that tied up there. Often, when he'd sold all he had, he helped men with their repairs. He began to gain some skill at carpentry himself.

In one of the quayside warehouses, a cooper had his business. He made, sold and repaired barrels. A lot of work goes into the cutting and shaping of wood to make a barrel. The cooper paid well for the salvaged staves Albrecht took him.

With some of his earnings, Albrecht bought a hand cart. On that he was able to take more and bigger timbers to the harbour. Some of the wood he used to build himself a shed against the side of the cottage. There he dried, cleaned and stowed what he found.

Chapter Four
Precious Amber

"Do you ever pick up anything else on the beach?" a man asked one day, as they stood talking on the quay, their deal agreed.

"Sometimes I find these," said Albrecht. From his bag, he took three or four pieces of amber.

"A good piece of that will fetch more than I've paid you for that length of oak."

"Really?"

"Yes, I'm not jesting. It's valuable stuff. You won't get any interest here, mind you. But take it to Lübeck and you'll find dealers there who'll pay well for it."

"What do they want it for?"

"Lots of things. Small pieces go to be made into jewellery—earrings, necklaces, rings and the like. Bigger bits they fashion into dice, chessmen, knife handles. And amber makes good rosary beads."

"You seem to know a lot about it."

"I'm no expert. It's not my line. But I did once serve on the ship of a merchant who traded out East. We used to come back with silks and spices. One of the things we traded them for was amber. Mind you, it had to be top stuff. Some of these pieces won't do."

"Why not?"

"Look at them. They're cloudy. That comes from the air bubbles trapped in the resin. What people want is the clear stuff. And they want it polished, not dull."

"I'm off to Lübeck tomorrow," Albrecht announced when he got home.

"Whatever for?"

Over supper, he shared with his mother what he had learned at the harbour.

"We have work to do," he said, as soon as they had cleared away the supper things. He spread the whole of his amber collection on the table. From a cupboard, his mother fetched a pot of beeswax and some rags she saved for dusters. They worked together cleaning and polishing the pieces.

"My favourites," said Albrecht, "are the bits with the flies and wasps trapped inside them. Those creatures will never rot away. Preserved in there, they'll live forever."

"Nothing lives forever, Albrecht," replied his mother. "They're lifeless bodies. For us to be able to see them now, they first had to die."

Chapter Five
Lübeck

"Here, put these in your bag," said Albrecht's mother. "There's bread, cheese and sausage. You'll need something to eat. You don't want to be paying Lübeck prices." Albrecht had risen early for his walk to the city.

"Are you sure you're going to be alright?" he asked. "I'd never forgive myself if anything happened to you when I wasn't here."

"Stop fussing. Of course I'll be alright. How do you think I managed when your father was away?"

It was a long tramp up river. Trade had always been Lübeck's business. Its merchants felt secure siting their homes and warehouses well inland, beyond the reach of the pirates who raided the coast.

On entering the city, Albrecht made for the market square. Sat on the wall of a fountain, he ate the food his mother had given him. Having satisfied his hunger, he walked round the market stalls and chatted to stall holders. Thirsty after his trek, he stepped into an inn for a beer. There, he took the opportunity to talk with fellow drinkers. Albrecht asked about Lübeck's dealers in amber.

He heard tales of sharp practice.

"If you shake hands with that one," a man told him, "be sure you count your fingers, to check you've still got them all."

But in talk of the amber trade, one name kept coming up, of a man respected for his honesty in dealing with people. Albrecht got directions to the man's house, in a street off the market square. He knocked. A young woman answered the door.

"What can I do for you, sir?"

"I'm told a dealer lives here. I'd like to speak with him, if I may."

"May I ask your business, sir?"

"I have some amber he may wish to buy."

"Please step inside, sir. My father has somebody with him. But if you'll wait, I'm sure he won't be long."

Albrecht sat on a bench in the passage, which ran from the front to the back of the house. He did not have to wait long. A door off the passage opened and two men came out. One left and at the sound of the front door closing, the young woman returned.

"Father, this young man would like to talk to you about amber."

"Come in, sir," he said.

Albrecht explained his purpose. He spread the contents of his bag on the table between them. The dealer examined the pieces one by one in silence. He rubbed them between his fingers, peered into them and held them up to the light of the window. He questioned Albrecht about how he came by the amber. He always took care, he said, to be sure about the origin of anything offered to him. At last, he sat back in his chair.

"You have some good pieces here, sir. I would be interested in buying them from you. May I ask, have you sold amber before?"

"No, I haven't."

"I ask that not because I want to draw on your inexperience. If we are to do business with one another, I need you to understand what I offer on my side."

"Go on," said Albrecht.

"You could take your amber and try to sell it directly to people who want it, without going through a dealer."

"I suppose I could."

"What I offer you is contacts. I deal in many things but I have been buying and selling amber in these parts for a long time. Over the years, I have built up many contacts. I have a network of craftsmen who are skilled at cutting amber to shape, at polishing it and fixing it in mounts. I know the men and women, not just in this city but round about, who are willing to spend their money on amber products.

"Most of them don't favour the pieces with spiders, beetles and bees trapped in them. But I also know wealthy collectors who are intrigued by such things. They like to have good specimens to display in their cabinets. I'm in touch too with the barges which take goods from here further inland.

"There are many communities far from our coast where amber from the Baltic is appreciated. Because of those contacts, I can pay well for good pieces.

But I charge for my contacts. That's the profit I take for myself from each deal. You understand me, sir?"

"Yes, that seems only fair."

"I'm glad you think so. What I promise is that I'll tell you if the price of amber goes down and I'll tell you too if I see it rise."

They needed no more talk. The dealer offered a sum and Albrecht accepted it. They shook hands.

The dealer's daughter must have stayed within earshot, for when she heard her father open the door of his room, she was there in the passage to show Albrecht out.

His business done, Albrecht had a long walk home ahead of him. But he put thoughts of his mother before his anxiety to get on his way. He returned to the market square to seek a stall which had caught his eye earlier.

Albrecht's mother had been a skilled lace maker. On many an evening, she used to sit working at her cushion, her pins and her bobbins. But age had dimmed her eyes and she had been forced to put lace aside.

Albrecht found the stall. Lace and linens of all kinds were laid out on the trestle top and hung from its awning. He chose a lace cap.

"For a young lady, perhaps?" asked the woman on the stall. Albrecht frowned.

"No, for my mother."

He set off, following the course of the river. The 'groak, groak' of a pair of ravens soaring overhead was a welcome sound. They roosted on the cliffs, so their calls told him he was nearing the coast.

Light was fading when he reached the cottage. He gave his mother a hug.

"A good day, son?"

"Very good. And I've got something for you." He drew the lace cap from his bag.

"Oh it's beautiful. But you shouldn't have, Albrecht. That must have cost a lot of money."

"For you, mother, only the best will do."

Chapter Six
Prosperity and Decline

That was the first of many trips Albrecht made to Lübeck. It was a small place in those days. People were curious and quickly got to know one another's business. Albrecht's visits to the dealer and the things he bought in the market were noted and talked about.

Albrecht's trading thrived, both in amber and timber. He saved enough to swap his hand cart for a horse and wagon. Some of the wood he salvaged, he set aside. He turned the shed on the side of the cottage into a workshop. A new stove meant he could busy himself in the workshop in all weathers and it was a help too in drying waterlogged timber.

Albrecht bought new tools to add to those left by his father. He discovered he had a flair for making and repairing things. The money he earned for doing that added to what he got from his trading in Lübeck and at the harbour, so that he was able to buy more ducks and geese and even a pig.

As Albrecht flourished, his mother declined. Walking became a struggle. Albrecht would set the fire for her in the morning before he went out. It lasted to the middle of the day. He tried always to return then, to prepare something for her to eat and to bank up the fire. His mother spent most of her time now sat by the hearth. No longer able to bustle about, she felt the cold, even on mild days.

"We need to talk, Albrecht," she said one evening.

"What about?"

"I'm not going to be around forever and you—"

"Nonsense," he interrupted. "I don't want to hear you talking like that."

"Listen to me, will you," she said. "It's time you started thinking about your own future."

"I do and look how well we're doing."

"I don't mean that. Most young men of your age have moved away and started to make lives of their own. You're stuck out here looking after me. Haven't you ever thought about setting yourself up in Lübeck?"

"Suppose I did," replied Albrecht, "and, mind you, I'm not saying for one moment I want to but, suppose I did, would you come with me?"

"Oh, Albrecht, you know I couldn't leave this place. Your father built the cottage with his own hands. I'll never leave it."

"That settles it then," said Albrecht. "If you're staying here, I'm staying here. I couldn't bear the thought of being parted from you."

His mother said nothing. She had not told him what was really in her heart. Above all else, she wanted to see her son happily married and bring grandchildren to her before she died. She realised she was getting nowhere and gave up.

Albrecht's mother was not the only woman thinking about his future. The dealer's daughter made sure she knew from her father when Albrecht was to pay a call. On those days, she put on her best cap and a clean pinafore. Letting him in and showing him out, she smiled and tried to draw him in talk.

In one of those chats at the doorway, she asked Albrecht if he had ever thought of suggesting to her father that the two of them might go into partnership. She had no mandate from her father for raising that. Indeed, he would have been cross if he had found out. In reality, it was a partnership with her, not with her father, that she had in mind.

In response, Albrecht was polite and friendly. He caught her drift but he made it clear he was not interested in taking their friendship further. There was only one woman in his life and that was his mother.

One afternoon, Albrecht crossed the market square on his way to the dealer's house. A group of young men were lounging on some bales of cloth. As Albrecht walked past, one of them asked.

"Are you getting anywhere with the dealer's daughter?" Albrecht ignored the question and kept walking.

The group sniggered. The young man said in a loud voice: "He might do better if he bought presents for her, instead of for his mother." Albrecht stopped. He turned and walked back to the huddle.

"I don't know you, friend," said Albrecht, smiling at the young man. "So I don't know why you want to mock me. But I like a laugh myself. To show I bear no ill feeling, here, let me give you a hug."

The young man was startled but before he could step back, Albrecht embraced him, pinning his arms to his sides. Albrecht tightened his grip and then tightened it still more. The young man went red in the face and began to gasp for breath.

Albrecht lifted him off his feet. The rest of the bunch looked on openmouthed. Albrecht barged through them, carrying the joker. He strode to the fountain in the middle of the square. Heaving him over the rim, he dropped the young man into the water. The stall holders round about cheered and clapped. From that day, no one in the city taunted Albrecht.

Albrecht's strength was in its prime but his mother was becoming ever weaker. When he went to Lübeck for the day, he paid a woman from the town by the harbour to sit with her. She spent more time dozing in her chair. Soon, her legs went altogether and she kept to her bed.

The dealer's daughter was not one to follow a hopeless cause. Soon, Albrecht learned she was betrothed to the choirmaster of the big church in Lübeck. In time, the dealer was blessed with the grandchildren Albrecht's mother had longed for.

Chapter Seven
Parting Words

Albrecht was an early riser, especially on days when there was an early high tide. He was eager to get out along the beach to see what the waves had washed in.

His first job of the day was to get the fire going. Once it was well ablaze, he hung a pan over it and warmed some weak beer for them both.

A day came when Albrecht found it hard to rouse his mother from her sleep. He knelt at her bedside with a beaker in his hand.

"Here, mother, have your drink. It'll set you up for the day."

"I can't, Albrecht."

"What's wrong?"

"I really don't feel good."

"Well, have a drink. Just a little. It'll make you feel better."

She took a few sips. That was all she could manage. It was as much as she could do to raise her head from the pillow.

"I'll stay with you today, mother."

"There's no need, Albrecht. You go." It strained her even to speak and she panted for breath.

"But you're ill. I can look after you."

"I'm not ill, Albrecht. I'm old and tired. No amount of looking after is going to change that. My end is near."

"Don't say that, mother. I couldn't bear for you to leave me."

His mother sighed. "Albrecht, I'm an old, old woman. You're a young man with your whole life before you. This cottage will be yours. Maybe you'll take a wife to share it with you."

"No, mother, I only want you."

"I'll not argue with you anymore. Death is coming for me. I'm sure of that. I'm tired now. I want to sleep. Go about your work. And leave me be."

She closed her eyes and turned her face to the wall.

"I'll be back in the middle of the day to bank up the fire," said Albrecht. He bent over and kissed her cheek.

Albrecht slung his bag over his shoulder and pulled the cottage door to behind him. The sun was rising far out over the sea but as he set off, his mood was dark.

Chapter Eight
Death Comes

Downcast though he felt, Albrecht was alert as he walked along the shore.

To his surprise, he saw a figure in the distance, walking his way. It was unusual for anybody else to be there that early in the morning. Albrecht was wary. Sometimes, pirates would land one or two men by boat to scout an area, looking for a merchant's house to sack or a village to raid.

The man continued to approach. Albrecht could see he had something over his shoulder. It might be a spear or a pike. At that distance, he couldn't make it out. Albrecht grew more suspicious. The man wore a long cloak and had pulled its hood down over his head, hiding his face.

Albrecht kept to his usual pace. He held his head down as if looking at the water but all the time, he glanced at the figure coming towards him.

Soon, the man was close enough for Albrecht to see he carried a scythe on his shoulder.

Albrecht thought that odd, for harvest time was still some way off.

They drew near one another. Under the hood, Albrecht could now see it was an old man, with a long grey beard. His cloak was ragged. The scythe matched the cloak, for its blade bore the marks of much use.

"Good morning, young man."

"Good morning," Albrecht replied, watching the old man.

"Can you tell me? Am I going the right way? I'm looking for a cottage by some pine trees. I have a call to pay there on an old lady."

His mother's words that morning flashed through Albrecht's mind.

"Death is coming for me," she had said. He lunged at the figure, grabbed the scythe and hurled it to the ground.

Death glared at Albrecht. "You're making a big mistake. There's nothing you can do to stop me."

"We'll see about that," shouted Albrecht. He knew it was either Death or his mother and he was determined that Death would be the one to die.

Albrecht leapt at him, knocking Death down and landing with all his weight upon him. He clamped both his hands around his neck and squeezed with all the strength at his command.

To Albrecht's astonishment, he felt Death's neck shrinking in his hands. As he tightened his grip, instead of resisting, the flesh became softer and more compacted.

He knew he had already done enough to kill any ordinary man. This was no ordinary man. Albrecht let go of Death's neck and wrapped his arms around his body, to hug the last breath out of him. But again, as he tightened his embrace, he felt Death's body growing smaller and softer in his arms. He strained his muscles all the more.

In a moment, Death was no bigger than a dog and moments later, the size of a rabbit. For all his amazement, Albrecht would not let go. Perhaps I can crush him to nothing, he wondered. He squeezed and squeezed until at last Death was the size of a pea. Albrecht held Death in one fist. He clenched it with all his might but that was as small as death would go. The old man was a tiny figure squirming under Albrecht's fingers.

"What do I do now?" Albrecht pondered. "If I let him go, he's sure to return to his normal size."

He looked around him. He spotted a whelk shell lying on the sand. The whelk had long since died. The shell was empty, bleached white by the sun and by the tides.

Albrecht picked it up. With care, he rammed death into the shell and clamped his thumb over the open end. Walking on a little way, he found a tar ball. He squeezed tar into the shell to seal it.

There was enough to shape it into a ball around the shell, with only the point of its spiral sticking out.

With all his power, Albrecht hurled the shell as far out into the sea as he could. He watched the splash as it fell into the water and sank.

"There!" he said aloud. "See if you can get out of that."

Albrecht went back and picked up Death's scythe.

A bit of work on this, he thought to himself, *and it'll fetch a good price in the market.*

He carried on along the beach. He found nothing of any worth. His meeting with Death took away his zeal for searching the shore, so he turned and made his way back to the cottage.

Chapter Nine
Recovery

Albrecht had been astounded to meet Death but he had more surprises to come that day.

Nearing home, he was startled to see smoke billowing from the cottage chimney.

That's strange, he thought. *The fire should have died down by now. Whoever can have banked it up?*

He stepped inside and there stood his mother. She wore her apron and had rolled up her sleeves, just as she used to when she bustled about her chores.

"You're up," he said. "How come? You were in bed and in a bad way when I went out."

"You tell me," she replied. "I'm as mystified as you. One moment I was lying there panting, I was finding it harder and harder to breathe. The next moment, I felt as if all my weariness had been blown away. I feel ten years younger. I just had to get up and get on."

"Well!" was all Albrecht could say.

"See. I've built the fire back up. You've looked after me well, Albrecht. But I can tell, you've had to let things go a bit. I've been giving the place a good clean and a tidy up."

Albrecht beamed. He took his mother in his arms and hugged her. She did not see the thoughtful look on his face. He decided to say nothing about his meeting with Death.

"Look at this." Albrecht held up the scythe. "I found it on the beach. I'm going to do it up."

"Let's have some lunch first," she said. "I can tell I haven't eaten well for days. I'm starving."

There was lentil soup left in a pot. She put some by the fire to warm. Albrecht fetched some cheese and a sausage.

Those who live close to a beach have to deal with its flies. The tides wash seaweed ashore and dump it in lines along the high water mark. The seaweed rots, particularly when it is warm and that attracts flies.

Smack! A fly had landed on the table. Albrecht was too quick for it. He brought his hand hard down. But when he took his hand away, the fly shook its wings and buzzed off to the cottage window.

Albrecht's mother chuckled. "You're losing your touch, son."

"I don't think so. I had him alright. These flies must be getting a lot tougher." They sat at the table and ate together.

"I don't mind admitting it. I was frightened this morning, mother. I thought I was going to lose you. I couldn't bear that."

"I thought I was near my end, myself. I can't account for it but I feel like a new woman now. Whatever it was, once we've done eating, I'm going to clean this place from top to bottom."

"In that case, I'll into the shed and see what I can do with that scythe."

Albrecht worked hard. He hammered away at the blade, beating all the dints out of it. With a whet stone, he sharpened it. One of the handles was cracked. He had a piece of beech, which he turned to make a new one. To finish it off, he oiled the shaft.

He re-joined his mother. "I've been thinking," he said. "We should celebrate. Why don't I kill the pig? We can have a joint of pork this evening."

"Good idea," she replied. "You get on with that and I'll get the stove ready."

Albrecht took a sharp knife and a bowl to catch the blood. Strong as he was, he had no problem seizing the pig and wrestling it to the ground. Pinning the pig down, he cut its throat. He drew the blade deep through the flesh of the pig's neck.

He was bewildered to see not a drop of blood. And when he withdrew the knife, the cut closed over, as if it had never been made. He tried again and the same thing happened. Albrecht cut many times but he could draw no blood and every time, the pig was unharmed.

He let the pig go. It trotted away, squealing in complaint.

From his look, Albrecht's mother could see something was amiss.

"What's up, Albrecht?"

"I've changed my mind. Let's leave the pig for now. We can finish off the sausage and cheese tonight. I'll go into Lübeck in the morning and get something special for us."

She smiled. "For all you're big and strong, you've a soft heart, Albrecht. I don't wonder you couldn't bring yourself to kill the pig. It's no bother. We can get somebody to do it for us, when the time comes."

Albrecht said no more and was quiet over supper.

Chapter Ten
Uproar

Lübeck's market square was in uproar. Crowds pressed around food stalls. People pushed and jostled to get to the front. Everywhere clusters of folks stood talking, shaking heads, waving arms and shrugging shoulders.

"What's going on?" Albrecht asked a man.

"Haven't you heard? There's neither fish nor meat to be had anywhere." Albrecht struggled through the throng to the shop of a butcher.

"I've nothing," said the butcher. "And what's worse, it looks as if I'll get nothing. My slaughter man says he can't kill a single beast."

A fishwife sat on a nearby step, an empty basket at her feet.

"This morning all the boats came back, safe and well," she told him. "But not a fish did they catch. Not a crab. Nothing."

Albrecht called at the dealer's house.

"Compared with some, we're not so badly off," the dealer said. "We've got a couple of hams and a barrel of salted fish. But we can't go through all our reserves. We don't know how long this will go on. My daughter is out scouring the city for food. She's worried for her children."

In the street by the dealer's house, Albrecht bumped into a miller he knew. The miller was the only man he saw smiling in Lübeck that day.

"People are crying out for bread. I'm shifting flour by the wagon load."

"But why is there no meat or fish?"

"There's something weird going on," answered the miller. "I've heard so many stories this morning. What they add up to I can't fathom. All I can tell you is what I've seen with my own eyes."

"In the barn where I store my grain, I keep several cats. I always have done. Where you have grain, you'll have rats."

"My best cat is a big brute. I call him Black Tom. He's fast and he's vicious. Black Tom is not one to toy with a rat once he's caught it. Killing is his game. In all my time, he's the best ratter I've ever had.

"Last night, I watched him catch one. As ever, he jumped on it. He stabbed his claws info the creature's back and sank his teeth into its neck. When he finally let go, what do you think happened? That rat shook himself and ran off. Black Tom caught it again and gave it more of the same with the same result.

"The other two cats must have heard the racket. Over they ran and joined in. They circled the rat and soon the three of them were taking turns to bite it. When they paused, the rat got back to its feet and looked at them, as if to say, you're getting nowhere, are you? So, why don't you just give up?"

Albrecht listened to the miller's tale with growing dismay.

"What do you make of it?" he asked.

"I don't know. But it must have to do with the fact nobody can kill any fish or slaughter any cattle. It seems nothing can die."

Chapter Eleven
Confession

On his way home, every thump of his horse's hooves hammered the miller's words into Albrecht's brain.

"Nothing can die."

Riding along the shore, he heard a din louder even than that in Lübeck's market place. Gulls in great numbers screamed at one another. They fought to get at the piles of rotting seaweed, frantic to tear off pieces to eat.

Albrecht's mother knew from his face there was something wrong as soon as he stepped through the door.

"Whatever's up?"

"There's no food to be bought. No meat, no fish, no fowl. Nothing."

"Why ever not?"

"Sit down, mother. There's something I need to tell you."

They sat at the table. Troubled by his frowns, she took Albrecht's hand in hers.

Albrecht unfolded what he had seen and heard in Lübeck. He told of his meeting with Death and how, having squeezed him almost to nothing, he had thrown him out to sea in a shell.

"So, you see, it's all my fault," he said. Tears filled his eyes. "I've put Death out of action and now no creature can die."

"Oh, Albrecht." His mother rose from her seat. She put her arms round him.

Albrecht sobbed. "I did it for you, Mother. I didn't want you to die."

"I know, I know," she said, patting his back.

She waited for Albrecht to settle himself.

"We all have to die, son."

"But you wanted to live on, didn't you?"

"Of course I did. But when Death comes, we've no choice. Think of all those flies and spiders caught in the amber. Just imagine if none of them had ever died. The world would have filled with insects long ago. They have their young and then they die to make room for them."

"But what am I to do now?"

"There's only one thing you can do, find that shell and release Death. Your sharp eyes on the beach have supported us all these years. Now you must use them to put things right. Get out there and start searching. We can only hope the tides will carry the shell back in."

Albrecht knitted his brows.

"Suppose I find it and set Death free. He'll come straight for you."

"If he does, I'll be ready for him. Never mind me. Think of all those frenzied folk in Lübeck. Enough of talking now. You be off and start looking."

Albrecht embraced his mother. He grabbed his bag and set off for the beach.

On the way, he pictured to himself where he was when he threw the shell. He had a good idea of the spot. Having found it, he made a pile of stones above the water line to mark the place. He sat down and turned his mind to the tides, the currents and the winds. After thinking for a while, he paced along the beach. Some way on, he stopped and built another pile of stones. Drawing on his knowledge of the coast, he reckoned that if the shell was to come ashore it was likely to wash up somewhere between his two markers.

The tide had turned and was beginning to go out. Albrecht walked the sand between the piles, tracing lines parallel with the sea, back and forth.

He was bothered all the time by swarms of flies but he kept at it. He scanned every patch of sand and turned every stone, to be sure of missing nothing. Working his way down the beach, he followed the waves as they washed back.

The hours passed. The light began to fade. No longer able to see well enough, he broke off his search. Before trudging home, he moved one of the piles of stones. When he renewed his hunt the next day, he would cover an even wider stretch.

"No luck," Albrecht said to his mother. "I've looked all over. Either I've missed it or it hasn't washed up yet. I'll try tomorrow as soon as it's light."

"I've been looking too," said his mother. "I couldn't sit here doing nothing. I've been out over the fields, me and scores of others, all of us foraging for things to eat."

She pointed to a heap on the table.

"That's our supper tonight. I'll make nettle soup and cook these mushrooms."

Theirs was a quiet supper. Neither of them felt in the mood to chat. Their thoughts were all of what the next day might bring.

Chapter Twelve
Death Goes

"I've got an idea," said Albrecht.

It was not yet dawn. He and his mother sat together eating their last piece of sausage.

"I'm going to take the scythe with me. It belongs to Death. Who knows, he might be drawn back to it somehow?"

"Go on," his mother replied. "It can't do any harm."

Early though it was the beach was fizzing with life. Every day, the sands were littered with dead shore crabs, broken by the waves. None of them died now. Everywhere they scuttled about, making back for the water. Stranded jellyfish used to meet their end in puddles. Now, they sat pulsing on the sand as they waited for the next tide to re-float them.

Albrecht planted the scythe in the sand. He began again to pace backwards and forwards, his head down and his eyes fixed.

Backwards and forwards he went, hour after hour. In a while, his head began to ache and his eyes became red but still he kept searching, backwards and forwards across the beach.

At last, with the afternoon drawing in, he sank down on the sand, weary. Rousing himself, he tramped back to the scythe. He threw himself down there for a moment to eat the crust of bread his mother had put into his bag.

As he lay propped on an elbow looking about him, he noticed a small, black blob sticking out of the damp sand. It was a tar ball. He jumped up. Scooping the sand away, he dug up a whelk shell, its open end rammed into the tar. That was it. He had found the shell.

Albrecht held it to his ear. He could hear no sound. He looked about for a flat stone. Placing the shell on the stone, he prised off the tar and stood back.

A tiny figure scrambled out of the shell; a figure no bigger than the nail of his small toe. Albrecht watched the figure grow and grow until before him stood Death, at his full height again.

Death rubbed his back and bent his knees.

"Ah, that feels better. Small I may have been but I was cramped in there and queasy too from being rolled about."

"I'm sorry for what I did," said Albrecht.

Death looked up and down the beach.

"I imagine you are by now, young man. You can see for yourself what happens when I am not about my business. I told you, did I not, that you were making a big mistake."

Albrecht nodded. "What now?" he asked.

"It looks as if I have a lot of catching up to do."

"Then you'll be needing this." Albrecht handed Death his scythe.

"Well, well. You've done a splendid job. This looks as fine as it ever did."

Albrecht said nothing. He feared now for his mother's life.

Death broke the silence.

"I know what you are thinking. I shall certainly go for your mother. But you have released me. You have restored my scythe. And, I believe, you have learned a lesson."

"Yes, I have."

"In return then, I shall give you more time with your mother. But make no mistake. I shall come for her when I choose and you will not see me. No, the next time you see me will be when I come for you."

"Thank you, until we meet again." For all Death's chilling words, Albrecht was able to smile, knowing his mother would be alive when he returned home.

Death hoisted the scythe onto his shoulder. Without another word, he turned and walked off, away from Albrecht's cottage.

Chapter Thirteen
A Story

Death kept his word. He let Albrecht's mother live for several more years. Every morning, when she woke well and lively, Albrecht was thankful for another day he would have with her.

When Death did come, he came in the night while she was sleeping. Albrecht bore his loss calmly. Those who knew how much he loved his mother were surprised to see how well he took her death. They did not know his brush with Death had prepared him. Albrecht's mother carried to her grave the secret of that encounter. And Albrecht vowed he would never tell a soul what he had done.

His friends had another surprise. Every year, in his mother's memory, Albrecht made a new scythe and gifted it to one of the local farming families. On top of that, he let it be known that he would repair, at no charge, any scythe brought to him. People were puzzled. Albrecht was known to make his living from the sea. He had never shown any interest in work on the land. They questioned him but he gave away nothing.

Over the years, Albrecht became close to the dealer's family. The dealer helped him take a share in one of the boats, which traded inland along the rivers.

To the dealer's grandchildren he became 'Uncle Albrecht'. When they had free time, they loved to spend it with him on the beach, in his workshop and on his wagon.

Some of Albrecht's wood found its way into Lübeck's church, once its choirmaster managed to collect enough money to restore his choir stalls.

The dealer's youngest grandchild was a girl. Her name was Lise-Lotte but everyone knew her as Lilo. She was devoted to Uncle Albrecht. She liked nothing more than to join him on his beachcombing walks.

One morning, Lilo was seven years old at the time, they were strolling together on the shore when they saw in the distance a mottled shape on the sand. Lilo raced ahead to look.

"It's a seal," she shouted over her shoulder as she got nearer.

It was a seal. It was a dead seal. It lay with its front flippers spread wide and its chin flat on the sand. When Albrecht caught her up, Lilo was kneeling at its side. Its eyes were closed in dark slits. It had been brought ashore on that morning's tide. Drops of water still hung from its whiskers.

"Isn't it lovely?" said Lilo. She stroked the back of one finger down its long snout and burst into tears. Albrecht put an arm round her.

"Every creature has to die sometime, Lilo."

"But it's not fair," she wailed.

"Here, come and sit with me."

Albrecht took her hand and led her up the beach to the edge of the dunes. They sat and he waited in silence for her sobbing to lessen.

"I'll tell you a story, Lilo," said Albrecht, once she was quiet. "One of the sailors at the harbour told it to me when I was a lad. It's a fanciful tale, to be sure. But it does have a message. Let me see if I can remember. It's about a young man who clung too much to his mother."

The Tale of Philippe Legrand – France

Chapter One
Philippe Lends a Hand

"This is a job for Philippe," the man said.

He spoke to his son. The two of them stood at the side of a track. They had climbed down from their wagon and were surveying the damage. A jolt caused by a rut had knocked one of the back wheels off its axle. The wheel lay on its side where it had rolled into a ditch. The wagon, loaded with barrels of apples bound for a press in the neighbouring village, now sagged in one corner.

"Run back, son, and ask him if he'll come and lend us a hand."

The boy trotted off down the track. As he neared his village, he heard the 'tink, tink, tink' of a hammer on iron. When closer, he picked up too the puff of bellows. Those sounds told him Philippe was at work in his forge.

The boy paused at the forge door. Gazing at the red glow of the coals in the furnace, he could feel their heat from there. He savoured the warm, sooty aroma of its smoke. He loved to watch Philippe working and was happy to wait for him to finish shaping a spade head on his anvil.

He told Philippe of their mishap and asked if he would break off from his job to come and help them.

Philippe was always ready to help. In a corner lay a bag made of old sacking, with rope handles. He kept it there for such times as this. Inside were things he might need for repairs away from the forge—mallets, hammers, chisels, wedges, crowbars, nails and bolts. It was a weight most men in the village would have strained to lift. Philippe swung it over his shoulder as if it held only goose down.

Before leaving, Philippe put his head round a wooden partition at the back of the forge.

"You keep an eye on things here, my dear," he called. "I'll be back soon."

At the wagon, the boy's father had wedged the three wheels with rocks to stop it from rolling. He had tried to shift the barrels but they were too much for him. He hauled the wheel out of the ditch, relieved to find neither it, nor its axle was broken. While he waited, he gave his horse a nosebag of oats.

With no thought of unloading the barrels, Philippe squatted with his back against the sagging corner of the wagon, put his hands behind him underneath its frame and straightened his knees. Having lifted the wagon, he held it up while father and son slid the wheel back on its axle. Philippe finished the job with his mallet, hammering two wedges into the hub to fix it in place.

"There you are, my friend," he said, not even puffing from the effort. "That'll hold to get you there and back. When you're home, call in and I'll do a proper job on it."

The man was loud in his thanks, which Philippe, no liker of fuss, put aside with a wave of his hand.

"One thing you can do for me," he said. "When it's ready, you can drop by at the forge and leave me a flagon of your cider."

Chapter Two
Labryte

"You keep an eye on things here, my dear."

Those had been Philippe's words as he made ready to leave the forge. He spoke them not to a wife, not to a daughter, nor even to his mother. He was speaking to Labryte, his horse.

Many times his neighbours smiled to hear Philippe address Labryte as he did. None, though, made fun of him for they had nothing but respect and affection for their village blacksmith.

Labryte had been with Philippe since she was a foal. She grew to be a sturdy mare, dapple grey in colour, with a deep chest, thick legs and powerful hindquarters.

She was intelligent, good-tempered and trustworthy. No slope, however steep, defeated her. She would pull a cart steadily, toiling the day long. When a place fell vacant in a ploughing team, she was ready to stand in and make up the numbers. She never needed a whip. A touch from Philippe and Labryte knew at once what he wanted her to do.

At the end of a day, when he had ridden her to a distant village and back or led her in drawing a load, Philippe loved to rub Labryte down, running his big hands over her silver coat and its many pale blotches.

Philippe was the village blacksmith but he served his neighbours in another way and for that he depended even more on Labryte. At intervals, he journeyed to get them salt.

Their village was in the territory of a powerful Count. This Count was the younger brother of the King of France. He both envied and mistrusted his brother. All the time, he was fearful the King would attack him, so he amassed military might of his own and built lots of defensive strongholds around his domain. He resented his brother's royal title, so he was ever campaigning to capture foreign lands and to be crowned their King.

To fund his armaments, his fortifications and his campaigns overseas, he made the salt trade across the whole of his territory a monopoly of his own. The profits he garnered from selling salt were huge, enough to resource his defences, his ambitions and a lavish lifestyle besides. Merchants dealing in salt could afford to pay the taxes he imposed but the prices he demanded were pushing ordinary people into poverty.

Chapter Three
Journey Plans

"We're getting low, Philippe. We need you to make another trip."

The wife of the village butcher was at the forge to speak with Philippe. She was one of a group of village women who handled the sharing of the salt Philippe brought back from his summer journeys.

Everyone needed salt. The villagers slaughtered many of their animals before winter came. Salt was essential for preserving the meat and curing the hams, which would sustain them through the dark, cold months. Without salt, they could make neither cheese nor bread. Families used salt in cooking, in cleaning pans and in washing clothes.

On the morning of his departure, many villagers gathered to wish Philippe well and to see him off.

"Let's check you've got everything," said the butcher's wife.

"I've got Labryte's nosebag and enough oats to see her through," said Philippe, patting the mare's neck.

"Your first thought is always of Labryte, eh, Philippe?"

"As it should be," he answered.

"You've got your sacks and your cloth bags?"

"Yes and my bag of sand."

"We'll wrap the sacks and the bags round the empty flagons," said the woman, "so they don't break."

"And I've got my other companion," said Philippe, waving his cudgel.

The sacks slung over Labryte's flanks were bulging but the woman managed to cram in some cheeses and a cask of cider. The mare was ready to go, newly shoed that morning and having emptied a whole trough of fresh hay. Philippe put on his cap and off they set together.

Another departure was about to take place elsewhere. The Count lay awake in his chateau. He had been woken when servants tiptoed into his bedchamber to light candles on the table, to put fresh logs on the fire and to draw back the drapes around the bed.

Adjusting his eyes to the dim light, he surveyed the wall hangings adorning the chamber. Their details he could not make out but the patches of blue and green and red seemed to give out warmth in defiance of the draught, which made them lift and fall against the walls.

The Countess lay at his side, pretending to be asleep. He knew her to be pretending, for she was unnaturally still. He kept silent for some time, nerving himself to broach his plans.

At length, he spoke.

"I shall be setting off soon, to oversee manoeuvres." The Countess sat up and looked at him.

"There seem to be lots of manoeuvres lately."

The Count avoided her stare, keeping his own gaze fixed at the candles on the table.

"There are, Countess, and all of them, I assure you, are necessary. I want to be ready for my campaign in Italy. Besides, our forces have to be alert all the time in case of attack from that wretched brother of mine."

"That surely is no way to speak of your King."

"I intend to be King myself one day and then I'll show you how a monarch conducts himself."

"Can we afford all this?" asked the Countess. "Would you not help our people more if you spent the money improving tracks and waterways?"

"Our people will only flourish in so far as their territory is strong."

The Countess sighed. "So, where are you going to watch these manoeuvres?"

"My generals keep the location of their forces secret. The King has spies everywhere. I don't want him picking up word of them. I'm expecting a message at any time. The messenger will tell me where they are and when I know, I shall set off at once."

The Countess frowned. "How easy is it to hide a whole army? If the King has spies everywhere, aren't they more likely to spot it than to overhear mention of its whereabouts?"

"I would not expect you to understand, Countess."

"We can at least agree on that," replied the Countess.

Chapter Four
Setting Out

In those days, the lanes of France were hazardous, particularly for those travelling on their own. There were desperate men about, watching for merchants and even pilgrims to rob.

Philippe always greeted strangers he met with, "Good day, my friend," Many a one who approached with a mind to waylay him, seeing Philippe's sturdy frame, the heft of his cudgel and the power of his horse, thought better of taking him on.

Once in a while, a foolhardy individual would risk it. Philippe never chose to use his strength against another but he would defend himself. Those encounters always ended the same way, with the robber fleeing to a nearby village in search of someone to set a bone broken by a kick from Labryte or a blow from Philippe's cudgel.

Philippe stopped at inns on his journey. However tired and hungry he was, he first watered and fed Labryte. He gave her a rub down and made sure she was comfortable in a stall of her own, with plenty of clean straw and fresh hay. Before retiring himself, he always visited the stables to bid Labryte good night.

Inns provided more than a bed and a meal. People stopping exchanged news with one another. Philippe took care to find out from fellow travellers if any of them had spotted the Count's tax collectors in the area. The Count employed troops of men to patrol his territory looking for anybody who had not paid him tax on their salt.

Robbers haunted the inns. Lurking about, they listened and chatted in the hope of picking up useful information. Having identified a likely victim, they would leave the inn early in the morning and lay an ambush along the route they had learned the traveller was to take.

One time, a robber weighed up Philippe as a target. In the inn, a couple of ostlers were struggling to move a large cider barrel.

"Here, let me have a go at that," said Philippe. The robber watched, amazed to see Philippe wrap his arms round the barrel, raise it to his chest and carry it inside. Doubting what he had seen, the robber guessed those ostlers must have been putting it on, to spare themselves a job. He stepped into the hallway of the inn. Making as if he was weary, he leaned against that barrel. To his surprise, he found it full and untapped. He was unable even to tilt it.

"I'll not tangle with him," he said to himself.

Philippe was making for the Salt Pans on the coast, a flat expanse of mud and water, which was once the delta of a river. Wooded hills looked down upon the Salt Pans. There, under the cover of the trees, Philippe made his camp. The summer nights were warm. He loved sleeping under the stars. And Labryte was able to find plenty of tasty grass in the open glades.

The Count, by contrast, had not one but twenty horses to choose from for his journey.

"Chamberlain," he called out. "Meet me in the stables, at nine of the clock."

"At your command, my Lord," came the Chamberlain's reply.

The Count's stables were set apart from his chateau. Their main range had an arch through it, high and wide enough to allow the passage of carriages. Above the arch was a bell-tower, topped with a weather vane. On both sides of the arch were vaulted bays where the Count's many carriages were parked. He possessed a whole fleet, from gilded coaches for ceremonial occasions to plain vehicles for driving about his estate. There were tack rooms too, hung with bridles, saddles and harness, smelling of old leather and of the beeswax rubbed in to keep it supple.

The arch led into a cobbled yard. The stables themselves filled the lower storeys of the other three ranges enclosing the yard. In each range was a line of stalls. Their partitions of wooden planking all ended in a post on which the Count's coat of arms was carved. Above, in the roof space, lit and ventilated by dormer windows, were hay lofts, store rooms and sleeping quarters for stable boys, grooms, coachmen and blacksmiths.

The Count met his Chamberlain. They stood where the arch opened out onto the yard.

Before them all was bustle. Grooms led horses by, their shod hooves clopping on the cobbles. Men heaved sacks of straw. Boys sloshed buckets of water and others pushed on brooms. A rhythmic creak sounded in one corner where a man was working a pump to fill a trough. Shouted orders came from those in charge to those whose job it was to do their bidding.

"I need a coach ready for an early departure tomorrow morning," shouted the Count. Then, even louder, "I'm going on manoeuvres," he bellowed, as if to make sure the whole yard heard his words.

"May I ask where, my Lord," said the Chamberlain.

"That must remain a secret until we are far beyond the estate."

"Your Lordship's caution is commendable. As you have told us many times, His Majesty's spies are everywhere. But I am afraid I must press your Lordship."

The Count interrupted him.

"Come, let us speak over there." He pointed to the centre of the yard, a spot beyond the hearing of those going about their work.

They walked across and the Chamberlain continued.

"The coachmen will need to know something of the distance and the terrain if they are to select the right horses, my Lord. They have to know whether to load fodder and whether the party is to stop overnight on the way."

"Very well. Very well."

The Count bent forward and whispered in the Chamberlain's ear the name of a Manor House.

The Chamberlain grasped at once that his master was set not on military, but on romantic manoeuvres.

"The coach is to bear no markings," the Count went on, still whispering. "I want blinds on all the windows and nobody is to wear livery. You understand me?"

The Chamberlain understood him very well. There were indeed to be army manoeuvres but the Count was not going to attend them. The Manor House he had named was the home of one of his generals. The general's wife had caught the eye of the Count at a recent chateau ball. While her husband was away conducting manoeuvres, she was to receive a visit from the Count.

Chapter Five
The Pans

"Good day," said the Sergeant of the Guard. He embraced Philippe. "Did you have a good journey?"

"Good day to you. Yes, a good journey and one all the better for having good company." Philippe patted Labryte's neck.

The Sergeant turned towards a doorway at the back of the guardroom and called.

"Come on out. Philippe and Labryte are here." Two men joined them and exchanged more embraces.

Philippe had risen early that morning. Near where he camped in the wood, he had a well concealed hiding place. There he stowed the things he wanted no one to see. He fitted Labryte with her nosebag of oats. Having reloaded her with some cheeses, all the empty flagons and the cask of cider, he walked her down to a spring at the foot of the hill. The flagons he filled with fresh water.

Philippe and Labryte went to the main gate into the Salt Pans. The way in was barred by huge wooden doors. At Philippe's knocking, a face appeared behind the metal grill in a small door set in the gate. The Sergeant opened the door. Stooping under the lintel, Philippe went into the guardroom.

Their greetings done, the four men stepped outside. The guards made a fuss of Labryte. Her muzzle was deep in the nosebag but she turned her ears forward and swished her tail to show she enjoyed their attentions.

"We'd better get on with it," announced the Sergeant. "Much as we'd like to, we're not allowed to make any exceptions."

"I know," said Philippe. "It's no problem." He unfastened the two bags which hung against Labryte's flanks.

"But first, I've got a little something for you, gentlemen." Philippe took out the cider. "When you've drained the cask, I'll have it back."

The men thanked him. The weather was hot and their hours were long. They grinned.

"This'll make the shift pass quicker."

They set about searching the two bags.

"As always with you, Philippe," said the Sergeant, "everything just as it should be. Open the gates, men, and let our friend through."

So jealous was he of the money he made from the Salt Pans, the Count had turned them into a fortress. On his orders, men had raised an earth rampart, some ten leagues long, to enclose the whole site. The rampart they had topped with a wooden palisade. A path behind it was patrolled by the Count's guards. At intervals stood watchtowers from which they looked down on those at work harvesting the salt.

"Just look at that, Labryte. That's an amazing sight, is it not, my dear?"

Philippe had seen the Salt Pans many times but when those gates banged to behind him, he would always stop and take in the view.

In the far distance, a line of blue showed where the sea lay. Scattered across the land were small, stone cottages. Harvesting the salt was seasonal work. Villagers from round about came to the pans for the whole summer, staying in the cottages. Families from the same village took clusters of cottages together.

The land was cut by a network of channels and canals. Amongst them were the pans themselves, some of them silver pools of still water reflecting the clouds above, some mottled by patches of salt starting to crystallise. Causeways skirted the pans, narrow paths on banked up mud. Against the causeways were heaps of salt, dotting the landscape with pyramids of sparkling white.

Everywhere people were at work. Men and women drew long-handled rakes through the water, dragging salt crystals into mounds. In places, figures were bent over the mounds, taking up dry salt between wooden paddles and dumping it into trugs. Boys and girls carried off the trugs, emptying them into wheelbarrows.

Gang planks bent under their weight as men and women pushed barrows across to tip into the holds of barges. Crewmen worked the tillers and tended the sails of the barges. When there was no wind, they hauled and punted them along the canals. The salt was heaped at the main gate, where a team of the Count's men weighed it, recorded amounts and stacked it by the sack full.

Chapter Six
Water and Salt

"Welcome, Philippe." The woman gave him a hug. "We've been looking out for you. And welcome to you too, Labryte." She reached up and fondled one of the mare's ears.

Having tethered Labryte in the shade, Philippe followed the woman into the cottage. He was glad to sit down in the cool. She placed a hunk of bread on the table before him and drew a beaker of wine from a barrel.

Philippe was one of a troop of water sellers who supplied the workers on the pans. There was not a drop of fresh water to be had there. All was brackish. The water sellers, searched on their way in and again on their way out, fetched freshwater from springs and wells in the countryside round about and sold it to the salt workers.

They brought in flour and yeast too. In every cluster of cottages, there was one with a bread oven. Each family would bring its dough to be baked there. Families had their own wooden stamps to mark the dough, so they could tell which loaves were theirs.

Some water sellers traded with any family but some, and Philippe was one, had developed ties of friendship with particular groups. Over the years, Philippe had become close to a group from a village in the hills. There was trust and affection on both sides.

The water sellers were not allowed to stop on the pans overnight but Philippe lingered each day as long as he could. He enjoyed helping with the work and was happy to mend anything that broke. Where the banks would bear her weight, Labryte pulled barges. When their day's work was done, she gave rides to the children.

Philippe mingled with the other water sellers but within his own circle of families, he took no money for his fresh water. He did sell the cheeses, accepting only enough to pay for Labryte's oats, food for himself and lodging on his journey. For the water he brought them every day, the families paid him in salt.

Labryte was a clever horse. Trained by Philippe, she played her part in his smuggling. Every morning, he packed a canvas bag at the bottom of her nosebag and covered it with a layer of oats. Labryte was to eat none until they were well inside the Salt Pans and clear of the guards. While at the gatehouse being searched, on the word 'oats' from Philippe, she pretended to be eating, moving her jaws and giving a snort of contentment from time to time. On the way back, she followed the same routine, except then the canvas bag was full of salt.

Philippe's trusted families varied their routes when carrying salt to the barges. They were able to pause behind cottages with a load, hidden from the scrutiny of the Count's men on the watchtowers. In no time, they would take a handful of salt, put it into the canvas bag and move on to the canal side. They needed few handfuls to fill it.

Back at his camp in the evening, Philippe took out the salt and emptied it into sacks. Those he kept hidden in a dry place he had made in the woods for just that purpose.

On most days, Philippe made more than one water run and he usually stayed at the pans five or six days at a time. That was enough to fill two sacks with salt, a quantity which saved his neighbours at home a lot of money. And they took care to buy some salt too in the regular way, for it would have looked strange if their village never purchased a grain.

Philippe was affable and generous towards the Count's guards. Sometimes, he lingered at the guardhouse and chatted with them. They knew how fond he was of Labryte and how he loved to talk of her, celebrating her qualities and relating her feats of strength.

One anecdote he always shared whenever new guards appeared. Philippe praised Labryte's gentle temperament. But he would tell the tale of a pedlar who had once tried to steal oats from her nosebag. The fellow had run off howling from the pain of a bite on his hand.

"Labryte's a sweet soul," said Philippe, "but mess with her nosebag and you'll find out she can be fierce."

Chapter Seven
Encounter on the Way

Both their trips over, the two men set out homewards, Philippe back to his village and the Count back to his chateau.

Both of them avoided busy ways, the Count to obscure where he had been and Philippe to evade the Count's patrols.

Philippe had no need to lead Labryte. They walked side by side, companions going at the same pace. Philippe talked to Labryte all the time. He spoke to her of the colours of the wayside flowers, of the sounds of the birds in the hedgerows and of the smells of the land.

They were brought to a halt by a carriage coming towards them. The carriage, pulled by two horses, was only just able to squeeze along the narrow track. It pulled up and the two parties faced one another.

The Count opened the carriage door and leaned out.

"You two!" he yelled at the coachmen holding the reins. "Get that oaf and his nag out of my way!"

Realising that in his anger he had shown himself, he ducked back inside in haste and slammed the door.

The Count need not have worried. Philippe had not recognised him. He had, however, heard the Count's words.

"Steady, my dear," said Philippe, patting Labryte's neck. "We may have to teach that person better manners."

With those words, he reached and drew out his cudgel from where he had wedged it between Labryte's bags. He stepped forward and planted himself square on the track before her.

Seeing the figure of the man confronting them and the size of his cudgel, the two coachmen did not move from their seats.

Inside the carriage, the Chamberlain spoke.

"If you will permit me, my Lord, I am sure I can settle this."

"Well, go on then. But be quick about it."

The Chamberlain got out. He walked to Philippe. Removing his hat, he bowed.

"Good day to you, Monsieur. That's a fine horse you have there."

Philippe was astonished. In all France, few gentlemen would address someone like him with such respect.

"Good day to you, Sir," said Philippe, removing his cap. "She's fine indeed and strong too."

"She must be. Those look heavy bags. May I ask what you carry?"

"Sand," answered Philippe. "Let me show you." The Chamberlain wore kid leather gloves, so Philippe plunged his hand into one of the sacks and drew out a fistful of red sand. It was for just such an occasion that he placed bags of sand on top of the salt.

The Chamberlain moved closer to Philippe and spoke in a hushed voice.

"Would you step back with me a moment, Monsieur, that we may talk out of earshot of the carriage?"

They paused together behind Labryte.

"I must apologise to you for my master's outburst. He is more used to commanding then to asking. I pray you will overlook his hasty words."

Philippe nodded and said nothing.

"This is a tight spot, Monsieur," the Chamberlain went on. "I wonder how we are to solve our problem."

Philippe looked around. It was narrow indeed, hemmed by high hedges topping steep banks. A little way behind them there was a ledge on one bank but a horse of Labryte's size would never be able to climb onto it, least of all one as heavily laden as she was.

Philippe studied the ledge.

"Back up a little way, my dear," he said to Labryte. "I'm going to see what I can do."

Labryte took a couple of paces backwards and drew level with the Ledge.

"Hold still," he whispered in her ear.

Philippe squatted down, spread his arms wide and placed them apart under Labryte's belly. Her weight was a strain even for him. He took a deep breath and with a grimace which told of the effort, slowly straightened his knees. He lifted Labryte from the ground and set her on the ledge.

Philippe gasped. "Stand still there, my dear. Once the coach is past, I'll lift you down and no harm."

It was the Chamberlain's turn to be astonished. He removed a glove and shook Philippe by the hand.

"I am honoured, Sir, to have met the strongest man in France."

Philippe smiled. "You'd better call the carriage past, sir, before your master has more rude words to say."

The Chamberlain whistled to the coachmen. They drove the carriage past Labryte. Having stopped, both of them stood, turned and looking back over the roof of the carriage, watched with open mouths as Philippe lifted Labryte from the ledge down onto the track.

"May I ask your name, sir and where you live?" Philippe hesitated.

"I give you my word. I shall not share your name with my master."

"My name is Legrand." Philippe was inclined to trust the man but not so far as to name his village. "I am the blacksmith at a place some twenty leagues from here."

The Chamberlain patted Labryte. He ran the hand from which he had taken his glove under the bottom of her bags. The two men walked back to the carriage. As they went, the Chamberlain raised his hand, as if to brush hair from his face. Unseen by Philippe, he licked the palm of his hand.

In parting, he doffed his hat again and bowed low to Philippe.

"I depart in your debt, sit and with the memory of your Herculean strength. And I wish you well with your load," he paused and smiled, "with your load of sand."

Chapter Eight
Returns

"To the inn, everybody," cried the butcher's wife.

Philippe had been embraced by all and Labryte rewarded with carrots. Their welcomes done, it was time to hand out the salt.

"Fetch the scales," she told her husband, "and set them up in the inn."

The village women weighed out amounts and poured the salt into small, cloth bags. Those they gave out. They always held some back in reserve, which they entrusted to the village baker. He stored it near his oven, to keep it dry. Some bags they made up too for cottagers living alone beyond the village.

The job of sharing the salt was once done by the men. But they quarrelled. Some tried to cheat and at times, they traded blows. Fed up with the strife, the village women stepped in and took over. They handled the job without argument.

With the salt parcelled out, the villagers gave themselves over to celebrating another trouble-free trip to the pans by their blacksmith. The dancing that evening was lively and the singing lusty. High spirits rose higher still on draughts of cider.

The next day, a bit later than usual, they resumed their routines, shaped for them, as always, by the seasons. They felt secure, knowing now they had enough salt to prepare for the winter and to see them through it. Families gathered wood from the forest, building up their log piles ready for the colder times to come. As summer waned, they looked forward to autumn and harvest.

Back in his forge, Philippe set about the jobs awaiting his return. Tools of every kind had to be made ready for the cutting, lifting and stacking of crops. Villagers brought him sickles and scythes for sharpening. There were spades and forks in need of new shafts. Wagons required attention and Labryte was kept busy moving them.

The Count, by contrast, found his return did not restore familiar routines.

"Whatever is that?" he exclaimed.

Once back within his estate, the Count had raised the blind and was looking through the window of his carriage as it neared the chateau.

"Who the devil has put up a tent on my land without my permission?"

The Chamberlain leaned forward to see for himself what had provoked the Count's wrath.

There, on an open stretch of grass in front of the chateau, was a pavilion. A black pennant flew from its top. By it stood a man attending to a black horse.

"I know nothing of this," said the Chamberlain. "But your Lordship can be assured, I shall try to find out who this discourteous intruder is, as soon as we arrive."

Chapter Nine
A Mysterious Challenge

The Countess, who had seen the carriage approaching, hurried down and met them in the entrance hall.

"You'd been gone only a short while," she explained, "when that fellow and his squire pitched their tent right there. I sent over some of the stable hands, with pitchforks, to see them off. The ruffian put them all to flight at sword point. Then he strode over and demanded to see you."

"He seems to be a knight of some kind. He would give no name, nor tell where he was from. He said only that he'd come to challenge you to single combat."

The Count gulped. "What are we to do?"

"I'll tell you what I did. I said I would send out your champion to take up his challenge."

"My champion? Do I have a champion?"

"I guessed you'd not want to fight the man yourself when you got back," replied the Countess. "I sent for your Marshall of Cavalry. By the way, the Marshall appeared not to have seen you at the manoeuvres. The Marshall picked the best man in his troop, a stout fellow, he assured me, of proven courage and fighting skill."

"I'm sorry to say the poor man is now nursing broken ribs. It'll be a time before he mounts horse again. The knight swatted him aside as if he was a fly buzzing round his platter."

At those words, colour drained from the Count's face.

His wife went on. "The Marshall was confident he had other men who would fare better. He was mistaken. In the time you've been away, that knight has vanquished the three most accomplished fighters in your cavalry."

Open mouthed, the Count looked to his Chamberlain.

"My Lord," said the Chamberlain, "I shall seek a parley with this knight. It may be that I can find out something to our advantage."

The Chamberlain was mistaken too. He learned nothing from the knight. From the look of the man and his speech, he guessed he was from the Northlands. The Chamberlain had floated the possibility of a payment to buy him from his purpose but the knight would have none of it.

"He is not to be swayed," the Chamberlain reported to the Count. "If you send champions out to face him, he said, he will tackle them one by one. But when you have run out of champions, he demands to meet you in single combat. Once he has slain your Lordship, he plans to take possession of your chateau and your lands."

"Without doubt, this knight is in the pay of my brother."

"He granted me only a brief talk," answered the Chamberlain, "but in all he said he came across as one little minded to do the bidding of another, even a King. His prowess in single combat seems to be matched by his arrogance."

"So?" snapped the Count. "What are we to do?"

The Countess spoke. "I have a suggestion. In that pavilion, there are just two men, the knight and his squire. Muster thirty of your soldiers and storm it. Surprise them by night, if that will make it easier. There need be no bloodshed. Thirty men ought to be able to overpower them and truss them up. If you really want rid of him, have him carried to the coast and pay the captain of a merchant ship to transport him as a prisoner to the Indies."

"You don't understand," replied the Count. "The knight has challenged me. Honour requires that his challenge be answered. If I did what you suggest, I should dishonour myself and this family for all time."

"What is honour?" the Countess asked. "Is honour going to comfort the mothers, the wives and the children of the men this knight has killed? Will honour knit the bones of those injured at his hand?"

"I would not expect you to understand matters of honour."

"You're right," snapped the Countess. "I don't."

She turned and without another word, went back to her chamber.

Chapter Ten
Finding a Champion

The chamberlain broke the silence.

"I too have a suggestion, my Lord. But I fear it may please you no more than that of the Countess."

"Go on. Let me hear it."

"You may remember, my Lord, we had to pause on our way back here."

"Well, what of it?"

"My Lord, in that narrow lane we met the strongest man I have ever seen."

"You mean that oaf with the dapple grey horse?"

"I mean, my Lord, the man who showed great courtesy in making way for us and great strength in doing so."

"You're surely not suggesting we get some peasant to be my champion?"

"We have tried courage, military experience and combat skill. The knight has overwhelmed them all. Perhaps sheer strength and native guile will serve your Lordship better."

"But I shall be a laughing stock if I send out a man like that to fight a knight."

"I repeat, my Lord—the strongest man I have ever seen. But if your Lordship is adamant, then make ready to fight the knight in single combat yourself."

The Count frowned. "Very well," he said. "Send for the man. After all, it will be no loss to me if he gets killed."

"It will be a loss to those who know him and who care about him, my Lord."

"Don't bandy words with me, Chamberlain. Send for him and let that be an end of it."

The Chamberlain bowed and withdrew. In his office, he wrote a letter. Having finished it, he sent for one of his trusted men.

"I would like you to find somebody for me," he said, "and, if he agrees, to bring him back here. I suggest you wear your working clothes and take one of the old wagons. Ask around for the big blacksmith with the dapple grey mare. He shouldn't be hard to track down. He must be well known. If you're challenged, say only that your master has a job he'd like to ask him to do. When you meet him, please give him this letter."

Acting on the Chamberlain's advice, the man found the lane where Philippe had met the Count's coach. Following the direction Philippe and Labryte had been taking, he began to ask after the blacksmith. The Chamberlain was right. He took little time to learn the name of the village and to locate its forge.

Philippe was astonished. He had never learned to read and no one had ever sent him a letter before. He asked the man to follow him and set off to seek the village Priest.

The Priest was at home and happy to read the letter to Philippe. He scanned it first. If it contained anything alarming he wanted to know, so as to strike the right tone.

"This is what it says, my son. It seems a fine letter, so listen with care."

'My dear Monsieur Legrand, we met but a short time ago in a narrow lane. On that occasion, you showed great courtesy in making way to let my master through. You showed great strength too in moving that splendid horse of yours to one side. I am indebted to you.

I gave you my word that I would share nothing about you with my master, the Count. But I write to you on his behalf. As I say, he knows neither your name nor your business but he has great need of a man with the strength you possess. He wishes to meet you and to ask your help.

If you decide to decline, you have my assurance you will suffer nothing. Should you agree to come with my man to the chateau, I shall be yet more in your debt.

I ask only that you decide without delay and if you are willing that you accompany my man with all possible speed.'

Philippe gulped. "Well," he said. And after a pause, again, "Well." He could think of nothing else to say.

The Priest prompted him. "Philippe, this man is waiting for your answer."

"I don't know what to say, Father. What do you advise?"

"The man you met in the lane, Philippe—what did you think of him? Do you believe he is to be trusted?"

"He spoke well to me, Father. And he was impressed by Labryte."

At that point, the Chamberlain's man put in.

"I have worked for the Chamberlain a dozen years," he said, "and I have ever found him to be a man of his word."

Still, Philippe was silent.

"Would you withdraw for a moment," said the Priest, "while I speak with Philippe in private?"

The Chamberlain's man left the Priest's study, closing the door behind him.

"Philippe, do you think the Chamberlain realised what you were carrying? The only thing that bothers me in the letter is his mention of 'your business'."

"I don't know, Father. But if he did and if he'd told his master, I'm sure the Count would have sent his inspectors to arrest me right away, however much the Chamberlain wanted to keep his word."

"So you don't think this is a trap, my son?"

"We didn't talk for long, Father but from what he said, I doubt he's one to pull a mean trick."

"In that case, Philippe, I advise you to go. You can at least see what the Count wants you to do. After all, if the Count is refused and becomes cross, he poses a risk to you and to our supply of tax-free salt."

The Priest called the man back and Philippe told him he would go to the chateau.

"Let's lose no more time then," said the man. "We can leave right now, for the Chamberlain will see you given all you need once we're there."

"Not yet," said Philippe. "I must see Labryte and say goodbye first."

On their way back to the forge, Philippe called on a neighbour, who agreed to make sure Labryte was watered, fed and exercised while he was away. The neighbour also undertook to keep the forge furnace alight until his friend returned.

Philippe topped up the fodder in Labryte's stall. Patting the mare's neck, he whispered in one ear.

"I shall miss you, my dear. But I shall be back soon."

Chapter Eleven
Martin

"A warm welcome to you, Monsieur." The Chamberlain had hurried to the stable block, as soon as word reached him that his man was back. He was eager to talk to Philippe before he met the Count.

The Chamberlain bowed. "I am most grateful to you for agreeing to come. Will you walk with me about the yard, while I explain what lies behind my letter?"

As they walked, the Chamberlain told Philippe of the knight, of his challenge to the Count and how he had defeated those so far sent against him.

"The Count knows your amazing strength. He wishes to ask you to be his champion and take on the knight on his behalf."

"I use my strength in my work," replied Philippe. "I am not a fighting man."

"I ask only that you do not set your mind against it. Sleep on the matter, Monsieur. Tomorrow I will bring you before the Count and the Countess. I beg you to give a hearing to his request."

"I will do as you ask," answered Philippe.

"Here, Martin!" called the Chamberlain, to a lad who was sweeping the cobbles. "Please show this gentleman to the loft and make a space for him to sleep tonight."

The Chamberlain had wanted to give Philippe a room at the chateau. The Count would not hear of it, insisting the blacksmith had to sleep in the stable loft with the other workers.

The Chamberlain bowed again to Philippe.

"Until tomorrow, Monsieur."

Martin led Philippe to a door in the corner of the square, at one end of a stable block. They walked along the line of stalls, the muscular bulk of Philippe dwarfing the gaunt frame of the boy at his side.

Martin paused at one stall. He slipped in beside a horse to stroke its muzzle and whisper in one ear. Knowing horses, Philippe could tell there was something ailing this one. The horse relaxed though under Martin's caresses, its lower lip hanging loosely down. While Martin was talking to it, one of the grooms appeared.

"Out of there, boy!" he barked.

Turning to Philippe, he said, "He's a soft one and that's the truth."

Glowering at Martin, he snarled, "You don't manage horses with sweet talk, boy. You've got to show them who is master." With that, he gave the horse a hard slap on its haunches. The horse laid back both its ears and stamped one hoof on the cobbled floor. Philippe and Martin said nothing. They turned and continued on their way.

Martin led Philippe up some wooden steps into the loft above the stalls. A small group of men was up there. Grooms and stable hands, they were taking a break from their work. They chatted to one another. Two of them played cards. While Philippe introduced himself, Martin took a broom, swept a space clean of dust and laid in it a straw-filled pallet.

One of the men, lounging on his own pallet, watched Martin at work. He picked up a grooming brush and threw it at the boy, catching him a sharp blow on the back of his head. The man guffawed and several others laughed too.

"You're handy with that broom," the man shouted. "Are you looking to become a chambermaid up at the chateau?"

More laughter followed from the group. Martin said nothing. He carried on preparing the space where Philippe was to sleep. Philippe looked at the man who threw the brush, noting his features.

Before turning in for the night, Philippe asked Martin to join him in taking a turn or two about the courtyard. He wanted to stretch a hand of friendship to the lad, for he could see that, as the youngest and the smallest there, he had a tough time of it.

"How do you come to be working here?" Philippe asked.

"The nuns sent me."

Philippe guessed the story behind those words.

"So you have no family then?"

"None that I know," replied Martin. "They told me I was left with them as a baby. It was the feast of St Martin the day they found me at the convent gate, so they called me Martin. I don't know when I was born but I've taken that day as my birthday. When I was ten, they put me to work here. I've been in the stables ever since."

"It looks like you get a fair bit of bullying."

Martin sighed. "At times. I've thought about running away. But where would I go? I'd end up begging on the road. That could be worse than this. When I'm feeling low, I think about the horses. If I went, I'd miss them. The horses don't give me any bother. I love them."

"The words of a man of my own mind," said Philippe. That was all the spur he needed to tell Martin about Labryte.

When he lay down to sleep that night, Martin felt happier than he'd been in a long while. For the first time in his life, someone had spoken of him as a man.

Chapter Twelve
Negotiations

Philippe rose early in the morning. He missed Labryte. Back at the forge, his first task on waking was to go and greet her.

Philippe went down the steps and across the yard to the pump. Having washed himself, he began to walk back when he saw Martin carrying a bucket to the drain in the middle of the yard. It was the slop bucket. Up in the loft, it stood in a corner ready for any man who needed to relieve himself in the night. It was Martin's job to empty it every morning.

One of the grooms was walking the other way. As he passed Martin, he gave the lad a shove, causing him to spill some of the slop over his feet. The man turned and said with a snigger.

"You need to be more careful, boy."

Philippe recognised him. It was the one who had thrown the brush. He strode over to Martin.

"Go and put the bucket down by the drain," he said. "But don't empty it. And then go to the pump and make yourself clean."

While Martin did as he was told. Philippe went after the groom, who had continued on his way across the yard. Catching him up, Philippe grabbed the man from behind in a hug and lifted him off the ground.

"I can see that you like to have a laugh, my friend," said Philippe. The groom could say nothing, for Philippe's hug had squeezed the breath from his lungs. After a few attempts to kick behind him, he became limp.

Philippe carried the man to the drain and dropped him from a height onto its grid. He picked up the slop bucket and poured its contents over the man's head.

When the groom's spluttering and cursing at last subsided, Philippe spoke.

"You're not laughing now, my friend. If I see you or any of your mates picking on young Martin, I'll give you even less cause to laugh."

Word of what Philippe had done was around the estate in little time. The Chamberlain had heard of it before he walked to the stables to escort Philippe to the chateau.

"Good day, Monsieur," he said when he found Philippe. "I hear you have already put your strength to good use."

Philippe returned the greeting. He smiled at the Chamberlain's words but said nothing.

The Count and Countess came to the Chamberlain's office to speak with Philippe. He removed his cap and wished them both.

"Good Day."

"My Chamberlain," began the Count, "believes you are the strongest man in France."

"I don't know about that, sir."

"Well, the task I want done will certainly require strength." The Count described the arrival of the mysterious knight, his challenge and his success in defeating those sent against him. He made much of his own feelings of outrage at the knight's intrusion and of the threat to everybody if the knight managed to take over the estate.

"I ask you to be my champion, for the honour of this noble house is in peril."

"In my village, Sir," replied Philippe, "we don't have much to do with honour. But we do know plenty about peril—when our crops fail, when cattle fall sick and when rents and taxes are raised."

"Well said," put in the Countess. "This is about something more real than honour. It is about bullying. That knight wears fine armour but inside it, he is no more than a bully. The silly rules of this honour game are what he uses to kill and to maim."

"He has brought grief and hardship to families here, causing them to fear how they will get by in the future. The Captain of a cavalry troop broke his back when felled by that knight and is unlikely to walk again. One of our best swordsmen lost three fingers. He will never more wield a tool, never mind a sword."

"This bully will continue his bloody campaign until he is stopped. My appeal to you, Monsieur, is based not on honour but on compassion. Have pity on those who have already suffered. Think of those who might yet fall victim to him. I beg you to do what you can to end the career of violence this knight seems determined to pursue."

Philippe looked into the Countess' eyes.

"Very well," he said. "For you, Madame, and for pity's sake, I will go out, face the man and see what I can do."

The Countess curtseyed to Philippe.

"Thank you," she said and withdrew.

The Count was appalled to see his wife curtsey to a blacksmith but a warning look from the Chamberlain restrained him from spluttering his outrage.

"Chamberlain," he said, "see him kitted out with armour, weapons and a horse." With those words, he turned and left.

Chapter Thirteen
Preparing for Combat

"Let the Count show his gratitude with his resources," said the Chamberlain, "if not with his words. You shall have the pick of his horses."

Philippe and the Chamberlain walked back to the stables. As they crossed the parkland, Philippe admired its trees, some of them familiar and some new to him.

They passed together along the stalls. Philippe scrutinised each horse in turn.

"Do you find one you like, Monsieur?"

"They're handsome horses, I admit that," said Philippe. "But I've not seen one that suits me. They're too slender in the leg. And I like a horse with a heavy head and a full face."

"You are loyal then to our French horses," said the Chamberlain. "Most of the Count's, it is true, have Arab blood in them."

"My own Labryte has spoiled me. I doubt I'll ever meet another to match her. I'm sorry I couldn't bring her with me."

They continued down another line of stalls.

"This one might just do," said Philippe. He squeezed into the stall and undid the horse's halter. The horse refused either to turn or to back out. It stood where it was and even shifted a little to push Philippe against the side.

"Ah, you have chosen the Count's most haughty mount," said the Chamberlain. "If it does not wish to go, you will not be able to move it."

"We shall see." Philippe barged out of the stall. He took the horse's tail in one hand. As an experienced blacksmith, he knew where to position himself behind a horse so as not to be kicked. Walking backwards, he pulled the horse out, its hooves slipping and skating on the cobbles.

"This one is not for me, after all," he declared. "I'll not take a horse I wouldn't want as a friend."

After a pause, he went on, "If I'm to meet the knight, I must be on Labryte."

"And so you shall be, Monsieur. I shall send my man to bring your horse. She will be back with you before the end of the day."

"She'll not leave the forge at anyone's bidding. I'd like Martin to go with your man."

The Chamberlain sent at once for Martin. Philippe told the lad of his neighbour and gave him instructions about Labryte's tackle and saddling.

"Here, take my cap with you. Give her a sniff at that and she'll know you came from me."

Martin was overjoyed. Here was a chance to see something of the world beyond the stable block. What was more, he was being trusted for the first time to manage a responsible task.

Martin and the man left straight away, while the Chamberlain took Philippe to the Count's armoury, in the chateau.

The Count had a lavish collection, both of weapons and of body armour. He had bought from the best makers in Germany and Italy. As one who worked in metal himself, though at the humbler end of the trade, Philippe marvelled at the craftsmanship. But in that hoard of poleyns, cuisses, greaves and coutes, he could find not one breast plate big enough to cover his chest. He turned to the weapons, gauging the weight and balance of spears, flails and maces.

"These are handsome things," he said to the Chamberlain, "but they are not my sort of thing."

"I do hope you will find something to suit you, Monsieur. Excuse me, but I must leave you to look some more. I have to visit the knight to tell him that tomorrow the Count's new champion will meet him."

Philippe strolled back to the stables. As he went he had an idea, which quickened his pace. From the stables, he fetched a woodman's axe and returned to the parkland. A tree there had caught his notice. It was new to him, a young tree, about his own height.

He wrapped his arms round the trunk, heaved and pulled it out of the ground. With the axe, he cut off the roots and upper branches and carried the trunk back to the stables, to hew it down to size and trim it more. Philippe was sorry he had not brought his cudgel from the forge but this tree, when shaped, would serve as well.

Philippe was still working at it when Martin and the Chamberlain's man rode into the yard, Martin astride Labryte. Delight lit his face. It was plain that the lad had been thrilled by his outing. And he and Labryte were clearly friends already.

Joyful was the reunion of Philippe and Labryte. He put his arms around her neck, kissed her muzzle and fed her treats he had been saving for just that time.

At that same moment, the Count was far from joyful. He and the Countess were taking exercise in the chateau, strolling up and down its long gallery. The Count loved to gaze out of the windows, musing with pleasure that all the land, for as far as he could see, belonged to him.

"My pomegranate!" he spluttered. "My pomegranate! It's gone!"

The Countess looked. He was right. Where the pomegranate tree had stood, there was a hole and beside it, a pile of cut branches and roots.

"Chamberlain! Chamberlain!" screamed the Count.

The Chamberlain ran the length of the gallery.

"What is the meaning of this?" the Count roared. "Where is my pomegranate tree?"

"I regret to say, my Lord, it has been uprooted and—"

"Idiot!" interrupted the Count. "I can see that. Who has done this?"

"Your new champion, my Lord. He was unable, it seems, to find a weapon to suit him in your armoury. He took the tree and has fashioned it, I am told, into a cudgel, to use in tomorrow's combat."

"This was all your idea, Chamberlain. I shall not forget that. I carried that pomegranate all the way back from my pilgrimage to Jerusalem."

"It is a pity you came back having gained nothing more than a souvenir tree," said the Countess.

Ignoring his wife, the Count continued to rant at his Chamberlain.

"Do you mean to tell me he intends to face a knight in armour with just a cudgel? I shall have him locked up at once."

"May I suggest, my Lord, that you do nothing until the combat is over? After all, if the man succeeds in ridding you of the knight, your Lordship may feel more inclined to reward than to punish him."

"And if the knight rids me of him," retorted the Count, "it will be divine retribution for his destruction of my pomegranate."

"If God does have a list of sinners to punish," said the Countess, "I imagine people who fell others' trees will feature lower on it than husbands who deceive their wives."

Chapter Fourteen
Challenger and Champion

The Count had ordered a row of seats to be placed for him and his courtiers to watch Philippe and the knight. On the far side of the field from them stood all the stable hands and chateau servants who could get away from their work. Amongst those from the stables, one groom in particular was hoping to see Philippe humiliated and slain. That man, though, kept his thoughts to himself, for all his colleagues, while not optimistic, were longing to see one of their own kind, a working blacksmith, defeat a high-born knight.

The knight was first onto the field. He rode back and forth, the black horse trotting with a haughty gait. His polished armour shone in the morning sunlight.

"Good day to you, Sir," said Philippe, joining him on Labryte.

The knight did not return the greeting. He thought it beneath him to be familiar with one from the lower orders.

"Go tell your master I am ready," he commanded, "if his champion dares to face me."

"I am the Count's champion, Sir."

"What? Is this the Count's idea of a joke?"

"I am no man's joke." said Philippe.

"I will not dishonour myself by joining combat with a peasant on a spotty carthorse."

"I understand little of honour," answered Philippe. "But I do know one of its rules. If you decline to face a champion, you must quit the field, as if defeated."

"Very well," snapped the knight. "I shall see this jest through to the finish. And by the finish, neither you nor the Count will be laughing, that I promise."

"Before we begin, Sir, let us move a little out of earshot of those who have come to watch. I would ask for a private word with you."

"If this is a trick to delay the moment of your death, it will be only a short delay. But I can afford to humour you." They moved into the middle of the field. "Now say what you have to say and no more. They will be the last words you utter."

"I am a peaceful man, Sir," said Philippe. "I wish you no harm, even for your insult to me and to Labryte. Suppose we just pretend to fight, to satisfy the crowd. We could make a show of going at one another for a while and then declare our combat to be a draw. That way, neither of us gets hurt, you can leave and boast of still being undefeated and we'll have put a stop to more bloodshed."

The knight glowered. "How dare you suggest such a thing to a warrior knight? We fight to the death—your death, peasant, when I slice that blockhead from your coarse shoulders."

The knight pulled away, turned his horse and rode at Philippe, waving his sword aloft.

Philippe and Labryte did not move. For a moment, it looked as if Philippe was in a trance, so still did he sit in the saddle. At the last instant, as the knight swung his sword towards his neck, Philippe jerked his cudgel up before him. The sword blade sank deep into the wood. With a twist, Philippe wrenched it from the knight's grasp. The impetus of the knight's horse carried him on, now empty handed, behind Philippe.

Philippe wrenched the sword out of the cudgel. Slipping one foot from its stirrup, he raised a knee and brought the blade down across it. The knight's sword was of the finest tempered steel but Philippe snapped it in two as if it was a branch of dead wood.

The knight had pulled his horse up. He turned and faced Philippe again.

"I beg you, sir," said Philippe. "Let us stop this now, before there is any hurt. We can unseat one another at the same time and make it appear we are evenly matched."

"I will parley no more with an oaf like you. I had thought to give you a swift end. I shall enjoy myself now, beating you to death slowly."

With these words, he reached behind his saddle and drew out a flail. It was a rod with a short length of chain at one end. On the chain hung an iron ball, stuck with sharp spikes.

Philippe watched but did not move.

"Now my dear," he said, patting Labryte's neck. "I think you can see what we'll need to do."

The knight rode again at her but Labryte stood her ground. As he came almost level, swinging the flail, she suddenly shied away with a sideways jump, just enough for the swirling ball of spikes to miss its target.

With a nimbleness surprising, given her bulk, Labryte turned and sped after the knight.

Catching him up, Philippe swung his cudgel and dealt a blow which knocked him from his horse. He hit the ground with a clatter heard all round the field.

Philippe dismounted and went to the knight who lay motionless. He raised the man's visor.

His fall at speed in full body armour had snapped the knight's spine. He was dead.

Chapter Fifteen
A Victor Rewarded

"As ever, my Lord, a brilliant decision on your part," gushed one of the courtiers.

"Indeed, your Lordship showed great judgement," another acclaimed, "in perceiving it would need an unconventional champion to defeat this knight."

The Count's courtiers pressed round him, trying to outdo one another in praising his wisdom. While he basked in their congratulations, the Chamberlain crossed the field to see what help the fallen knight might need and to talk to Philippe.

"The knight is dead," Philippe said. "And I am sorry for it. I never wanted to take the man's life."

The Chamberlain bowed his head.

"It is pity indeed," he said, "that a life should be thrown away on such a wild quest. But you should not blame yourself, Monsieur. I believe nothing but death would have put a stop to this knight's mad ambition."

Philippe looked doubtful.

"The Count is busy at present," went on the Chamberlain. "But once you have returned Labryte to her stall, may I ask you to come to the chateau. I will give instructions for you to be shown to the library."

Philippe nodded. The two men parted.

To the Chamberlain's amazement the squire, leaving his master's body where it lay, had led the knight's horse back to their pavilion and was already taking it down. Within the hour and without a word to anyone, the squire had gone. The Chamberlain had the knight's body carried to the chapel in the chateau.

When Philippe entered the library, he found the Count, the Countess and the Chamberlain seated at a table. The Count waved a hand, directing him to sit. On the table was a flagon and two silver goblets. Philippe winced when he saw what was next to them, the knight's helmet.

"Some wine for you, fellow," said the Count. His slurred voice boomed in the hush of the book lined chamber.

The Chamberlain poured him some wine. To be polite, Philippe took a sip and smiled his thanks, but the rough cider of his village was more to his taste than any vintage from the Count's cellars.

"Well done, fellow. I was sure your strength would win the day."

At those words, the Chamberlain fixed his eyes on one of the bookshelves, avoiding Philippe's gaze. The Countess, though, looked at Philippe and smiled.

"I shall reward you richly," went on the Count, after draining his goblet and gesturing for it to be refilled. "Take the knight's helmet. My Chamberlain will conduct you to my treasury. You may fill the helmet with what you wish—gold pieces, silver ingots, precious stones."

If the Count was expecting glee to light Philippe's face, he was disappointed.

"What is the matter, fellow? Is my offer not handsome?"

"Pardon me, sir. I am a simple man, content with a simple life. I want nothing that riches can buy."

"Very well, then, take nothing," snapped the Count.

The Countess spoke. "Let us not be hasty. You have done something for us, Monsieur, and we should be churlish not to recognise that. If you do not want things, is there some service the Count can render you?"

Philippe smiled. "There is, Madame. In my village, we are put to hard straits to buy our salt, what with the tax upon it. I ask the Count to grant us exemption from his salt tax. We are a small village. That would make little dent in the amount he gathers."

"Very well, Monsieur," responded the Countess, getting in before the Count could speak. "That would be a fitting reward. Do you not agree, husband?"

"Er, yes. I suppose so," said the Count. He downed another gulp of wine.

"You have done well for your neighbours," continued the Countess. "Is there nothing we can persuade you to have for yourself?"

Philippe looked to the Chamberlain, who gave him a nod of encouragement.

"I have been thinking lately I should look for somebody to help me with my work. There is a lad in your Lordship's stables. Martin is his name. He is good with horses and the two of us seem to get along well. May I ask him to come and work with me?"

"As you wish," said the Count. He neither knew their names, nor cared much about any of the men in his stables.

"See to it, Chamberlain," he said. "We have kept you too long from your work. Good day to you." The Count took the flagon and refilled only his own goblet. With a raised finger, he pointed Philippe to the door.

Chapter Sixteen
A Triumphant Homecoming

"Do you mean that?"

"I do," said Philippe. "I need some help at the forge. If I'm any judge of folk, I think you and I will get along fine. And I can see Labryte is at ease with you. To me that counts for a lot."

Martin was too overjoyed to speak.

Meanwhile, the Chamberlain was busy in his office. He was keen to act quickly, while the Count was still in a mood mellowed by wine.

Having dictated a certificate of exemption from the salt tax, the Chamberlain had his scribe produce two fair copies. One was for Philippe to carry with him. The other was to be lodged in safe keeping with Philippe's village priest. The Count signed and sealed them without a glance.

The Countess acted with speed too.

"You were willing to give away a helmet full of money," she said, lending the Count her arm as he walked unsteadily into his chamber. "Let me fill it anyway and share the money between the families of the men killed and injured by the knight."

The Count grunted. He was no longer able to speak.

"You rest now, while I sort it out. Let me draw your chair by the fire. See, I've brought your wine and your goblet."

The Count sat down heavily. He slumped back against the velvet cushions, plumped up by his wife and gazed with unfocused eyes at the flames flickering in the hearth.

The Countess hurried back to the library. She collected the helmet and made for the treasury, bent on carrying out her plan before the Count could give it sober thought.

When Philippe had left the village accompanied by the Chamberlain's man, his neighbours feared for him. When that same man returned, only with Martin and then took Labryte, they were anxious, for neither told them anything. Great was their relief when Philippe and Labryte returned and their relief became jubilation when Philippe told them they would no longer have to pay tax when they bought salt.

The villagers welcomed Martin amongst them. Philippe's fondness for the lad was ample to ensure their acceptance of a stranger.

Chapter Seventeen
A New Team at the Forge

Philippe lost no time in making his confession to the village priest. The knight's death at his hands was a heavy weight upon his conscience and one he carried for the rest of his days.

He spoke to no one else of his combat with the knight. When pressed by his neighbours, Philippe would say only that he had been able to render the Count a service which needed some strength. Martin had too much regard for his friend ever to spill a word of what had passed at the chateau.

No one came forward to claim the knight's body. The Count would not hear of burying him in his chapel. A grave was dug where his pavilion had stood. The Count had a headstone set there bearing the words, 'Here lies a challenger defeated'. At the insistence of the Countess, some words were added, 'May God Grant him Peace'.

The Count had the knight's helmet mounted on a wall of his dining chamber. Over dinner, he would tell guests the story of the challenge. As the years went by, Philippe's role shrank in his telling and his own part grew.

Philippe resumed his visits to the Salt Pans. He was relieved that he no longer put his friends there at risk by smuggling.

From that date, the guards at the gatehouse helped Philippe load Labryte with sacks of salt at the end of his stay, all of it bought tax-free. Martin always went with him. After years of knowing nothing but the inside of a convent and a stable yard, the young man relished seeing a new part of the country. At the pans, he threw himself into the work of raking, bagging and hauling salt.

Philippe, it turned out, was a good judge of folk. He and Martin did get along fine and Martin became second only to Philippe in devotion to Labryte.

Martin thrived in his new life. He grew taller and gained weight, though he never acquired Philippe's strength at the anvil. His was a good hand for the finer work. Tackle and saddles became his speciality. Taught by the Priest, he learned to read. Philippe declared himself too old to learn. He had got by well enough without it, he said.

In no time, the people of the village, when they had a problem, found themselves saying:

"This is a job for Philippe and Martin."

Notes

Plum Brandy – Poland

19. *the river Nile*: all Leon's stories come from the Hebrew Bible. Chapter 41 of the Book of Genesis tells how Joseph impressed the Pharaoh of Egypt by being able to explain to him the meaning of his dreams. As a reward, the Pharaoh appointed Joseph to be his second-in-command.

20. *We have a meal together*: dinner on Friday evening is the first of three Shabbat meals for which Jewish people and their families come together.

23. *a stretch of his woodland*: many nobles who owned estates found the income they got from their crops and their tenants was insufficient to support the kind of lifestyle they felt entitled to maintain. A common practice was to sell off areas of woodland from time to time to raise cash.

23. *Krakow*: one of Poland's oldest cities. It became the country's royal capital and seat of government in 1037 and remained so for over 500 years. It was an important centre of commerce in Eastern Europe.

25. *the story of Samson*: the Philistines were a people living on the south-west coast of Israel. Samson, a Jewish man of exceptional strength, waged war against them. The Philistines, having managed to capture him, put him in chains. Samson took revenge by pushing down the pillars of the Philistines' temple, killing many of them and himself. The story is in Chapter 16 of the Book of Judges.

34. *We already know a recipe*: many families made their own plum brandy, by steeping plums in sugar and vodka and leaving the mixture to ferment. Different recipes included different ingredients in addition to the basics—for example, elderflower, strawberries and lemon zest.

35. *mysterious writing*: Leon's story is from Chapter 5 of the Book of Daniel. It tells how Daniel explained the mysterious writing which appeared on a wall in the palace of Belshazzar, king of Babylon.

36. *the language of these stories*: at his school, Leon would have been taught Hebrew, the original language of the Book of Daniel. Hebrew is written from right to left.

42. *the Songs of David*: Leon begins to sing one of the Psalms, Number 15, which is said to have been composed by David, a king of Israel. The Psalm begins with a question, "Lord, who may dwell in your sanctuary?" It goes on to answer that question—those 'who speak the truth' and those 'who do their neighbours no wrong'.

42. *a man who sings*: the Cantor was a trained soloist whose job it was to lead the singing in a synagogue.

44. *a man who tried to steal*: the Old Testament Book of Joshua, in Chapters 5, 6 and 7, relates the story of the defeat of Jericho by the Israelites. One episode in that account is Achan's theft of some of the treasure reserved for God's temple.

53. *a glass of plum brandy*: Polish people are celebrated for their hospitality. They have a saying, "When a guest enters your house, God enters too." It is common to welcome a visitor by offering them a drink, of plum brandy or of vodka.

56. *sour cabbage*: some people added pepper and juniper berries for extra flavour. Depending on the temperature, a batch of sour cabbage would be ready after about two months of fermentation. It might be eaten on its own, made a filling in dumplings or served with wild mushrooms or smoked sausage. In much of Europe, it is known by its German name, Sauerkraut.

The Castle of Soria Moria – Norway

65. *the wooden racks*: called 'hjell' in Norwegian, these racks stand on the foreshore of many coastal villages. Fish which have been caught, usually cod, are gutted, split along their spines and hung on the racks to dry in the wind and cold air.

68. *a troll*: trolls were believed to live in remote places, amongst mountains and caves. They were usually hostile towards humans. Often they kidnapped people, taking over their lands and belongings.

72 *My name is Aurea*: the name means, 'the golden lady'

82. *Bari, Cologne, Galicia*: relics of the body of St Nicholas are kept in the Basilica in Bari, Southern Italy. Cologne Cathedral has a shrine believed to contain the bones of The Three Wise Men. The Cathedral of Santiago de Compostela in Galicia, north-west Spain, houses a shrine enclosing relics of St James, one of the Twelve Apostles. All three drew pilgrims in great numbers from all over Europe.

92. *whom they named Favonia:* they named her after Favonius, the West Wind. That wind was called the favourable one, because it was associated with the start of spring and new growth.

The White Mountain – Slovenia

97. *a learned scholar who lived in a far-off castle*: Janez Vajkard Valvasor (1641–1693) was a scholar who for a time lived in Bogensperk Castle. There he kept the books and materials he had collected and he carried out scientific experiments.

97. *He is embarked upon a great work*: Valvasor wrote 'The Glory of the Duchy of Carniola', a book in a number of volumes which brought together much about the history, the geography and the folklore of the land that is now Slovenia.

99. *She excels in grammar, logic and rhetoric*: these three subjects, called in Latin the 'Trivium', were the core curriculum of medieval education.

101. *a programme of work*: another cluster of subjects in the educational curriculum, the 'Quadrivium', consisted of arithmetic, geometry, astronomy and music.

101. *galls from the oak trees*: galls, often called oak apples, grow on the leaves and twigs of oak trees. They were collected, crushed and mixed with rain water to draw out their tannic acids, one of the core ingredients of the medieval ink recipe.

102. *the shrine of St James*: the shrine, containing relics of St James, attracted many pilgrims. People undertook pilgrimages for a variety of reasons—out of personal piety, to give thanks for prayers answered or for the pleasure of travel. Many were made as acts of penance for wrongdoing.

105. *lakes which disappear and reappear*: the land in that part of Slovenia rests upon porous limestone. Over time, the action of water upon the limestone has created sinkholes and, in places, large underground caverns. As a result lakes and ponds, which form on the surface fed by rain and snowfall in winter, can disappear during dry weather, only to reappear the following winter when replenished.

107. *baked dumplings*: called 'strukljii', these dumplings are a traditional dish in Slovenia.

108. *Nu, come inside*: "Nu" is a Yiddish word with a range of meanings. It is sometimes used, as here, to voice mild impatience. Its sense is, "Don't dither, get on with it."

111. *were any creatures swept along*: a type of salamander lives in some of the caves, having adapted to the extreme conditions underground. In darkness, it needs neither colour nor sight, so it has lost both skin pigments and the use of its eyes. Able to tolerate the cold of the water and having no predators down there, it can live for over fifty years.

120. *to improve the local breed*: Slovenia's Lipizzaner horses are a breed which has been improved by crossing Andalusian horses from Spain and Neapolitan horses from Italy.

120. *maps and engravings*: when published 'The Glory of the Duchy of Carniola'

was illustrated with over five hundred copperplate engravings and included many maps.

The Giant with Golden Hair – Scotland

127. *a man wading*: the man was following a way of fishing traditional at estuaries. The hurdles, set in the water in vee formations, directed fish into putchers, cone-shaped baskets woven with willow twigs. Once inside a putcher, fish had difficulty escaping.

128. *floating timber*: men would float timber down rivers, for that was an easier way of getting heavy trunks to sawmills than trying to move them by cart.

130. *he fished the river*: a traditional way of fishing rivers was to build dams, by heaping rocks out from islands and gravel banks along the river's course. The dams steered fish towards nets fixed in the water with hazel poles and weighed down with stones.

131. *Hush your blether*: blether is a Scottish dialect word for idle talk which goes on too long.

132. *wolves*: it is thought that wolves became extinct in Scotland early in the seventeenth century.

149. *white flowers*: Mossy Saxifrage has pure white flowers with five petals. It is common in upland Scotland.

152. *the sauce*: pike was usually soaked in salt water for several hours to take away its muddy taste. If cooked soon after being caught, it would be doused in a sauce thickened with breadcrumbs and flavoured with herbs.

154. *a water spirit*: Seonaidh was a water spirit who could be malevolent if not propitiated with offerings. Her name seems to be Scottish Gaelic.

162. *the loch*: Loch-an-Eilean, on the Rothiemurchus estate in the Scottish Highlands, has a small island on which, long ago, a castle was built.

Maria and the Goat – Italy

167. *a small town deep in a valley*: Maria's parents lived in Mazzano Romano, in the Lazio region of Italy. Its founders might be thought unwise to have settled deep in a valley, where they could be at risk of being flooded. But back then, the Mediterranean was beset by Saracen pirates. They would land and venture far in from the coast, in search of places to plunder. People reacted by building in hidden spots where they hoped pirates might not see them.

167. *A stretch of marshes*: the Pomptine Marshes, in the south of Lazio, were infested

with malaria-carrying mosquitoes.

168. *Her husband had worked at a quarry*: there were and still are, quarries in Lazio where Travertine is extracted. It is a cream-coloured form of limestone, much used for buildings in Italy.

171. *there was a tiny chapel*: in the Chapel of San Sebastiano fragments of frescoes can still be seen on one of its side walls and in the space above the altar.

173. *the doorway of his cantina*: cantina in Italian means wine cellar. Much of the rock around Mazzano Romano is tuff. Being somewhat porous, tuff is easy to cut into.

174. *they soon smell awful*: male goats, known as Billy goats, have a strong smell. Most people find it unpleasant but it is thought to attract female goats.

179. *The river*: the valley of the River Treja is rich in vegetation and supports lots of wildlife.

179. *a porcupine*: the Crested Porcupine is found in many African countries but in Europe only in Italy and Sicily.

179. *a line of hills*: the Sabatini Hills are to the south-west of Mazzano Romano.

182. *the waters of a lake*: Lake Bracciano is a circular lake. It is believed to have filled a patch of land which sank long ago when an underground chamber, once holding molten rock, collapsed.

189. *A kite sitting in a tree*: Black Kites live in Africa, Asia and Australia. The European sub-species breeds across central, southern and eastern Europe. They do hunt but most of their food they take by scavenging.

189. *the river*: the River Tiber runs through Rome to the coast. Some stretches of its bank sides were lined with wharves and warehouses. It was an important trade route. Ships were once able to sail 100 kilometres up river. They carried grain, produce, stone and timber. Since then silting has made that impossible.

189. *the University of Bologna*: founded in 1088, it is the oldest university in Europe. The city of Bologna is the capital of the Emilia-Romagna region, in northern Italy.

Leaping Ferghal – Ireland

195. *Connemara*: in the west of Ireland. That region played a big part in shaping and keeping alive traditional Irish culture. To this day it is home to many who speak Gaelic.

195. *a ford across the stream*: fords feature a lot in old Irish stories. They are often the borders between territories and so places where challenges and conflicts occur.

195. *Peat bogs*: peat is the remains of dead plants which build up over centuries. In boggy places, where the ground stays wet all the time, plants do not rot down. They

pile up and form a layer, which is black or dark brown in colour. Peat can be cut into oblong blocks and, once dried, it can be burned. There were large areas of peat bog in Connemara.

196. *travelling bards*: bards earned their livelihood by travelling around performing stories, reciting poems and singing songs. They told of clan sagas, local history, heroes of the past, voyages to distant lands, wondrous happenings, the trickery of fairies, ghostly apparitions and the deeds of gods

197. *from the Skelligs to the Giant's Causeway*: the Skelligs are rocky islands off the south-west tip of Ireland, in the province of Munster. At the opposite end of the country, on its north-east coast, lies the volcanic rock formation known as the Giant's Causeway.

202. *heather beer*: brewed from barley, beer was flavoured with heather.

204. *Bull Ford*: in Irish folk tales places are often given names to commemorate events which happened there. By that practice, landscape becomes a map celebrating and preserving deeds of the past.

212. *the barking of dogs*: in those days villagers kept dogs to combat wolves. Sometimes they took them out on hunting parties to track the wolves and run them down. Within villages dogs guarded livestock, especially when winter hunger drove wolves down from the hills to try to take a sheep or a calf.

215. *Do you see my loom?:* Both wool and linen cloth were woven on wooden looms. On a loom, a line of warp yarns hung down from a horizontal beam. Each yarn was weighted with a stone tied on at its end to keep it taut. Weaving was done by passing weft threads horizontally in and out through the line of warp threads. If the loom was knocked, the warp yarns might swing together and become tangled with one another.

215. *carding*: people carded raw fibre by hand to prepare it for spinning. They used carding paddles, flat pieces of wood into which rows of short metal spikes had been set. With the paddles they combed the fibre, untangling it into straight threads and pulling out any impurities.

216. *She named him Ferghal*: the name Ferghal seems to mean brave, courageous.

218. *a small lake with an island*: in Irish Gaelic a dwelling built for defence on an island in a lake was called a crannog.

220. *the berries and the lichens*: elderberries will dye fabric light blue and Common Orange Lichen yields a yellow/orange colour.

221. *stretch my legs into Ulster*: Connacht lay in the west of Ireland, Ulster in the north.

223. *Maeve*: the name of the Queen of Connacht, one of the ancient provinces of Ireland. She plays a big part in the story of The Tain, Ireland's great epic. The name Maeve seems to mean cause of joy.

229. *One stick doesn't make a fire*: in The Tain the story's hero, Cu Chulainn chants a verse which includes this proverb.

236. *she reckoned he was Lug*: at one point in The Tain Cu Chulainn, wounded and alone, is facing a whole army of enemies when the Celtic god, Lug, miraculously appears to help him. Lug is described as a tall, good-looking man, wearing a green cloak over a tunic. He is said to have curly, yellow hair and a square-cut beard.

243. *in the peat*: in modern times archaeologists have found bodies buried in peat bogs. Some of them seem to have been deliberately placed close to the borders of territories in spots overlooked by hills. One theory is that they may be the bodies of leaders who had been deposed.

251. *I hope my tale*: the narrator's closing words are similar to those used by the storyteller, Seán O'Conaill, at the end of his tales.

All of You – England

255. *the Feldon country*: an area of Warwickshire which lies to the south and the east of the River Avon.

255. *Draycote way*: Draycote Meadow still has the ridges and furrows which show it was once an 'Open Field', farmed by a group of local villagers.

264. *Tu-whit, tu-whoo*: William Shakespeare, who was born in Warwickshire, put into words the call of the tawny owl. In his play, Love's Labour's Lost, he wrote:

> nightly sings the staring owl:
> Tu-whit, tu-whoo!   (5.2.910-911)

In fact, it is the female which makes the tu-whit call, while the male bird hoots tu-whoo.

266. *The Raven*: in his poem, The Parliament of Fowls, written towards the end of the fourteenth century, Geoffrey Chaucer gives a brief description of the character of each bird taking part—the Jay is scornful, the Raven wise, the Goose watchful, the Cormorant greedy and the Lapwing deceitful.

267. *Nebula*: an old word for anything that is cloudy, misty or foggy.

276. *ale*: families regularly brewed their own ale. Water clean enough to drink safely was hard to find. Ale had the advantage of being boiled as it was made.

276. *a charcoal pit*: made by digging a big hole, filling it with logs and setting them alight. The pit was covered with earth so that, having little air, the wood burned slowly and turned to charcoal, not to ash. Charcoal was valuable because when burned it produced the high temperatures needed to smelt iron ore.

Death in a Shell – Germany

279. *balls of tar*: in some places natural oil seeps out of the sea bed. It congeals to form tar and the tides wash little balls of tar ashore.

279. *the nearby town*: Albrecht and his parents lived close to the town that is now called Travemunde, on the north coast of Germany.

281. *bits of amber*: what is now the Baltic Sea was once a great forest. When glaciers melted at the end of one of the Ice Ages, the level of the sea rose and the forest disappeared below the waters. Baltic amber is the fossilised resin of those submerged trees.

284. *tiny blooms*: the flowers Albrecht picked were Sea Rocket. It grows along the tops of beaches, where its deep roots in the sand draw nourishment from the organic material dumped by waves at the high tide mark.

289. *their cabinets*: some wealthy individuals had in their home a display cabinet or even a whole room, in which they showed off to visitors the curious objects they had bought from dealers or collected on their travels. Those might include minerals, coins, seeds, bones, dried animal specimens or small artefacts. Some were simply fascinated by unusual things but some were taking their first steps in studying science.

290. *a skilled lace maker*: lace makers worked to a pattern. The pattern was fixed onto the flat surface of a cushion with lots of tiny pins. The threads being woven together hung down over the sides of the cushion. They were wound around bobbins. As the work went on, more thread was unwound from each bobbin.

293. *the big church in Lübeck*: the Marienkirche is the largest church in Lübeck. It was begun in the early thirteenth century. Built of brick, its interior was decorated with wall paintings.

The Tale of Philippe Legrand – France

319. *Labryte*: Labryte is a Percheron draught horse. Percherons were first bred to be war horses but their strength made them ideal for heavy work of all kinds.

322. *Salt*: in the thirteenth century the Count of Anjou and Maine collected all the salt produced in his territories and sold it to local people with a heavy tax on top, which earned him enormous profits. Jealous of his brother, King Louis IX of France, the Count fought many campaigns overseas. He eventually made himself King of Sicily.

325. *the Salt Pans*: coastal salt pans yield salt by the evaporation of sea water. Channels are dug to direct incoming tidal water into shallow pools. The sea water is

held there and evaporated by the heat of the sun. As the water evaporates, the salt in it becomes solid crystals. Those salt crystals are raked up into heaps. Once dry, the salt is loaded into sacks.

328. *leagues*: a league is nearly five kilometres.

337. *Martin*: the festival of St Martin of Tours was celebrated on 11th November.

343 *poleyns*: the poleyn and the couter were hinged pieces of body armour. Made of a number of separate plates joined together, they flexed as the wearer bent his knee or elbow. The cuisse and the greave were single pieces. The former protected the thigh and the latter the shin.

344. *my pomegranate*: a small fruit tree of the Middle East. To flourish, it needs hot days and cool nights, so a lot of care would be needed to keep one alive in the west of France.

344. *my pilgrimage*: a pilgrimage to Jerusalem took a long time and cost a lot of money. A pilgrim from France would travel first to Venice. There he would board a ship to sail down the Adriatic Sea and eastwards across the Mediterranean. Many pilgrim ships stopped in Cyprus, before continuing and heading for the coast of the Holy Land. An overland trek took him to Jerusalem. The goal of most pilgrims was the Church of the Holy Sepulchre, believed to have been built over the site of Jesus' crucifixion and his empty tomb.